TABLE OF CONTENTS

Ch. Five: Magic
Page 4
- Cadixtat…6
- Daenthar…11
- The Hidden Lord…16
- Justicia…20
- Malotoch…24
- Pelagia…29
- Shul…33

Ch. Six: Quests & Journeys
Page 36
- In-Between Escapades…40
- Capsule Campaign…43

Ch. Seven: Judge's Rules
Page 48
- Carnifex…50
- Dzzhal…56
- Hekanhoda…64
- Horned King…72
- Klarvgovok…78
- Magog…84
- Nhool…92
- Obitu-que…98
- Serbok…104
- Yila-Keranuz…110

Ch. Eight: Magic Items
Page 118
- Crafting Magic Rings…120
- Patron Weapons…128
- Mysterious Manuscripts, Monographs & Manuals…133
- Named Swords…136

CREDITS

Writers: Steven Bean, Julian Bernick, Daniel Bishop, Jobe Bittman, Tim Callahan, Colin Chapman, Michael Curtis, Edgar Johnson, Brendan LaSalle, Stephen Newton, Terry Olson, Harley Stroh

Endsheet artists: Doug Kovacs, Peter Mullen

Cover art: Doug Kovacs

Interior artists: Chris Arneson, Tom Galambos, Friedrich Haas, Jim Holloway, Doug Kovacs, Cliff Kurowski, William McAusland, Brad McDevitt, Jesse Mohn, Peter Mullen, Russ Nicholson, Stefan Poag, Chad Sergesketter, Mike Wilson

Cartoons: Chuck Whelon

Editors: Jen Brinkman, Rev. Dak Ultimak

Proofreader: Jen Brinkman

Development, layout & art direction: Joseph Goodman

Layout: Matt Hildebrand

DCC RPG Created by Joseph Goodman
www.goodman-games.com

CH. NINE:
Monsters
Page 148
Making Bugs More Interesting...150
Chaos Lords, Mutants, Degenerates,
Sycophants, Servitors, and Juggernauts...153
DCC Constructs...158
Giants...161
Make Your Freak Unique (Mutations)...165
Reptiles...170
DCC Therianthropes...174
Monstrous Patronage...177

APPENDIX M:
Moustaches
Page 184
The 'Stache Stash: Magic
Moustaches for DCC RPG...186
Doug's d200 Random Stuff Chart...190

INTRODUCTION

DCC RPG is a game founded in principle. Important amongst those principles is an aversion to rules bloat. The DCC RPG core rulebook is but a single book. There are no splatbooks, sourcebooks, character books, monster manuals, or other supplements for DCC RPG. They are not needed. Incumbent upon the judge is the need to create: yon horizon is filled with adventure, and it is *your adventure*. You have worlds inside you: find them.

Yet the urge to create is a hungry god, and gods demand nourishment. It was originally conceived that an annual publication would exist in some form to showcase the brilliance of the DCC RPG community. This would be the DCC RPG Annual, published each year to distribute these gaming creations.

The best of things happened: the DCC RPG Annual was never needed. The DCC community burst forth a verdant jungle of inspiration, with ripe fruit on every limb. Blogs and personal posts; zines; community publications; the Gongfarmer's Almanac; officially licensed third-party works: there is a vast supply of inspiration from whence the DCC judge can draw and iterate.

And thus I introduce a volume which has no place. If you are a DCC fan, you absolutely do not need this book. Should you to desire to read it, however, you shall witness a book that has become a legend, despite never before being published.

Spoken about for half a decade in hoary whispers, at long last Goodman Games brings you: the DCC RPG Annual. Much of the material for the DCC Annual was written between 2012 and 2014, when the original need was perceived. In many ways, it springs forth from the original inspirations of DCC RPG, which were psychically close at that time. There are magic swords. There are patrons. There are even more tables for making monsters unique. There are rules for making cleric deities more distinctive. There are rules for patron weapons and magic rings. There is the lost continent of Mu, and the hidden places between worlds. And there are rules for magical moustaches.

This DCC Annual is organized in the same manner as the DCC RPG core rulebook: chapter five is magic, chapter eight is magic items, and chapter nine is monsters, just as in the core rulebook. There is no chapter two, because the skills section of the core rulebook has no expansion material in the Annual.

You absolutely do not need the DCC Annual to play DCC RPG, nor does any material in this Annual supersede or otherwise change the baseline game experience as expressed in the core rulebook. There is no rules bloat: only new vistas of imagination.

If you enjoy this book, I strongly encourage you to familiarize yourself with the world of third-party DCC publications. If you wish to join their ranks, we offer a free license to those DCC fans who would share their creations. You can find more information at www.goodman-games.com.

– *Joseph Goodman, April 2019*

Chapter Five
MAGIC

Dark arts breed dark deeds.

CADIXTAT

The Chaos Titan, the Sundered Lord, the Severed Chaos, Cadixtat was once the fearsome champion of Zhuhn, the Great Enemy, embodiment of destruction and discord. In a battle of the gods, Cadixtat's hand was severed by an angelic agent of Law, his mighty *Axe of Unmaking* cast down upon the world. Useless as a combatant, Zhuhn finished what the forces of order had begun and slashed his own failed champion's body to pieces, sending the remaining fragments of Cadixtat to fall to Aereth where they remain buried beneath the surface of the planet.

Imbued with the essence of the demigod, Cadixtat's nine parts each contain remnants of his power, and though some say his sentience has dissipated in this sundered form, true believers know that his divinely fragmented consciousness imparts abilities upon his most trusted followers and implores the willing to spread the prophecy of the means of his resurrection.

Followers of Cadixtat believe in proving themselves worthy through combat, tending to value action over inaction and violent resolutions over negotiation. Though no official Church of Cadixtat is known to exist, a growing cabal of believers has formed into the self-proclaimed Weavers of the Divine Flesh. Convinced that the nine pieces of the holy corpse of Cadixtat lay beneath the surface of the world, awaiting reunification, the members of this pseudo-society have begun expeditions far across the seas and deep into the darkest ravines. The Weavers are sages and explorers, wizards and adventurers, relic hunters and lost souls seeking redemption. They lack any centralized leadership and are more than willing to murder and deceive to gain any shred of possible information about the whereabouts of the pieces of Cadixtat.

Clerics of Cadixtat are often suspicious of the intentions of the Weavers, though the resurrection of the Severed Chaos is the outwardly stated goal of each. The clerics tend to be wandering priests, spreading news of Cadixtat's imminent rebirth while sowing the seeds of violence and discord at every opportunity. If they seek adventure with allies of Law or Neutrality, they do so to further the larger goals of dissent and disorder. After all, what could be more chaotic than a band of tomb-robbing murderers?

The preferred weapon of any cleric of Cadixtat is the battleaxe, in tribute to the Sundered Lord's all-powerful *Axe of Unmaking*. The deity's symbol is a series of crisscrossed slashed lines, representing his wounds caused by failure against the forces of Law, often emblazoned in red on a black tunic worn over chainmail armor.

SPECIAL TRAITS

Lay on Hands

When the cleric of Cadixtat successfully casts *lay on hands* roll 1d6 to determine its unique manifestation: (1) the cleric's fingernails grow obscenely long and dig into the chest of the target, pumping healing energy straight into the heart; (2) flames swirl around the hands of the healer, causing flesh to bubble as the target is healed; (3) icy mists shoot from the cleric's fingers, freezing the skin and hair of the target before the rapid thaw reveals the healing; (4) nine-legged insects crawl from the ears, nose, and mouth of the cleric and quickly suture the torn skin of the target; (5) the wounds of the target overflow with pus and blood before congealing into yellow-red gelatin which offers healing; (6) beneath the skin of the target, bones pop and sinews reform as the limbs grow and contract back to normal.

Divine Favors

Will of the Axe: Once per 1d10 days, the cleric may attune to the rippling chaotic emanations of the legendary artifact *The Axe of Unmaking* and increase his or her attack die by +1d for 1d6 rounds. The manifestation of such enhanced offensive power also temporarily transforms the cleric in the following manner (roll 1d4): (1) the cleric's eyes glow in an irregular, pulsating rhythm; (2) anything said by the cleric is spoken with his or her words out of order; (3) the cleric's weapon arm bulges with throbbing muscle expanding any armor worn along with it; (4) the cleric alternates between shrinking and enlarging to 20% of his or her normal size. These effects end when the attack bonus runs out.

Heart of Chaos: Once per month, the cleric may invoke the word of Cadixtat to attempt to inspire listeners toward savagery and destruction. Up to 10 targets within 50' may be persuaded in this way, potentially turning frightened villagers or likely pacifists into violent xenophobes. The targets must not yet be engaged in hostile actions, and the cleric must speak the language of the targets for the effect to work and must succeed on a DC 15 Personality check. If successful, each target must make a DC 15 Willpower save or become enraged with hatred toward those whose outward appearance differs from those affected. Targets unable to resist the *heart of chaos* will ferociously attack (with a +2 bonus to hit and damage) the nearest humanoids of a race different than theirs or whomever is closest and most unlike themselves. This enraged state lasts for 1 turn or until no obvious target is within 100' of the affected.

Cleric of Cadixtat Titles

Level	Title
1	Prophesier
2	Sunderer
3	Veil-slasher
4	Sower
5	Unifier

Disapproval

Those who believe in the eternal sentience of the sundered lord have been granted powerful gifts, but those who displease him will suffer until they learn their proper role in his resurrection. Fragmented in form though he may be, Cadixtat still retains the divine might of a demigod and he needs his followers to prove themselves strong enough to unite his component parts into one. The disapproval table below is customized for clerics of Cadixtat.

Roll	Disapproval
1	The cleric must fall to the ground and begin crudely slashing at the ground for 10 minutes with an edged weapon in penance to the sundered lord, as soon as possible (e.g., during combat, the cleric can wait until after the battle).
2	Cadixtat's essence psychically bellows to his believers and the cleric must immediately recite the following prophecy, repeatedly, for 10 minutes: *The nine shall weave and become one. Cadixtat will rise again as the unmade son.* Failure to do so will cause the loss of all spells for the rest of the day.
3	The cleric must prove his usefulness to Cadixtat and the forces of chaos. If the cleric does not kill a law-aligned creature within the next hour, he suffers a -1 to spell checks for the rest of the day.
4	The cleric's ineptitude has caused Cadixtat's power to wane. Until the cleric converts a new follower to the ways of the Severed Chaos, his spell check bonus is reduced by ½ (rounded down).
5	Two of the cleric's spells are forgotten for the rest of the day and replaced by another randomly-determined spell of the same level.
6	The cleric may not use the *lay on hands* ability until he severs a limb from a living victim in the name of Cadixtat.
7	The pain of Cadixtat's wounds overwhelms the cleric, immediately inflicting 1d4 damage per level of the cleric. This damage will not cause the cleric's hit points to fall below 1.

Roll	Disapproval
8	Cadixtat demands upheaval and unrest. The cleric must attempt to use the *heart of chaos* as soon as possible. If the divine favor is not used immediately (or as soon as one or more targets are within range), the cleric suffers a cumulative -2 penalty to all physical actions and attacks until the *heart of chaos* is used.
9	The cleric must roll 1d6 along with each spell check for the next 24 hours. The result of the d6 is deducted from the spell check before determining the spell effect.
10	The cleric suffers minor corruption (roll 1d10 on Table 5-3 in the *DCC RPG rulebook*) and loses one randomly-determined spell for 24 hours.
11	Cadixtat ignores the cleric for the remainder of the day, prohibiting the use of canticles, class abilities, or spells beyond level 1. The only way to regain the favor of the severed chaos, until the next morning, is to deliver the killing blow to nine or more enemies.
12	The cleric loses all class abilities for 1d6 turns or until he deals 10 points of self-inflicted damage, whichever comes first.
13	The cleric must destroy or discard his primary weapon and find a new battleaxe. For each day the cleric does not find and/or use this new weapon to draw blood, he suffers 1d6 damage that cannot be healed by *lay on hands*. A week-long ritual dedicated to Cadixtat removes this disapproval effect.
14	Cadixtat finds the cleric unworthy until he displays proven combat durability. The cleric's arms and legs grow in a crude, disproportionate manner, causing a -2 penalty to all attacks and physical checks until the cleric loses ½ of his hit points to enemies in melee combat. After that, the cleric's limbs return to normal.
15	Cadixtat strikes the cleric blind and fills his mind with images of violence. The cleric is at -4 to all actions and spell checks until a "4 dice" result is rolled on a *lay on hands* check. This may be done via self-healing or by another Chaos-aligned cleric.
16	Angered by the cleric's incompetence, Cadixtat reverses the cleric's ability to *turn unholy*. Every attempt to use the ability results in "turned" creatures becoming focused on the cleric's presence and focusing all attacks on him. Damage results on the turn unholy table provide healing to the targeted creatures instead, and kill results double their hit points. To return the *turn unholy* ability to normal, the Cleric must slay a Law-aligned human or humanoid in single combat.
17	The cleric cannot use any canticles or divine favors for the next 1d8 days.
18	The cleric suffers major corruption (roll 1d10 on Table 5-4 in the *DCC RPG Rulebook*) and loses one randomly-determined spell permanently.
19	The cleric immediately vanishes from his current plane of existence and flies through the black void where the nine severed parts of Cadixtat can be seen spread apart in the distance. The cleric returns to his original location in 1d3 hours and suffers a -1d penalty to all saving throws until getting a full night's rest.
20+	The cleric cannot cast any spells or use any class abilities until he cuts off one of his own fingers and crushes it with an axe in tribute to Cadixtat. For every two fingers missing from the primary hand, attack rolls suffer a -1d penalty. If all fingers have been removed, the cleric must find one of the severed parts of Cadixtat and beg for forgiveness in person.

CANTICLES OF CADIXTAT

Cadixtat favors songs of discord and disarray, improvised tunes of imperfect skill, sung with passion. More potently, though, are the hymns and chants his clerics have passed down through the generations since his fall. These canticles are not spells, though they may replicate spell-like effects. Instead, these are additional class abilities unique to clerics of Cadixtat.

Level 1: *Metamorphosis* Level 3: *Tattered Veil of Chance* Level 5: *Hand of Chaos*

METAMORPHOSIS

A zealot of Cadixtat learns this hymn of self-transformation at 1st-level. Rolled as a normal spell check action with all corresponding bonuses and penalties, the canticle of metamorphosis must be sung loudly while swinging a battleaxe in a crisscross motion, with the fervor of a true believer of the resurrection of the Sundered Lord.

Spell check	Result
1-15	Failure. Roll disapproval if applicable. Increase disapproval range otherwise.
16-17	The cleric's fingernails grow as if to become small blades. For 1d6 rounds, the cleric may deal 1d8 damage with an unarmed slashing attack, and gains one additional attack per round at -1d as long as the additional attack is the unarmed slash.
18-23	The palm of the cleric's right hand tears open to reveal a gaping mouth filled with jagged teeth. The maw remains for 1d3 rounds and may be used as an unarmed attack at an additional +2 to hit, dealing 1d8+2 damage, or it may be used to cast the *scare* spell (as the level 2 wizard spell) with a spell check equal to the Personality modifier of the cleric.
24-25	The cleric and everything in his possession grows to twice their normal size for 1 turn. While enlarged with the power of the Chaos Titan, the cleric gains +5 to attacks and damage, plus one of the following additional benefits (roll 1d5): (1) gain +20 hp; (2) gain +5 AC; (3) gain infravision and the ability to see 5x normal distance; (4) gain the ability to perform Mighty Deeds of Arms as a warrior of one level below the cleric's own level; (5) gain +1d to spell checks.
26+	Cadixtat's power ripples through the believer. For 1d3 turns, the cleric gains an additional +2 modifier to two of the following abilities (roll 1d5 twice, reroll duplicate results): (1) Personality; (2) Intelligence; (3) Stamina; (4) Agility; (5) Strength.

TATTERED VEIL OF CHANCE

At level 3, a cleric devoted to Cadixtat gains the ability to see the patterns in the chaos of life. Cadixtat's defeat was all part of the larger plan of the cosmos, just as his prophesied resurrection has already been written in the Book of Fate. For the cleric, it is as if a veil has been torn from his or her eyes and the world looks different. This new divine awareness allows the cleric to continue to manipulate Luck as normal, but also in a way that he or she has not been able to before. Immediately upon achieving 3rd level, and *upon advancing to any additional levels,* the cleric re-rolls his or her Luck ability score as indicated below:

Current Luck	New Luck Ability Score*
1-3	Roll 1d6+1 to determine
4-7	Roll 2d6+3 to determine
8-11	Roll 3d6+2 to determine
12-14	Roll 3d6+4 to determine
15+	Roll 4d6 to determine (Maximum Luck score: 18)

Note that the cleric may end up with a lower Luck score in some instances. Such is the whim of the divine.

In addition to determining a new Luck ability score at each level starting at level 3, the cleric also gains the ability to spend one Luck point to increase a die roll by +1d. This use of Luck, and the amount of Luck points spent, must be declared *prior* to rolling the die. In play, this should be declared via a recitation to Cadixtat developed by the player and verbalized. "Through the Severed Chaos, I see three fingers of Cadixtat," would mean the PC was declaring the use of 3 Luck points, for example. For each point of Luck declared this way, the cleric adds +1d to the roll. Thus, a level 3 cleric who spends 3 points of Luck prior to rolling damage with his or her battleaxe would roll 1d16 for damage instead of 1d10. A level 3 cleric who spends 2 points of Luck prior to an attack roll would roll 1d30 for that attack. This use of Luck may also be used to increase the die roll of a chaos-aligned ally, granting, for example, a d24 spell check to a chaotic wizard with a single point of Luck.

HAND OF CHAOS

Granted at level 5, this ability allows the cleric of Cadixtat to summon one of many possible manifestations of the severed right hand of the Sundered Lord. Imbued with chaotic energies, the hand is a formidable, unpredictable weapon. To summon the Hand of Chaos, the cleric must bury a severed right hand in the dirt and chant prayers to Cadixtat for one full turn. Anytime for the rest of that day, the cleric may roll a spell check as an action to see what emerges from the spot at which the severed hand was buried.

The spell check is modified by the type of right hand buried as part of this ritual (if the type of hand does not match those below, the judge should determine the closest equivalent):

Hand from a Chaos-aligned human: +1d

Hand from a Neutrality-aligned human: +2

Hand from a Law-aligned human: +1

Hand from an elf or orc: -2

Hand from a dwarf or lizardman: -1

Hand from a halfling or kobold: -1d

Hand from any other humanoid race: -2d

Hand from a demon or an angel: +2d

Spell check	Result
1	Failure, deity disapproval, and worse! Roll 1d6 (1-2) Cleric rolls deity disapproval an additional time, using a d20; (3) the cleric's right hand shrinks to half size for 1 hour, causing all one-handed weapons to become two-handed weapons, and providing a -1 penalty to Strength checks and melee damage; (4) the cleric's right hand appears as glass for the next hour, providing a -1 penalty to AC and Agility checks; (5) the cleric's right hand gains a gelatinous sheen for the next hour, causing held items to slip out of the hand unless a Reflex save is made vs. the cleric's Personality score; (6) the cleric's right hand withers and falls off, causing -1d to all physical actions until the hand grows back in 1d4 days.
2-19	Failure. Roll disapproval if applicable. Increase disapproval range otherwise.
20-23	A human-sized hand with six fingers digs its way back to the surface under the command of the cleric. The hand looks strong and may balance objects on its "back" while it crawls around, with a Strength equivalent to 18. It may climb up surfaces as if using a *spider climb* ability in constant effect. If thrown as a weapon, this hand can grab any victim it hits for 2d6+3 damage. Any attack against it that would hit AC 18 or higher will cause the hand to disappear from this plane of existence. If not attacked, it will vanish after 2d6 rounds.
24-27	Crawling from the ground, like an uncoordinated flesh-covered spider the size of a panther, this hand with five fingers features demonic, long fingernails. Not dexterous enough to attack effectively with its blade-like nails, it has enough essence of the sundered lord to imbue the cleric with the following wizard spells at a +6 spell check as long as the cleric is in contact with the hand: *magic missile, ward portal, fire resistance, scorching ray*. These spells may be cast at +1d if the cleric successfully rides the hand like a mount, by performing a successful DC 15 Agility check and a successful DC 15 Personality check. The hand may move at 20' per round. Treat the hand as AC 18 with 20 hit points. After being reduced to 0 hp, or after 2d6+CL rounds, the hand disappears.
28-29	Erupting from the ground, the size of a covered wagon, the hand darts quickly toward the cleric like a panicked spider before following the commands of its summoner. The palm of this huge hand features a gaping mouth with gnarled teeth, and each finger is distinct. The index finger is coated with putrescent slime, the middle finger's nail is long and curved like a scimitar, the ring finger wears a giant ring and the tip of the finger has sprouted a half-dozen small hands of its own, and the little finger throbs with bloody veins. This hand behaves as a ferocious creature under the control of the cleric. **Lesser Hand of Cadixtat:** Init: +3, Attack middle fingernail slash +8 melee (2d6+6) or leaping bite +6 (2d6+2 and special); AC 16; HD 7d8+20; hp 58; MV 30'; Act 2d20; SP leaping bite knocks victim prone, may cast the following wizard spells at +8 spell check: *spider climb, invisibility*; SV Fort +6, Ref +3, Will +4; AL C. The hand disappears after 1d8+CL rounds or until it slays 6 Law-aligned enemies, whichever comes first.
30+	Erupting from the ground, the size of a small cabin, this hand is a larger version of the hand described above. This "greater" hand moves more methodically and with some divine intelligence as contrasted with the frantic "lesser" hand in the previous entry, even though they share similar superficial appearances. **Greater Hand of Cadixtat:** Init: +1, Attack middle fingernail slash +14 melee (3d6+6) or leaping bite +8 (2d6+3 and special); AC 18; HD 8d8+30; hp 73; MV 40'; Act 2d24; SP leaping bite knocks victim prone, may cast the following wizard spells at +10 spell check: *flaming hands, spider climb, invisibility*; SV Fort +8, Ref + 2, Will +6; AL C. The hand disappears after 2d6+CL rounds or until it slays 9 Law-aligned enemies, whichever comes first.

DAENTHAR

Stern and unwavering is Daenthar, the Lord of the Hallowed Forge. He is the god of the earth, or industry, of those who work in crafts, or who seek to draw the riches from the earth in terms of stone, metal, or gems. He is said to have crafted the first dwarves from raw earthstuff when the world was young, and to guide and guard them while they tunnel deep beneath the earth. Although dour and solemn, the Mountainlord is called upon by those who venture into the high mountain passes as well as those who delve into the deepest of mines. Daenthar is said to protect those who serve Him well.

Temples dedicated to Daenthar are rare, although the god himself is offered prayers and sacrifices widely. Where they are found, the Mountainlord's clerics create heavily protected stone-walled holdfasts dedicated to their god. These act both as fortress and temple, and may extend deep beneath the ground. Travelers are happy to find such places, which offer respite from the dangers of the high passes.

The clergy of the Hallowed Forge wear full battle armor for ceremonies. When not offering sacrifices, conducting rituals to Daenthar, or faced with enemies, they dress instead in holy accoutrements resembling nothing so much as well-made workman's clothing. The god uses an upright forging hammer, placed before a cracked mountain, as his holy symbol.

Daenthar is depicted as a stout human or a tall dwarf, often arrayed in full battle armor or standing over a forge or an anvil. Depictions of the Mountainlord are always carved in stone; any other depictions are considered blasphemous. Daenthar is among the most severe proponents of Law. He never breaks his sworn word, and demands that His clerics likewise hold their vows. Thus, while the direct proponents of Daenthar are lawful, neutral – and even chaotic – beings will call upon the Mountainlord to bind an oath.

Sacrifices to Daenthar are made in service and wealth. Money and time are given to public service, and to glorify (or strengthen) the fortress-temples of the Mountainlord. A cleric in need may reduce his disapproval by promising such works, but woe to he who breaks an oath to the Lord of the Hallowed Forge! Even promises made without a reasonable time frame to complete (as determined by the judge) act to increase, rather than decrease, disapproval.

There is never any doubt when Daenthar speaks to His faithful. The voice of the Lord of the Hallowed Forge may be heard in the crack of stone and the rumble of avalanches. He may cause a carven image of Himself to move and speak. His face may appear in the hot coals of the forge, or His voice in the ringing of hammer on iron. His identity is never in doubt, and the meaning of His words is always clear. Daenthar does not equivocate.

The Mountainlords's favored weapon is the warhammer.

SPECIAL TRAITS

Lay on Hands

When a cleric of Daenthar attempts to heal a chaotic dwarf, the recipient is treated as being "adjacent" on the *lay on hands* chart (page 31 of the DCC RPG rulebook). A neutral dwarf is treated as "same", while a lawful dwarf is healed with a +1d bonus on the dice chain to the spell check.

A cleric of Daenthar can use this ability to repair animated objects and similar constructs. This works in exactly the same way that healing for living creatures does, save that the will of the Mountainlord causes damage to the object to reverse. Rust may be removed as if healing a disease, and broken mechanisms may be treated as broken bones. Because animated objects and constructs are never truly "alive", they can be "healed" even centuries after being reduced to 0 hp.

Finally, by spending 10 minutes with appropriate tools, a cleric of Daenthar may attempt a *lay on hands* check to repair any mechanical device. This does not actually call upon divine power, and cannot alter or result in disapproval. If the check fails, the cleric may try again if he spends 1 hour on the next check. Another check may be allowed after 4 hours work, and a final check after 1d3 days work. This check is modified by the cleric's Intelligence, rather than Personality.

The judge may require specific materials (or their equivalents) be available. For example, making a rusted portcullis move may require both a lubricant and a hard object to knock apart metal that has been rusted together. The judge may also rule that repairs are not complete and/or temporary (i.e., perhaps the rusted portcullis can be raised, but thereafter cannot be lowered again).

Check	Result
1-13	Failure.
14-19	A small, relatively simple device may be repaired.
20-22	A larger simple device, or a small device of medium complexity, may be repaired.
23-25	A large simple device, a medium-sized device of average complexity, or a small very complex device may be repaired.
26-28	A very large simple, a large device of average complexity, or a medium-sized very complex device may be repaired.
29-30	Any simple device, a very large device of average complexity, or a large very complex device, may be repaired.
31+	Any device may be repaired.

Turn Unholy

In addition to the normal creatures a lawful cleric can turn as unholy, clerics of Daenthar may attempt to turn animated objects and constructs, such as golems and beings made of clockwork. On a result of "K", the cleric may instead choose to command the constructed beings for up to 1d3 turns. The cleric may not command more HD in constructs than twice his level in this manner. The constructs described in the *Psalm of the Hallowed Forge* are immune to this ability.

Cleric of Daenthar Titles

Level	Title
1	Aspirant to Stone
2	Fellow of the Forge
3	Journeyman of the Mountain
4	Craftsman of the Hallowed Forge
5	Master Craftsman of the Hallowed Forge

These level titles are not gender-dependent. A 3rd-level female cleric is called a Journeyman of the Mountain, just as a male cleric is.

Disapproval

It is the role of clerics to be mortal embodiments of a higher power, extolling their deities' virtues and shepherding the ignorant into the flock. In exchange for a life of devotion, deities grant great powers to their most favored disciples. Those who show disrespect by ineptly invoking holy power or acting in a manner contrary to their deity's wishes run the risk of punishment. The table below contains a deity disapproval tailored for followers of Daenthar.

Roll	Disapproval
1	The cleric has lost his connection to the solid stone of the earth, and must spend 10 minutes meditating to restore this bond, as soon as possible (e.g., during combat, the cleric can wait until after the battle).
2	No mortal can encompass the profundity of Law enough to please Daenthar at all times. Now the cleric must pray and mediate for at least one hour to reestablish himself as an agent of the Law. If he fails to do this within 120 minutes, he takes a -1 penalty to all spell checks until the hour's mediation and prayer is complete.
3	The cleric must donate 100 gp or 8 hours of labor to community service – building or repairing walls, designing irrigation systems or aqueducts, performing smithwork or stonework, etc. If these conditions are not met within 24 hours, the cleric takes a -1 penalty to all spell checks until they are.

Roll	Disapproval
4	The cleric immediately incurs an additional -1 penalty to all spell checks that lasts until the next day.
5	Daenthar demands that the cleric undertake the twin tests of humility and righteousness. For the next 24 hours, the cleric must obey the orders of others, if they do not further the aims of Chaos, but must eschew those orders which would work against Law. Each time he fails to obey an order he should, or obeys an order he should not, he takes a cumulative -2 penalty to all spell checks.
6	The cleric immediately incurs a -1 penalty to *lay on hands* attempts. This penalty remains in place until the cleric completes a quest to heal the sick or crippled. The quest must be of the cleric's own devising, and any profit he gains from the quest must be donated to public works.
7	The cleric must endure a test of faith. For the next 24 hours, he cannot use his *lay on hands* ability to heal himself, although he can still heal others. If the cleric endures this test without complaint (judge's determination), his ability to heal himself is thereafter restored. If not, his disapproval increases by 1 for the next 24 hours.
8	The cleric immediately incurs a -4 penalty to spell checks on the specific spell that resulted in disapproval (including laying on hands and turning unholy, if those were the acts that produced disapproval). This lasts until the next day.
9	Daenthar wishes the cleric to rely less upon his spells and more upon himself. The cleric immediately incurs a -2 penalty to all spell checks that lasts until the next day.
10	No magic is used without consequence. The caster immediately loses the power to cast one random spell until the following day, lest the energy released aid the forces of Chaos.
11	The cleric has lost spiritual position with regards to community, immediately incurring a -2 penalty to all spell checks. This remains until the spiritual link is restored. For every full day spent performing public works for which the cleric gains no compensation, he may attempt a DC 15 Willpower save. Success means that he has regained his connection to the community, and the penalty is removed.
12	Daenthar turns His face from the cleric. Until Daenthar is mollified, the cleric cannot gain XP or levels as a cleric. This requires a public donation of no less than 100 gp per level the cleric has acquired. Once such a donation is made, the cleric can again gain XP and levels, but does not accrue "back pay" (so to speak) for XP missed while he was disowned.
13	The cleric loses access to two randomly determined level 1 spells, which cannot be cast until the next day.
14	The faithful of Daenthar rely upon skill of hands and strength of limb, even more than reliance upon divine power. This is a lesson the cleric must learn. For each spell cast, he takes 1 point of temporary damage to Strength, Agility, or Stamina per spell level (e.g., a level 3 spell causes 3 points of temporary ability damage). The cleric may decide which ability score to apply each point of this damage to, but may not use magic to heal it.
15	Daenthar is not forgiving this day. When the cleric rests for the night, he does not "reset" his disapproval range at the next morning – it carries over from this day to the next. The disapproval range resets as normal the following day.
16	For some broken vow in thought or deed, Daenthar removes the cleric's ability to *lay on hands* for 1d4 days. Only after this time does the cleric regain his healing abilities.
17	The cleric loses access to 1d4+1 spells, randomly determined from those he knows. He cannot cast those spells for the next 24 hours.
18	The cleric learns what it means to be caught between the hammer and the anvil! Every time the cleric calls upon Daenthar to *turn unholy*, *lay on hands*, or cast a spell, the cleric takes 1d5+3 points of damage under the gentle ministrations of the Lord of the Hallowed Forge, which cannot be magically healed. This condition lasts for 24 hours.
19	For the next 24 hours, the cleric may only attempt to *lay on hands* on any given creature once.
20+	Only the extremely arrogant or foolish would push the unyielding Mountainlord so far! The cleric immediately loses all access to spells, the ability to turn unholy, and the ability to *lay on hands*. As an act of penance, each day (including the first), the cleric may give away his worldly possessions. The percentage of worldly possessions given away (based on the cleric's possessions at the time the disapproval occurred) is the percent chance that Daenthar relents and restores the cleric's divinely-granted abilities on the following day. For example, a cleric who donates half his worldly goods has a 50% chance of being restores to Daenthar's good graces on the next day. If Daenthar does not relent, and the cleric then donates half of what remains, he has a 75% chance of being restored on the following day. If no additional sacrifice is made, there is no chance of Daenthar relenting on a subsequent day.

CANTICLES OF DAENTHAR

Music and ritual play central roles in many worship services. Raised in prayer, the voices of the faithful can invoke minor powers of their deity, much like a spell. The following powers may be learned by clerics of Daenthar:

Level 1: *Chaunt of the Unmoving Mountain*

Level 3: *Song of Stone*

Level 5: *Psalm of the Hallowed Forge*

CHAUNT OF THE UNMOVING MOUNTAIN

All clerics of Daenthar are able to sing the *Chaunt of the Unmoving Mountain*, granting them great stability when his feet are in contact with earth or stone. Direct contact is not necessary; a cleric wearing boots or foot armor is equally able to utilize the *Chaunt*. Starting on the second round, while chanting prayers to the Mountainlord, the cleric gains the following benefits. However, the cleric cannot otherwise speak or cast spells, and every instance of using the *Chaunt of the Unmoving Mountain* (or for each 10 minutes of continual use) causes the cleric's disapproval to automatically increase by 1.

- The cleric adds his level to Strength checks and Reflex saves to avoid falling, tripping, or being moved against his will.
- The cleric subtracts his level from Mighty Deeds, such as trips, throws, or pushbacks, intended to move him.
- If the cleric is moved (for example, due to a giant's critical hit), he subtracts his level in feet from how far he is moved. If the result is 0 or less, the cleric is not moved.

SONG OF STONE

This low, droning song allows a cleric of Daenthar to harden his flesh to a stone-like consistency. The cleric must anoint himself with holy mineral oils (costing 15 gp) while singing, a process which takes a full turn to complete. The cleric then makes a spell check and consults the table below. It should be noted that any AC bonus received does not stack with armor; the cleric gains only the better of the two bonuses.

Spell check	Result
1-15	Failure.
16-17	Cleric gains +2 bonus to AC for the next hour.
18-23	Cleric gains +2 bonus to AC for the next hour, and any damage the cleric takes is reduced by 1 point.
24-25	Cleric gains +4 bonus to AC for the next 2d6 hours, and any damage the cleric takes is reduced by 2 points.
26+	Cleric gains a +6 bonus to AC until the next dawn. Any damage the cleric takes is reduced by 5 points.

DWARVES AND THE MOUNTAINLORD

Normally, only humans can become clerics, but Daenthar is the creator-god of the dwarves and allows them among his faithful. The judge may rule that dwarven priests of Daenthar are NPCs only, using the stat blocks below.

If the judge desires, lawful dwarves may choose to become clerics of Daenthar upon reaching 1st level. In this case, the dwarf retains the racial characteristics possessed as a 0-level character, but gains no further Dwarf class abilities.

Dwarven acolyte: Init +0; Atk warhammer +1 melee (1d8) or harmful spell (see below); AC 10; HD 1d8; MV 20'; Act 1d20; SP harmful spell 2/day; SV Fort +1, Ref +0, Will +2; AL L.

Dwarven priest: Init +0; Atk warhammer +3 melee (1d8) or harmful spell (see below); AC 15; HD 1d8; MV 20'; Act 1d20; SP harmful spell 3/day; SV Fort +3, Ref +0, Will +4; AL L.

The harmful spells of dwarven followers of Daenthar take several forms:

1d5	Spell
1	*The Fist of Daenthar:* Stone fist flies from the caster up to 30', striking with a +3 attack bonus for 1d4+2 damage.
2	*Heat of the Forge:* Target within 60' takes 1d3 damage on the first round, 1d4 damage on the second round, 1d5 damage on the third round, and so on up the dice chain until a DC 12 Fort save succeeds. Characters in metal armor suffer +1 damage per round.
3	*Hammer of the Mountain:* The caster can hurl his warhammer up to 50', with a +5 bonus to hit, and doing 1d8+4 if successful (DC 15 Ref save for half). The warhammer is consumed by the spell, potentially leaving the caster weaponless.
4	*Weight of Stone:* Target within 100' feels its weight increased by 150%, slowing the target's movement by -10' per round and reducing its initiative by -1d3. The effect lasts 1d5+2 rounds. DC 10 Will save negates.
5	*Visage of Stone:* Target within 30' is transformed into stone, unless a DC 10 Fort save is made. The effect lasts only 1d3 rounds.

PSALM OF THE HALLOWED FORGE

This psalm allows a favored cleric of Daenthar to request the aid of the Mountainlord in the form of one or more constructed servants created by the Lord of the Hallowed Forge. All of these creatures appear to be made of burnished black metal, which burns elves for 1 point of damage per round of contact (or +1 damage per successful attack). All of these creatures are extreme representations of Law. They are obedient to the cleric so long as they are not asked to oppose Law or bolster Chaos, and they may turn on a cleric who wishes to use them for sinful purposes.

Minor constructs are human-sized. Major constructs are 8' tall. When a construct is reduced to 0 hp, or the time it has been sent for expires, it simply fades away.

Spell check	Result
1	Failure and worse! A minor construct is sent to chastise the cleric, attacking for 2d6 rounds before fading away. The wounds caused by the construct cannot be magically healed, but the cleric need not succeed in a Luck check to be recovered if reduced to 0 hp. **Minor construct:** Init +0; Atk warhammer +3 melee (1d8+2); AC 15; HD 2d12; MV 20'; Act 1d20; SP immune to mind-affecting, half damage from heat or cold, all damage taken reduced by 2 points; SV Fort +5, Ref +0, Will +7; AL L.
2-19	Failure.
20-21	A minor construct is sent to aid the cleric for 1 turn. **Minor construct:** Init +0; Atk warhammer +3 melee (1d8+2); AC 15; HD 2d12; MV 20'; Act 1d20; SP immune to mind-affecting, half damage from heat or cold, all damage taken reduced by 2 points; SV Fort +5, Ref +0, Will +7; AL L.
22-27	2d5 minor constructs are sent to aid the cleric for 1 hour. **Minor construct:** Init +0; Atk warhammer +3 melee (1d8+2); AC 15; HD 2d12; MV 20'; Act 1d20; SP immune to mind-affecting, half damage from heat or cold, all damage taken reduced by 2 points; SV Fort +5, Ref +0, Will +7; AL L.
28-29	A major construct is sent to aid the cleric for 1d3 hours. **Major construct:** Init +0; Atk warhammer +5 melee (1d8+3); AC 20; HD 4d12; MV 30'; Act 2d20; SP immune to mind-affecting, half damage from heat or cold, all damage taken reduced by 5 points; SV Fort +10, Ref +0, Will +12; AL L.
30+	1d3 major constructs are sent to aid the cleric until the next dawn. **Major construct:** Init +0; Atk warhammer +5 melee (1d8+3); AC 20; HD 4d12; MV 30'; Act 2d20; SP immune to mind-affecting, half damage from heat or cold, all damage taken reduced by 5 points; SV Fort +10, Ref +0, Will +12; AL L.

THE HIDDEN LORD

Mysterious are the ways of The Hidden Lord, God of Secrets. The Chaotic god's true name itself is shrouded in mystery. The Cloaked One, the Keeper of Forbidden Lore, and He of Many Names are but a few of the masks worn by The Hidden Lord. Indeed, many of the dark cults that skulk in the shadows of civilization's light unknowingly worship the same unseen master though it is said the upper echelons of the various sects are aware of their common bond.

The God of Secrets' high priests have forged a secret society—The Hidden Path—dedicated to furthering their dark master's evil schemes. These high corruptors infiltrate rival houses of worship, seeding ruin and shepherding the weak-willed into darkness. Seekers of forbidden knowledge and those willing to trade their souls in exchange for occult powers will find kinship, for a time, within the walls of The Hidden Lord's black temples.

The Hidden Lord is a being dedicated to Chaos in its purest form. His followers are mostly aligned with Chaos, though some remain neutral in the eternal battle between light and dark. The Hidden Lord has neither tenets nor iconography. The deity is never depicted in any form (unless the purpose is to deceive) though the truly devoted may sometimes receive visions of screaming owls with glowing eyes. Clerics of The Hidden Lord can invoke His power using the holy symbol of any other Neutral or Chaotic god. When The Hidden Lord does make His presence known, it is through seemingly random acts of entropy: glasses shatter for no apparent reason or spontaneous flames burst to life. The Hidden Lord's favored weapon is a curvy-bladed ceremonial dagger.

SPECIAL TRAITS

LAY ON HANDS

Followers of the Hidden Path mask their abilities under the guise of other neutral or chaotic gods, emulating their specific manifestations. Clerics of The Hidden Lord also have access to the *Death Touch* canticle (see below).

Cleric of The Hidden Lord Titles

In order to mask their true nature, clerics of The Hidden Lord assume standard cleric titles or the titles of other Neutral or Chaotic clerics.

Disapproval

It is the role of clerics to be mortal embodiments of a higher power, extoling their deities' virtues and shepherding the ignorant into the flock. In exchange for a life of devotion, deities grant great powers to their most favored disciples. Those who show disrespect by ineptly invoking holy power or acting in a manner contrary to their deity's wishes run the risk of punishment. The table below contains a deity disapproval tailored for followers of the Hidden Lord.

Roll	Disapproval
1	The cleric has offended The Hidden Lord and must spend 10 minutes prostrate and groveling before the deity, as soon as possible (i.e., during combat, the cleric can wait until after the battle).
2	The Hidden Lord is angered and commands the cleric to immediately spend 1d3 rounds groveling and prostrate, unable to take any other action. Those who disobey this order incur a -5 penalty to all spell checks for 10 minutes.
3	The cleric must commit an act of treachery or deceit before midnight, or incur a -1 penalty to all checks on the following day.
4	The cleric suffers a cumulative -1 penalty to all spell checks until the next day.
5	The Hidden Lord demands penance in blood. The cleric suffers a -2 penalty to all spell checks until he or she slays a foe with The Hidden Lord's favored weapon, the curvy-bladed ceremonial dagger. All attacks with the favored weapon gain a +1 bonus to attack rolls and damage. Multiple rolls of this result increase the requisite body count before the hex is lifted.
6	The cleric loses access to one randomly determined canticle until the next day.
7	The cleric incurs a -3 penalty to spell checks with the specific spell or canticle that resulted in disapproval until the next day. Additional rolls of this result increase the penalty by -1.
8	The cleric is forbidden to cast one randomly determined level 1 spell until the next day. Should the cleric disobey this stricture, a phantom bolt of spectral energy strikes the cleric for 2d6 damage and the deity disapproval range increases by +2.
9	The cleric suffers a cumulative -2 penalty to all spell checks until the next day.
10	The cleric loses access to one randomly determined spell from each level known until the next day.
11	The Hidden Lord demands a test of faith. Whenever the cleric is unoccupied, he or she must self-flagellate with a cat o' nine tails until midnight (e.g., the cleric may stop the flagellation during combat, but must resume the beating afterwards while walking through the dungeon). The whipping causes 1d8 points of damage per hour and inflicts a -2 penalty to Fort, Ref, and Will saves.
12	The cleric loses access to 1d3 randomly determined spells until the next day.
13	The Hidden Lord believes His worshiper is unclean. The cleric is unable to *lay on hands* or *turn unholy* until he is baptized. The cleric must be fully immersed in clean water to perform the rite.
14	The cleric's deity is enraged by the cleric's sinful uses of His power. The cleric's *lay on hands* ability only works on creatures of chaotic alignment for the next 1d4 days.
15	The Hidden Lord will not be placated on this day. When the cleric rests for the night, the deity disapproval range is not reduced. Starting on the following day, the cleric must make a successful DC 15 Will save before resting for the night to regain the deity's favor. The disapproval range will not reset until a nightly Will save succeeds.
16	The Hidden Lord devotes His attention to worthier champions. The cleric's *lay on hands* and *turn unholy* abilities are weakened. For the next 1d4 days, the effects of those abilities are halved and rounded down (e.g., if the cleric heals 7 hit points of damage, the hit points restored are reduced to 3.)
17	The cleric loses the ability to turn unholy creatures for 1d6 days.
18	The Hidden Lord believes the cleric's holy symbol is tainted. The cleric must immediately throw away all holy symbols in possession. The cleric will be unable to cast any spells until a new holy symbol is obtained. The value of tainted holy symbols cannot be counted as sacrifice to the Hidden Lord.
19	The cleric cannot cast any level 1 spells or canticles until the next day.
20+	The cleric's voice doth offend the Hidden Lord. The deity demands a vow of silence until the following day. The cleric may not speak or cast spells. Disobedience is met with swift retribution. A phantom bolt of spectral energy strikes the cleric for 4d6 damage and the cleric's vow of silence is extended an additional day.

CANTICLES OF THE HIDDEN LORD

Music and ritual play central roles in many worship services. Raised in prayer, the voices of the faithful can invoke minor powers of their deity, much like a spell. True believers that walk The Hidden Path will be rewarded with the following canticles during their spiritual journey:

Level 1: *Death Touch*   Level 3: *Psalm of Secrets*   Level 5: *Black Temple Prayer*

DEATH TOUCH

All adherents of The Hidden Lord learn *Death Touch*, a reversed form of the cleric's *lay on hands* ability. The cleric recites a baleful dirge while physically touching the target using an action. *Death Touch* inflicts wounds on the living. Animated creatures, such as elementals or constructs, do not take damage.

The damage die used scales according to the cleric's level. Consult the following table:

Level	Damage Die
1-3	1d3
4-8	1d6
9-10	1d12

The effect is reversed on un-dead creatures, instead restoring hit points equivalent to the damage inflicted.

Before rolling the spell check, the cleric may elect to impose a single debilitating condition from the list below instead of causing full damage. "Overflow" dice become normal damage, but if the damage dice are too low, there is no effect at all.

Effect	# of Die	Condition
Twist limb	1	Opposed Fort saves, or move at half speed 1d3 rounds
Bruise organ	2	-1 cumulative penalty to melee attacks and damage
Boil blood	3	Opposed Fort saves, or blinded or deafened 1d4 rounds
Pinch nerve	4	Opposed Fort saves, or paralyzed 1d6 rounds

The difference between the alignment of the cleric and the target defines the amount of devastation wrought by the attack. The dark power is more lethal against living creatures of differing alignment.

Spell check	Same	Adjacent	Opposed
1-11	Failure	Failure	Failure
12-13	1 die	1 die	2 dice
14-19	1 die	2 dice	3 dice
20-21	2 dice	3 dice	4 dice
22+	3 dice	4 dice	5 dice

PSALM OF SECRETS

This song is laden with double meanings and holds the power to reveal secret doors. To call down The Hidden Lord's boon, the cleric must swing a brass censer smoldering with incense for 1 turn while intoning the solemn song. When the psalm ends, the cleric makes a spell check and consults the table below.

Spell check	Result
1-15	Failure.
16-17	The cleric receives a sign the next time a secret door is within 10' of the cleric. The sign can take many forms: a section of masonry smashing to the ground; an ominous whistling sound; or a pebble rolling across the floor, coming to rest before the hidden portal.

18-23	The cleric receives a sign whenever a secret door is within 20' of the cleric for 1d6 turns. The sign can take many forms: a section of masonry smashing to the ground; an ominous whistling sound; or a pebble rolling across the floor, coming to rest before the hidden portal.
24-25	The cleric receives a sign whenever a secret door is within 50' of the cleric for 2d6 hours. The sign can take many forms: a section of masonry smashing to the ground; an ominous whistling sound; or a pebble rolling across the floor, coming to rest before the hidden portal.
26+	Until the hour strikes midnight, the air around the caster remains tinged with incense smoke. Whenever the cleric comes within 100' of a secret door, the smoke snakes into a wispy trail leading to the portal. The cleric also sees a ghostly outline of the opening when within 20'.

BLACK TEMPLE PRAYER

By reciting this prayer, the cleric opens a portal to an extradimensional temple consecrated to The Hidden Lord. After each verse, a platinum ceremonial bell (costing at least 1,000 gp) must be struck. Invoking this power requires 5 minutes of total concentration.

The first time this canticle is used, the judge should hand the player a single piece of graph paper with a 40'x40' square room at the center. The room contains a 10' wide entry portal and an altar atop a 10'x10' dais. Future invocations of this prayer allow the player to expand the temple to his or her liking.

The chaotic Hidden Lord only reveals the *Black Temple Prayer* to his most loyal servants. Clerics should never forget they are only visitors to this quasidimension.

The Hidden Lord may refuse to answer this prayer should the cleric be disfavored.

Spell check	Result
1	Failure and worse! Hostile creatures takes up residence in the extraplanar temple, laying claim to all its wealth. The judge rolls privately and notes the intruders. Roll a d6: (1) 2d6 zombies; (2) 1d8 ghouls; (3) 1 mummy; (4) 1d3 randomly-generated type III demons; (5) 1 randomly-generated type IV demon; (6) extradimensional analogue of cleric.
2-19	Failure.
20-21	A 10'x10' archway of black stone is summoned for 1 turn. Any creatures or items that pass through the archway fade away and are transported to a linked archway in the cleric's extraplanar temple. The cleric can dismiss the portal with a thought.
22-27	A 10'x10' archway of black stone is summoned for up to 1d6 turns. Any creatures or items that pass through the archway fade away and are transported to a linked archway in the cleric's extraplanar temple. The cleric can dismiss the portal with a thought. The cleric can also expand, reallocate, or contract the temple floor plan by 2d6 × 10'. The floor plan is constrained to a total area of 160' x 200' or roughly the size of a single sheet of quadrille paper.
28-29	A 10'x10' archway of black stone is summoned for up to 1d12 hours. Any creatures or items that pass through the archway fade away and are transported to a linked archway in the cleric's extraplanar temple. The cleric can dismiss the portal with a thought. The cleric can also expand, reallocate, or contract the temple floor plan by 2d8 × 10'. The floor plan is constrained to a total area of 160' x 200' or roughly the size of a single sheet of quadrille paper.
30+	A 10'x10' archway of black stone is summoned for up to 1 day. Any creatures or items that pass through the archway fade away and are transported to a linked archway in the cleric's extraplanar temple. The cleric can dismiss the portal with a thought. The cleric can also expand, reallocate, or contract the temple floor plan by 2d12 × 10'. The floor plan is constrained to a total area of 160' x 200' or roughly the size of a single sheet of quadrille paper.

JUSTICIA

To name Justicia of the Helmless Vigil is to invoke one or both of her twin aspects: righteousness and mercy. Justicia appears in the mortal world as a statuesque, powerful, warrior bearing a flaming, golden longsword. She is clad in an ornate, gilt-engraved suit of full plate mail, but never wears a helm, so no visor or eye-slit can impede her perception of the just path. Divinity defines her features: from her high, angled cheekbones to the noble's point from which her long, raven-gloss hair sweeps back across fine, fluted ears. Her smile conveys the deepest empathy or the sharpest vindication, depending on what lies within the heart of the viewer. The Knight-Chaplain Raedia, speaking of when she was first called to Justicia's service, describes the presence of the goddess thusly: "grace incarnate and unfathomable in her splendor…"

Her followers are lawful clerics, cavaliers, guardsmen, sheriffs and anyone who enforces fairness through strength, tempered by mercy and humility. This humility stems from the belief that all mortals, no matter how evil-seeming, can find redemption. Entering Justicia's service means joining one of the many militant religious orders founded in her name. All members learn to wield the sword and to use it as the holy symbol through which they can channel the favor of Justicia. Members wear a white tabard with the symbol of the goddess embroidered in red – a flaming longsword held point-down. Individual Orders are permitted to expand upon this insignia. Tabards of the Order of the Sundered Scale (paladins dedicated to slaying evil dragons and giving recompense to victims out of the hoards they recover) depict the sword of Justicia pressing against a shield ringed with vigilant eyes, with the blade piercing a dragon head.

Within these orders a devout follower might rise to earn a high title: for clerics, Knight–Chaplain Proper; for warriors, Knight-Templar; and for wizards, Knight-Arcanist Argent. Members of such orders are much sought after to serve as magistrates, for they are known for wisdom, fairness and for being incorruptible. Such magistrates, whether cleric, warrior or mage, are given the title Knight-Justicar Blazon.

Justicia is legendary for avenging wrongs done to her faithful servants. A high-priest of Bobugbubilz once sacrificed one of her Knight-Chaplains to the Toadfiend. Justicia answered this injury by sending a landslide that buried the toad-priest's mountainside temple under countless tons of rock.

SPECIAL TRAITS

Lay on Hands

When the cleric of Justicia successfully casts *lay on hands* roll 1d4 to determine its unique manifestation: (1) the cleric is enveloped in a nimbus of golden light; (2) The cleric must pass a sword or dagger over the patient. When she does, the blade radiates a heatless, healing flame; (3) A long, amber-tinted, sword-shaped shadow falls across the recipient. There is no source for this shadow and it is visible even in dim light; (4) The wounded, ill or afflicted individual becomes encased in an illusory suit of plate mail formed from starshine.

Divine Favors

Absolve: The cleric can relieve an individual of the guilt that she feels about a minor wrongdoing and remove the stain of that wrongdoing from the individual's conscience or spiritual self. Using this minor blessing, a cleric of Justicia can absolve actions such as small or "white" lies, cheating others out of small amounts of money or passing off poor quality goods. Significant, major or mortal spiritual and ethical transgressions cannot be absolved with a minor blessing – they must be purified through a powerful ritual or the transgressor must receive divine punishment or accept a divine quest appropriate to the seriousness of the transgression.

Cleanse: The cleric can remove all dirt, stains, scratches and cosmetic blemishes from items by immersing said item in a water-filled basin that the cleric has consecrated to the goddess. This minor blessing cannot repair items or restore functionality.

Cleric of Justicia Titles

Level	Title
1	Acolyte-Guard
2	Sword-Cleric
3	Knight-Cleric
4	Knight-Chaplain
5	Sword-Saint

Disapproval

Like all deities, Justicia expects her mortal agents to be unwavering in their faith and potent in the work they do in her name. She knows that to err is to be mortal and she has sympathy for her followers who fall short of the mark. But the consequences she metes out to steer those followers to the right path are at once loving, instructive and *firm*. Below is a deity disapproval table specific to clerics of Justicia.

Roll	Disapproval
1	The cleric must swear to walk everywhere for the next month; she cannot utilize mounts, wagons, boats, or any conveyance other than her own feet to travel.
2	The cleric must swear to a comrade that, in the event of that comrade's death, the cleric will lay her body to rest in her homeland.
3	The cleric must immediately begin a six-day fast. Each day of fasting beyond the first reduces the cleric's Stamina by one point. These points are regained on the second day after the cleric breaks this fast.
4	The cleric is lent out by Justicia to the service of another god and must complete that service as part of her current quest. The god and the service are determined by the judge. Most likely it will be a Lawful god, though Justicia might give her follower's service over to a Neutral god as part of an exchange that she sees as providing a net benefit to Law.
5	The cleric is given an object lesson in humility. Justicia names one of the cleric's compatriots. The cleric cannot refuse a request or direction from that individual for two hours. However, if that compatriot does not show wisdom or mercy in commanding the cleric, Justicia reverses their roles for 10 minutes.
6	The cleric must recite the names of all the stars and constellations she knows in the heavens. Before the recitation, the judge will give the player five seconds to estimate how many he or she knows. At the end of the recitation, the player will roll the die on the die chain closest to the number that he or she estimated. If the die roll is greater than the number of stars named, the cleric temporarily loses one point of Personality for two hours of in-game time.
7	The cleric must load up a shield with three stone extra weight (36 pounds) and bear this on her shoulders for the next two hours of in-game time. The cleric may only set this load down to engage in combat, cast spells, *lay on hands* or *turn unholy*.
8	The cleric is teleported to an extradimensional space where she must confess to all transgressions and mistakes that she has made during the past 48 hours of serving Justicia.
9	The cleric must go barefoot for the next two hours.
10	At the next safe opportunity (e.g., not in the middle of a battle or other encounter) the cleric must run a "gauntlet" comprised of the cleric's compatriots, who strike the cleric with fists or the "flat" of their weapons. The cleric must run the gauntlet as many times as it takes to successfully reach the end.
11	The cleric must swear an oath to defend a person or cause of his or her choice. If the judge determines that the cause is not in accordance with the work and goals of Justicia, the cleric loses 4 points of Stamina until after the next time the cleric acts in defense of the declared person or cause.

Page 21

Roll	Disapproval
12	The cleric forgoes the wearing of armor for the next four hours. The cleric must carry her armor on her back in a bundle or heaped upon her shield like a dish tray.
13	The cleric must break her own sword and cannot use it as a weapon or holy symbol (e.g., cannot *turn unholy*) until it is re-forged. The cleric can still cast spells and *lay on hands*.
14	The cleric loses the *Templar's Might* canticle for the next two hours. If the cleric is not sufficient level to know this canticle, then he or she suffers as -1 penalty to hit and damage rolls instead.
15	The cleric loses the Templar's Might canticle for the next eight hours. If the cleric is not sufficient level to know this canticle, then he or she suffers as -1d penalty to hit and damage rolls instead.
16	During the next combat encounter, the cleric must engage an enemy in single combat and refrain from striking until the third round following the start of the engagement. If an ally joins the combat, the cleric loses ½ of his or her remaining hit points at the end of the engagement.
17	In order to relieve another follower of danger, Justicia teleports the dangerous encounter to the cleric's own location for the cleric and his or her allies to deal with. The encounter is determined by the judge and can be anything with a difficulty or challenge level appropriate to the cleric and his or her allies.
18	Justicia lends the divine aid she would give the cleric to other followers who are presently more needy and/or efficacious. The cleric cannot cast 1st level spells until after a night has passed.
19	Justicia's confidence in the cleric simply cannot be restored on this day. When the cleric rests for the night, his or her deity disapproval range is not reduced. Starting on the following day, the cleric must make a successful DC 15 Will save every eight hours to regain the deity's favor. The disapproval range will not reset until the cleric's Will save succeeds.
20+	For two hours of in-game time following the onset of disapproval, the cleric may accept *nothing* from an ally or another creature: no food, no water, no beneficial spells, no help in combat, etc. Nothing beneficial an ally does *can even affect the cleric*. If the cleric dies as the result of this isolation, then his or her spirit travels to Justicia's Celestial Fane where one of the goddess' Lawful Primes will decide what happens next…

CANTICLES OF JUSTICIA

Oaths of service and honor-vows are the heart's blood of militant religious orders. As an incantation effects wizardry, so do vows and oaths call forth aide from the deities — if spoken with devotion. Justicia's Knight-Chaplains go through their service chanting their oaths and vows which manifest as divinely-powered canticles:

Level 1: *Righteous Freedom*

Level 3: *Templar's Might*

Level 5: *Martyr's Reward*

RIGHTEOUS FREEDOM

It is Justicia's will that none of her knights be more encumbered in their efforts to mete out justice than they need to be. She sends them a tiny spark of her divine power, one that lightens the load of their chosen armor and gives them freedom of movement when wearing armor in battle. This canticle reduces a cleric's armor check penalty by 1 for every level the cleric has attained. It also reduces the cleric's armor speed penalty by 5' and lowers the fumble die by one step on the dice chain. Finally this canticle lends divine strength to whatever armor the cleric wears, increasing the armor's AC bonus by +1 with an additional +1 for every three levels above 1st that the cleric has attained (see table).

TEMPLAR'S MIGHT

All of Justicia's clergy are battle-priests trained in the arts of warfare by the militant religious order to which they belong. When a cleric of Justicia attains third level, he or she can perform Mighty Deeds as a 1st level warrior. The cleric declares the deed and rolls the appropriate deed die, but the deed die is only used to determine whether or not the cleric's deed succeeds. The deed die never adds to the cleric's attack or damage rolls. As a cleric of Justicia advances in level, so does his or her ability to perform Mighty Deeds; the cleric always rolls a deed die as if he or she was a warrior two levels lower than his or her cleric level (see table).

MARTYR'S REWARD

By achieving 5th level or higher, a cleric of Justicia becomes especially valued by the goddess. Such high-level clerics are invaluable to Justicia's divine cause and their loss is not taken lightly. If a 5th level or higher cleric of Justicia is killed, and Justicia regards the activities of that cleric at the time of his or her death to have been directly pursuant to her divine cause, the goddess will deliver retribution to the agents of the cleric's death. (The exact form of retribution is determined by the judge.)

Level	Attack	Templar's Might Die	Armor Check Bonus	Armor Speed Bonus	Armor Bonus	Unarmored	Padded, Leather, Studded	Hide, Scale, Chain	Banded, Half-Plate, Full Plate	Shield
1	+0	N/A	+1	+5'	+1	d4	d6	d10	d14	d6
2	+1	N/A	+2	+5'	+1	d4	d6	d10	d14	d6
3	+2	d3	+3	+5'	+1	d4	d6	d10	d14	d6
4	+2	d4	+4	+5'	+2	d4	d6	d10	d14	d6
5	+3	d5	+5	+5'	+2	d4	d6	d10	d14	d6
6	+4	d6	+6	+5'	+2	d4	d6	d10	d14	d6
7	+5	d7	+7	+5'	+3	d4	d6	d10	d14	d6
8	+5	d8	+8	+5'	+3	d4	d6	d10	d14	d6
9	+6	d10	+9*	+5'	+3	d4	d6	d10	d14	d6
10	+7	d10**	+9*	+5'	+4	d4	d6	d10	d14	d6

At +9 Armor Check Bonus, a cleric of Justicia can wear full plate and carry a shield with no armor check penalty.

**Because a cleric of Justicia's Templar's Might die only determines whether or not the cleric accomplishes a deed and does NOT modify attack or damage rolls, it tops out at a straight d10 roll.*

MALOTOCH

Most folk shudder at the sight of gore and recoil from the scent of rotten flesh. These prodigies serve notice of mortality and inevitable death, and we deny and shun them, lest somehow we, ourselves, be tainted and marked for Death. And, so, we fail to appreciate the manifold benefits we reap from the fertility of flesh-become-Earth, and notice not that corpses fail to accumulate in piles and windrows, but instead nourish worm and raven, feed mold and rot, become bone and dust, and, so, revert to the base forms of Life itself. Only a few give reverence to the Carrion Crow Goddess, Malotoch, who some call "demon." Only a few worship Our Lady of Dissolution, the crow-headed goddess of the battle's aftermath, the taloned Mother of Disease, the Devourer of Flesh made holy by death. Malotoch appeals to those mortals who recognize that it is fitting to consume the flesh of one's fellows, to close the circle of life so poignantly. These are the cannibals who eat of their brothers' flesh, not because they fear starvation, but because it is righteous that they do so.

Malotoch's aspect is of a beauteous human woman of ideal proportions, with the head and legs of her most blessed avatar, the carrion crow. Like the crow, She is wily and her memory is long; and her vengeance is patient and sure. Her sacred places are battlefields, crypts and sepulchers, plague pits, and anywhere else were the reek of blood-rot is high and the sweet scent of decaying flesh lingers long. She is called "Crow Mistress" by those who fear her and "The Mother" by those who worship at her scaled and taloned feet. Few are those who name her Malotoch, for most people fear to draw the Crow Mistress's unblinking eye. Those few are her clergy, and they keep sacred her holy places through sacrifice and ritual, visit her vengeance upon those who profane them, and partake in her holiest rites and rituals.

The sacred symbol of Malotoch is the crow and, in her sacred iconography, crows usually are depicted perching upon a gibbet, gallows, or perhaps a broken battle standard. Her clergy carry or wear tokens like crows' feet, feathers, or bones. Among the laity, sometimes these holy symbols are made of metal or stone, but the priests of the Crow Mistress always bear the veritable remains of her sacred messengers. Most of the time, though, the priests of Malotoch dress like any other person, but will always bear a token sacred to their goddess (e.g., a crow's feather in a hat, a crow's skull on a thong about the neck).

The clergy of Malotoch are secretive and insular as a rule, as they are hated and feared by most. So Malotoch's clerics often travel in murders of three or more rather than singly. During her holy-days the clergy of Malotoch dress in ragged black vestments, sometimes besmirched with grave dirt or stained with blood or with the effluvium of corrupted flesh. The highest of her priests wear flowing, winged cloaks, black as night, and masks in the likeness of crow's heads with feathers of blackened iron and beaks of sharpened bronze, their eyes hidden behind black metal grilles or lenses of obsidian. The short sword is their sacred weapon, and those clerics of Malotoch who can afford to do so pay handsomely for finely crafted weapons adorned with effigies of crows and other scavenger birds.

The holiest days of the cult of Malotoch fall on the new moon, when darkest night blankets the world, and her high holy-day is the last new moon of the year, when Death is strongest. During these holy-days, clerics and worshipers of Malotoch gather in lonely, forgotten places, to make bloody sacrifices to her and consume the flesh thereof. Places sacred to the Crow Mistress can be found near any human habitation, whether in the great cities or in the lonely wilds: graveyards with crumbling stones, ancient barrow lands, killing grounds and execution yards, and the sites of great battles, half-forgotten. In her holiest places, carrion crows of all kinds gather together, muttering and crying out in their croaking tones. They perch there and watch, and wait, and remember. It is perilous indeed to intrude on these places when her guardians await, lest you come bearing a toothsome gift, living or dead… but preferably dead. The ignorant common folk may forget the history of these places but Malotoch remembers, and She knows the names of the fallen. During the dark of the moon, good folk stay far away from her sacred enclaves, and try not to think about what happens there. Occasionally, though, some cleric of another faith or a foolish, righteous king might seek to disrupt the rites and kill these priests and worshipers. Just as often, Malotoch's vengeance falls upon them and theirs, and people learn anew why Malotoch's people are not to be trifled with, and why crows, alone among the beasts, are counted in *murders*.

SPECIAL TRAITS
Lay on Hands

When the cleric of Malotoch successfully casts *lay on hands* roll 1d4 to determine its unique manifestation: (1) a tarry black stain spreads from the fingers of the cleric and seeps into the flesh of the target's wounds, before fading away over the next hour; (2) A murder of shadow crows descends and perches on the cleric and target, obscuring both, then fly away into nearby shadows when the healing is done; (3) The fetid odor of rotting flesh surrounds the cleric during the healing and lingers around both healer and healed for 1d3 turns afterward; (4) Threads of blackness emanate from the fingers of the cleric and crawl, writhing, into the flesh of the person being healed.

Divine Favors

Raven Moon: Upon the night of the new moon, clerics of Malotoch receive +1 to any spell check, and +2 for her canticles and for the spells most sacred to her (*darkness, curse, speak with the dead*). On the night of the last new moon of the year, they may use a d24 to cast any spell or perform any other rite (including canticles). The clerics of the Crow Mistress find themselves similarly thwarted, and roll at -1 to any spell check during full moons, and on the longest day of the year they roll a d16 for any spell casting, rites, or canticles.

Speak with Messenger: Once per day, clerics of Malotoch may seek out a crow, raven, rook, or jackdaw, and ask it any question, but will receive only a croaking, one-word answer in response. This response will be true according to the knowledge and understanding of the bird in question.

Blessing of the Flesh: Consumption of dead or dying flesh is Malotoch's most sacred rite. Once per day, provided that she has consumed human flesh that day, a cleric of Malotoch may halt her own "bleeding out," when reduced to zero hit points. However, the cleric still remains out of action and unconscious until she is healed to 1 or more hit points.

Cleric of Malotoch Titles

Level	Title
1	Fledgling
2	Corbie
3	Raven
4	Rook
5	Murder-Mother (or Father)

Disapproval

The priests and priestess of Malotoch are fanatical in their worship, and have been granted access to her powers, including the ability to cast spells, conduct sacred rites, and provide healing and succor to the faithful. However, even the Crow Mistress's clergy may fall into error. Should they earn her disapproval, whether by misusing the powers granted them or by failing to keep her sacraments, the clergy of Malotoch are subject to the following penalties as a result of her vengeance for their trespass.

Roll	Disapproval
1	The cleric has offended the Crow Mistress, and must recite 10 unique prayers to her during the darkest hour of the night. (This takes 10 minutes, but must be done at the correct time.) If not done, then cleric must roll on the Disapproval table again, and add 10 to the result.
2	Malotoch is angered by the cleric's transgression. To atone the cleric must scavenge for meals for the next week. 20% chance of acquiring a food or water-borne illness.

Roll	Disapproval
3	The cleric must acquire and burn a feather from a crow or other corvid, or suffer a -1 penalty to all saving throws on the following day.
4	Malotoch turns her regard from the cleric. For the next day, *lay on hands* attempts must be made with a d16 instead of a d20.
5	Malotoch requires a sacrifice. Until the cleric slays a foe and exposes it for a feast of crows, she suffers a -2 penalty to spell checks with the spell or canticle that resulted in disapproval. Additional rolls of this result should be ignored and re-rolled, until the required sacrifice has been made.
6	Malotoch must feed. The cleric must carve flesh from her own body and feed it to a crow. Roll 1d4, and take that much damage. Until this sacrifice is completed, the cleric cannot use *lay on hands* on herself.
7	Convert the unbeliever. The cleric must convert someone to the worship of Malotoch, or suffer a -3 penalty to spell checks with the specific spell or canticle that resulted in disapproval. Additional rolls of this result increase the penalty by -1 and increase by +1 the number of converts she must make. Conversion requires willing consumption of human or demi-human flesh.
8	Malotoch harvests the vital fluids from her worshiper as atonement. The cleric's skin shrivels and she loses 2 points of Stamina which must be left to heal naturally.
9	For the next week, any attempt to use *lay on hands* will fail automatically if the target is not a worshiper of Malotoch, consecrated by the willing consumption of human or demi-human flesh.
10	The cleric loses the ability to *lay on hands* until the next day.
11	For 1d5 days, each time the cleric casts one randomly determined spell (including *lay on hands*), she loses access to it until she prays for one hour.
12	Before the next new moon, the cleric must build a shrine to Malotoch, in a place where none exists. Failure to do so will result in the loss of 1d4 randomly determined spells (including *lay on hands*) until the shrine is built.
13	Malotoch requires her priest to bathe in the blood of a lawful cleric. Each day that goes by until this occurs, the cleric will lose 1 point of (roll 1d7): (1-2) Strength; (3-4) Agility; (5-6) Stamina; or (7) Luck. This loss will be restored once the cleric's baptism is complete.
14	Malotoch sends a murder of crows to bedevil the cleric for 1d3 days. Every moment that the cleric is not praying to the goddess, or doing something to benefit her, the birds will swoop down and peck at the cleric, befoul her robes with their ordure, and otherwise distract her. Sleep will be next to impossible, and she will not be able to heal hit points or attributes during this time. -2 to any spell checks.
15	The goddess requires her cleric to complete an important errand for her (something that can be completed in just a couple of days, chosen at judge's discretion). For each day that passes before the task is completed, the base disapproval range rises by +1. It will drop to 0 when the task has been completed.
16	The cleric loses access to all spells until she successfully casts *Psalm of the Flesh-Eater*. Completing the canticle and consuming the consecrated flesh will have no other effect but grant access to those spells.
17	For the next week, the priest will be afflicted with a horrible disease, frightful to behold (e.g., oozing sores on the face). Any attempts to traffic with normal folk will end poorly (-5 to any rolls made as a result of interaction with NPCs) until the disease heals naturally. Any attempt to heal the disease with *lay on hands* will increase the length of the ailment by 1d10 days.
18	Malotoch withdraws her favor from the cleric, granting only a fraction of her power. Until the cleric atones through righteous penance, results for any spell checks (including *lay on hands*) or attempts to *turn unholy* will count as one step lower in effects (e.g., 2 dice of healing become 1 die, go one result lower on spell results, etc.).
19	Malotoch's wrath descends upon the cleric, striking her dumb for 1d3 days, and making it impossible for her to cast spells.
20+	The cleric must use the *Murder Hymn* canticle to summon an anathaema eagle, and ride it to the peak of Tol Morda. There she must cut off her own hand and lay it upon the Altar of Bones as a sacrifice.

CANTICLES OF MALOTOCH

Level 1: *Murder Hymn* Level 3: *Psalm of the Flesh-Eater* Level 5: *Requiem of the Surrendered Flesh*

MURDER HYMN

With a ghastly, croaking chant, the cleric of Malotoch summons murders of carrion crows. At the highest level, this canticle allows the cleric to choose to summon a small number of anathaema eagles, instead.

Spell check	Result
1-11	Failure.
12-13	1d6+1 live carrion crows appear. They will obey simple instructions of up to two words, for 1 turn, before flying away.
14-23	CL+1 *dozen* diseased carrion crows appear, and may be ordered to attack any single individual within sight range. The crows persist until the creature is dead or until 5+CL combat rounds pass, before flying away. See stat block below. **Diseased carrion crows**: Init +3; Atk swarming bite +1 melee (1 hp x one quarter the number of birds, rounded down, plus disease); AC 12; hp 1 per bird; MV 5' or fly 50'; Act special; SP half damage from non-area attacks, armored areas of targets not damaged but 10% chance per round that unprotected eye is blinded, disease DC 9+CL Fort save or contract grave rot (-1 Stamina per day until healed or dead); SV Fort +0, Ref +7, Will -2; AL C.
24-31	1d6 per CL *score* diseased carrion crows (as above) appear, and may be ordered to attack up to CL different targets. The crows persist for 1 turn, or until dismissed. The cleric may command them to switch targets or attack new targets.
32+	Either CL anathaema eagles or 1d10 per CL *score* diseased carrion crows appear. Either may be ordered to attack up to CL targets. The creatures persist for 1d4 hours, or until dismissed. The cleric may command them to switch targets or attack new targets. If the cleric summons anathaema eagles, one may be ridden as a mount by the summoning cleric. **Anathaema eagle**: Init +4; Attack claw +6 melee (1d6+3) or bite +6 melee (1d8+3, disease); AC 16; HD 4d10+4; MV 10' or fly 80'; Act 3d20; SP disease DC 12+CL Fort save or contract filth fever (DC 12 Fort save or take 1 point Agility and Stamina damage per day for 1d3 days); SV Fort +5, Ref +8, Will +3; AL C.

PSALM OF THE FLESH-EATER

The cleric sings a vile, croaking prayer over the flesh of a deceased human or demi-human. Upon successful completion of the prayer, the cleric may partake of this grisly feast, and receive from The Mother a measure of divine protection or other powers. On a successful casting, the cleric or worshiper may choose to take a lower but potentially more desirable result from the table. Any non-worshiper who eats this flesh should make a DC 10+CL Willpower save or take an amount of damage equal to the spell check. Should any cleric of another deity sup from the blessed corpse, she should be subject to divine retribution by her own deity, per the judge's discretion.

Spell check	Result
1-15	Failure.
16-17	The cleric receives +2 to melee damage and saving throws for 1 turn.
18-20	The cleric receives +CL to her next spell check of another spell (but not another canticle).
21-23	All the cleric's senses are sharpened, providing a CL+1 bonus to any checks requiring sight, hearing, smell, taste, or touch. In addition, she gains 1d3 points of temporary Luck which must be used before dawn of the next day.
24-25	The cleric's body becomes resistant to mundane and magical damage. She may ignore damage taken (1d6+CL) a number of times equal to CL. Alternately, she can spellburn (as wizard) a number of points equal to her CL+1, to be applied her next spell check. These points are not burned from her own physical attributes, but from those of the corpse upon which she fed.
26+	The cleric may choose any two results, below, including all effects listed, even if they are optional.

REQUIEM OF THE SURRENDERED FLESH

At level 5 the cleric gains access to a complex chant whereby her body is transformed, temporarily or permanently, into un-dead flesh. The thousand names of the Crow Mistress are sung, and runes, sigils, and inscriptions appear on the failing flesh of the caster. While hideous and terrifying to behold, the results of this canticle provide the cleric with damage resistance and protection against turning and/or purifying magics. At the highest result, this canticle allows followers of Malotoch to rise as un-dead creatures, if killed. The results of the spell makes the cleric unsuitable for the company of most normal beings, who will react with fear and, potentially, violent hostility to her changed form. On a successful casting, the cleric or worshiper may choose to take a lower but potentially more desirable result from the table.

Spell check	Result
1	Failure and worse! A misstep in the ritual has caused it to backfire. Roll 1d4: (1) take CL damage which cannot be healed except by natural healing; (2) the cleric's flesh is so weakened that the next successful attack counts as a critical hit on the appropriate table; (3) the cleric's flesh begins to rot and she will take 1d8+CL damage per day until a *lay on hands* from another worshiper of Malotoch results in 3 or more dice of healing; (4) the cleric's flesh withers as she ages 1d10 years per caster level, and permanently loses 1d3 points of Strength, Agility, or Stamina, plus 1 additional point per 10 years aged (spread evenly across the attributes).
2-19	Failure.
20-21	The cleric's flesh withers to mummy-like consistency for 1d10+CL turns. She need not eat or drink, and non-magical weapons do half damage to her. She also receives +2 to any saving throw against magical effects, or reduces the damage dice for magical damage from spells one step on the die chain (d8 becomes d7, d6 becomes d5, etc.).
22-27	The cleric's flesh begins to seethe with corruption. For the next CL hours, the cleric enjoys the following benefits: Any damaging attack only does half damage. She adds CL/2 (rounded down) additional HD beyond her own when determining results of *turn unholy* attempts made against her. Any normal human or demi-human attempting to approach her must make a DC 8+CL Fort save or be driven back retching with nausea from the reek of her rotting flesh.
28-29	The cleric's flesh begins to weep blood and corruption and her eyes blaze with unholy fires. For the next CL+6 hours, she may ignore damage from any attacks made with mundane weapons, and the damage dice for magical weapons or spells are reduced two steps on the die chain (d8 becomes d6, d6 becomes d4, etc.). She also gains a ranged gaze attack against anyone at whom she looks directly (even if only in reflection). The target must make a DC 10+CL Willpower save or flee in unreasoning fear, until a successful Willpower save is made.
30+	The cleric's body appears as normal except that it is covered in thousands of lines of tiny script, like a full-body tattoo the color of old blood. For the next CL+1 days, the cleric's saving throws against magical attacks receive +CL bonus. Additionally, if she is slain, she will rise as an un-dead creature with a number hit points equal to normal, plus CL. The cleric acquires the normal un-dead traits (does not eat, drink, or breathe; is immune to critical hits, disease, and poison, as well as to the *sleep*, *charm*, and *paralysis* spells, other mental effects, and cold damage). The cleric also rolls critical hits on *Crit Table U: Un-dead* (see DCC RPG rulebook, p. 390).

PELAGIA

Woe to those whose livelihoods depend on the graciousness of the oceans, who do not show deference to the Goddess of the Singing Sea. As goddess of the seas, oceans, travel, and music, Pelagia is respected by bards, sailors, merchants, and pirates alike. Through the years, sailors and singers have respectfully created monikers for Pelagia which have become as varied as the oceans themselves: The Singing Sea, The Coral Queen, and The Maiden Voyager.

Pelagia's motivations are focused on the health of the oceans—to keep them accessible to as many creatures as possible, as well as free from pollution, destruction, and the unnatural taint of magic. In her eyes, the forces of Law and Chaos are mere currents in her vast waters; as symbiotic together as the remora is to the shark, or the hermit crab to the sea snail. Pelagia has an uneasy truce with Ithha, Prince of Elemental Wind, and scorns both Azi Dahaka and Nimlu-run for their corrupting effects in Her waters.

While many may find it wise to make offerings to Pelagia to ensure good fortune on their journeys, the truly devout dedicate themselves to a lifetime of service to advance the goals of the Singing Sea. Clerics commonly cover themselves in elaborate tattoo patterns which symbolize the sea. It's not unusual to find a follower of Pelagia covered in curved tattooed lines that give the appearance of rolling waves when the cleric walks. Clerics of Pelagia typically clothe themselves in blue garb adorned with necklaces of shells or pearls and use rapiers as their preferred weapon. As part of their servitude, the cleric will work a lifetime on their personal Map of the Known World, focusing on the seas and coastlines the cleric has traveled to, which can also be used as their holy symbol.

Servants of Pelagia ardently protect the oceans, and are known for their effective pirate hunting, which pleases the goddess by keeping travelers safe on her waters. Sacrificial offerings typically consist of valuable shells and pearls returned to the ocean in her name. Shrines erected in her honor range from humble sea coves, to the majestic mythical holy site whose hidden location is known only to the highest of clerics of her order, the Temple of the Sacred Wave.

SPECIAL TRAITS

Lay On Hands

When the cleric of Pelagia successfully casts *lay on hands* roll 1d4 to determine its unique manifestation: (1) A soft wave of sea-foam washes out of the cleric's hands and covers the wounds of the victim. When the wave subsides, the wounds are healed; (2) The cleric begins to sing a beautiful and enchanting melody. As the pitch and tempo rise, the wounds miraculously evaporate into mist; (3) Barnacles suddenly appear firmly affixed to the body of the wounded. After a few minutes, they can be peeled away revealing tender, healed skin underneath; (4) The cleric vomits forth gelatinous slime—miraculous jellyfish ooze—which heals wherever it is applied.

Divine Favors

Water breathing: The cleric is able to breathe underwater for 3d6 rounds, once per day.

Summon minor sea life: Once per day, when near any pool of water, the cleric can summon 1d6 small to medium sized fish or crustaceans (up to 12 inches in length) to the water's surface where they can be easily fetched.

Hold liquid: Once per day, the cleric is able to hold liquid (primarily water) like a solid (i.e., without the need of a container like a flask or waterskin). The cleric can hold one quart per caster level for up to 1 round per caster level.

Cleric of Pelagia Titles

Level	Title
1	Shantyman
2	Minstrel
3	Skald
4	Merman
5	Siren

Disapproval

The clerics and followers of Pelagia are expected to faithfully serve their goddess, and will refer to performing Her plans using phrases such as "swimming with Her current" or sometimes as "spreading Her song". Alas, fragile mortals are not always capable of understanding the complex demands of deities. Those who "wander from Her path" are reminded of Her higher purpose via the following punishments when they go astray.

Roll	Disapproval
1	Cleric must spend the next 15 minutes working on drawing a map of the known worlds.
2	Cleric must sing the 20-minute epic poem "Our Maiden of the Sea" to an audience of at least two members, or suffer -1 to spell checks for remainder of day.
3	Within the next 12 hours, the cleric must bathe herself (preferably in sea water) for at least 60 minutes.
4	To pay homage to the sleek creatures of the sea, the cleric is asked to remove all visible hair from her body.
5	Pelagia demands that the cleric must hold their breath underwater for 1d3 +1 rounds. After 1 round, cleric must make DC 10 Fortitude save each round or take -1 temporary Stamina damage.
6	Within the next 2 days, the cleric must add 2 square inches of tattoo to their skin (DC 10 Fort save or 1 hp damage).
7	Pelagia feels your song is unworthy. Cleric loses their voice for remainder of day. Ability to *lay on hands* remains available, but spell casting is not.
8	Pelagia asks the cleric to write a haiku dedicated to a fallen comrade and then recite it to her party (the player is encouraged to do so in game). PC makes spell checks at -1d penalty until complete.
9	The cleric must be punished for his continued hubris. Cleric loses 1 random 1st-level spell for remainder of the day.
10	The cleric's voice has offended the goddess. Cleric's tongue becomes engorged, forcing her words to slur and resulting in -3 to spell checks for 3d4 hours.
11	Pelagia questions their focus, and demands the cleric offer 20% of wealth to a temple, guild, or secret society dedicated to the worship of Pelagia.
12	Pelagia demands cleric to make a pilgrimage to an ocean or lake within 1d3 days lest they lose all abilities until pilgrimage is complete.
13	Pelagia feels cleric is not performing to full potential; cleric's *lay on hands* healing is limited to 1 die maximum for remainder of day.
14	Shame of the bottom feeder! Cleric is forced to the bottom of the initiative order until one full day of mediation is performed.
15	It pleases Pelagia to transform the cleric's face into that resembling more of a fish—cleric's eyelids are removed resulting in bulbous fish eyes. Cleric incurs -3 penalty to spell checks for remainder of day.
16	Pelagia reminds cleric of the power of Her holy gifts by revoking ability to *turn unholy* for 2d3 days.
17	The strain of failed prayer has resulted in the cleric forgetting how to cast 1d4 randomly selected spells.
18	It pleases Pelagia to transform the cleric's face into that resembling more of a fish—non-functional gills are inserted into the cleric's neck. In addition, cleric incurs -4 penalty to spell checks for remainder of day.
19	Blasphemer! Pelagia randomly selects one spell from cleric's known spell list and casts it against cleric (treat as spell check 22 with no save).
20+	Pelagia suspects the profane cleric wants to be closer to the Afterlife. Pelagia smites cleric by permanently advancing her physical age 1d5 years.

CANTICLES OF PELAGIA

For years, sailors have understood the power of work songs to motivate an ornery crew. Clerics of Pelagia are masters of the ancient sailor tradition of the sea shanty. Even the lowest level cleric of Pelagia has memorized and mastered a variety of sea shanties to perform a variety of tasks, all of which advance Pelagia's goals.

Level 1: *Motivational Shanty* Level 3: *Siren's Call* Level 5: *Water's True Name*

MOTIVATIONAL SHANTY

Even as young acolytes, the clerics of Pelagia learn a number of well-known sea shanties such as "All for 'me Dwarven Ale" and the salacious "Ladies of Dundraville" to improve morale, incite bravery and increase strength. However, with Pelagia's divine blessings, the Pelagian shantyman can boost a crew's (or parties') motivations, providing superhuman bonuses to Strength checks or Willpower saves. The effectiveness of the particular shanty depends on the level of the cleric:

Cleric Level	Shanty Effect
1-3	+1 to Strength checks and Willpower saves
4-6	+1d3 to Strength checks and Willpower saves
7+	+1d3 +CL to Strength checks and Willpower saves

SIREN'S CALL

One of Pelagia's most revered creatures is the Siren – the songstress of the sea. The Pelagian cleric who achieves the rank of Skald (3rd level) will be truly rewarded by the Coral Queen: the goddess will permanently transform the vocal chords of the cleric such that they are capable of reproducing the magical call of the siren. When the cleric exercises these divine chords, she will find all those within range will lose hostility towards the cleric and approach to stand before her mesmerized for as long as the cleric maintains the tune. Attacking a target enraptured with the siren's call will break their mesmerization. Targets may attempt a Willpower save to negate.

WATER'S TRUE NAME

Only the most pious of Pelagia's followers who have dedicated a near lifetime of service vanquishing hundreds of Her foes will be blessed with the most precious of gifts that Pelagia can bestow upon a mortal: *Water's True Name* and physical transformation of the cleric's body to be able to enable its pronunciation. With the ability to call the water, the caster is able to perform miraculous feats that demonstrate Pelagia's awesome power and strike fear in Her foes. Pelagian clerics fully comprehend that invoking *Water's True Name* is an event that ripples the very fabric that separates men from the divine and holds the potential to awaken sea demons and raise the attention of jealous patrons — it is not a *task* to be undertaken lightly.

On successful spell checks, the PC may substitute any effect at a lower spell check result.

Spell check	Result
1	Failure and worse. The PC's pathetic attempt at controlling nature has irritated the elemental elders. The PC accidentally conjures a violent air elemental which immediately begins to attack the caster.
2-19	Failure.
20-21	Walk on Water. The PC is able bind water beneath his feet so that he may stride across it. The PC may travel 10' per caster level.
22-27	Water Bridge. The PC is able to bind water beneath the feet of himself and his allies so that they may stride across it. The PC and up 2d6 companions may travel 10' per caster level.
28-29	Summon water elemental. The cleric is able to summon a fearsome sentient water elemental which obeys the Pelagian cleric for 2d6 rounds.

30-35	Minor Water Miracle. The cleric is able to channel the favor of Pelagia to control water and make it bend to the caster's will creating awe-inspiring miracles that sailors and bards will weave into tales for generations. As far as what makes a "minor" miracle, it is up to the judge's discretion, but as a general rule, it should be an event that could affect up to 20 or so individuals, several large ships, or creatures 5 HD and lower. Examples include: raise or lower tides in a harbor, create a whirlpool that could swallow a ship, or create an ocean wave that could speed the voyage of a vessel. In addition, the cleric has the ability to *turn unholy* against any water-based creature which is 5 HD or less within a 100' radius for 2d6 rounds.
36+	Major Water Miracle. The cleric demonstrates that he is truly one of Pelagia's chosen servants and has the full power of the Singing Sea at his command. In a booming voice resembling whale song, the Pelagian cleric is able to command waters and seas to obey his every command. The scope of the water miracle that the priest is able to control will be written about in religious texts and history scrolls for eons. The extent of the water miracle is up to PC's imagination and judge's discretion, but as a general rule, it should be an event that could affect hundreds of individuals, entire navies or fleets, or creatures up to 9 HD and lower. Examples might be: the cleric is able to part a sea enabling an entire town to flee an enemy, create a giant tsunami capable of devastating a coastal town, or create an ocean whirlpool capable of swallowing a fleet.

SHUL

Most societies revere orbiting moons, which hold power over their lands. These celestial orbs illuminate the night, but occasionally shroud the day in darkness. Their orderly motions influence the oceans, cause madness, transform beings into beasts, and provide precise measures of time (e.g., a calendar). Consequently, many attribute Law and wisdom to lunar powers. Although the Purple Planet's Kith worship one moon god, while the Shudder Mountains' Shudfolk revere another, all such deities are manifestations of the Watcher in the Sky, Shul.

Shul is god of the moons, measurement, knowledge, and literacy. Additionally, some consider him the pure embodiment of Law, naming him "Lawgiver", though other deities may disagree. He is the divine force behind calendars and almanacs, and created Ur, the oldest written language. Among Shul's followers, one typically finds alchemists, astrologers, barristers, farmers, herbalists, navigators, sages, scribes, and others adhering to strict regimens. Shul's influence is governed by the combined phases of the multiverse's moons, waxing and waning in seemingly random pattern. Only Shul, and perhaps The Fates, can predict these motions.

In some realities, Shul allies with Choranus, while in others, with Valdreth the Unchanging One; in each case, followers carefully measure and track events, hoping to predict Chaos' uprisings. Occasionally there are causes shared with the nature god Ildavir and the sea god Pelagia, but the friction between Law and Neutrality limits these alliances. The Watcher's primary enemy is The Hidden Lord, whose manifestations of pure Chaos, spontaneous acts of entropy, and corruption of forbidden knowledge are anathemas to Him. It is sinful for Shul's clerics to aid The Hidden Lord's followers; this incurs increased deity disapproval. Other sinful transgressions include aiding any who would destroy written works, alter the flow of time, or refuse to share knowledge with Shul's followers. The Watcher's followers treat chaotic lycanthropes (and chaotic therianthropes) as unholy, in addition to those considered unholy by Law.

Shul usually appears as a glowing, featureless humanoid, driving a silver chariot pulled by two winged oxen, one black as the new moon, the other white as the full. Shul's clerics dress in blacks and whites according to a moon's phases; when the moon is full, they wear white; when it is new, they wear black; when it is half waning or waxing, they dress symmetrically in both colors. Traveling clerics typically carry 3 different robes to ensure they always match the moon's phases. Shul's holy symbol is a crescent moon with half a man's face emerging from the inner arc, though some primitive cultures use an eye within a circle instead. His clerics favor a moon-phase mace, which has a large metallic sphere at one end of the haft (silvered, if possible), and a similarly-sized metal ring at the other. Some use the ring to disarm opponents; others attach a chain to the ring, swinging the mace larger distances, and using it to entangle opponents.

The holiest events for Shul's followers are solar and lunar eclipses. Solar eclipses are good omens (+1d to spell checks), with Shul proving that he can block the sun. Lunar eclipses, with Shul's brightness being shadowed, are bad omens (-1d to spell checks), and require fervent prayer. Other holy days include new moons and full moons. Sacrifices are favored by Shul if they contain large amounts of silver. His clerics always begin first level with the spells *second sight* and *comprehend languages*, with the rest of their allotted spells determined randomly. Note that since *comprehend languages* is an arcane spell, inept invocations cause misfires and corruption as well as deity disapproval.

SPECIAL TRAITS
Lay on Hands

A cleric may choose or roll (1d4) among the following unique manifestations to describe the healing power of Shul: (1) A glowing sphere orbits the wounded area, bathing it in healing light. The wound heals as the miniature moon slowly dims and vanishes; (2) The cleric's hands exude a mist that coalesces into a radiantly swirling cloud. The wound absorbs the luminous cloud as it heals; (3) Taking blood from herself, the cleric writes words of mending, encircling the wounded area. The words glow and join together as the wound heals; (4) With his eyes slowly changing from white, to black, to white again, the cleric focuses on the wound. The faint sounds of tinkling crystal bells emit from the wound as it heals.

Divine Favors

Shul bestows the following favors among his most faithful. Note that these may become unavailable if one falls into disfavor (i.e., incurs Deity Disapproval).

Moonsense: Once per day, the cleric can commune with Shul to gain knowledge regarding any event that involves the moon. Examples include knowing when the tide will be lowest, when will the moon be brightest, when is the best time to plant a particular crop, whether or not the moon is involved in removing a curse, etc. This power is not limited to the cleric's homeworld.

Reckoning Braid: A vital tool for Shul's clerics is a short, thin rope, triple-braided with black, gray, and white strands. Each cleric makes her own reckoning braid, an arm span's length or shorter. Although the braid itself is mundane, it is a conduit for Shul's power in the hands of its maker. Once per day, the cleric may use the braid to miraculously measure one thing accurately (length, weight, time, volume, etc.). For example, a cleric could measure the height of a mountain, the duration of a rainstorm, the weight of a cow, the temperature of a fire, etc.

Cleric of Shul Titles

Shul's clerics have their own level-dependent titles, with the highest ranking members adding the prefix "Moon" to their name, e.g., "Moon Farah."

Level	Title
1	New
2	Crescent
3	Waxing
4	Gibbous
5	Moon

"No, it looked better with the beard."

DISAPPROVAL

The Watcher in the Sky knows when his subjects fail to be beacons. Shul carefully measures failure and sets them on a path from waning to waxing favor. The following table contains Deity Disapproval results customized for the Watcher's clerics. Penalties are cumulative unless otherwise noted.

Roll	Disapproval
1	The cleric must appease Shul by doing nothing except dancing Moon Sirvarn's Moondance for at least a full turn, as soon as possible (e.g., immediately, or at the end of combat).
2	The god of literacy demands written penance. The cleric must write an apology to Shul for 1 hour, as soon as possible (e.g., immediately, or at the end of combat). Failure to complete it within the next 2 hours incurs a -1 spell check penalty until the full hour's writing is done.
3	For the entire duration of moonrise to moonset, the cleric must preach the gospel of Shul to at least one listener. Failure incurs a -1 spell check penalty until moonset of the following day.
4	The cleric suffers a cumulative -1 penalty to all spell checks until the next moonrise or moonset (whatever takes longer).
5	Until moonset of the following day, the cleric gains an ever-present luminescent moonshadow. During this time the cleric must not use his hands, except for combat and clerical powers. Failure results in 1d4 damage and the loss of all clerical abilities until the moonshadow disappears.
6	The cleric immediately incurs a -1 penalty to all lay on hands attempts. This penalty remains until the cleric removes a curse that involves the moon.
7	The Watcher forbids the cleric from using divine favors until she spends the entire night watching the moon, moonrise to moonset.
8	Until the next moonrise or moonset (whatever takes longer), the cleric is troubled by a bad moon rising. He suffers -2d to spell checks on the specific spell or ability that resulted in disapproval.
9	Until moonset of the second day, the cleric gains an ever-present luminescent moonshadow. During this time the cleric must not use his eyes (-8 to attack rolls, move in random direction at half speed). Failure results in 2d4 damage and the loss of all clerical abilities until the moonshadow disappears.
10	The Watcher forbids the cleric from using *second sight* for the next 1d3 days.
11	The cleric must prove to be a worthy beacon. She radiates an inextinguishable light equivalent to torch-light, and grants a +1d bonus to attacks and spell checks targeting her. The cleric must take the lead in marching order, make leadership decisions, etc. Deity disapproval does not reset to 1 until Shul is satisfied (judge's discretion).
12	The Watcher forbids the cleric from using *comprehend languages* for the next 1d3 days. During this time, anything the cleric writes is unintelligible to all readers except the cleric.
13	Until moonset of the third day, the cleric gains an ever-present luminescent moonshadow. During this time the cleric must not use his legs. Failure results in 3d4 damage and the loss of all clerical abilities until the moonshadow disappears.
14	Shul restricts the cleric's *lay on hands* to be used only on lawful beings (unless they worship Shul). The restriction lasts for 2d3 days.
15	The cleric must endure the eclipse. He is the center of an inextinguishable 20' radius sphere of darkness, through which none can see. The cleric must significantly further Shul's cause, despite this hindrance. Deity disapproval does not reset to 1 until Shul is satisfied (judge's discretion).
16	The cleric immediately incurs a -1d penalty to all *lay on hands* attempts, and all successful uses of the ability heal 1 HD less damage. These penalties remain until the cleric removes a curse that involves the moon.
17	Until moonset of the fourth day, the cleric gains an ever-present luminescent moonshadow. During this time the cleric must not use his mouth (no eating, speaking, casting, etc., though drinking water is permitted). Failure results in 4d4 damage and the loss of all clerical abilities until the moonshadow disappears.
18	The god of knowledge demands a victory against The Hidden Lord. The cleric suffers a -1d spell check penalty until he acquires a tome containing secret knowledge of The Hidden Lord.
19	Shul demands that the cleric redeem himself by bestowing the gift of literacy on another. Until he teaches someone beginner's skills in reading and writing (in any language), he suffers a -1d spell check penalty. Checks for success may be made weekly, with the cleric rolling less than or equal to his Personality, and the student rolling less than or equal to his intelligence.
20+	The cleric receives the brand of the Moonless, and suffers a -2d spell check penalty until he completes the quest of the moonchild: speak with the trees draped in moonspider's webs; sleep on the steps of the moonpool; coax the black owl to land on a silver branch; view the new moon from Crimson Mountain's peak.

CANTICLES OF SHUL

Observing the subtleties of Shul's path, clerics learn holy canticles unique to the Watcher. As the moon has motion but is silent, these canticles are mouthed soundlessly. As the moon has a cycle of phases, these canticles are repetitive mantras. The player is encouraged to make up her own mantras for each of the following. Here is an example specific to Shul:

Silent Heavens Under Light
Holy Umbra, Lunar Sight
Utter Law, Sounding Height
Lifetimes, Seasons, Hours Unite

Canticles of Shul are gained at cleric levels 1, 3, and 5. They are not spells, though they may have spell-like effects.

Level 1: *Lunar Glow* Level 3: *Shul's Shining One* Level 5: *Nigodow's Septichromatic Orbs*

LUNAR GLOW

As the moon priestess soundlessly repeats his canticle, his holy symbol glows with a radiance that depends on his spell check. After the first round, this canticle requires concentration to be maintained (see DCC RPG rulebook, pg. 106).

Spell check	Result
1-11	Failure.
12-13	Waxing Crescent. The holy symbol radiates a faint glow in a 1' radius sphere.
14-23	First Quarter. The holy symbol radiates a pale blue glow in a 20' radius sphere. The light remains 1 round after the cleric ceases concentration.
24-31	Waxing Gibbous. The holy symbol radiates a creamy glow in a 40' radius sphere. Searching checks (secret doors, traps, etc.) gain a +1d bonus within. The light remains 1d3 rounds after the cleric ceases concentration.
32+	Full Moon. The holy symbol radiates a bright white glow in an 80' radius. Within the light: creatures unholy to Shul suffer -1d to attacks and spell checks; clerics of Shul (except the one chanting this canticle) receive +1d to spell checks; searching checks (secret doors, traps, etc.) gain a +1d bonus. The light remains 2d3 rounds after the cleric ceases concentration.

SHUL'S SHINING ONE

At level 3, the cleric learns this transformative mantra, during which she becomes a shimmering, semi-corporal cloud of moon energy, Shul's Shining One. It moves slowly on the surfaces of ground and water; however, direct exposure to moonlight enables it to fly rapidly via moonbeams. This holy form evolves depending on the cleric's spell check, but requires one uninterrupted turn of chanting for the transformation. In most cases, the cleric may not use any of her abilities while in this form. As an embodiment of Law, the Shining One can only damage, and be damaged by, beings of Chaos; it reverts to the bleeding-out cleric if slain, with the cleric's deity disapproval increased by 10. The Watcher does not grant this form to any who currently suffer deity disapproval effects.

Shining One: Init as cleric; Atk (per spell check); AC (per spell check); HD as cleric; MV 10' on air/water if no moon, fly 50' if exposed to moon; Act as cleric; SP immune to fire, immune to Law and Neutrality, only affects Chaos; SV as cleric; AL L.

Spell check	Result
1	Failure and corruption (as wizard). Roll 1d6: (1-3) minor; (4-5) major; (6) greater.
2-13	Failure.
14-21	Duration: 1d3 rounds. AC 14; Atk spectral tendril +3 melee (1d4+3)
22-29	Duration: 2d3 rounds. AC 15; Atk scintillating vortices (chaotic beings within melee range make DC 14 Will save or stand helplessly entranced for 1 round) or spectral tendril +CL melee (1d4+CL)
30-33	Duration: 1d3 turns. AC 16; Atk scintillating vortices (chaotic beings within melee range make DC 15 Will save or stand helplessly entranced for 1 round) or spectral tendril +CL melee (1d5+CL, cleric is healed +CL hp)
34+	Duration: 2d3 turns. AC 17; Atk scintillating vortices (chaotic beings within melee range make DC 16 Will save or stand helplessly entranced for 1 round) or spectral tendril +CL melee (1d6+CL, cleric is healed +CL hp, cleric may roll for *turn unholy* on target if applicable)

NIGODOW'S SEPTICHROMATIC ORBS

Nigodow was the first high priest to learn the canticle of the septichromatic orbs. Since this knowledge is gained at level 5, it is rarely witnessed, and is almost mythic among Shul's followers. The mantra requires the cleric to have 7 particular gems of different colors. Each must be worth at least 1,000 gp, and acquired either through a holy quest or through donations for Shul, personally collected by the cleric. When he first learns the canticle, his body absorbs the gems, his skin gaining a permanent opalescent sheen thereafter. The canticle must be repeated for 1 round, after which spectrally glowing miniature moons orbit the cleric. On his next successful spell check, or the next time he is successfully attacked, roll 1d7 on the table below and apply the result. Thereafter, for each successful spell check (or successful incoming attack), choose the next moon on the list, wrapping around to 1 (black) if necessary. Note that effects on the attacker occur after the attack (i.e., it is not negated). The corresponding moon disappears upon activation. Incurring deity disapproval dispels all remaining moons. This canticle may be used once per day.

d7	Moon / Gem	Cleric Makes Successful Spell Check	Cleric is Successfully Attacked
1	Black / Opal	Success eclipses disfavor; reduce disapproval rating by 1d3.	Attacker makes DC 15 Will save or falls magically asleep for 1d3 rounds.
2	Red / Ruby	Gain +10' to MV through next round.	Attacker makes DC 15 Ref save or takes 2d4+CL fire damage.
3	Orange / Tourmaline	+2 bonus to AC through next round.	Attacker makes DC 15 Will save or attacks his ally on his next attack.
4	Yellow / Topaz	+1d to melee attacks with the moon-phase mace (through next round).	Attacker makes DC 15 Will save or inflicts the same damage upon himself.
5	Green / Emerald	Cleric is healed 1d8+CL damage.	Cleric is healed 1d8+CL damage.
6	Blue / Sapphire	+1d to saving throws through next round.	Attacker makes DC 15 Ref save or takes 2d4+CL electric damage.
7	White / Diamond	Spend a free action die right now.	Attacker makes DC 15 Fort save or is blinded for 1d3 rounds (-8 to attacks, move half speed in random direction)

Chapter Six
Quests & Journeys

The journey will end as it begins.

IN-BETWEEN ESCAPADES
TURNING DOWNTIME DOWNRIGHT INTERESTING

The lives of adventurers are rife with danger. Their escapades place them in harm's way on a daily basis and death is but a misstep away. But this courting of danger is not without its benefits, as the adventurer who survives is certain to see more marvelous sights and lay hands upon treasures undreamt of by the common-folk.

Because of their daring and unusual occupations, adventurers tend to attract the attentions of the ineffable entities that lurk in the higher (and lower) realms of the multiverse. These powers, often cruel, capricious, or mischievous, ensure that the lives of those who embrace adventure never lack excitement. Even when seeking a respite from the dangers of dungeon and wilderness, an adventurer's life might suddenly turn thrilling and potentially hazardous, plunging them without warning into twisting plots, horrible accidents, strange whims of fate, and other unforeseen discomforts.

The following table provides the judge with twenty-four interesting occurrences that might strike a PC or party while they're enjoying some downtime in a safe locale. The table assumes the party is enjoying their rest and relaxation in a somewhat civilized settlement (a town or city), but the events can easily be customized to accommodate other settings.

These events are not intended to be full-fledged adventures (although they can easily become so!), but short, interesting, and fun—for the judge at least—incidents designed to keep the adventurers' lives thrilling.

Interesting Occurrences In-between Adventures	
1d24	**Event Description**
1	A common animal (horse, dog, cat, cow, etc.) speaks to one of the PCs, engaging in casual conversation as if nothing were extraordinary about the situation. The animal asks the character to perform a minor task for it, acting as a proxy to complete a labor it can't otherwise do. Is the animal a mutant, a sentient being transformed by magic, or is this an elaborate hoax perpetrated by someone with an uncanny skill at ventriloquism?
2	The party is accosted by members of a small cult seeking to sway the band into joining their ranks. The cultists follow an obscure but generally harmless deity and are quite sincere in their faith—even if their tenets are a bit unorthodox. The cultists make a nuisance of themselves until driven off or one or more of the PCs agree to attend a moonlit religious service. There, the party discovers the cult has several important individuals in its ranks, some of whom will be willing to help their fellow cult-brethren down the line if the PCs become members of the sect.
3	Tentacles lunge from an open sewer drain or through the bars of a covered culvert, attempting to drag one of the PCs into the underworld. What creature these tentacles are attached to and why it desires the character (a tasty meal, a servant, someone to engage in friendly discussion, etc.) is left to the judge to decide. If there are several of these creatures and they have nefarious plans, the party may find themselves hired to rid the sewers of this stinky subterranean threat.
4	A relative of one of the PCs dies and chooses to haunt a surviving family member. The character is the focus of the specter's haunting. The spirit can be helpful, a hindrance, or malicious, depending on what sort of relations the PC maintained with his relatives. A character who regularly visits his family and remembers all their birthdays is likely to enjoy the benefits of a supernatural ally, while one who never bothers to write may find himself nagged (or even subject to ghostly violence) for his negligence.
5	Dimensional sailors (DCC RPG core rulebook, p. 405) suddenly appear above the street the PCs are strolling down, intent on plundering the landlubbers below. They swing down from their aerial skiffs in true swashbuckler fashion with knives in their teeth and cutlasses in hand. They fight, loot, and plunder, targeting the PCs first, until they either assuage their lust for booty or suffer significant losses. They then depart back from whence they came.

Interesting Occurrences In-between Adventures

6	Time-travelling assassins arrive in the present era determined to kill one of the PCs. That character's future descendant poses either a severe threat or substantial obstacle to the assassins and they seek to remove him from the time-space continuum by slaying his ancestor. The assassins may be limited to time-period appropriate technology or arrive bearing fantastical death-dealing armaments from the future. They give no reasons for their attack on the character, but if captured and interrogated, reveal their purpose. This information can potentially lead to interesting developments if the PC's future offspring is a vile tyrant whose death would indeed be a blessing to the world.
7	A door, window, skylight, etc. bursts open or breaks, heralding the arrival of a dark-clad figure. A group of armed individuals is hot on the the heels of a black-dressed rival and appear intent on violence. Is the sudden intruder a thief being pursued by the city watch, an assassin who just successfully murdered his target and in flight from the victim's security detachment, a clandestine lover caught in the act with his paramour and hunted by angry relatives, or some other interesting individual? The party can choose to become involved or merely watch the proceedings, but both choices could have potential ramifications later on down the line at the judge's discretion.
8	A demon appears in a puff of brimstone, its eyes scanning the crowd. The evil minion has been dispatched to collect thirteen people possessing the same certain physical attributes (brown skin, blue eyes, nine fingers, no sense of humor, etc.) by its sorcerous master and it senses the presence of one such person at this location—one of the PCs, naturally. The demon attempts to abduct the chosen individual, carrying him off to its master's lair.
9	An accidental collision with a passerby in a crowded place is no coincidence. The person the PC bumped into was a desperate thief, hounded spy, fleeing murderer, or other ne'er-do-well who needed to ditch incriminating evidence. He slips the object onto the PC in passing and then disappears into the crowd. Those searching for the criminal employ supernatural means to discern his location and these measures quickly target the object planted on the PC, putting him in their sights. Being of a "kill first, ask questions later" mentality, the PC (and the rest of the party) may have to survive an attack or two by powerful foes before the matter is straightened out. Once the deception is uncovered, the PC may desire his own revenge on the individual who got him into this mess!
10	The dead start to rise from their graves whenever the party is nearby, shambling out of cemeteries and burying grounds to follow them. The ambulatory deceased don't attack the party or other bystanders, but do persist in trailing along behind the party until turned or destroyed. Suffice to say, the relatives of the deceased, the local authorities, inn-keepers, brothel madams, and others aren't pleased with masses of rotting corpses following the PCs around and demand something be done. But determining why this is happening is no simple matter, let alone finding a solution to the problem.
11	While in an antechamber, study, inn room, or other private chamber, a rotted plank gives way beneath a PC's foot, revealing a dusty, cobweb-filled cavity beyond. Inside the hollow is a sealed bottle, a weapon covered in old bloodstains, a mummified corpse, or other mysterious object, secreted there long ago. The object has no immediate use to the party, but the circumstances of its condition beg to be investigated. Should the PCs pursue the mystery, they may ultimately be rewarded for their efforts—but not before rousing the attentions of those who want to keep the circumstances secret!
12	A mysterious stranger approaches the party in a public place and casts a baleful eye upon them. "We shall meet again, you foul malefactors," the figure hisses, "when the cock crows six times atop the Needle of Arguntus and the Lost Heir is finally revealed!" The stranger forks his fingers at the band and then vanishes into the crowd. In the days (or weeks or months) ahead, the party keeps overhearing references to the Needle of Arguntus and/or the Lost Heir (or whatever else the judge wishes to use in their place), but no further information is forthcoming about these objects, people, or the identity of the stranger. If the party doesn't pursue this mystery, nothing ever comes of it, but if they choose to dig deeper, it results in a self-fulfilling prophecy with both horrific and fantastic consequences.
13	The PCs are enjoying a fine meal in a tavern when the Great Slumbering Beast (or hibernating alien sorcerer or Thousand Year Demon Cicadas or whatever else the judge wishes to bedevil his players with) suddenly awakens. Unknown to everyone, the tavern stands directly above the menace's nesting place, putting the party at ground zero of this new cataclysm, unaware and unprepared.
14	A surreptitious race of human impersonators (serpent-men, doppelgängers, servants of the Subterranean Empire of Deros, etc.) needs impromptu disguises to continue their war against humanity. They decide that the PCs' flesh would make suitable costumes and contrives to lure the party to a secluded spot where they can flay their flesh and wear it like a body suit. The gambit could involve slipping soporifics into the party's food and drink, employing comely-seeming agents to coax the PCs into a private liaison, or impersonating officials offering employment. A party that is successfully ambushed but overcomes their attackers discovers clues to a large plot in the making…and signs of infiltration at the highest levels of society.
15	The party finds themselves the subject of a catchy but utterly derogatory new ballad that's on the lips of everyone in town. The PCs find themselves subjected to stifled laughter, ill-concealed sneers, and embarrassing questions everywhere they go. A local minstrel recently debuted the tune, but has already moved on to the next town. Is the musician in the employ of enemies seeking to defame the party or does he, himself, have a bone to pick with the adventurers? Perhaps it's all just a coincidental case of mistaken identity? In any event, the PCs are about to discover how difficult it is to combat a popular song rather than flesh-and-blood opponents!

	Interesting Occurrences In-between Adventures
16	Rats begin spying on the party. Wherever they go, a wary PC detects beady eyes peering at them from holes in the wall, sewer grates, the edges of rooftops, etc. The rodents display a cunning that seems to exceed that of normal rats, acting almost in concert with one another as if obeying secret instructions. Has the party offended the Secret Rat Lords that rule under the city or are the scurrying creatures the servants of a supernatural force or agency? What do the rodents or their secret master want from the party? Or is there nothing unusual happening at all and the rats' apparent cunning and interest in the party merely paranoia on the PCs' part?
17	A careless alchemist's assistant discards the waste byproducts of his master's experiments out an open window just as the party walks by below. The alchemical liquid waste can range from the foul and infectious to the caustic and damaging to the utterly bizarre and trasmutative. Whoever is struck by the liquid will undoubtedly have a few choice words for the unthinking assistant!
18	A random person in the vicinity of the party suddenly dies, his life snuffed out by a strange, devouring magical energy. This casualty was the result of a wizard utilizing a spell with a mercurial magical effect that slays someone the caster knows each time the spell is cast. If the PCs investigate the magical death, they'll eventually meet the wizard responsible. Unfortunately, meeting the wizard now means the sorcerer knows them, making them possible victims of the mercurial magical effect should the caster ever draw upon the spell in the future!
19	The party makes a turn down a narrow street and suddenly finds themselves in the middle of a tense stand-off between rival gangs with weapons bared. Any sudden movement might be enough to turn the showdown into a frenzied melee. Making matters worse, just before the PCs can choose to cautiously withdraw, spell-hurling sorcerers from yet another rival faction arrive, turning the street into utter chaos. It looks like big trouble for the party!
20	An ominous portent is glimpsed in the midst of some ordinary activity. The PCs witness a sign of obvious supernatural origin (a burning eye appears on a passerby's forehead, a ghostly parade marches through a marketplace, golden stallions ride over rooftops, etc.) that no one else is able to see. Powerful, possibly godlike forces are alerting the party to events shortly about to occur, perhaps for weal or woe. If one or more of the party has a patron, these omens may be signs from that entity that it has deeds that need doing and it is attempting to attract his servant's attention. The omen might be related to an upcoming event in the campaign, guised in cryptic symbolism, to whet the players' appetites for adventure or to instill unease in their characters.
21	A mundane object in the party's possession (a necklace worn by one of the PCs, a sheathed sword, or a tankard on their tavern table, for example) springs to life with malignant power and attempts to murder one of the PCs. The object is not difficult to defeat (unless specifically made for man-slaying like a sword), but once overcome the question of where its sinister power came from remains. Was it a hither-to unknown enchantment possessed by the item or is it the work of sorcerous enemies?
22	A discrete messenger approaches one of the PCs with a sealed missive. He claims to not know the sender, being instructed to deliver it to the PC by anonymous agents. If opened, the message is a personal invitation for the PC (and that individual alone) to meet clandestinely with the sender, who is a good-looking and moderately powerful noble. The message may be an invite for a romantic rendezvous stemming from the noble sighting the recipient about town or to discuss a delicate matter of another subject…or a trap. If the PC brings along his companions, the noble is insulted and the PC loses an opportunity. If it is a trap, however, going alone might have fatal consequences.
23	A piece of decorative statuary or other architectural embellishment falls from above, potentially striking and maiming a PC. An inspection of the resulting smashed rubble reveals it appears aged and worn, and may have fallen accidentally. It might have also been shoved intentionally. If this is the case, was the party the intended target or did it fall too early or too late to hit another passerby? Possibly more ominously, the statue is a representation of a god or goddess, one who the party's recent actions have potentially angered. Was this an act of subtle divine vengeance?
24	One of the PCs receives an unusual coin as change during an ordinary business transaction. The coin is of small value (copper or silver) and appears largely normal. The only remarkable characteristic is the short message and strange symbol inscribed on the reverse side of the coin. The inscription appears meaningless to the casual viewer, but sorcery or a knack for cryptography can decipher the message. If revealed, the inscription provides directions or instructions to the meeting place of a secret conspiracy. The coin was meant for a visiting agent, but it accidently reached the PC's hand. The conspirators become aware of the mistake and now seek to recover the coin and perhaps silence the PC permanently to protect their cabal.

CAPSULE CAMPAIGN
THE LOST CONTINENT OF MU

apsule campaigns are a basic premise for a DCC RPG game that judges can use as a starting point to build new and exciting stories for their players. You won't find scads of details and new rules here, just the bare bones to get an amazing campaign started. The judge will have to provide the final details, allowing him to create a campaign uniquely his own.

CAMPAIGN BACKGROUND

n the middle of a vast, warm ocean lies a land shrouded in secrecy. Said by those who protect the ancient wisdom of old to be the original home of humanity, this clandestine world is difficult to reach and nearly impossible to find. It is the lost continent of Mu.

This verdant land is home to many mysteries, phenomenon incomprehensible to the cultures who dwell in the world beyond Mu's wave-kissed shores. From networks of powerful ley lines, to crystalline technology, to secret cults dedicated to alien forces, Mu is a place unlike any other.

It is said that Mu was the first continent to rise from the primordial oceans of the ancient past and that it was here that life began. In time, mankind arose from the ranks of animals and came to dominate the primeval land. The high priests of Mu preach that their forefathers were chosen by the Sky Gods to lord over this world and it was these mysterious figures who elevated the first men above the animals. To this day, the residents of Mu, who call themselves Murn, still pay homage to the Sky Gods and have erected sacred spaces to await their return.

Blessed by the gods, the Murn transformed their land into a paradise. Dwelling in harmony with nature and gifted with powerful and clean crystalline technology (see below), the Murn made miraculous advances in science and magic, laying the foundations for much of what the outside world today knows of these arts. Even into the modern era, the Murn continue pushing the boundaries of science, experimenting into areas of knowledge outsiders might consider immoral. The Murn disregard such concerns, placing enlightenment above the suffering of the creatures (and even lesser specimens of humanity) that must endure their often cruel and painful experiments.

Eventually, the Murn looked beyond their shores. Daring explorers and fearless colonists departed their ancestral home for unknown lands, taking with them the Murn's knowledge, magic, and technology. These bold adventurers founded the great civilizations of the outside world, teaching the primitive tribes they discovered there the arts of agriculture, writing, and sorcery. But as the centuries passed, the colonies become isolated from their motherland, forced to concentrate on meeting the challenges and threats these new lands presented. Communication broke down, trade failed, and the descendants of the Murn forgot their origins, replacing history with myth.

Three hundred years ago, the prodigals of Mu returned. The far-removed descendants of the original colonies, now grown debase and savage (as the Murn people saw them), rediscovered their forgotten homeland. They came back not as long-lost kin, but as raiders and pirates. The first ships sacked a half-dozen coastal towns and cities, shocking the pacific people of Mu. Once the shock faded, however, Murn sorcerers and soldiers rallied and drove off the plunder-seeking outsiders with magic and crystalline weapons.

In the wake of this unexpected assault, the priests and kings of Mu decided that protective measures needed to be enacted. The ley lines were tapped and the powers of air, water, and ether invoked. The magician lords of Mu encircled the continent with a mighty field of magic, one that obscured the land behind clouds of mist, created strong currents to drive away or sink ships that blunder into Murn waters, and could transport unlucky vessels far off-course and away from the secret land. In addition to these elemental wards, titanic slumbering guardians were erected on four shores of the continent to defend against invasion. In times of danger, these stony sentinels animate and rise from their earthen beds, striding into the ocean to repel attackers.

Despite these defensive measures, the Murn have not completely shuttered themselves away from the outside world. The High Queen has allowed a small number of foreigners entrance into the paradisical land over the past century. Seekers of esoteric wisdom and emissaries from nations with something to offer the Murn are welcome in small numbers.

These visitors find a seeming paradise awaiting them and fall sway to the charms of Mu and her High Queen. What they do not know is that Mu possesses a darker side and the outsiders that discover all is not as it appears on Mu seldom live to warn others.

REACHING MU

Mu is nearly impossible to locate intentionally. The magical wards and elemental safeguards protecting its shores readily demolish, delude, or delay ocean-going vessels seeking the

lost continent. A handful of foreigners arrive accidentally, cast up on Mu's beaches when their ships sink or are dashed to bits on the coastal reefs by typhoons. An elite selection of foreign ambassadors, usually representing powerful magical potentates or quasi-mystical religious cults, are granted leave to dwell in Mu in a special settlement designed for visitors while they treat with the Murn.

PCs wishing to explore the fabled land should approach a representative of these foreign powers and inquire about the possibility of acting as agents or functionaries on behalf of these groups or to serve as bodyguards for envoys heading to Mu. Adventurers filling such roles will find they enjoy a greater degree of freedom—although not complete permission—to sample the wonders of Mu.

Adventurers failing to win a posting on Mu can either attempt to breach the elemental wards via sorcery or by flying to the mysterious land (airborne travel is not as greatly affected by the magical defenses, but neither is it immune to them). Lacking these options, they can simply set sail and hope they wreck close enough to swim to the land's strange shores!

CLASH OF RELIGIONS

The majority of the Murn people worship the Sky Gods, delicate beings who dwell on high and are believed to have blessed the denizens of Mu long ago with intelligence and the wherewithal to dominate their world through sorcery and technology. Beautiful temples, many of them tiered pyramids, stand in the cities throughout the continent. At some confluxes of ley lines, escpecially those of fire and air, sacred spaces dedicated to the Sky Gods are situated. These spaces are broad, flat plazas of fitted flagstones surrounded by statuary. The plazas bear sacred imagery and inscriptions facing upwards so that the Sky Gods might admire them from their heavenly abodes. At night, shining beacons of crystalline technology are lit to guide the Sky Gods back to Mu so that they might once again bless their devoted worshippers.

Not all in Mu venerate the Sky Gods. Some of the Murn people have grown tired of waiting for the Sky Gods to return and have turned to the worship of less wholesome forces. Secret temples dedicated to foul gods such as Tulhu, Vhrumor, and Bash'narabet-duum have emerged in the bowels of the cities or in far-flung regions away from prying eyes. The devotees of the Sky Gods strive to crush these darker rival sects, but they often vanish into the shadows when discovered only to resume their black worship elsewhere. Most unsettling are stories that the nobles of Mu—including the High Queen, herself—are allied with the dark cults, clandestinely supporting them in return for magical gifts the Sky God priests cannot provide.

INHABITANTS OF MU

The Murn people are without exception humans. No demihumans exist on the continent and the inhabitants are extremely curious about such races (perhaps too curious in some cases, leading to the demihuman being imprisoned for study and even vivisection so that Murn science might properly categorize the creature).

The Murn are dark of complexion, ranging in coloration from nearly ebony to reddish-brown. Hair and eye coloration is also dark, but rare individuals possess red hair and green or

lemon-yellow eyes. The Murn dress in flowing robes, light gowns, toga-like wraps, sarongs, and short tunics, wearing sandals or low shoes on their feet. Ceremonial and decorative facial and body make-up is commonly worn by both sexes. Thanks to the curative powers of Mu crystal technology, disease is almost unknown and longevity is commonplace. A lowly laborer might live two hundred years and suffer few adverse effects from aging. The elite members of society regularly live for five hundred years or more.

Although a beautiful people on the whole, there is an inherent ugliness hiding behind the comely faces of the Murn. After millennia of dwelling in paradise with their needs and whims catered to by sorcery and crystalline science, the Murn have become a debauched, amoral people. They seek pleasure and entertainment wherever they can find it, searching for new means to allieviate the boredom that afflicts them all. The Murn have discovered that unsuspecting visitors to their land prove to be delightful subjects to practice their debase recreations upon. Having sampled most of life's pleasures, the Murn's great malaise can only be alleviated by the pain, humiliation, and oftentimes death of others. When outsiders are unavailable, the elite of Murn society use underlings and servants as playthings, pawns, and patsies in byzantine games of politics and social maneuvering. The High Queen is a master of manipulation and poltical backstabbing, and her lesser nobles aspire to be her equal.

Aside from the Murn people, there are few known denizens on the continent other than animal life. Tropical and subtropical plant and animal life thrives across the land and several large swaths of the continent are designated as natural preserves left untouched by the people of Mu.

Monstrous races such as orcs, ogres, trolls, etc. are not found on seemingly-paradisiacal Mu, but the land is not completely free of unwholesome occupants (see below).

CRYSTALS OF MU

The Murn have mastered a form of technology and magic unseen outside its protected borders. Crystal and gem deposits abound on Mu and the people have devised a means to enchant and empower these crystalline structures to produce unexpected results. Most Murns believe the Sky Gods taught them the secret of using crystals as technology.

Mu crystal technology varies in size from shards small enough to be held in one hand to entire chambers constructed of the gleaming, transparent material. Drawing power from the native ley lines that crisscross the continent, Mu crystals never lose power so long as they remain on the continent. The rare artifact that leaves the land rapidly becomes nothing more than a semi-precious or ornamental stone.

Mu crystal technology is commonplace. Even the lowest of farmers might possess a crystal that preserves food or heals minor injuries. Soldiers wield crystals that discharge blasts of magical power or create defensive shields to protect them from attack. The elite of Mu have access to special chambers located in the temples and palaces. These rooms are said to improve body and mind, grant temporary magical prowess, and even raise the dead.

In game terms, Murn crystalline technology allows for magical spells to reproduce predictable results without the variance of spell checks. A crystal weapon might consistently create a *scorching ray* with a 26 spell check result, for example, or a crystalline chamber may always heal those inside as if the subject of a 20 spell check *lay on hands* effect. The exact nature and effect of these crystal devices is up to the judge to determine, but they lose their properties once outside of Mu.

LEY LINES

The continent of Mu is traversed by a network of magical power lines located within the earth and flowing through the air. These paths are ley lines and each bears a connection with one of the five elements: air, earth, ether, fire, and water. Magic practiced at the confluxes of these lines are charged with elemental power, allowing the magicians of Mu to produce spectacular and long-lasting results.

A ley line conflux can be recognized by the increased presence of the associated elements. A conflux where fire and water cross is a steamy place filled with constant water vapor, while a site where air and earth intersect is strewn with strange rocky growths that seem to sing as the wind blows through their hollow cavities. Although a conflux is in theory open to all practitioners of magic, some are home to experimenting wizards who have cajoled writs of law from the elite class granting them ownership of the confluence until their experiments have concluded. Given the long lifetimes of the Murn, this might mean the wizard owns the site for centuries.

Spells on ley lines are amplified by the land's inherent magic. A fire-based spell cast along a fire ley line might enjoy anything from a +1 to a +1d bonus and might grant additional effects such as reduced spellburn costs, at the judge's discretion. Confluxes should be especially powerful—and possibly just as unpredictable!

RUINS OF MU

The continent of Mu is ancient beyond comprehension. In the hundreds of millennia since mankind arose on the mysterious land, cities have grown from tiny villages into vast metropolises. In many cases, each generation has built atop the constructions of the past, creating a strata of buried buildings and ancient passageways beneath the cities. Largely forgotten or ignored, these subterranean realms are the home of dark cults, discarded experiments, and inhuman aberrations spawned from errant magical forces. Occasionally the underworld of Mu vomits up some of the corruption it contains, forcing the Murn to address the problem (usually by a wide scale slaughter), but the terrible forms of life always recover and grow anew.

In other parts of the continent, nature has been allowed to reclaim formerly civilized portions of the land. Farmland is permitted to lie fallow so that nature might replenish the soil and towns and cities that have become obsolete in purpose are simply abandoned. These forgotten structures and renewed wilderness become home for terrors that emerge from the underworld to seek sanctuary from the burning crystal weapons of humanity. Relics of Mu's distant past can also be found in the ruins. Although old-fashioned to the current Murn, these artifacts possess powers far beyond those known in the outside world and would fetch a small fortune in foreign markets.

PLACES OF INTEREST

The Crystal Mines: At the base of a chain of volcanoes are countless diggings that wind deep into the earth. A hundred thousand men and women work these mines every day, excavating the myriad varieties of crystals and gems that (often literally) power the land of Mu. These workers are largely unwilling laborers, sentenced to toil in the crystal mines for criminal acts, outstanding debts, or simply offending the wrong political power. A handful of foreigners work alongside the Murn, forced to serve as slaves for their temerity of breaching Mu's sacred borders. To the outside world, the precious gemstones that emerge from these mines on a daily basis are worth a king's ransom, but the Murn value them more for their technological use than monetary value. A daring raid of the mines would accrue enough treasure for the robbers to live like emperors—or earn a prolonged and painful death if they're caught.

Muin: The capital city of Mu, this great metropolis sits in the center of the continent. The city is a paradise of green vegetation and white marble. Water flows in decorative cataracts and through canals that divide the various sections of the city. Roads from outlying cities terminate in Muin, leading there like the spokes of a wheel. From her crystal palace, the High Queen of Mu rules, unchallenged and beloved. Outsiders wishing to remain in the land must be granted the leave of the High Queen, but gaining an audience requires them to navigate a sea of minor functionaries and lesser nobles, all of whom have their own agendas that might prove lethal to the foreign visitors.

The Sentinels: On each of the four shores stand almost two score massive stone heads gazing out beyond the ocean breakers. Expressionless and weathered, the apparent statues keep unblinking vigilance against invaders. Only the Mu know that each head is but the visible portion of a massive animated guardian buried in the earth below. When the land is endangered, the rocky sentinels unearth themselves to battle the enemies of Mu. It is said that no Murn commands the sentinels; they act when necessary and perform as they deem best to carry out their duties.

H'lah-buu: Loosely translated as "the place for filthy savages," H'lah-buu is a small town inhabited solely by outsiders granted permission to remain in Mu by the High Queen. An eclectic mix of shrewd traders, enlightenment-seeking ascetics, and diplomats from foreign kingdoms, this settlement is the only place on the continent where outsiders can live for extended periods. A garrison of Murn soldiers prevents the residents from straying beyond the town borders without written permission.

Xotchyuthl: This name for the region beyond the eastern mountains means "the Veiled Land," and it is an expanse concealed behind towering volcanic mountains and cloaked in steaming jungles. Two hundred millennia ago, it was an inhabited land, but it is now abandoned by the Murn for reasons no outsider can deduce. What is known is that the people of Mu seldom venture into the Xotchyuthl. Rumors that foreigners have established a toe-hold in this expanse are disregarded by the Mu, who seem convinced of the Veiled Land's ability to destroy those who dare enter it.

She: In the midst of a broad floodplain there squats a timeless sculpture, weatherworn and ancient. Although the details are faded from a hundred million rainstorms, the figure appears feminine and faces almost defiantly towards the west. The Murn do not speak of this monumental statue to outsiders and patently ignore it as much as possible. They refer to it only (and always in hushed voices) as "She." Many attempts have been made to understand the origin of this titanic statue, but the results all point to the unsettling fact it was erected before mankind walked the primordial continent of Mu. Those who have caught a glimpse at the statue's secrets and plumbed the labyrinthine network of secret chambers located beneath the stone giantess claimed the Sky Gods had no role in She's creation, shuddering at the thought of who or what might be responsible.

Vryllhalh: High in the mountains stands a crystalline city far removed from the mundane worries of everyday life. Only those Murn who have achieved the highest level of magical mastery or mental acumen are granted entrance into Vryllhalh. Within the walls, they take their studies to heights undreamt of by archmages or madmen. Vryllhalh is considered a paradise-within-paradise by the Murn, but there are darker whispers about the crystal city. Some say the residents are no longer truly human, transformed body and soul by their lofty pursuits. Rumors of magical and physical cannibalism practiced to sustain the occupants are common, as are tales of a sinister cabal with their sights set on the utter mastery of the lost continent.

ADVENTURING ON MU

Adventures set on Mu have a common theme: the dark secrets of paradise. At face value, Mu is a land filled with magic, beneficial crystal technology, harmonic coexistence with nature, and longevity and health for all its inhabitants. However, lurking beneath the perfect exterior of the land are myriad evils.

A DCC RPG campaign set on the lost continent of Mu could be run with the PCs as either outsiders recently arrived in the mysterious land or as native Murns seeking to navigate the unseemly side of their home paradise. The adventurers will quickly discover that Mu is not the paradise it appears. Foul monsters, either the result of callous experimentation or summoned up by the black cults that venerate them, lurk in the underbelly of the cities and prowl the crumbling ruins in the wilderness. Wizards and mental adepts seclude themselves from outsiders, ostensibly for privacy, but far too often to conceal what their delving into unexplored mystical realms has wrought upon them. Even the noble class, seemingly benevolent and gifted with the wisdom of their ancient land, are scheming, debauched, and bored, and find no small pleasure in using others as pawns or reveling in wanton violence and bloodshed. Making matters worse, escape from the lost continent is nearly impossible due to the elemental wards that ring the land. The political and sorcerous powers of Mu can turn these powerful natural forces against any who try to sail beyond their grasp.

For best effect, a judge wishing to introduce Mu to his DCC RPG campaign should first drop hushed whispers and seemingly tall tales about the wonders of Mu. Make it seem to be an El Dorodo of crystalline wonders and unfettered magical power and gently encourage the PCs to learn more of the land. Their efforts confirm the legends and hopefully entice the adventurers to seek out the continent. Once there, they initially find it a paradise—until the true face of the land reveals itself and the PCs find they are trapped in the belly of the beast. The challenge then becomes to escape from paradise, hopefully with a few magical souvenirs or purloined gemstones to remind them of their stay!

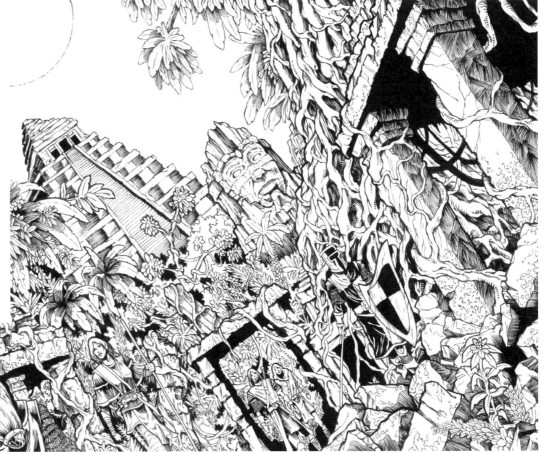

Chapter Seven
JUDGE'S RULES

Yet a paradox is afoot, for the judge knows no rules.

CARNIFEX

When gods turn their affections to the mortal realm, it must invariably end in tragedy. The mortal vessel is unfit for divinity, and the gaze of any god is both a gift and a curse. Yet some gods delight in toying with the lives of mortals, and may – for a short while – even fall in love.

The Carnifex is one such goddess. Once a millennium, the saint of executioners, lepers and outcasts takes a mortal for her own. But should the character make overtures to another patron or — worse — share his or her affections with another mortal, the wrath of the spurned goddess will know no bounds.

As a rule, the Carnifex only bestows her affections upon one character at a time. Entire empires may rise, fall, and fade from memory before she favors another. Note that the Carnifex's tastes span the multiverse and all its children, and her chosen one may be of any sex or race.

Invoke Patron check results:

12-13   The ground erupts with heaving maggots exhaling the stench of corpse-breath. The PC can direct specifically where the maggots emerge, designating one 5' square per CL. Human-sized or smaller characters within the area must succeed on DC 10 Ref saves or slip beneath the earth to drown in a pool of maggots (escape requires a DC 10 Strength check, modified by armor). With a large enough area of effect, walls and foundations can be undermined, halls or corridors can be blocked, etc. The maggots vanish after 1d5+CL rounds, leaving gaping holes in their wake.

14-17   The fickle goddess delights in the petitioner's plea, and sends a swarm of rats to her lover's defense. All foes within 30' take 1d5 damage, and must make DC 10 Fort saves or contract flesh rot, losing 1d4 hit points per round until succeeding on the Fort save. The rats attack for but a single round, and refuse to attack any character bearing fire (e.g., torches or flaming brands pulled from a campfire).

18-19   Death and disease come to all that harm the Carnifex's favorite. The PC is "blessed" with a flesh-eating disease that infects anyone he touches: lesions erupt within and without the victim, flesh blackens within moments, and fingers and toes peel off like scabs. Anyone struck by, or striking, the caster must succeed on a DC 15 Fort save or be infected. Infected PCs suffer 1d10 damage per round until healed or succeeding on a Fort save.

20-23   The Carnifex conjures a murder of crows that descends in a swirling, cawing cloud of feathers and talons. Sight is obscured to less than 5' for all but the caster. Foes must succeed on DC 15 Ref saves each round or take 1d8 damage; on a natural roll of 1-3, the target's eyes are plucked from his skull. The murder attacks for 1d5 rounds before dispersing.

24-27   The mask of death descends over the caster. All foes and non-magical animals within line of sight of the caster must attempt a morale check or be shaken, suffering a -5 penalty to attacks for the remainder of the battle.

28-30   The Carnifex sends an envoy to aid the caster. A tide of rats appears, bearing a hideous rat king (composed of 1d30 + CL rats). The rat king can be spellburned (with the caster receiving 1 point per rat) or it can answer 1d5 questions posed by the caster. The rat king is incredibly knowledgeable, being able to report anything that a rat or mouse might have reasonably overheard.

30-31   Soul-Burn: The caster feeds off the death of his foes and allies alike, using their dying energies to fuel his own powers. For 1d14+CL rounds the Carnifex's champion receives 1 point of spellburn for each HD of creature that dies within 30'. The spellburn must be spent the following round or be lost. *Example: A 5 HD creature dies, granting the caster 5 points of spellburn. The caster must then spend the 5 points the following round. If the caster fails to spend the 5 points, they are lost.* Note: If the champion elects to spend the souls of fallen allies, these PCs **cannot** be saved by further healing or by recovering the body.

PATRON TAINT: THE CARNIFEX

Champions of the Carnifex are invariably transformed by their experience. A jealous mistress, the Carnifex demands that she be exalted above all others; even the PCs' peers and friends are potential rivals for her lover's affections. When patron taint is indicated, roll 1d6 on the table below.

Roll   Result

1   The PC acquires a wasting disease, ensuring that only the Carnifex finds him attractive. Over the course of 1 month the character is reduced to naught but skin and bones, resembling a walking skeleton held together by sinew and skin. If the result is rolled a second time, the PC's skin is covered with leprous lesions, boils and scabs, and he constantly gives off the stink of rotting flesh. If the result is rolled a third time (and every time thereafter) one of the PC's limbs withers, rots and falls from the body.

2   The Carnifex desires obeisance. At the next reasonable opportunity, the PC must create a shrine dedicated to the goddess, including statuary, precious metals, and stones worth no less than 500 gp, along with sufficient staffing to guard the same. If the result is rolled a second time, the champion must design and commission a chapel with opulent icons and relics worth no less than 5,000 gp. If the result is rolled a third time, the champion must erect a cathedral in her honor. A worth of 50,000 – 500,000 gp is suggested, but left to the judge to determine specific to the campaign. Regardless of the actual worth, the construction must be built to inspire fear and awe in worshippers down through the ages.

3   The Carnifex desires a new trophy for her demesne; a lesser scion of Law will do. The first Law-aligned creature the champion meets with HD matching or exceeding the champion's HD must be slain and offered up in sacrifice. (At the judge's discretion this may include Law-aligned PCs.) If the result is rolled a second time, the champion must seek and destroy a Law-aligned creature with CL + 5 HD. If the result is rolled a third time, the character must sacrifice a Law-aligned creature with CL +10 HD.

4   The Carnifex desires that her champion sire an heir. A godling fetus is conceived within the PC; the godling's presence grants the PC +1 to all Will saves, while draining the PC of 1d3 hp daily. If the result is rolled a second time, the godling has grown significantly in size, protruding from the PC's stomach or back, and distending the PC's flesh to the point where sleep is almost impossible. The nascent godling grants a +2 bonus to all Will saves, while consuming 1d5 hp daily. If the result is rolled a third time, the godling bursts from its sire, forcing a DC 20 Fort save to avoid death. If the PC survives, he earns 1d3 points of Luck and forever more receives a +3 bonus to all Will and Fort saves.

5   The Carnifex doubts the PC's affections and demands a sign of fealty. The PC must carve the sign of the Carnifex into his body, smearing a mix of salt, ashes and dye into the wound, inflicting 1d5 damage and requiring a DC 10 Will save to retain consciousness. If the PC successfully completes the act without succumbing to the pain, he earns 1 Luck point. If the result is rolled a second time the PC must peel back patches of his own flesh to illuminate the sigil, inflicting 1d14 damage and requiring a DC 20 Will save to remain conscious. If the PC completes the ritual without succumbing to unconsciousness he earns 1d3 Luck points. If the result is rolled a third time, the PC must drain all of his own blood, reducing himself to 0 hp and forcing a DC 25 Will save. If by some miracle the PC survives, he is henceforth sustained not by blood, but by his own force of will. Mundane attacks on his physical body are reduced by two on the dice chain. (For instance, a longsword would be reduced from 1d8 damage to 1d5, and a dagger would be reduced from 1d4 to deal a mere 1d2). Magical weapons, spells, etc. are unaffected.

6   The Carnifex craves the PC's company. At the earliest opportunity the PC must enter a trance to commune with his patron. Once entered, the trance lasts for 1d5 hours. Ending the trance prematurely (e.g., shaking the caster awake) inflicts mental trauma as the PC is shorn from distant realms; the PC must succeed on a DC 15 Will save or lose the ability to cast spells for an additional 1d3 hours. The second time the result is rolled, the trance lasts for 1d5 days. Awoken early, the PC takes 1d20 damage and must succeed on a DC 20 Will save or lose the ability to cast spells for 1d3 days. The third time the result is rolled, the caster mentally retreats to the Carnifex's realm for 1d5 years. Ending the trance early inflicts 3d20 damage, and the caster must succeed on a DC 25 Will save or be unable cast spells for an additional 1d3 years. If the result is rolled a fourth time, the caster vanishes from existence, whisked away to the gray, shadow realm of the Carnifex, never to return.

PATRON SPELLS: THE CARNIFEX

The chosen of the Carnifex may learn three unique spells, as follows:

Level 1: *Cloak of the Carnifex*

Level 2: *Executioner's Blade*

Level 3: *Shroud of Death*

SPELLBURN: THE CARNIFEX

The Carnifex delights in sacrifices offered up in her name; gifts of blood and flesh are especially welcomed. When a caster utilizes spellburn, roll 1d4 and consult the table below or build off the suggestions to create an event specific to your home campaign.

Roll   **Spellburn Result**

1   The Carnifex demands amorous service, whisking the PC to her realm. While but an instant has passed before he returns, the caster has aged 1 year for every point of spellburn.

2   The Carnifex demands material tribute: the PC must cut off a body part (an ear, finger, eye, nose, etc.) and offer it up to his mistress.

3   The caster must make a gift to his patron, valued at no less than 100 gp per point of spellburn. The items vanish with the burn.

4   His jealous mistress expects absolute devotion. In the next 24 hours the PC must track down and slay a former lover. Failing to do so doubles the points of the spellburn (i.e., if the caster had burned 4 Strength, he is treated as having burnt 8 instead).

Cloak of the Carnifex

| Level: 1 (Carnifex) | Range: Self | Duration: Varies | Casting time: 1 action | Save: Varies |

General	The caster conceals and protects the caster from harm.
Manifestation	Roll 1d4: (1) a voluminous black cloak, like a void cut from reality; (2) a crimson half-cloak that radiates ruby light; (3) a gossamer robe woven of stardust; (4) a tattered patch-cloak, sewn from the flesh of the Carnifex's lovers.
1	Lost, failure, and patron taint.
2-11	Lost. Failure.
12-13	Foes must succeed on a DC 10 Will save to see or hear the caster. The effect lasts for 1d5+CL rounds, or until the caster attacks another creature (either directly or by spellcasting).
14-17	Foes must succeed on a DC 10 Will save to see or hear the caster. The effect lasts for 1d10+CL rounds, or until the caster attacks another creature (either directly or by spellcasting). Additionally, mundane projectiles (save silver) are automatically absorbed by the cloak, and inflict no harm upon the caster.
18-19	Foes must succeed on a DC 15 Will save to see or hear the caster. The effect lasts for 1d12+CL rounds, or until the caster attacks another creature (either directly or by spellcasting). Additionally, attacks made against the caster with mundane weapons (save silver) are automatically absorbed by the cloak, and inflict no harm upon the caster.
20-23	Foes must succeed on a DC 20 Will save to see or hear the caster. The effect lasts for 1d14+CL rounds, or until the caster attacks another creature (either directly or by spellcasting). Attacks made with mundane weapons (save silver) are automatically absorbed by the cloak, and the caster may attempt a DC 25 Ref save to avoid damage from a magical weapon or spell.
24-27	The caster may cloak himself and one ally touched. Foes must succeed on a DC 20 Will save to see or hear the cloaked PCs. The effect lasts for 1d16+CL rounds, or until a character attacks another creature (either directly or by spellcasting). Attacks against the cloaked characters with mundane weapons (save silver) are automatically absorbed by the cloaks; cloaked characters may attempt a DC 20 Ref save to avoid damage from a magical weapon or spell.
28-29	The caster may cloak himself and 1d3 characters within 25'. Foes must succeed on a DC 20 Will save to see or hear the cloaked PCs. The effect lasts for 1d20+CL rounds, or until a cloaked character attacks another creature (either directly or by spellcasting). Attacks made against cloaked characters with mundane weapons (save silver) are automatically absorbed by the cloaks; cloaked characters may attempt a DC 15 Ref save to avoid damage from a magical weapon or spell.
30-31	The caster may cloak himself and 1d4 characters within 100'. Foes must succeed on a DC 20 Will save to see or hear the cloaked PCs. The effect lasts for 1d24+CL rounds, or until the caster attacks another creature (either directly or by spellcasting). Attacks made with mundane weapons (save silver) are automatically absorbed by the cloak; cloaked characters may attempt a DC 10 Ref save to avoid damage from a magical weapon or spell.
32+	The caster may cloak himself and 1d5 characters within the caster's sight. Foes must succeed on a DC 20 Will save to see or hear the cloaked PCs. The effect lasts for 1d30+CL rounds, during which time the cloaked characters may make attacks and cast offensive spells without ending the dweomer. Attacks against the cloaked characters made with mundane weapons (save silver) are automatically absorbed by the cloak; cloaked characters may attempt a DC 10 Ref save to avoid damage from a magical weapon or spell.

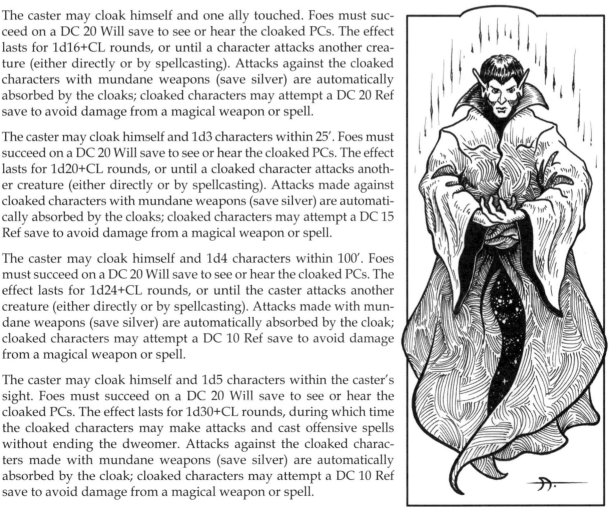

Executioner's Blade

| Level: 2 (Carnifex) | Range: Varies | Duration: 1d5 rounds +CL | Casting time: 1 action | Save: None |

General	The caster conjures a flying weapon to aid him in combat.
Manifestation	Roll 1d4: (1) a headsman's axe; (2) an executioner's sword; (3) a flying guillotine; (4) a scything pendulum.
1	Lost, failure, and patron taint.
2-11	Lost. Failure.
12-13	Failure, but spell is not lost.
14-17	The caster conjures a single flying weapon that can be directed to attack a foe within 30'. The weapon attacks as the caster, inflicting 1d5+CL damage per blow. The caster must concentrate to maintain the conjuration and cannot otherwise attack or move more than half speed. The attack may be blocked by certain magic (e.g., *magic shield*).
18-19	The caster conjures 1d3 weapons that can be directed to attack a foe within 60'. The weapons attack as the caster, inflicting 1d7+CL damage per blow. The caster must concentrate to maintain the conjuration and cannot otherwise attack or move more than half speed. The attacks may be blocked by certain magic (e.g., *magic shield*).
20-23	The caster conjures 1d4 weapons that can be directed to attack any foe within 100'. The weapons attack as the caster, inflicting 1d10+CL damage per blow. The caster must concentrate to maintain the conjuration and cannot otherwise attack or move more than half speed. The attacks may be blocked by certain magic (e.g., *magic shield*).
24-27	The caster conjures 1d5 weapons that can be directed to attack any foe within 500'. The weapons attack as the caster, inflicting 1d12+CL damage per blow, and can strike astral, gaseous or otherwise immaterial targets. The caster must concentrate to maintain the conjuration and cannot otherwise attack or move more than half speed. The attacks may be blocked by certain magic (e.g., *magic shield*).
28-29	The caster conjures 1d6 weapons that can be directed to attack any foe within 1000'. The weapons attack as the caster, inflicting 1d14+CL damage per blow, have a crit range of 19-20, and can strike astral, gaseous or otherwise immaterial targets. The caster must concentrate to maintain the conjuration and cannot otherwise attack or move more than half speed. The attacks may be blocked by certain magic (e.g., *magic shield*).
30-31	The caster conjures 1d7 weapons that can be directed to attack any foe within line of sight. The weapons attack as the caster, inflicting 1d14+CL damage per blow, have a crit range of 18+, and can strike astral, gaseous or otherwise immaterial targets. The caster must concentrate to maintain the conjuration and cannot otherwise attack or move more than half speed. The attacks may be blocked by certain magic (e.g., *magic shield*).
32+	The caster conjures 1d8 weapons that can be directed to attack any foe within line of sight. The weapons attack as the caster, inflicting 1d20+CL damage per blow, have a crit range of 17+, and can strike astral, gaseous or otherwise immaterial targets. The caster need not concentrate to maintain the conjuration, but if the spell is recast while the first spell is in effect, all the conjured blades attack random targets (including the caster) and neither spell may be ended prematurely.

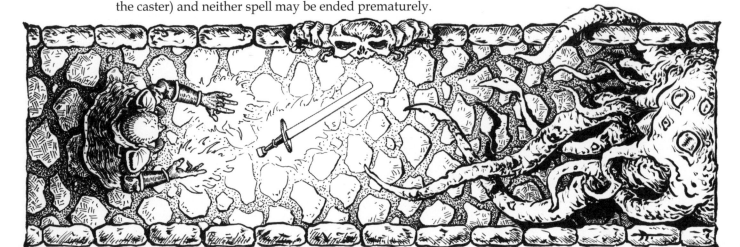

Shroud of Death

Level: 3 (Carnifex) Range: Varies Duration: 1d5 rounds +CL Casting time: 1 round Save: Varies

General	The caster steps into the plane of Death, assuming the powers of the un-dead.
Manifestation	Roll 1d3: (1) the caster becomes faint and translucent; (2) the caster takes the form of a material shadow, (3) the caster dons a gray veil of cobwebs that obscures his face.
1	Lost, failure, and patron taint.
2-11	Lost. Failure.
12-15	Failure, but spell is not lost.
16-17	The caster steps into the Realm of Death; viewers on his home plane see the caster as a shadowy, immaterial form, much like a ghost or phantasm. He can fly at twice his normal speed, can pass through solid objects, and is immune to physical attack from mundane weapons, though he can be harmed by spells and magical attacks. The caster can be turned as an unholy creature.
18-21	The caster's physical attack paralyzes his target for 1d6 rounds (DC 15 Will save to avoid), and immediately forces the victim to make a morale check. He can fly at twice his normal speed, can pass through solid objects and is immune to physical attack from mundane weapons, though he can be harmed by spells and magical attacks. The caster can be turned as an unholy creature.
22-23	The caster's physical attack drains his target of CL Strength, paralyzes his target for 1d6 rounds (DC 17 Will save to avoid), and immediately forces the victim to make a morale check. He can fly at twice his normal speed, can pass through solid objects, and is immune to physical attack from mundane weapons, though he can be harmed by spells and magical attacks. The caster can be turned as an unholy creature.
24-26	The caster gains the ability to shriek as a banshee 3/day, inflicting 1d14 sonic damage and aging living creatures by 1d20 years. The attack affects friend and foe alike, within 100'. The caster's physical attack drains his target of CL Strength, paralyzes his target for 1d6 rounds (DC 20 Will save to avoid), and immediately forces the victim to make a morale check. He can fly at twice his normal speed, can pass through solid objects, and is immune to physical attack from mundane weapons, though he can be harmed by spells and magical attacks. The caster can be turned as an unholy creature.
27-31	The caster gains the ability to possess another living creature within 100' (DC 20 Will save to repulse). For the duration of the spell, the caster is able to command the possessed creature as if its body were the caster's own. The caster can shriek as a banshee 3/day, inflicting 1d14 sonic damage and aging living creatures by 1d20 years. The attack affects friend and foe alike, within 100'. The caster's physical attack drains his target of CL Strength, paralyzes his target for 1d6 rounds (DC 20 Will save to avoid), and immediately forces the victim to make a morale check. He can fly at twice his normal speed, can pass through solid objects, and is immune to physical attack from mundane weapons, though he can be harmed by spells and magical attacks. The caster can be turned as an unholy creature.
32-33	Un-dead treat the caster as one of their own, and refuse to attack. The caster can possess another living creature within 100' (DC 20 Will save to repulse). For the duration of the spell, the caster is able to command the possessed creature as if its body were the caster's own. The caster can shriek as a banshee 3/day, inflicting 1d14 sonic damage and aging living creatures by 1d20 years. The attack affects friend and foe alike, within 100'. The caster's physical attack drains his target of CL Strength, paralyzes his target for 1d6 rounds (DC 20 Will save to avoid), and immediately forces the victim to make a morale check. He can fly at twice his normal speed, can pass through solid objects, and is immune to physical attack from mundane weapons, though he can be harmed by spells and magical attacks. The caster can be turned as an unholy creature.
34+	As spell check result for 32-33, save the caster's un-dead self is so powerful that he cannot be turned.

DZZHALI

Many sages say of Dzzhali (also called The Strangled Bride) that she was once a mortal. They say that after being murdered by her husband on their wedding night, she sent her own soul into the Abyss rather than go to her rest leaving the wrongs done to her unanswered. Legend has it that she crawled out of the Sea of Chaos and then conspired and clawed her way to power in the Courts of Chaos.

But many seers tell a different tale. *They* say Dzzhali was *never* mortal. They say that she is the pure essence of cold, singular, rage made manifest, a primal response to all the betrayals across history given form, voice and power.

What is undisputed is that Dzzhali endeavors to deliver vengeance, malice and anguish wherever she can reach, spreading mistrust and doubt to all caught up in her never-ending reprisals. Mortals cannot persuade Dzzhali to provide patronage - *she* decides whose hearts have been well and truly rent by betrayal and binds them to her service with the gift of potent powers; powers that often do not discriminate among hated enemies, devoted followers, loyal supporters and innocent bystanders.

Invoke Patron **check results:**

12-13   Dzzahli helps the caster look into the heart of one opponent and learn his hidden weaknesses. The caster goes up two steps on the dice chain for the next action die roll he makes against that opponent. In turn, that opponent gets a +1 bonus to *his* next action die roll against one of the caster's allies.

14-17   Dzzhali sends a blade of invisible force that strikes a visible opponent chosen by the caster, from behind. The strike does 2d4 damage and the victim must make a DC 12 Ref save or receive a critical hit (roll 1d12 on Table II). If the opponent survives the strike, he will attribute the attack to the nearest of the caster's allies and relentlessly attack that individual until either the target or the caster's ally is defeated. The opponent gets a Will save each round to cancel this compulsion.

18-19   The caster's opponents become uncertain about who is friend and who is foe. All enemies and one ally (chosen by the judge as an expression of Dzzhali's malice) within a 30' radius of the caster must make a DC 13 Will save each time they target an ally of the caster with a hostile action. If they fail the save they are uncertain whether their intended target is friend or foe and change their choice of targets. If an opponent is already engaged in melee when he becomes confused, he will withhold his attack rather than breaking off from melee to change targets.

20-23   The caster's opponents are plagued with self-doubt. All enemies within 30' of the caster drop down two steps on the dice chain for all action die rolls for 4d4 rounds (DC 18 Will save to drop down one step on the dice chain instead). One of the caster's allies (chosen by the judge as an expression of Dzzhali's malice) takes a -1 penalty to all action die rolls during the same time period (no save).

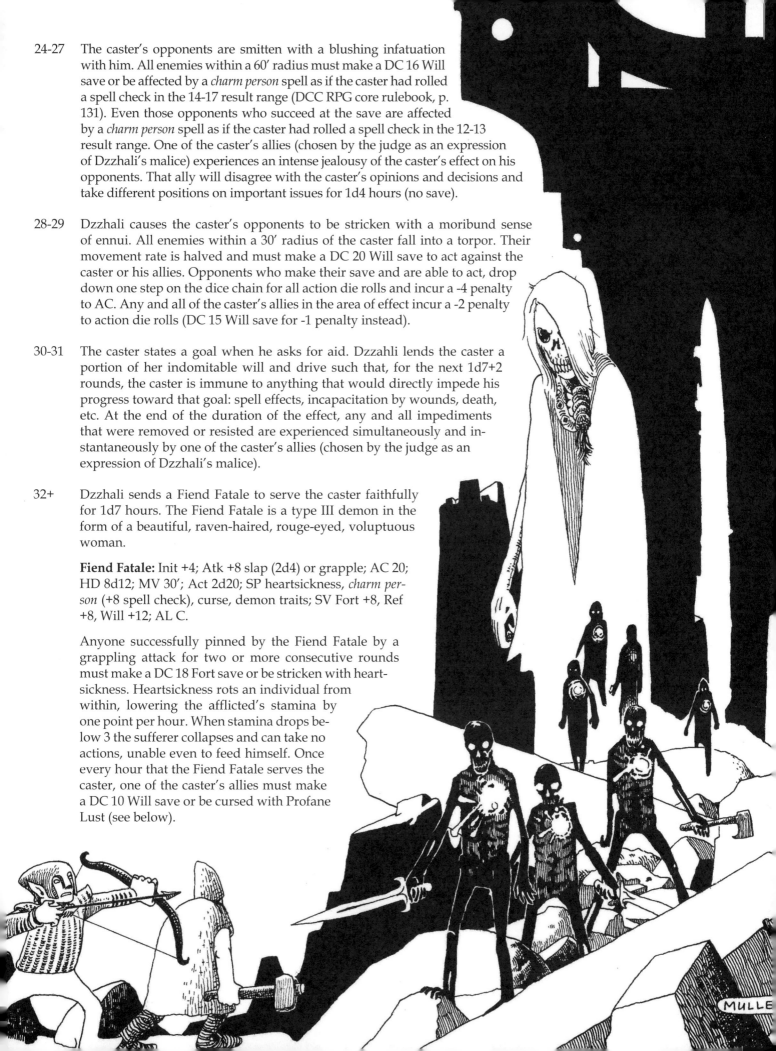

24-27 The caster's opponents are smitten with a blushing infatuation with him. All enemies within a 60' radius must make a DC 16 Will save or be affected by a *charm person* spell as if the caster had rolled a spell check in the 14-17 result range (DCC RPG core rulebook, p. 131). Even those opponents who succeed at the save are affected by a *charm person* spell as if the caster had rolled a spell check in the 12-13 result range. One of the caster's allies (chosen by the judge as an expression of Dzzhali's malice) experiences an intense jealousy of the caster's effect on his opponents. That ally will disagree with the caster's opinions and decisions and take different positions on important issues for 1d4 hours (no save).

28-29 Dzzhali causes the caster's opponents to be stricken with a moribund sense of ennui. All enemies within a 30' radius of the caster fall into a torpor. Their movement rate is halved and must make a DC 20 Will save to act against the caster or his allies. Opponents who make their save and are able to act, drop down one step on the dice chain for all action die rolls and incur a -4 penalty to AC. Any and all of the caster's allies in the area of effect incur a -2 penalty to action die rolls (DC 15 Will save for -1 penalty instead).

30-31 The caster states a goal when he asks for aid. Dzzahli lends the caster a portion of her indomitable will and drive such that, for the next 1d7+2 rounds, the caster is immune to anything that would directly impede his progress toward that goal: spell effects, incapacitation by wounds, death, etc. At the end of the duration of the effect, any and all impediments that were removed or resisted are experienced simultaneously and instantaneously by one of the caster's allies (chosen by the judge as an expression of Dzzahli's malice).

32+ Dzzhali sends a Fiend Fatale to serve the caster faithfully for 1d7 hours. The Fiend Fatale is a type III demon in the form of a beautiful, raven-haired, rouge-eyed, voluptuous woman.

Fiend Fatale: Init +4; Atk +8 slap (2d4) or grapple; AC 20; HD 8d12; MV 30'; Act 2d20; SP heartsickness, *charm person* (+8 spell check), curse, demon traits; SV Fort +8, Ref +8, Will +12; AL C.

Anyone successfully pinned by the Fiend Fatale by a grappling attack for two or more consecutive rounds must make a DC 18 Fort save or be stricken with heartsickness. Heartsickness rots an individual from within, lowering the afflicted's stamina by one point per hour. When stamina drops below 3 the sufferer collapses and can take no actions, unable even to feed himself. Once every hour that the Fiend Fatale serves the caster, one of the caster's allies must make a DC 10 Will save or be cursed with Profane Lust (see below).

CURSE OF PROFANE LUST

This curse is carried by demons — such as succubae and vampires — whose other-worldly sensuality and mesmerizing allure directly contrasts with their utter lack of real emotions, most notably love. The curse descends on the victim when the issuer chants — usually in one of three languages: Chaotic, Demonic or Ageless Necrotic — the following lines:

> *Lust slithers forth forbidden*
> *To caress with writhing glee*
> *Then lust crawls back to fawning dark*
> *With blackened heart you gave it free*

The curse carries a -2 Luck penalty and also reduces the victim's Personality by 2. It fills the victim with obsessive self-loathing, leading the victim to compulsively self-inflict minor wounds (scratching himself bloody, pulling out hanks of hair, abrading himself against rough surfaces, etc.). This self-harm prevents the victim from benefitting from naturally occurring healing (i.e., from overnight rest).

The curse can be remedied by the victim bathing a newborn child in Waters of Forgiveness brought from the Plane of Law and then performing ablutions using that wash water.

PATRON TAINT: DZZHALI

When patron taint is indicated for Dzzhali, roll 1d6 on the table below. When a caster has acquired all six taints at all levels of effect, there is no need to continue rolling anymore.

Roll   Result

1   The caster's soul is marred with chaotic corruption. The caster rolls on Table 5-3: Minor Corruption (DCC RPG, p. 116). The caster's soul takes on this appearance even though the corruption does not appear on the caster's body and is not externally visible. Creatures can sense the taint on the caster's soul, however, and react to the caster being marked by Chaos in accordance with their alignment and/or nature. If this result is rolled a second time, the caster's soul is corrupted by the result of a roll on Table 5-4: Major Corruption (p. 118). If this result is rolled a third time, the caster's soul is corrupted by the result of a roll on Table 5-5: Greater Corruption (p. 119).

2   The caster's magic is tainted with Dzzhali's general malevolence. Every time the caster successfully casts a spell that causes damage to an opponent, 1d3 damage is dealt to an ally of the caster chosen by the judge as an expression of Dzzhali's malice. The second time this result is rolled the damage caused to an ally increases to 1d4. The third time this result is rolled the damage increases to 1d5.

3   Anytime PCs perform a formal appraisal or begin to spend treasure gained from their last adventure, the caster's share of treasure is mysteriously and unexpectedly worth 10% (rounded up) more than originally believed and one ally's share (chosen by the judge as an expression of Dzzhali's malice) is worth 15% less (rounded down, of course!). If this result is rolled a second time, the caster's share of treasure is worth 15% more than originally believed (rounded up) and one ally's share (chosen by the judge) is worth 25% less than originally appraised (rounded down). If this result is rolled a third time, the caster's share of treasure is worth 10% more than originally believed (rounded up) and ALL the caster's allies' shares are worth 20% less (rounded down). These inequities are made mystically and manifest no matter how a party tries to adjust for them when they divide treasure amongst themselves.

4   The caster's magic is tainted with Dzzhali's general antipathy towards living beings. Anytime the caster successfully casts a spell that directly benefits one or more of his allies, one ally (chosen by the judge as an expression of Dzzhali's malice) must make a DC 12 Will save or forego the benefits of the spell. (Examples of *direct* benefits include such things as making an ally invisible or increasing an ally's armor class. This is in contrast to *indirect* benefits, such as damage that *may* kill or incapacitate opponents so they can't attack the caster's allies.) The second time this result is rolled, the Will save increases to DC 14. The third time this result is rolled the Will save increases to DC 16.

5   The caster's magic is imbued with the indiscriminate nature of Dzzhali's power. Any time the caster is healed by magical means, one point per hit die of healing is added to the hit point total of one opponent (chosen by the judge) in the next encounter involving the caster or his allies. (Healing that removes conditions does not invoke the taint.) The second time this result is rolled, when the caster benefits from magical healing that restores hit points, 1d3 hit points are added to the hit point total of *all* opponents in the next encounter that involves the caster or his allies. The third time this result is rolled, 1d3 hit points *per hit die of healing* are added to the hit points of all opponents in the next encounter involving the caster or his allies.

6   The caster becomes unnaturally attractive to a specific type of creature and simultaneously repulsive to that creature's antipode. For example, the caster may be attractive to elves but repulsive to dwarves, or attractive to children but repulsive to the children's parents, or the caster may become attractive to cats but repulsive to dogs. The attraction is a form of fascination that stops short of being a magical charm: creatures attracted to the caster will follow him around, take a positive interest in his activities, and be willing to perform small tasks in exchange for small favors. Creatures attracted to the caster will not otherwise go against their nature, perform services to their own detriment, take risks or put themselves in harm's way. Creatures repulsed by the caster will react negatively to the caster's arrival, communicate their displeasure to others, avoid and shun the caster, and attempt to impede the caster in any way that the creatures do not think will draw the caster's attention to them directly. The second time this result is rolled, the caster becomes unnaturally attractive/repulsive to a new pairing of creatures. The third time this result is rolled, the caster becomes unnaturally attractive/repulsive to yet another pairing of creatures.

PATRON SPELLS: DZZHALI

This patron of mindless, relentless vengeance grants three unique spells, as follows:

Level 1: *Detect Deception*

Level 2: *Inflict Anguish*

Level 3: *Excoriate Energy*

SPELLBURN: DZZHALI

Dzzhali spreads bitterness, distrust and discord. When a caster utilizes spellburn, roll 1d4 and consult the table below. Expand on these examples to create spellburn conditions that fit with Dzzhali's nature and are unique to your home campaign.

Roll   **Spellburn Result**

1   Dzzhali requires that the caster dissolve relationship ties as part of drawing needed magical energy. The caster must publically renounce a formal bond of friendship, fealty, fellowship or kinship. Examples of this include disowning a family member, resigning a membership in an Order, or cancelling all obligations – explicit or tacit – to an adventuring companion. The bond is forsaken until or unless it is formally and ritually renewed on terms both agreeable and beneficial to the other party.

2   Dzzhali allows the caster to draw the needed magical energy out of the creation of conflict. The caster must oath-swear a blood-feud against a clan, tribe, race, etc. The caster has fulfilled his oath when he has killed, maimed or enslaved a member of the clan, tribe or race with whom he feuds.

3   Dzzhali demands that her followers understand personal suffering. A caster who uses spellburn must forsake a human comfort for one month. The expenditure of magical energy through the use of spellburn takes all pleasure out of the chosen comfort, making the caster experience it as hollow, meaningless and mildly unpleasant: music sounds thin and flat, all food and drink tastes bland or even ashen, the touch of another person brings no warmth or comfort, etc. This results in a permanent -1 penalty to the caster's Fort saves.

4   Dzzhali demands that her followers overcome serious setbacks and still achieve their goals. Casters who use spellburn lose 1 XP + 1 XP/level of the spell. If losing XP for spellburn would cause the caster to lose a level, the caster experiences a different one of Dzzhali's spellburn effects.

Detect Deception

| Level: 1 (Dzzhali) | Range: 15′ or more | Duration: Instantaneous | Casting time: 2 actions | Save: Varies |

General
: Dzzhali wards her followers against others' deceptions and betrayals, lest these hinder her followers from spreading her gospel of malice. Through this spell the caster can attempt to detect deceptions of all kinds including lies, hidden properties of objects, traps, and concealments. The caster must be aware of the target in order to attempt a casting. On a successful casting, the wizard may choose to invoke any effect equal to or less than his spell check, allowing a range of options that include a weaker but potentially more useful result. The spell will not reveal any information about the specific nature of – or the truth behind – any deceptions, it will only alert the caster to the fact that they exist.

    When non-living enchanted objects, constructs, or structures are targeted, the judge secretly rolls a Fort save for the target, assigning a saving throw bonus appropriate to the level of enchantment of the item. (For example, an enchanted sword with a +1 bonus and no other special abilities would get a +2 bonus to its save, whereas a bonus of +8 to +12 would be appropriate to the sanctum of an archmage).

Manifestation
: Roll 1d4: (1) flies buzz around a 5′ area surrounding the target of the spell; (2) the sound of wedding bells tolling manifests during the casting; (3) a fetid breeze – the last breath of a dying man – washes over the caster and target; (4) the target of the spell turns a pallid white color during casting.

1
: Lost, failure, and patron taint.

2-11
: Lost. Failure.

12-13
: The caster can target one "person" within 60′ – an intelligent humanoid with whom the caster shares at least one common language. The person must make a Will save or the spell will instantaneously detect mundane, non-magical deceptions intrinsic to, or being carried out by, the target. At this level of effect the spell will alert the caster to verbal deceptions, lies and impersonations that occur during a single conversation, false appearances and physical disguises, and the presence of concealed objects on the targeted individual.

14-17
: The caster can target one mundane "monster" within 30′ – an animal or other creature that, while it may be extraordinary, is native to the world and not un-dead, a construct, extra-planar, supernatural or intrinsically magical in origin (e.g., ghosts, shadows, elementals, et al.). The target must make a Will save or the spell will instantaneously detect mundane, non-magical deceptions intrinsic to, or being carried out by, the target. At this level of effect the spell will alert the caster to deceptive communications or body-language (e.g., "playing possum"), camouflage, concealed appendages (e.g., retractable claws) or hidden attacks (e.g., poison spittle).

18-19
: The caster can instantaneously detect mundane, non-magical deceptions inherent to objects or structures within 15′. At this level of effect the spell will alert the caster to things hidden within an object or structure, falsehoods in writings, carvings, drawings or inscriptions, hidden functions (e.g., traps, secret doors) or the fact that an object has been made to look like something else.

20-23
: The caster can target one "person" within 60′ - an intelligent humanoid with whom the caster shares at least one common language. The person must make a Will save or the spell will instantaneously detect mundane and magical deceptions intrinsic to, cast upon, or being carried out by the target. At this level of effect the spell will alert the caster to verbal deceptions, lies and impersonations that occur during a single conversation, false identities, physical disguises or magical alterations to appearance, the presence of concealed objects, and hidden spell effects on the targeted individual.

24-27
: The caster can target a supernatural or inherently mystical being within 30.′ Gods, demi-gods and primal servants of Chaos and Law are immune to this spell. The target must make a Will save or the spell will instantaneously detect mundane and magical deceptions intrinsic to or being carried out by the target. At this level of effect the spell will alert the caster to deceptive communications or body-language (e.g., hostile intent by a zombie appearing to be an inanimate corpse), altered or illusory appearance, concealment (e.g., a Shadow hiding in the shadows), and otherwise undetectable weapons and attacks (e.g., invisible mind control; spellcasting and spell-like abilities with observable manifestations or that are not concealed by design do not constitute deceptions simply by being in an inactive state).

28-29
: The caster can target an enchanted object, construct, or structure within 30′. Legendary or "named" mystical locations and artifacts as well as objects and structures imbued with powerful divine magic are immune

to the effects of this spell. Despite being inanimate objects, enchanted targets get a Fort save (see spell description). At this level of effect the spell will alert the caster to things hidden within an object or structure, falsehoods in writings, carvings or inscriptions, hidden functions (e.g., traps, secret doors, spell triggers) or the fact that an object has been made to look like something else.

30-31	The caster chooses one of the weaker spell effects. If the target of the effect gets a saving throw, the roll drops one step down on the dice chain. If the save is missed, the caster gets the normal spell effects and may also obtain the answer to one yes-or-no question about the nature of/intent behind one of deceptions detected by the spell.
32+	The caster chooses one of the weaker spell effects. If the target of the effect gets a saving throw, the roll drops one step down on the dice chain. If the save is missed, the caster gets the normal spell effects and may also choose to ask up to three yes-or-no questions about the nature of/intent behind deceptions detected by the spell, or ask one open-ended question about the nature of/intent behind one of the deceptions detected.

Inflict Anguish

Level: 2 (Dzzhali)   Range: 120′   Duration: One round or more   Casting time: 1 action   Save: Will vs. spell check

General	The Strangled Bride likes nothing better than to spread the "joy" of her wedding night. This spell creates a psychic connection between the caster and one individual. The connection channels emotional anguish, wracking the target with pain and making concentrating on anything other than the anguish difficult. Once successfully cast on a target, the effects of this spell can be continued in subsequent rounds. As soon as the caster chooses an action other than maintaining the spell or the target successfully saves, the spell ends. At higher result levels the caster can perform other actions while also maintaining the spell.
Manifestation	Roll 1d4: (1) indistinct spectral images of beings the target creature has harmed swirl around it; (2) the caster is visibly wracked with the anguish he is channeling: sweating, tremors, facial contortions, etc.; (3) rope-like tendrils of blue-white force stretch out and wrap around the target's throat; (4) a magical viewport opens in the target's chest allowing others to see his/her heart writhe from anguish.
1	Lost, failure, and patron taint.
2-11	Lost. Failure.
12-13	Failure, but spell is not lost.
14-15	The caster can attack one target within range, which must make a Will save or take 1d4 points of damage and a -1 penalty to die rolls on its actions in the following round. If the target fails its save during the round the spell takes effect, then in subsequent rounds the caster can choose to take no other action and continue inflicting 1d4 damage and imposing the -1 penalty to the target's actions for that round. The target receives a save during each of these subsequent rounds with a cumulative +1 bonus to each consecutive save after the initial one. A successful save cancels all effects.
16-19	The caster can attack one target within range, which must make a Will save or take 1d4+1 points of damage and a -1 penalty to die rolls on its actions in the following round. If the target fails its save during the round the spell takes effect, then in subsequent rounds the caster can choose to take no other action and continue inflicting 1d4+1 damage and imposing the -1 penalty to the target's actions for that round. The target receives a save during each of these subsequent rounds with a cumulative +1 bonus to each consecutive save after the initial one. A successful save cancels all effects.
20-21	The caster can attack one target within range, which must make a Will save or take 1d6 points of damage and drops one step down on the dice chain when rolling for actions in the following round. If the target fails its save during the round the spell takes effect, then in subsequent rounds the caster can choose to take no other action and continue inflicting 1d6 damage and imposing the -1d penalty on rolls for actions for that round. The target receives a save during each of these subsequent rounds with a cumulative +1 bonus to each consecutive save after the initial one. A successful save cancels all effects.
22-23	The caster can attack one target within range, which must make a Will save or take 1d6+1 points of damage and drops one step down on the dice chain when rolling for actions in the following round. If the target fails its save during the round the spell takes effect, then in subsequent rounds the caster can choose to take no other action and continue inflicting 1d6+1 damage and imposing the -1d penalty on rolls for actions for

	that round. The target receives a save during each of these subsequent rounds. After the third consecutive round of saves, the target receives a cumulative +1 bonus to each consecutive save. A successful save cancels all effects.
24-25	The caster can attack one target within range, which must make a Will save or take 1d4 points of damage and a -1 penalty to die rolls for its actions in the following round. If the target fails its save during the round the spell takes effect, in subsequent rounds the spell continues to inflict 1d4 damage and imposes the -1 penalty to the target's actions for that round. Meanwhile the caster can take other actions. The target receives a save during each of these subsequent rounds with a cumulative +1 bonus to each consecutive save after the initial one. At this level of results the spell only ends when the target successfully saves or the caster voluntarily cancels the spell.
26-29	The caster designates a single target within range, which must make a Will save or take 1d4+1 points of damage and a -1 penalty to the die roll for its actions in the following round. If the target fails its save during the round the spell takes effect, in subsequent rounds the spell continues to inflict 1d4+1 damage and to impose the -1 penalty to the target's actions for that round. Meanwhile the caster can take other actions. The target receives a save during each of these subsequent rounds with a cumulative +1 bonus to each consecutive save after the initial one. At this level of results the spell only ends when the target successfully saves or the caster voluntarily cancels the spell.
30-31	The caster designates a single target within range, which must make a Will save or take 1d6 points of damage and drops one step down on the dice chain when rolling for actions in the following round. If the target fails its save during the round the spell takes effect, in subsequent rounds the spell continues to inflict 1d6 damage and to impose the -1d penalty on actions for that round. Meanwhile the caster can take other actions. The target receives a save during each of these subsequent rounds with a cumulative +1 bonus to each consecutive save after the initial one. At this level of results the spell only ends when the target successfully saves or the caster voluntarily cancels the spell.
32-33	The caster designates a primary target within range and the spell affects all opponents within a 15' radius of that primary target. All targets within the area of effect which must make a Will save or take 1d6 points of damage and drop one step down on the dice chain when rolling for actions in the following round. All targets that fail their saves during the round the spell takes effect may be subject to ongoing spell effects. In subsequent rounds the caster can choose to take no other action and continue inflicting 1d6 damage and to impose the -1d penalty on actions for that round. Targets receive a save during each of these subsequent rounds. The target receives a save during each of these subsequent rounds with a cumulative +1 bonus to each consecutive save after the initial one. At this level of results, as soon as the caster chooses an action other than maintaining the spell or the target successfully saves, the spell ends.
34+	The caster designates a primary target within range and the spell affects all opponents within a 15' radius of that primary target. All targets within the area of effect which must make a Will save or take 1d6+1 points of damage and drop one step down on the dice chain when rolling for actions in the following round. All targets that fail their saves during the round the spell takes effect may be subject to ongoing spell effects. In subsequent rounds the caster can choose to take no other action and continue inflicting 1d6+1 damage and imposing the -1d penalty on actions for that round. Targets receive a save during each of these subsequent rounds. After the third consecutive round of saves, the target receives a cumulative +1 bonus to each consecutive save. At this level of results, as soon as the caster chooses an action other than maintaining the spell or the target successfully saves, the spell ends.

Excoriate Energy

Level: 3 (Dzzhali) Range: Touch or more Duration: Instantaneous Casting time: 1 action Save: Fort vs. spell check

General	Dzzhali grants power to her followers, but the price of this power is paid by the followers' friends, allies, companions, and loved ones. The caster can use spellburn by draining the attributes of allies. Opponents cannot be targeted, nor can creatures acting as allies because of magical compulsion (e.g., *charm person*). An ally subject to the spell does not suffer effects of spellburn other than temporary attribute point loss. The caster cannot lower any of the target's ability scores below 4. If the target has a patron or serves a divinity, the caster may incur the displeasure of that entity for using the life energy of the target for his own purposes and to further Dzzhali's aims. 
	The caster must use the drained attribute points as spellburn in a casting by the end of the next round or the drained attribute points return to ally in the following round. Spellburn energy drained from an ally cannot be combined with additional spellburn by the caster when the next spell is cast. The caster suffers other effects of spellburn besides attribute point loss as if he had burned his own attribute points. The caster experiences these non-attribute loss effects of spellburn even if he fails to cast a spell in time and the drained attribute points return to the caster's ally.
Manifestation	Roll 1d4: (1) maggots erupt from the target's skin; (2) a spectral image of the target is drawn from its body and into the body of the caster; (3) the topmost layers of exposed skin on the target's body instantly rot and slough off; (4) the caster's insides expand radically from the inside out, causing his entire body to bulge until his eyes, blood vessels, and skin are on the verge of bursting.
1	Lost, failure, and patron taint.
2-11	Lost. Failure.
12-15	Failure, but spell is not lost.
16-17	The target of the spell must be a wizard or elf, must be touched by the caster, and can choose to make a Fort save or the caster drains up to two attribute points from across the three attributes that are eligible for spellburn: Strength, Agility, or Stamina.
18-21	The target of the spell must be a wizard or elf, must be touched by the caster, and can choose to make a Fort save one step down on the dice chain or the caster drains up to two attribute points from across the three attributes that are eligible for spellburn: Strength, Agility, or Stamina.
22-23	The target of the spell must be a wizard or elf, must be touched by the caster, and can choose to make a Fort save or the caster drains one point from each ability score eligible for spellburn: Strength, Agility, or Stamina.
24-26	The target of the spell must be a wizard or elf, must be touched by the caster, and can choose to make a Fort save at one step down on the dice chain or the caster drains one point from each ability score eligible for spellburn: Strength, Agility, and Stamina.
27-31	The target of the spell must be a wizard or elf within 15' and the target can choose to make a Fort save or the caster drains up to two points from each ability score eligible for spellburn: Strength, Agility, or Stamina.
32-33	The spell can target a wizard, elf, or cleric up to 15' away. The target can choose make a Fort save at one step down on the dice chain or the caster drains one point from each ability score eligible for spellburn: Strength, Agility, and Stamina.
34-35	The spell can target a wizard, elf, or cleric up to 30' away. The target can choose to make a Fort save at one step down on the dice chain or the caster drains up to two points from each ability score eligible for spellburn: Strength, Agility, and Stamina.
36+	The spell can target a wizard, elf, or cleric up to 30' away. The target can choose to make a Fort save or the caster drains up to 10 points from across the three ability scores eligible for spellburn - Strength, Agility, or Stamina - apportioned any way the caster chooses.

HEKANHODA

Hekanhoda: the Lord of Grotesques, Viscount of Corruption, Caliph of the Unclean, Duke of Deformities and Avatar of Afflictions. Hekanhoda's body evidences every deformity known to man, as well as many that are unknown. He dresses in courtly robes that do not cover his deformities, they accentuate them. His finery is no affectation: Hekanhoda has perhaps the most pedigreed lineage amongst the Host of Chaos. He is the bastard son of the Dark Fey Queen and sired by Bobugbubilz himself. The Annals record that the King of Elfland deposed the Dark Fey Queen and Hekanhoda makes no secret of the fact that he has oath-sworn enmity against the White-Bearded Regent. The heraldry of Hekanhoda's robes – purple for royalty, yellow for Elfland and red for his avowed blood-feud – are but one of the outward signs of his lineage. Another is his ownership of the eternal *Grimoire of Endless Night*, smuggled out of Ffumoria, his mother's former realm.

Through the mixing of his mother's and father's bloodlines Hekanhoda wields the power of the Nine Mortal Afflictions. Each affliction is fueled by a character flaw inherent in mortals and each finds physical expression in a life-threatening disease or infirmity. This makes them terrible weapons at the disposal of Hekanhoda and his followers.

Invoke Patron check results:

12-13   Hekanhoda gives the caster insight into the mortal flaw of arrogance, which manifests in the body as bubonic plague. The caster can select one visible creature within 240' and cause pustules to erupt from the target's skin, covering its body. The pustules are painful and it is difficult to avoid chafing them. This imposes a -4 AC penalty and a -2 penalty to Agility. If the target makes a successful DC 15 Fortitude save these penalties are halved. The pustules burst and scab over in 2d3+1 turns, ending the effect.

14-17   The caster understands the mortal inclination toward bitterness and resentment and knows how this expresses itself as evil humors in the joints. The caster can select one visible creature within 240' and cause painful swelling in the target's joints. The joint inflammation makes it painful and difficult to move, resulting in the target dropping down two steps on the dice chain when rolling Action dice. Furthermore, the target's movement is reduced by 10'. If the target makes a successful DC 15 Fortitude save these penalties are halved. The target's joints remain impaired until the disease causing the inflammation is cured.

18-19   The caster grasps that a seed of contempt lives in the hearts of all mortals. Nurturing this seed causes it to grow into a malignancy in the body. The caster can select one visible target creature within 240' and cause a huge tumor to grow impossibly fast inside the target's body. The growth of this tumor has the effect of an immediate critical hit. The caster rolls 1d8+16 on Crit Table II to determine the effects of the hit. Targets make saves against the effects of this hit using a die two steps up on the dice chain (e.g., they roll a d30 if they would normally roll a d20).

20-23   Hekanhoda reveals to the caster how envy inculcates itself in the spirit. The caster sees the acrid bile that builds up in the gut when envy festers. The caster can void this bile from himself in the form of a vomitus spray. The spray inflicts 4d4 damage on up to three creatures within a cone 15' long and 15' wide. Target creatures that succeed at a DC 15 Fortitude save take half damage (rounded up). The spray also degrades any clothes, equipment, or possessions that it comes in contact with that would be negatively affected by acid. The caster can spray acid bile three times and then the spell is expended.

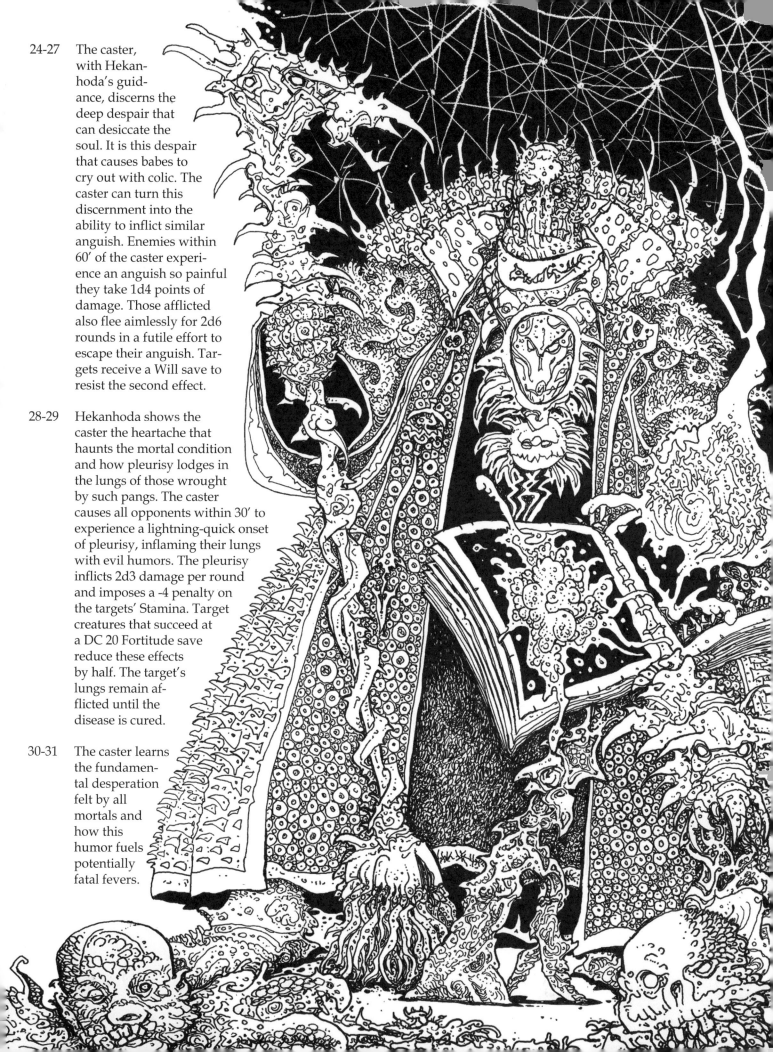

24-27 The caster, with Hekanhoda's guidance, discerns the deep despair that can desiccate the soul. It is this despair that causes babes to cry out with colic. The caster can turn this discernment into the ability to inflict similar anguish. Enemies within 60' of the caster experience an anguish so painful they take 1d4 points of damage. Those afflicted also flee aimlessly for 2d6 rounds in a futile effort to escape their anguish. Targets receive a Will save to resist the second effect.

28-29 Hekanhoda shows the caster the heartache that haunts the mortal condition and how pleurisy lodges in the lungs of those wrought by such pangs. The caster causes all opponents within 30' to experience a lightning-quick onset of pleurisy, inflaming their lungs with evil humors. The pleurisy inflicts 2d3 damage per round and imposes a -4 penalty on the targets' Stamina. Target creatures that succeed at a DC 20 Fortitude save reduce these effects by half. The target's lungs remain afflicted until the disease is cured.

30-31 The caster learns the fundamental desperation felt by all mortals and how this humor fuels potentially fatal fevers.

The caster instantly afflicts all opponents within 60′ with a preternatural, raging, burning fever. The fever inflicts 2d3 heat damage per round. Spells, abilities or magic items that allow a creature to resist fire mitigate the effect. Target creatures that succeed at a DC 20 Fortitude save reduce the damage by half. On the third round following affliction, targets experience the onset of delirium. Each round, delirious creatures roll a DC 15 Willpower save. If they fail their save they cannot correctly perceive reality and their actions that round are directed at a random creature or object. Targets are afflicted until the fever is cured.

32+   Hekanhoda lays bare the barrenness of the human soul and shows how this leads to sterility and impotence. All enemies within 120′ of the caster must succeed at a Willpower save or be weakened by impotence and extreme lethargy. Targets that fail their save lose 4d3+4 points of Strength. Creatures reduced to Strength 3 or lower can take no action except movement, which is reduced to 5′. Creatures reduced to Strength 0 must make a second DC 20 Will save or slide over the edge from lethargy into death.

PATRON TAINT: HEKANHODA

When patron taint is indicated for Hekanhoda, roll 1d6 on the table below. When a caster has acquired all six taints at all levels of effect, there is no need to continue rolling.

Roll   **Result**

1   The caster's spine deforms, the vertebrae enlarging to form a large crest of ridges protruding 6″ out of the caster's back. The second time this result is rolled, the caster also develops a pronounced hunchback. When this result is rolled a third time the caster's tailbone lengthens and protrudes, giving him a thick, bony tail.

2   The caster's fingers migrate from one hand to the other. When this result is first rolled, one finger falls off of one hand and the other hand grows an extra that is disproportionately-sized and located in a random spot on the caster's hand or wrist. The second and third times this result is rolled the process repeats. The deformity has no effect on spellcasting but if one hand is reduced to two fingers, that hand loses a great deal of its ability to manipulate objects, resulting in a two-step drop down on the dice chain for rolls for actions that require manual dexterity (wielding a weapon, tying a knot, etc.).

3   A corpuscular face develops on some part of the caster's body. First roll a d16 to determine its location.

The face has its own personality and can interact with the caster and the outside world. A face also knows one spell and can cast this spell on the caster's behalf in lieu of the caster's own action. The caster rolls his spell check – including taking into account the level of the spell — as normal for this casting and experiences any effects of misfire, corruption, etc. If the caster already knows the same spell as the face, this benefit is negated. Roll 1d16 to determine the personality of the face and the spell it knows:

d16	Location	d16	Personality	Spell Known
1	Head	1	Haughty, Arrogant	*Chill touch*
2	Forehead	2	Cloying, a Sychophant	*Choking cloud*
3	Cheek or Chin	3	Inappropriate, Insulting	*Ventriloquism*
4	Neck	4	Chatty, Talkative	*Magic mouth*
5	Shoulder Blade	5	Indecisive, Absent-minded	*Forget*
6	Upper Back	6	Boring	*Sleep*
7	Lower Back	7	Seductive, Charming	*Charm person*
8	Side	8	Poetic, Artistic	*Color spray*
9	Rump	9	Suspicious, Paranoid	*Ward portal*
10	Upper Arm	10	Cunning	*ESP*
11	Forearm	11	Cultured, Well-traveled	*Comprehend language*
12	Hand	12	Critical	*Scorching ray*
13	Thigh	13	Enthusiastic, Bombastic	*Enlarge*
14	Knee	14	Narcissistic	*Mirror image*
15	Shin	15	Shy, Insecure	*Invisibility*
16	Foot	16	Mad, Delusional	*Invisible companion*

4   Bone spurs 1d6+2" in length erupt from the caster's body (the sub-table in result 3 can be used to randomly determine a location). Each of three times this patron taint result is rolled, 1d3 spurs emerge. Spurs can be used as melee weapons. They benefit from the caster's attack bonus and do 1d3 damage.

5   Anytime the caster encounters creatures with corruption, he may absorb that corruption unto himself. If the caster is within 60' of a corrupted creature he must succeed at a DC 12 Fortitude save or one of the creature's corruptions transfers to him. The second time this result is rolled, the Fortitude save increases to DC 14. When this result is rolled a third time, the save increases to DC 16.

6   Sunlight becomes anathema to the caster. The first time this result is rolled, the caster cannot stand full sunlight. Exposure drains one hit point per hour, unless a DC 12 Fortitude save is made. When this result is rolled a second time, overcast skies drain one hit point per hour unless a DC 15 Fortitude save is made. The third time the result is rolled the caster cannot be outside during the day at all or he will be drained one hit point per hour, unless a DC 15 Fortitude save is made.

PATRON SPELLS: HEKANHODA

The Lord of Grotesques teaches his followers three spells out of the *Grimoire of Endless Night*, as follows:

Level 1: *Hekanhoda's Homunculus*

Level 2: *Wracking Plague*

Level 3: *Baneful Gaze*

SPELLBURN: HEKANHODA

Hekanhoda celebrates his "uniqueness" – what others call deformities – and demands that his followers make themselves over in his image. When a caster utilizes spellburn, roll 1d4 and consult the table below. Use these to inspire you to create special spellburn conditions for Hekanhoda in your home campaign.

Roll   Spellburn Result

1   The caster must pour burning pitch onto his body. The pitch raises blisters and also cools and hardens into tumor-like clots that resemble the leprosies that mark Hekanhoda's body.

2   The caster must break one joint on either a finger or a toe for every attribute point he uses for spellburn. For every two broken finger joints (rounded down) the caster incurs a cumulative -1 penalty to his attack rolls in combat. For every four broken toe joints the caster incurs a -5' penalty to movement.

3   The caster must affix a metal screw clamp to the nerve cluster in one of his arms. The application of the clamp to this pressure point effectively immobilizes the extremity, making the caster unable to use it. The caster must keep the clamp in place for one hour for every attribute point used for spellburn.

4   The caster must affix a metal screw clamp to the nerve cluster in one of his legs. The application of the clamp to this pressure point effectively immobilizes the extremity. As a result, the caster's movement rate is halved. The caster must keep the clamp in place for one hour for every attribute point used for spellburn.

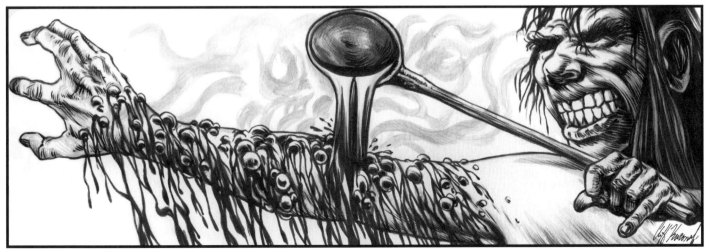

Hekanhoda's Homunculus

Level: 1 (Hekanhoda)   Range: Self   Duration: Lifetime   Casting time: 1 day   Save: N/A

General	This alchemical formulae from the *Grimoire of Endless Night* guides the caster in constructing a humanoid homunculus out of body parts and animating it with the spirit of a demon. The spell check is made upon the completion of construction and if the check is successful the homunculus animates and functions in every way as the caster's familiar.

The basic form of the homunculus is that of a humanoid roughly 2' tall, but the specifics can deviate substantially from that starting point by using an animal head, multiple legs, a single leg or no legs, multiple arms, etc. Judges should role-play with the caster the process of gathering body parts, designing and constructing the homunculus. On the basis of the design and construction process the judge should customize the basic stat block, below, to make the construct's physical abilities match the caster's design. The judge can also use the Variety in Humanoid Tables 9-1 and 9-3 (DCC RPG rulebook pg. 380) and the Unique Demons Tables 9-11, 9-12 and 9-13 (DCC RPG pg. 404) to randomly determine some of the parts the caster is able to acquire for assembling the homunculus.

The caster gains hit points equal to the homunculus' total and the homunculus has the powers of **both** an Arcane **and** a Focal familiar (see DCC RPG rulebook pg. 317).

Once the caster has constructed and animated a homunculus, he cannot construct and animate another until the current one dies and a fortnight-minus-a-day passes. If the homunculus dies, the caster immediately acquires patron taint and suffers a -2 spell check penalty until a fortnight-minus-a-day passes.

Hekanhodan Homunculus (type I demon-construct, Hekanhoda): Init +1; Atk TBD (judge's discretion or Table 9-13, DCC RPG rulebook pg. 404) +4 melee (1d8); AC 14; HD 4d4; MV 30'; Act 1d20; SP TBD (judge's discretion or Table 9-14, DCC RPG rulebook pg. 404) + infravision, *darkness* (+4 check), speaks common and infernal, crit threat range 20; lacking demon immunities; SV Fort +2; Ref +2; Will +2; AL C. |
Manifestation	Varies.
1	Lost, failure, and patron taint.
2-11	Lost. Failure.
12-13	Per judge.
14-17	Per judge.
18-19	Per judge.
20-23	Per judge.
24-27	Per judge.
28-29	Per judge.
30-31	Per judge.
32+	Per judge.

Wracking Plague

Level: 2 (Hekanhoda)	Range: Varies	Duration: Varies	Casting time: 1 round	Save: Fort vs spell check

General	The caster infects one or more creatures with a painful, debilitating illness.
	Creatures who fail their save versus this spell lose the ability to heal damage through rest or other normal means (herbal poultices, bandages, etc.) — it can only be healed magically.
	Because of the magical nature of this plague, it requires 5 hit dice of healing to be cured by a cleric's *lay on hands*. The cleric spell *neutralize poison or disease* affects it per the spell check result of the casting.
Manifestation	Roll 1d4: (1) the caster exhales foul-looking humors that envelop the target(s); (2) target(s) go pale, shiver and break out in a foul-smelling sweat; (3); a swarm of smoky, spectral rats emerge from the ground and scamper around the feet of the targeted creatures; (4) a miasmic odor permeates the area of the spell's effect, causing all who smell it to gag and retch briefly.
1	Lost, failure, and patron taint.
2-11	Lost. Failure.
12-13	Failure, but spell is not lost.
14-15	The caster's touch infects one visible target with a painful, debilitating illness that lasts for a day. The target must succeed at a Fortitude save or take 1d4 damage and suffer a -2 penalty to an attribute score of the caster's choice.
16-19	The caster's touch infects one visible target with a painful, debilitating illness that lasts up to a week. The target must succeed at a Fortitude save or take 2d3 damage and suffer a -2 penalty to two attribute scores of the caster's choice. Anyone who maintains close proximity to a creature infected with an illness from this spell at this result level for one hour or more must make a DC 12 Fortitude save or become infected, suffering the effects of the spell as if it had been cast upon him.
20-21	The caster infects all visible enemies within 15' with a painful, debilitating illness that lasts up to a week. The target must succeed at a Fortitude save or take 2d3 damage and suffer a -2 penalty to two attribute scores of the caster's choice. Anyone who maintains close proximity to a creature infected with an illness from this spell at this result level for one turn or more must make a DC 12 Fortitude save or become infected, suffering the effects of the spell as if it had been cast upon him.
22-23	The caster infects all visible enemies within 30' with a painful, debilitating illness that lasts up to a month. Targets must succeed at a Fortitude save or take 2d3 damage and suffer a -2 penalty to two attribute scores of the caster's choice. Infected creatures lose one hit point per hour until they are healed or they perish. Anyone who maintains close proximity to a creature infected with an illness from this spell at this result level for one turn or more must make a DC 13 Fortitude save or become infected, suffering the effects of the spell as if it had been cast upon him.
24-25	The caster infects all visible enemies within 60' with a painful, debilitating illness that lasts up to a month. Targets must succeed at a Fortitude save or take 2d4 damage and suffer a -3 penalty to two attribute scores of the caster's choice. Infected creatures lose one hit point per hour until they are healed or they perish. Anyone who maintains close proximity to a creature infected with an illness from this spell at this result level for one turn or more must make a DC 14 Fortitude save or become infected, suffering the effects of the spell as if it had been cast upon him.
26-29	The caster infects all visible enemies within 120' with a painful, debilitating illness that lasts until the infected person is cured or dies. Targets must succeed at a Fortitude save or take 2d4 damage and suffer a -3 penalty to two attribute scores of the caster's choice. Infected creatures lose one hit point per turn until they are healed or they perish. Anyone who maintains close proximity to a creature infected with an illness from this spell at this result level for half a turn or more must make a DC 14 Fortitude save or become infected, suffering the effects of the spell as if it had been cast upon him.
30-31	The caster infects all visible enemies within 100 yards with a painful, debilitating illness that lasts until the infected person is cured or dies. Targets must succeed at a Fortitude save or take 2d4 damage and suffer a -3 penalty to two attribute scores of the caster's choice. Infected creatures lose one hit point per turn until they are healed or they perish. Anyone who maintains close proximity to a creature infected with an illness from

	this spell at this result level for half a turn or more must make a DC 14 Fortitude save or become infected, suffering the effects of the spell as if it had been cast upon him.
32-33	The caster infects all visible enemies within 100 yards with a painful, debilitating illness for up to a month. Targets must succeed at a Fortitude save or take 3d3 damage and suffer a -3 penalty to four attribute scores of the caster's choice. Infected creatures lose one hit point per turn until they are healed or they perish. Anyone who maintains close proximity to a creature infected with an illness from this spell at this result level for a minute or more must make a DC 15 Fortitude save or become infected, suffering the effects of the spell as if it had been cast upon him.
34+	The caster infects all visible enemies within 200 yards with a painful, debilitating illness for up to a month. Targets must succeed at a Fortitude save or take 3d4 damage and suffer a -4 penalty to four attribute scores of the caster's choice. Infected creatures lose one hit point per turn as well as one additional point from an attribute score (rolled randomly) until they are healed or they perish. Anyone who maintains close proximity to a creature infected with an illness from this spell at this result level for a minute or more must make a DC 16 Fortitude save or become infected, suffering the effects of the spell as if it had been cast upon him.

Baneful Gaze

Level: 3 (Hekanhoda)　　Range: Sight　　Duration: 1 round or more　　Casting time: 1 action　　Save: Fortitude vs. spell check

General	The caster channels the power of Hekanhoda's evil eye to immobilize and torture opponents.
Manifestation	Roll 1d4: (1) one of the caster's eyes grows to four times its normal size and bulges out of its socket; (2) the caster removes one of his eyes from its socket and brandishes it like a wand at the target(s) of the spell; (3) a target's eyes roll back up into its head and its body shakes with convulsions (4) a huge third eye with a sickly, ochre yellow iris appears in the center of the caster's forehead.
1	Lost, failure, and patron taint.
2-11	Lost. Failure.
12-15	Failure, but spell is not lost.
16-17	The caster makes eye contact with one target. The target receives a Fortitude save. If it fails, the target immediately takes 1d4 hit points of life-drain damage and is paralyzed. In subsequent rounds, if the caster concentrates fully on the target and maintains the eye contact, the target must succeed at a Fortitude save or remain paralyzed and take an additional 1d3 damage each round. Any successful subsequent save cancels the spell's ongoing effect on that target.
18-21	The caster makes eye contact with one target. The target receives a Fortitude save. If it fails, the target immediately takes 2d3 hit points of life-drain damage and is paralyzed. In subsequent rounds, if the caster concentrates fully on the target and maintains the eye contact, the target must succeed at a Fortitude save or remain paralyzed and take an additional 1d4 damage each round. Any successful subsequent save cancels the spell's ongoing effect on that target.
22-23	The caster makes eye contact with one target. The target receives a Fortitude save. If it fails, the target immediately takes 2d4 life-drain damage and is paralyzed. In subsequent rounds, if the caster concentrates fully on the target and maintains the eye contact, the target must succeed at a Fortitude save or remain paralyzed and take an additional 1d6 damage each round. Any successful subsequent save cancels the spell's ongoing effect on that target.
24-26	The caster makes eye contact with up to three targets in quick succession. The targets must all be within a field of vision in front of the caster and defined by a cone 30' long and 20' wide. Targets receive Fortitude saves. Any target that fails immediately takes 2d4 hit points of life-drain damage and is paralyzed. In subsequent rounds, if the caster concentrates fully on the targets that failed their initial saves and maintains eye contact, those targets must succeed at a Fortitude save or remain paralyzed and take an additional 1d6 hit damage each round. Any successful subsequent save cancels the spell's ongoing effect on that target.
27-31	The caster makes eye contact with up to three targets in quick succession. The targets must all be within a field of vision in front of the caster and defined by a cone 30' long and 20' wide. Targets receive Fortitude

saves. Any target that fails its save immediately takes 3d3 hit points of life-drain damage and is paralyzed. In subsequent rounds, if the caster concentrates fully on the targets that failed their initial saves and maintains eye contact, those targets must succeed at another Fortitude save or remain paralyzed and take an additional 2d4 damage each round. Any successful subsequent save cancels the spell's ongoing effect on that target.

32-33   The caster makes eye contact with up to six targets in quick succession. The targets must all be within a field of vision in front of the caster and defined by a cone 40' long and 30' wide. Targets receive Fortitude saves. Any target that fails its save immediately takes 3d3 hit points of life-drain damage and is paralyzed. In subsequent rounds, if the caster concentrates fully on the targets that failed their initial saves and maintains eye contact, those targets must succeed at another Fortitude save or remain paralyzed and take an additional 2d4 damage each round. Any successful subsequent save cancels the spell's ongoing effect on that target.

34-35   The caster makes eye contact with up to six targets in quick succession. The targets must all be within a field of vision in front of the caster and defined by a cone 40' long and 30' wide. Targets receive Fortitude saves. Any target that fails its save immediately takes 3d6 hit points of life-drain damage and is paralyzed. In subsequent rounds, if the caster concentrates fully on the targets that failed their initial saves and maintains eye contact, those targets must succeed at another Fortitude save or remain paralyzed and take an additional 3d3 damage each round. Any successful subsequent save cancels the spell's ongoing effect on that target.

36+   The caster makes eye contact with up to ten targets in quick succession. The targets must all be within a field of vision in front of the caster and defined by a cone 60' long and 40' wide. Targets receive Fortitude saves. Any target that fails its save immediately takes 3d6 hit points of life-drain damage and is paralyzed. In subsequent rounds, if the caster concentrates fully on the targets that failed their initial saves and maintains eye contact, those targets must succeed at another Fortitude save or remain paralyzed and take an additional 3d3 damage each round. Any successful subsequent save cancels the spell's ongoing effect on that target.

HORNED KING

The Horned King rules from the Thrice-Tenth Kingdom, venturing across the mutiverse on his Wild Hunts. A solemn and grim lord, he delights only in the hunt, testing his martial prowess against the deadliest foes. A patron of the old ways, the Horned King bestows his blessing upon heathen witches, barbarian shamans, and warriors who exalt the wild savage hidden within.

Invoke Patron check results:

12-13   Hounds bay on the shrill wind, striking fear into the hearts of the hunted. One target within the caster's sight must make a DC 12 Will save or succumb to paralyzing terror. If the target fails the save, it cowers in the shadows, too terrified to move. Unintelligent creatures flee for their lives. The effect lasts 1d6 rounds or until the creature is forced into action (such as by being attacked or threatened).

14-17   The wolfish demeanor of the predator overtakes the caster, infusing his soul with the spirit of the Wild Hunt. The caster can unerringly track creatures (Luck check, DC 5) through the most harrowing of conditions for 24 hours (or until the power is dismissed). Henchmen are unnerved, suffering a -2 morale penalty for the duration of the effect.

18-19   A long, haunting howl fills the air, followed by driving wind. The caster knows the location and most direct route to one living target within 50 miles. (The caster is not inherently aware of perils in the path.) If the caster reaches the target within 24 hours, the target suffers a -2 penalty to AC and saves for the duration of the encounter.

20-23   The Horned King sends six hounds to assist the caster. They appear from a cloud of darksome soot or billowing snow. They remain for 2d6 rounds, before vanishing back to the Thrice-Tenth Kingdom. **Hound:** Init +4; Atk bite +4 melee (1d8+4); AC 15; HD 3d8; hp 15; MV 45'; Act 1d20; SV Fort +4, Ref +2, Will +4; AL C.

24-27   The caster and his allies are chilled by a driving wind, and the howls of hounds erupt all around. All enemies within 50' must make a DC 15 Will save or succumb to paralyzing terror. Targets failing the save cower in the shadows, too terrified to move. Unintelligent creatures flee. The effect lasts 1d6 turns or until a creature is forced into action (such as by being attacked or threatened).

28-29   *Spear of the Horned King.* A shimmering spear appears in the caster's hand; the silvery tip of the spear is marked with the sigil of the Horned King. If the spear does not taste blood before the next moonrise, it vanishes. If the spear is used in battle (either melee or ranged combat) the target must attempt a DC 20 Will save or be struck instantly and permanently dead. The caster can employ the spear but once in his entire lifetime.

30-31   *Crown of the Horned King.* A scintillating aura rings the caster's brow, sparkling gray and silver. During the span of the next 24 hours, the caster has the ability to summon up to 1d20+10 hounds to serve his will. If sent on the hunt, the hounds can track any being across the multiverse, finding their prey within 1d12 rounds. The hounds remain 24 hours before vanishing back to the Thrice-Tenth Kingdom. **Hound:** Init +4; Atk bite +4 melee (1d8+4); AC 15; HD 3d8; hp 15 each; MV 45'; Act 1d20; SV Fort +4, Ref +2, Will +4; AL C. This ability is available only once in a caster's lifetime. If this result is rolled again, the caster may choose the *Spear of the Horned King* (as above) if it is available; otherwise, the Horned King is unable to assist the caster.

32+   Mark of the Horned King. The caster places the mark of the Horned King upon a target within sight. On the next moonrise, the target receives a DC 25 Will save. On a failed save, the Horned King and his hounds appear and carry away the target. This ability is available only once in a caster's lifetime. If this result is rolled again in the future, the caster may choose the *Crown of the Horned King* or *Spear of the Horned King* (as above) if either is available; otherwise, the Horned King is unable to assist the caster.

PATRON TAINT: THE HORNED KING

When patron taint is indicated for the Horned King, roll 1d6 on the table below. When a wizard has acquired all six taints at all levels of effect, there is no need to continue rolling any more.

Roll   Result

1   The caster is overtaken by the call of the hunt. If a foe retreats, the caster must make a DC 10 Will save. On a failed save, the caster gives chase for 1d7 rounds. The second time this corruption is rolled, the Will save DC increases to 15.

2   The caster takes on the attributes of the Horned King's minions. Roll 1d4: (1) wide antlers; (2) a thick coat of fur; (3) elongated muzzle; (4) fangs and claws.

3   Only the strong survive in the Thrice-Tenth Kingdom, and the caster cannot tolerate weakness among his pack. If, after a combat, a fellow character hovers at 1 hp or is unconscious, the caster is overcome by the powerful desire to finish off his ally (DC 10 Will save or slay the downed character).

4   Following a victorious battle, the caster must make offerings to his grim patron. The caster is driven to make an altar, totem, or marker of some sort adorned with the grisly remains of the vanquished. This is unique to each servitor of the Horned King, and can vary from a simple head impaled upon a staff to bloody offerings burnt atop a pyre. There is a slim chance (1% per caster level) that the Horned King is pleased by the offering, granting his servant a +1 bonus to Luck. If the caster should fail to make an offering, there is a similar chance (1% per caster level) that the Horned King is displeased, withdrawing his patronage until the caster can make worthy amends.

5   The caster is driven to care for his entire adventuring party (now regarded as a pack). Any attack on a fellow PC, henchman, or hireling is treated as an attack on the caster. The caster employs whatever force needed to eliminate the threat.

6   The caster refuses to accept the authority of any party member who has not bested him in combat. The battle need not be to the death

but the caster is driven to use every tool at his disposal in an effort to win. If the caster is defeated, he will follow the new pack leader to the very gates of Hades, but if the caster wins the bout, he assumes leadership of the pack.

PATRON SPELLS: THE HORNED KING

The master of the Thrice-Tenth Kingdom grants his followers three unique spells, as follows.

Level 1: *Slaying Strike*

Level 2: *Name of the Quarry*

Level 3: *Call of the Wild Hunt*

SPELLBURN: THE HORNED KING

The Horned King is a difficult and capricious patron, who delights in subjecting his devotees to tests of the will and of the flesh. Whether his whims turn to weal or woe depends entirely on the courage and fortitude of the caster. When a caster spellburns in the name of the Horned King, roll 1d4 and consult the table below. Alternately, use the table as inspiration for results better suited to your own campaign.

Finally, note that many of these results expect a caster to be engaged in mortal combat. Pity those that call upon the Horned King without need, or attempt to gain his blessing under false pretences.

Roll	Spellburn Result
1	A pack of black spectral hounds appears, but can only be seen or heard by the caster. The pack gives a mournful howl that drains the stats spent in the spellburn.
2	To complete the spellburn, the caster must carve the name or sigil of a foe into his body, marking the target as his prey. Following the battle, if the caster offers up a trophy cut from his quarry, and burns the trophy in honor of the Horned King, there is a 5% chance of regaining the stats spent in the spellburn.
3	Following the conclusion of the battle, the caster must collect sufficient remains to construct a totem to his dark lord. The totem should be built of the corpses of the slain, a task that takes 1d4 turns to complete (additional party members may aid in the task, at the judge's pleasure). Failing to construct the offering results in a -5 penalty to the caster's Luck until the Horned King's demands are appeased.
4	The Horned King expects that his followers display courage in the face of danger. Following the spellburn, the caster has 1d4+1 rounds to strike a foe (or be struck) in melee combat. If the caster fails to do so, he or she suffers twice the stat loss of the original spellburn. (For example, if the caster has burned two Strength, at the end of allotted time the caster would suffer a total loss of four Strength.) If the caster somehow scores a critical hit within the time span, he regains all the stats spent in the spellburn.

Slaying Strike

Level: 1 (Horned King) Range: Touch (one melee weapon) Duration: Varies Casting time: 1 round Save: None

General	Invoking the malefic Wild Hunt, you dedicate a chosen melee weapon to the slaying of a specific creature, your quarry. You must have personal knowledge of the quarry but do not need a physical trace; mere knowledge is enough. If the chosen weapon is used against another target before striking the quarry, the enchantment is discharged, without effect. If the caster attacks his quarry and misses, the spell is not discharged. Unless noted otherwise, the indicated weapon can only be wielded by the caster. A caster may possess only one such weapon at a time.
Manifestation	Roll 1d4: (1) an apparition of the Horned King appears before the caster, blessing the chosen weapon; (2) dozens of silent phantom black hounds rush past the caster, disappearing in pursuit of his quarry; (3) a mournful horn sounds in the distance; (4) a horned crown appears on the caster's brow as he assumes a grim and ominous mien.
1	Lost, failure, and patron taint.
2-11	Lost. Failure.
12-13	The caster's next strike to the quarry inflicts an additional 1d3+CL damage. If the caster fails to strike the target within 3 rounds or before the quarry is slain, the spell discharges on the caster, inflicting 1 point of damage.
14-17	The caster's next strike to the quarry inflicts an additional 2d5+CL damage, and the quarry's actions suffer a -2 penalty until the end of the next round. If the caster fails to strike the target with the enchanted weapon within 5 rounds or before the quarry is slain, the spell discharges on the caster, inflicting 1 point of damage.
18-19	The caster's next strike to the quarry inflicts an additional 3d8+CL damage, and the quarry is knocked prone. If the caster fails to strike the target with the enchanted weapon within the next hour or before the quarry is slain, the spell discharges on the caster, inflicting 1 point of damage.
20-23	The caster's next strike to the quarry inflicts an additional 4d10+CL damage, and the quarry loses its next action. If the caster fails to strike the target with the enchanted weapon within the next day or before the quarry is slain, the spell discharges on the caster, inflicting 1 point of damage.
24-27	The caster's strike to the quarry inflicts an additional 5d12+CL damage. Additionally, the quarry loses its next turn. If the caster fails to strike the target with the enchanted weapon within the next day or before the quarry is slain, the spell discharges on the caster, inflicting 1 point of damage.
28-29	The caster's next strike to the quarry inflicts an additional 6d14+CL damage. Additionally, the quarry is struck unconscious for 1d3 rounds (divine, un-dead, and powerful extraplanar beings are immune to this effect). If the caster fails to strike the target with the enchanted weapon within the next week or before the quarry is slain, the spell discharges on the caster, inflicting 1d4 points of damage.
30-31	The caster's next strike to the quarry inflicts an additional 6d20+CL damage. Additionally, the quarry falls into an unconscious stasis, and cannot be roused for 1d100 years (divine, un-dead, and powerful extraplanar beings are immune to this effect). If the caster fails to strike the target with the enchanted weapon within the next year or before the quarry is slain, the spell discharges on the caster, inflicting 1d8 points of damage and leaving the caster in an unconscious stasis from which he cannot be roused for 1d10 weeks.
32+	The caster charges a melee weapon with the slaying strike. This weapon may be wielded by a character other than the caster. The weapon's next strike to the quarry slays the target. If the weapon fails to strike the target in the next 100 years or before the quarry is slain, the spell discharges, slaying the caster and any character possessing the enchanted weapon.

Name of the Quarry

Level: 2 (Horned King) Range: Varies Duration: Varies Casting time: 3 rounds Save: Will vs. spell check

General	The caster invokes the target's True Name, to weaken and bind the subject. The spell relies on specific components for its efficacy — a casting can only be as powerful as its components allow. However, more potent components allow for stronger castings. Example: If the caster has blood from the target, she can successfully cast any iteration of the spell. But if the caster only has line of sight to the target and no other components, the best she can hope for is a 14-17 result, regardless of her spell check.
Manifestation	Roll 1d3: (1) a blazing sigil hovers above the target; (2) a black brand appears on the target's forehead; (3) target is limned in green flames.
1	Lost, failure, and patron taint.
2-11	Lost. Failure.
12-13	Failure, but spell is not lost.
14-17	**Required Component:** Line of sight to target. Target suffers -1d to initiative rolls. Duration: 1d7+CL rounds. Range: line of sight.
18-19	**Required Component:** Memory of target speaking his or her own name. Caster knows general direction of target. Target suffers -1d to initiative rolls and -1d to saving throws. Duration: 1d10+CL rounds. Range: 1 mile.
20-23	**Required Component:** An object once touched by the target. Caster knows general location of target. Target suffers -1d to initiative, saving throws, attacks, and damage rolls. Duration: 1d12+CL rounds. Range: 5 miles.
24-27	**Required Component:** Object or article of clothing once belonging to the target. Caster knows specific location of target; target cannot move more than 1 mile from location at time of casting. Target suffers -1d to initiative, saving throws, attacks, and damage rolls. Foes receive +1d to attack and damage rolls against target. Duration: 1d7+CL rounds. Range: 10 miles.
28-29	**Required Component:** A bit of hair or nail trimmings. Caster knows specific location of target; target cannot move more than 250' from location at time of casting. Target suffers -1d to initiative, saving throws, attacks, damage rolls, and spell checks. Foes receive +1d to attack and damage rolls made against target. Duration: 1d16+CL rounds. Range: 50 miles.
30-31	**Required Component:** A bit of target's flesh. Caster knows specific location of target; target cannot move more than 100' from location at time of casting. Target suffers -2d to initiative, saving throws, attacks, damage rolls, and spell checks. Foes receive +2d to attacks, damage rolls, and spells cast against target. Duration: 1d20+CL rounds. Range: same plane.
32+	**Required Component:** Blood of target. Caster knows precise location of target; target cannot move more than 10' from location at time of casting. Target suffers -2 to initiative rolls, saving throws, damage rolls, and spell checks. Target's foes receive +2d to attacks, damage rolls, and spells cast against target. Duration: 1d50+CL rounds. Range: unlimited.

Call of the Wild Hunt

Level: 3 (Horned King)   Range: Self   Duration: Varies   Casting time: 1 round   Save: Will vs. spell check

General	The caster imbues himself with the contagious, frenzied energy of the Wild Hunt. Caster declares a target, the Hunt's quarry. If the Wild Hunt fails to slay its quarry before the end of the spell, any infected members turn on the caster in a frenzy of hyper-violence lasting 1d20+CL rounds. The enchantment lasts for 1d16+CL rounds, when the caster attempts another spell, or when the quarry is slain — whichever comes first. The caster may spellburn to extend the duration by 1d5 rounds per point of burned. Points burned in this manner do not otherwise improve the spell. Characters at 0 hp or less at the end of the spell collapse and begin bleeding out.
Manifestation	Roll 1d5: (1) caster takes on dark, shadowy cast and grows enormous horns; (2) spectral wolves coalesce from the shadows, howling the quarry's name; (3) shadows lengthen and deepen and the caster takes on the appearance of towering huntsman, clothed in bloody skins; (4) a hunting horn sounds in the distance, and is answered by the mournful howls of a hundred wolves; (5) a fearsome black warhorse with eyes like coals emerges from the gloom, stomping its hooves impatiently as it awaits the caster.
1	Lost, failure, and patron taint.
2-11	Lost. Failure.
12-15	Failure, but spell is not lost.
16-17	Caster gains movement of 45' and +1d to attack rolls against a single declared target (the Hunt's quarry).
18-21	Caster gains movement of 60' and +1d to attack and damage rolls against the quarry. Nearby allies must make Will saves or be caught up in the Hunt, forsaking all other actions to chase the quarry. Up to 3 allies may succumb to the fervor, gaining the same bonuses as the caster.
22-23	Caster gains movement of 75', ignoring all difficult terrain (i.e., the caster is flying, but only at ground level). Caster also gains +2d to attacks and damage rolls against the quarry. The caster may continue to make actions until he reaches -5 hp. Nearby allies must make Will saves or be caught up in the Hunt, forsaking all other actions to chase the quarry. Up to 6 allies may succumb to the fervor, gaining the same bonuses and powers as the caster. The Hunt is joined by one eldritch hound (acting with the same initiative, movement, saves, and alignment as the caster). **Eldritch hound:** Init --; Atk bite +8 melee (2d6); AC 18; HD 4d12; MV --; Act 1d20; SV Fort --, Ref --, Will --; AL --.
24-26	Caster gains movement of 100', ignoring all difficult terrain (i.e., the caster is flying, but only at ground level). Caster gains +2d to attacks and +3d to damage rolls against the quarry. The caster may continue to make actions until he reaches -10 hp. The Hunt is joined by 1d3 eldritch hounds (see above for stats). Friends and foes alike within 50' must make Will saves or be caught up in the Hunt, forsaking all other actions to chase the quarry. Up to 10 other characters may succumb to the fervor, gaining the same bonuses and powers as the caster.
27-31	Caster gains flight at a speed of 150', +2d to attacks, and +3d to damage rolls against the quarry. The caster may continue to make actions until he reaches -15 hp. The Hunt is joined by 1d5 eldritch hounds (see above for stats). Friends and foes alike within 100' must make Will saves or be caught up in the Hunt, forsaking all other actions to chase the quarry. Up to 25 other characters may succumb to the fervor, gaining the same bonuses and powers as the caster.
32-33	Caster gains flight at a speed of 200', +2d to attacks, and +3d to damage rolls against the quarry. The caster may continue to make actions until he reaches -20 hp. The Hunt is joined by 1d6 eldritch hounds (see above for stats). Anyone viewing the Hunt must make a Will save or be caught up in the fervor, forsaking all other actions to pursue the quarry. Up to 25 characters may succumb to the frenzy, gaining the same bonuses and powers as the caster.
34-35	Caster gains flight at a speed of 300', +2d to attacks, and +4d to damage rolls against the quarry. The caster may continue to make actions until he reaches -25 hp. The Hunt is joined by 1d7+CL eldritch hounds (see above for stats). Anyone viewing the Hunt must make a Will save or be caught up in the fervor, forsaking all other actions to pursue the quarry. Up to 100 characters may succumb to the frenzy, gaining the same bonuses and powers as the caster.
36+	Caster gains flight at a speed of 400', +2d to attacks, and +5d to damage rolls against a the quarry. The caster may continue to make actions until he reaches -30 hp. The Hunt is joined by 1d12+CL eldritch hounds (see above for stats). Anyone viewing the Hunt must make a Will save or be caught up in the fervor, forsaking all other actions to pursue the quarry. An unlimited number of characters may succumb to the frenzy, gaining the same bonuses and powers as the caster.

KLARVGOROK
The Merciless Gaze

Klarvgorok resembles nothing more than a tremendous blood-shot and dual-lobed eyeball perched almost comically on a pair of birdlike legs. He never blinks and sees beyond time and space. (Refer to *DCC #80 Intrigue at The Court of Chaos*, p. 5)

Those who seek Klarvgorok do so only at great need: need for secret knowledge and true-seeing; need for devices and abilities to divine the truth in a world of lies and deceptions; need to find a path when there seem only to be dead-ends. Klarvgorok's aid always comes at a price, for his appellants must provide him with new knowledge and betray the secrets they hold most dear.

Invoke Patron check results:

Note: Klarvgorok recognizes that the correct tool must be used to ferret out the secrets of the universe. The caster may make a Personality check (DC 10) to influence how Klarvgorok responds to his invocation. If successful the PC may choose between the result rolled and any lower result.

12-13   Klarvgorok's gaze is focused elsewhere, now, but he sends a minion to aid the petitioner. The creature is an unnatural rat (or other rodent of the judge's choice) whose large eyes glitter with malevolent intelligence. It will observe and/or inspect a creature, object, or location for up to one hour. It is up to the player to provide the specifics of its task. For example, "Look around the house," would be less likely to locate a hidden grimoire than, "Search the study, first, including every cabinet, chest, and compartment, hidden or otherwise." The creature will return after one hour to report what it has learned in a shrill, chittering, evil-sounding language that is somehow intelligible to the caster but to no one else.

14-17   Klarvgorok warps the caster's senses, imbuing them with the power of Chaos. For 1d3 turns the character gains infravision and the ability to see through up to 3 feet of wood, 2 feet of stone, or 1 foot of metal, if it is not somehow magically warded against intrusion.

18-19   Klarvgorok grants the appellant access to forbidden lore. The caster may learn, temporarily, the cleric spell *second sight*. The spell may be cast with automatic success at the 12-13 result; or the caster may make a spell check at +5 in hopes of achieving a higher result.

20-23   Klarvgorok provides intimations of the immediate future for 1d6 rounds, granting the caster a +4 to any single roll.

24-27   For the next 1d6+CL rounds, the caster's touch provides understanding of occulted information about any object or creature touched. If an object, the origins, purpose, or properties of the object are revealed, including magical properties, if any. If a creature, the caster gains insights about its personality, intentions toward the caster, and general motivations. If it is an intelligent creature, the caster can, with an opposed Will check, learn something the creature would like to keep secret (where it hid the gold, who sent it to kill the caster, etc.).

28-29   Klarvgorok grants the caster unerring ability to locate any single object, creature, or location hitherto unknown. The character may determine its direction and approximate distance, but not what might lie between the caster's location and that of the item in question. This ability lasts for 1+CL days, or until what is sought is located.

30-31   The power of Klarvgorok's piercing gaze is granted to the caster. For the next 1d3+CL rounds, the character's eyes (including the Third Eye) blaze with blackest light, granting the ability to see with great clarity for a mile in any direction, unimpeded by any interposing substance or object. During this time, the caster also may focus the gaze on any single object or creature and either inflict 1d10+CL damage (no save) or determine 1d3 specific facts about its origins, purpose, motivations, intentions, or other properties.

32+ Klarvgorok's gaze sees all. The caster gains the ability to get true answers to 1d3+CL questions asked of any creature. The specificity of the answer, of course, depends on the specificity of the question asked. However, the information provided will address, as specifically as possible, the question asked, to the best ability of the creature to answer it. Creatures of hit dice equal to or greater than the caster may attempt a Will save against any question asked, but those with fewer hit dice must answer without saving, truthfully and to the best of their ability. The answers are understandable to the caster, even if the creature's language is not known.

PATRON TAINT: KLARVGOROK

Klarvgorok's power is great, but he is a creature of Chaos. Over time, those who traffic with him may be affected by the bending of reality and perception through his manipulations.

When a patron taint result is indicated, roll 1d4 on the table below. Repeated results may amplify a particular effect, depending on the entry in question. When a caster has been affected by all four results, then only those results that still may increase should be heeded.

Roll   Result

1   There are no secrets, now. The first time this result is rolled, the caster must answer truthfully the first question he or she is asked, no matter who asks it or at what risk the true answer is given. The second time this result is rolled, the caster must make a Will save (DC 8) to lie, no matter the circumstances. Each time this result occurs, the Will save must be rolled at +2 to the original value—DC 8 becomes DC 10, DC 10 becomes DC 12, etc.

2   Avian extremities. The first time this result is rolled, the caster's legs elongate and become thinner and bonier, with scaly patches on some parts of the flesh. The second time this result is rolled, the caster's feet elongate, and the toes fuse such that there are three digits instead of five, and the caster's legs become more birdlike, with yellow, squamous lower parts, and partly-feathered upper parts. Roll 1d8 for type of bird: (1) chicken; (2) turkey; (3) crow or raven; (4) ostrich or emu; (5) flamingo; (6) vulture; (7) swan or goose; (8) heron or crane. The third time this result is rolled, the caster's feet and legs are fully transformed into bird legs, and the PC's proportions and gait match those of the type of bird whose legs she has gained (i.e., a crow may hop instead of walking, while a heron takes long, graceful steps). Judges may also grant PCs with appropriate animal parts (e.g., rooster or ostrich) a melee kick attack which causes 1d4 damage (normal Strength modifier applies).

3	The eyes have it. The first time this result is rolled, the caster's eyes become more sensitive to light, granting limited infravision (20 feet, but not in total darkness); however, in bright sunlight, any check involving vision must be made at -2. The second time this result occurs, the caster gains true infravision (60'); in normal lighting, he or she must make visual checks at -2, and at -4 in bright sunlight. The third time this result occurs, the caster's eyes swell and grow (including the surrounding bones and muscles) to become like those of a nocturnal mammal (e.g., a cat, a rat, an opossum, an owl) of the judge's choice. These changes, if not hidden, make it difficult for the caster to interact with anyone other than another wizard, and Personality checks with non-wizards must be made at -2. The fourth, fifth, and sixth rolls of this result should cause the caster's whole head to transform into an enormous, single eyeball. On the fourth roll, the existing eyes merge into one. On the fifth roll, the eye begins to swell and bulge from the caster's skull, and the caster's neck begins to elongate and become more mobile. On the sixth roll, the skull itself swells to encompass the eyeball, which is approximately 12 inches in diameter. The caster's powerful and flexible neck allows the eyeball to look in any direction, and to dart rapidly from position to position.
4	The light of his eyes. The first time this result is rolled, the caster's eyes acquire a glow, though it's difficult to see except in dim light or darkness. Roll 1d6 for color: (1) red; (2) orange; (3) yellow; (4) green; (5) blue; (6) purple. The second time this result is rolled, the caster's eyes glow more brightly, and the glow can be seen in all but the brightest of sunlight. The third time this result occurs, the caster's gaze will be able to cause minor damage if it lingers on anyone or anything (1 point per round). If the thing it lingers upon is combustible, the object will catch on fire after 3 rounds of continuous attention. This effect does not occur if the eyes are closed.

PATRON SPELLS: KLARVGOROK

Klarvgorok, the Merciless Gaze, grants three unique patron spells, as follows:

Level 1: *Accountancy of the occulted eye*

Level 2: *Klarvgorok's merciless gaze*

Level 3: *Klarvgorok's astounding artificer*

SPELLBURN: KLARVGOROK

Klarvgorok's aid doesn't come without a price. He demands that the caster sacrifice something of herself for the privilege of his intervention. Each time a caster uses spellburn, roll 1d4 on the following table. Several of the results provide potentially interesting ways to connect the caster to Klarvgorok as a patron, and to expand and flavor the judge's campaign world.

Roll	Spellburn Result
1	A vision of the Merciless Gaze strikes the caster blind for 1d3 turns, as Klarvgorok steals her eyes, for a time, for his own inscrutable purposes. This blindness cannot be healed by normal means or a cleric's *lay on hands*, as the eyes are not damaged, but simply gone for a time.
2	Klarvgorok requires a mortal shell with which to wander the material plane. At some point in the near future, the caster must grant Klarvgorok the use of her body for a period of 3d24 hours. During this time, Klarvgorok may do things the caster will come to regret, but may also provide the caster with entrée into the hidden world of the powers that hold sway in her locale. Judges are encouraged to use this result to create links between the caster and various NPCs (e.g., an acolyte within a local temple, a noble in the ruler's court, a ship's captain) to establish connections to organizations or institutions (e.g., the thieves' guild, conclaves of wizards, nameless death cults), or otherwise to integrate the caster and her adventuring party with the people and things that are happening beyond their immediate attention, and to immerse them in the larger affairs of the game world.
3	Klarvgorok requires your knowledge. The caster loses a random spell already known for 1d6+1 days. She cannot relearn the spell until the time has passed, even if she rests. It is unknown what happens to such spells, where they are taken, or what Klarvgorok does with them. When the spell is returned, the caster should make a Luck check. If successful, the caster may thereafter cast that spell with a +1 bonus. If it is failed, the caster must thereafter cast the spell at a -1 penalty. On a critical success (natural 1 on the Luck check) the caster may instead opt to cast that spell with an improved die (+1d on the dice chain). On a critical failure (natural 20 on the Luck check), the caster may choose either to cast that spell at a permanent -2 penalty or to cast it using a diminished die (-1d on the dice chain).
4	The caster takes on the Merciless Gaze for 2d24 hours. Though it is beyond mortal comprehension why he would do so, Klarvgorok wishes to observe the world from his minion's perspective. During that time, Klarvgorok will take no overt action, but the character's uncompromising stare alienates her from normal folk, who sense her otherworldly connection to Klarvgorok, even if they don't know why they feel that way. Any interactions with NPCs during this period (except for attempts to intimidate) are at a -4 penalty. Attempts to intimidate, however, are at a +2 bonus.

Accountancy of the Occulted Eye

Level: 1 (Klarvgorok)   Range: Self   Duration: Permanent   Casting time: 1d10 turns   Save: None

General	This spell allows the caster to channel the knowledge of Klarvgorok, and record it on some permanent medium—e.g., a tome or scroll of some kind. On a successful casting, the caster may select any lower result in place of the result rolled. *Note to judges:* Some of these spell results can aid the judge in providing the players with useful information for resolving patron quests, finding lost artifacts or rare material components for spells, or to accomplish other things in the campaign world. Some other results (those providing protection or those allowing the learning of new spells) might be abused by wily players. It is best that the judge discourage such abuses through use of Klarvgorok, himself, who always is looking for a means to better exploit those who seek his aid. Should the players abuse the power of Klarvgorok, then Klarvgorok will abuse his minions.
Manifestation	The caster is seized in a mania of frantic scribing, her hands moving with dizzying speed as she records the revelations of Klarvgorok. The resulting text is written in her own blood, which magically replaces the ink she would have used, and endows the resulting writings with sorcerous potency. The loss of blood causes Stamina loss as noted below.
1	Lost, failure, and patron taint.
2-11	Lost. Failure.
12-13	The caster inscribes the specific details of a shameful secret of an NPC, including the name and location of the NPC, and the name and location of another NPC who would like to know this information. It is up to the player whether or not she will use this information, sell it, or disregard it. It is up to the judge what repercussions might follow from its use by the caster, or its provision to others who might find it useful. 1 point of Stamina is temporarily lost.
14-15	The caster inscribes a single 1st-level spell already known, on a scroll. The caster may use this scroll to cast the spell even after it has been lost through a failed casting attempt. 1 point of Stamina is temporarily lost.
16-17	The caster inscribes a single 1st- or 2nd-level spell already known, on a scroll. The caster may use this scroll to cast the spell even after it has been lost through a failed casting attempt. 1 point of Stamina is temporarily lost.
18-19	The caster inscribes a single spell already known, up to 3rd-level, on a scroll. The caster may use this scroll to cast the spell even after it has been lost through a failed casting attempt. 1 point of Stamina is temporarily lost.
20-21	The caster inscribes a single spell already known, of any level, on a scroll. The caster may use this scroll to cast the spell even after it has been lost through a failed casting attempt. 1 point of Stamina is temporarily lost.
22-23	The caster inscribes 1d2+1 spells already known, of any level, on separate scrolls. The caster may use these scrolls to cast any of these spells even after they have been lost through a failed casting attempt. 1d2+1 points of Stamina are temporarily lost.
24-25	The caster draws a map of a locale not already visited (or some unexplored feature of a familiar locale). The map provides general locations of 1d3 of the following (roll 1d8): (1) a magical artifact; (2) a hidden library or other repository of knowledge; (3) a portal leading to a place not accessible by normal means; (4) someone who can provide what is needed (though not necessarily what is desired); (5) something desired by Klarvgorok (or some other patron with whom the caster might forge a bond); (6) a magical creature; (7) a material component to aid the casting of a spell (e.g., sword magic or monster summoning); or (8) the True Name of some wizard, demon, or other creature. 1d2+1 points of Stamina are temporarily lost.
26-27	The caster inscribes a powerful ritual to bind or banish a creature or spirit, or to dispel a persistent magical effect. The ritual grants the caster a +1d10 bonus to her spell check and +1 per ally who helps to cast it (judge determines the target number for success of the ritual). 3 points of Stamina are temporarily lost.
28-29	The caster inscribes her own body with runes and wards, granting protection against 1d4×d14 damage from (roll 1d4): (1) normal weapons or traps; (2) heat or cold; (3) magical spells or effects; or (4) all of these. The damage taken lowers the total number of points available in this "pool." When there are no more points left, the spell is ended, and the inscription disappears. 4 points of Stamina are temporarily lost.
30-31	As results for 28-29, and the amount of protection offered also can be drawn upon, on a point-for-point basis, to increase a Fort or Will save. The damage taken or the number of points used for a save lowers the

	total number of points remaining in this "pool." When there are no more points left, the spell is ended, and the inscription disappears. 4 points of Stamina are temporarily lost.
32+	The caster inscribes a scroll with a random spell not already known (roll 1d5 for level of spell). If the PC later casts the spell with a result of 18 or more, the spell can be added permanently to the caster's spellbook. If the result is less than 18, then the spell is not transferred successfully to a permanent record. 1 point of Stamina is temporarily lost.

Klarvgorok's Merciless Gaze

Level: 2 (Klarvgorok) Range: Varies Duration: Varies Casting time: 1 round Save: Varies

General	The caster may see what is hidden with the penetrating gaze of Klarvgorok. On a successful casting, the caster may select any lower result in place of the result rolled.
Manifestation	A third eye emerges from the caster's forehead. Roll 1d6: (1) a normal, humanoid eye; (2) a goat's eye; (3) a reptilian eye; (4) a compound eye, like that of a fly or other insect; (5) an eye just like the caster's regular eyes, but with the colors inverted from normal (black for white, red for blue, etc.); (6) a mechanical eye on a telescoping appendage.
1	Lost, failure, and patron taint.
2-11	Lost. Failure.
12-13	Failure, but spell is not lost.
14-15	The caster has infravision (30' range) for 1d6 turns. If caster already has infravision, the range is doubled.
16-19	The caster can see normally, through up to 10 feet of intervening substance (e.g., stone, dirt, or smoke) for 1d3 turns.
20-21	The caster can see invisible beings or objects for 1d6 turns.
22-24	The caster can detect magical effects and their natures and magnitudes, as per the *detect magic* spell, for 1 turn (use the current spell check result to determine *detect magic* effect).
25-27	The caster can comprehend things she normally would not, including languages, runes of power, and magical writings of all kinds. This effect lasts for 1d12 turns.
28-29	The caster's gaze can locate what is not present, allowing her to "see" an object or creature she is seeking, within one mile. The caster may not, however, see anything but the object and its precise location. Any intervening objects, substances, or creatures are rendered effectively invisible. When the caster stops looking at the object or creature located, the spell effect ends.
30-31	The caster's gaze can locate what is not present, allowing her to "see" an object or creature she is seeking, within fifty miles. This vision includes the ability to see any intervening objects, spaces, substances, or creatures, but the caster must focus on these things in order to see them. When the caster stops looking at the object located and any related details, the spell effect ends.
32-33	The caster's gaze can locate what is not present, allowing her to "see" an object or creature she is seeking, at any range. This vision includes the ability to see any intervening objects, spaces, substances, or creatures, and the caster need not focus specifically on these things in order to see them. When the caster stops looking at the object located and any related details, the spell effect ends. Judges should be willing (within reason) to allow the caster an Intelligence check to determine whether or not she remembers the minutiae, especially if such details become salient to the adventure at some later time. (Example: "You recognize this coffer from your augury, and realize that it must contain the Golden Skull of Bragox the Terrible.")
34+	As results for 32-33. Additionally, the caster may focus on the object or creature located, and attempt to cast a spell as if she were within melee range. A creature thus targeted also may make an appropriate save versus the spell result (Will or Fort, as applicable).

Klarvgorok's Astounding Artificer

Level: 3 (Klarvgorok)   Range: 30'   Duration: Varies   Casting time: 1 round   Save: None

General	The caster summons into being a power that creates an artifact that allows her to learn secrets and discover hidden things. For this spell, the caster must provide various material components in keeping with the artifact she is trying to create. For example, a telescope that allows the caster to see through walls might require metal tubing and lenses to begin with, but other, weirder materials as well (e.g., the eye of a Roc or immaculate jewels of the purest water). Judges should consider asking their players to quest for these items. The artifact created is considered chaotic, if it has an Intelligence (see spell results, below).
Manifestation	Roll 1d6: (1) a cloud of sparkling dust which forms a whirlwind around the materials until it disappears with a flash of light and a clap of thunder; (2) a blob of darkness which obscures the materials until dispersing into nothingness and revealing the completed artifact; (3) a host of rapidly-moving, tiny workers, which move in a blur around the materials, constructing the artifact before dispersing upon the shrilling of a steam whistle; (4) a viscid blob of ectoplasmic goo which envelops the material components and evaporates after the spell is complete; (5) an avian being which eats the materials presented and lays a jewel-toned egg before flying away (the artifact is inside the egg); (6) a demon, dressed in the height of court fashion, arrives with a valise, in which it rummages for a time before removing a device and proffering it the caster, then disappearing in a cloud of sulfurous smoke.
1	Lost, failure, and patron taint.
2-11	Lost. Failure.
12-15	Failure, but spell is not lost.
16-17	The artifact works, but only once per day. The second time it is used, there is a 5% chance that it ceases to function (roll before use). After the second use, each subsequent use increases the chance that the artifact will cease to function by 5% (roll prior to next use).
18-20	The artifact works three times per day. Each time it is used, there is a 25% chance that the result is unreliable in some way. (A device for determining the number of beings in a closed room may provide an incorrect number, or may suggest that the room is empty when it is not.)
21-23	The artifact works as it should, an unlimited number of times per day. However, it must be powered every 1d10 uses through provision of either living blood (via 1 point of spellburn by the caster) or some rare and/or precious substance determined by the judge.
24-26	The artifact functions perfectly, but each time it is used, there is a 10% chance that it has strange resonance with the local phlogiston currents, resulting in a Phlogiston Disturbance, as per the DCC RPG core rules, p. 103 (treat the artifact as the "opposing caster" when referring to Table 4-7: Phlogiston Disturbance).
27-31	The artifact functions perfectly, but is intelligent (roll 2d6+2 for its Intelligence) and communicates via empathy with the caster. The caster may have to convince it to function, if it believes she is acting in error or against the interests of Klarvgorok (at judge's discretion).
32-33	As results for 27-31, but the artifact's Intelligence is 3d6, and it is capable of speech. It also has 1 additional power: roll d% on Table 8-7: Sword Powers, Type I: Natural Powers (DCC RPG p. 370).
34-35	As results for 27-31, but the artifact's Intelligence is 3d6+2, and it is capable of telepathy with the caster. The artifact has 2 additional powers: roll d% on Table 8-7: Sword Powers, Type I: Natural Powers (DCC RPG p. 370).
36+	As results for 34-35, but the artifact's Intelligence is 3d6+4, and the artifact is capable of both speech and telepathy with the caster. The artifact has 1d4 additional type I powers (roll d% on Table 8-7: Sword Powers, Type I: Natural Powers, DCC RPG p. 370), and a 50% chance of a type III power (roll d% on Table 8-9: Sword Powers, Type III: Magical, p. 371). Judges may want to exclude the demon-binding and un-dead touch results, unless the artifact was created as a weapon of some kind. Alternately, the caster must use the artifact as a weapon to achieve those results, perhaps making it vulnerable to damage or destruction.

MAGOG

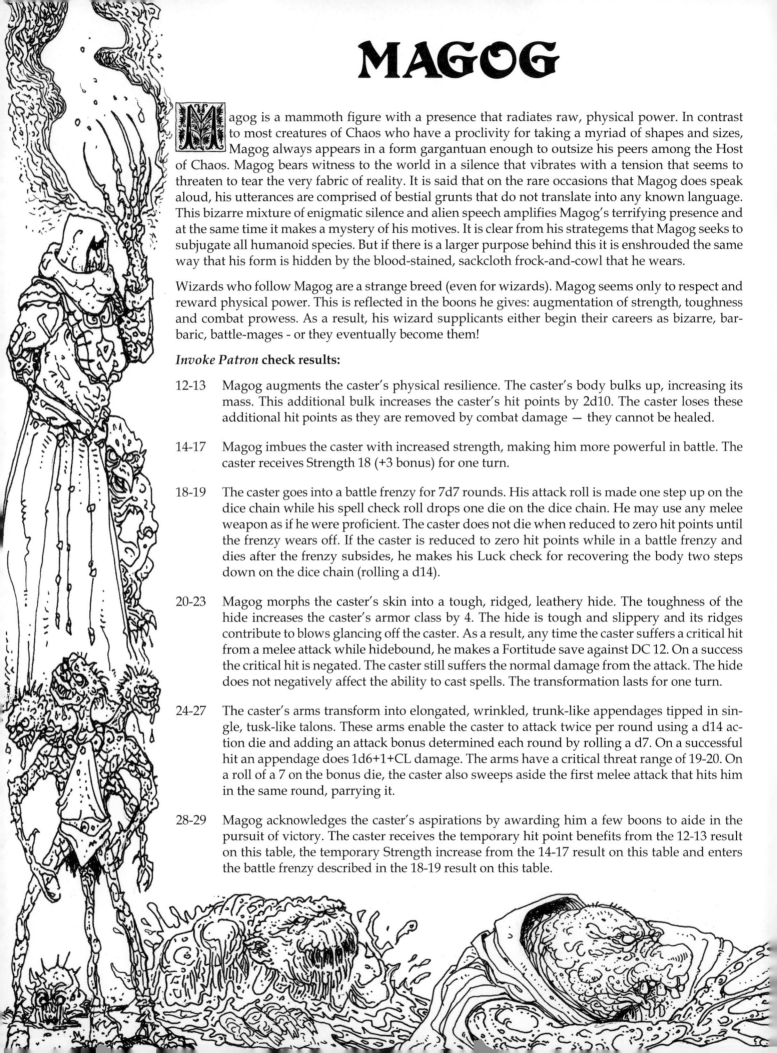

Magog is a mammoth figure with a presence that radiates raw, physical power. In contrast to most creatures of Chaos who have a proclivity for taking a myriad of shapes and sizes, Magog always appears in a form gargantuan enough to outsize his peers among the Host of Chaos. Magog bears witness to the world in a silence that vibrates with a tension that seems to threaten to tear the very fabric of reality. It is said that on the rare occasions that Magog does speak aloud, his utterances are comprised of bestial grunts that do not translate into any known language. This bizarre mixture of enigmatic silence and alien speech amplifies Magog's terrifying presence and at the same time it makes a mystery of his motives. It is clear from his strategems that Magog seeks to subjugate all humanoid species. But if there is a larger purpose behind this it is enshrouded the same way that his form is hidden by the blood-stained, sackcloth frock-and-cowl that he wears.

Wizards who follow Magog are a strange breed (even for wizards). Magog seems only to respect and reward physical power. This is reflected in the boons he gives: augmentation of strength, toughness and combat prowess. As a result, his wizard supplicants either begin their careers as bizarre, barbaric, battle-mages - or they eventually become them!

Invoke Patron check results:

12-13   Magog augments the caster's physical resilience. The caster's body bulks up, increasing its mass. This additional bulk increases the caster's hit points by 2d10. The caster loses these additional hit points as they are removed by combat damage — they cannot be healed.

14-17   Magog imbues the caster with increased strength, making him more powerful in battle. The caster receives Strength 18 (+3 bonus) for one turn.

18-19   The caster goes into a battle frenzy for 7d7 rounds. His attack roll is made one step up on the dice chain while his spell check roll drops one die on the dice chain. He may use any melee weapon as if he were proficient. The caster does not die when reduced to zero hit points until the frenzy wears off. If the caster is reduced to zero hit points while in a battle frenzy and dies after the frenzy subsides, he makes his Luck check for recovering the body two steps down on the dice chain (rolling a d14).

20-23   Magog morphs the caster's skin into a tough, ridged, leathery hide. The toughness of the hide increases the caster's armor class by 4. The hide is tough and slippery and its ridges contribute to blows glancing off the caster. As a result, any time the caster suffers a critical hit from a melee attack while hidebound, he makes a Fortitude save against DC 12. On a success the critical hit is negated. The caster still suffers the normal damage from the attack. The hide does not negatively affect the ability to cast spells. The transformation lasts for one turn.

24-27   The caster's arms transform into elongated, wrinkled, trunk-like appendages tipped in single, tusk-like talons. These arms enable the caster to attack twice per round using a d14 action die and adding an attack bonus determined each round by rolling a d7. On a successful hit an appendage does 1d6+1+CL damage. The arms have a critical threat range of 19-20. On a roll of a 7 on the bonus die, the caster also sweeps aside the first melee attack that hits him in the same round, parrying it.

28-29   Magog acknowledges the caster's aspirations by awarding him a few boons to aide in the pursuit of victory. The caster receives the temporary hit point benefits from the 12-13 result on this table, the temporary Strength increase from the 14-17 result on this table and enters the battle frenzy described in the 18-19 result on this table.

30-31 Magog rewards the caster's successful supplication by increasing his combat prowess to a level inspired by Magog's own might. The caster receives the temporary hit point benefits from the 12-13 result on this table and the temporary strength increase from the 14-17 result on this table. The caster is sent into the battle frenzy described in the 18-19 result on this table and also acquires the leathery hide and trunk-like appendages described in the 20-23 and 24-27 results on this table.

32+ Magog is immensely pleased by the caster's invocation and sends the caster a warband of Magog's subjugated enemies, the Makiz'hi to fight on the caster's behalf. When the spell succeeds, seven Makiz'hi crawl from the ground or slide out of the shadows. Emerging into the material world requires their full efforts for one round after the spell is cast and results in a -2 penalty to their armor class during that round. The Makiz'hi will defend and serve the caster until they are slain or the caster releases them, at which time they magically return to Magog.

Makiz'hi: Init +3; Atk bite or claw +3 melee (1d3 plus disease) or kick (only one per round) +3 melee (2d3); AC 13; HD 3d6; MV 25'; Act 3d18; SP disease, rabid, weapon-ready, half-living; SV Fort +3, Ref -3, Will +3, AL C.

The Makiz'hi are three-headed, three-legged, three-armed, rabid, quasi-human cannibals who originated in the Dun Primeval. Their skin is scaly and mottled with flecks of gray, olive, and brown. Their hair is the color of dried blood and is always caked with dung and tangled with sticks and bracken. They were nemeses of Magog before he attained rank in the Host of Chaos; one of his first acts as a member of the Host was to subjugate and enslave them. The Makiz'hi are afflicted with a rabid disease that keeps them in a constant state of mania. This mania makes them immune to Will-affecting spells that control the conscious mind such as *charm person*. They are affected by other Will-affecting spells such as *sleep* and *hold* but their disease-induced state of mind makes them highly resistant to such spells. Their extra heads give them 360-degree vision making them difficult to surprise and giving them excellent combat awareness, which boosts their initiative. Their extra limbs enable them to attack up to three times in a round but only one of these attacks may be a kick. Any opponent who takes damage from a Makik'hi bite or claw must make a DC 13 Fort save or contract an extremely virulent strain of rabies. Anyone failing the save begins to experience serious symptoms in 3d3 rounds: frothing at the mouth, violent muscle contractions, and hallucinations. Every round after the symptoms begin, the victim must make a DC 13 Fort save to fend off the effects of the disease and be able to act. As soon one of these saves is failed, the victim falls to the ground, overcome by delirium. If the disease is not cured within one turn of this collapse the victim dies. Though the Makiz'hi do not normally carry weapons, they can be quickly instructed in their use and will wield any with which their masters arm them. When a battle is over, they feast on the flesh of fallen foes who are recognizably humanoid. Any attempt to compel them to leave off this practice will enrage them and turn them against that person.

PATRON TAINT: MAGOG

When patron taint is indicated for Magog, roll 1d6 on the table below. When a caster has acquired all six taints at all levels of effect, there is no need to continue rolling anymore.

Roll	Result
1	The caster's nose and upper lip begin to transform and fuse into one another. The first time this result is cast, the caster's nose and lip lengthen and enlarge to three times their normal size and begin to roughen and take on an extremely ruddy hue. If the result is rolled a second time, the nose and lip lengthen, enlarge and fuse into a snout 12"-18" long with noticeable ridges and blotches. If this result is rolled a third time, the snout enlarges and lengthens further until it is 2'-3' long with thick wrinkles and a mottled greyish-green color.
2	The caster begins to devolve, his bone structure and posture morphing into an apish form. The first time this result is rolled, the caster's legs bow noticeably outward, his back arches and his hips settle, giving him a distinctly squat appearance. The caster loses one point of Intelligence. The second time this result is rolled, the caster's arms elongate, his neck shortens, he grows a protruding pot belly and his back arches further causing his arms to drape forward. The caster loses a second point of Intelligence. If the result is rolled a third time, the caster's brow thickens, his knees assume a slightly bent position, his arms lengthen again and he cants still further forward such that his knuckles are dragging on the ground when he walks. The caster loses a third point of Intelligence.
3	The caster's speech becomes increasingly inflected with the Primeval Din, one of the "first languages" of Chaos on the mortal plane. The first time this result is rolled, the caster's speech becomes regularly punctuated by grunts, bleats, groans, and hisses. These punctuations are beyond the control of the caster. While they do not interfere with his spell casting, they make it harder for the caster to be understood. Anytime the caster tries to communicate something to another creature, that creature must make a DC 10 Intelligence check or be unable to act on the knowledge or advice the caster is trying to convey. If this result is rolled a second time, the caster's speech comes out as equal parts intended language and Primeval Din, requiring a DC 15 Intelligence check to be actionable. The third time this result is rolled, the caster can only ever speak in Primeval Din, requiring fluency in this lost language or magical assistance (e.g., *comprehend languages*) to understand him.
4	The caster's hands begin to manifest Masticata – a mystical maiming of the hands that makes them appear as if they had been gnawed on or chewed by a beast or creature. The first time this result is rolled, bite marks and gnaw spots appear as minor bleeding wounds on both the caster's hands, requiring constant bandaging to avoid infection or contamination of whatever the caster touches. The second time this result is rolled, the wounds worsen. The bandaging required to tend these wounds makes it difficult for the caster to handle objects, tools, and weapons. Routine manipulations, such as lacing a boot, using a quill pen, or opening a door require a DC 10 Agility check to complete and tasks requiring fine motor skills require a successful DC 15 Agility check. If this result is rolled a third time, the wounds of the Masticata worsen still further. Tasks requiring fine motor skills are impossible for the caster to perform. Routine tasks require a DC 13 Agility check. Spellcasting incurs a -1 penalty to all spell check rolls.
5	The caster requires the freshly butchered flesh of his *own race* to sustain him. The first time the result is rolled, the caster must consume a pound of flesh from a member of his own race on one day of the week. The meat must be fresh - butchered from an individual slaughtered within the past day. If this result is rolled a second time, the

nutritional requirement increases to one pound consumed every three days. The third time the result is rolled, the nutritional requirement increases to one pound consumed every other day. For every half day that passes after the caster has missed the required sustenance, he loses one point of Stamina. If the caster's Stamina drops to three he cannot perform actions that require any significant effort. If his Stamina drops *below* three, the caster cannot exert himself in any way. If the caster's Stamina drops to zero he dies of malnutrition.

6   The caster loses more and more of the trappings of a civilized person, growing increasingly barbaric in custom and behavior. The first time this result is rolled, the caster abandons all grooming and hygiene habits and loses any knowledge he had of manners and decorum in polite society. The caster will have a difficult time gaining entry into high society: courts, balls, manor houses, etc. The caster also drops down one step on the dice chain when rolling Personality checks required for interactions or negotiations with individuals from high society. The second time this result is rolled, the caster loses his taste for tailoring and clothes in general, garbing himself in furs, skins, loin cloths, etc. He ceases to launder this garb. The caster eschews the use of utensils when eating and adopts course language and frequent cursing. The caster will be barred from polite society unless a person with status and prestige vouches for him. His appearance and manner drop him down two steps on the dice chain when rolling Personality checks required for interactions or negotiations with individuals from high society. If the result is rolled a third time, the caster embraces barbarism fully in his dress and manner: wearing necklaces strung with the ears of his slain foes, piercing himself with sharpened bones, adorning himself with tattoos and scars, painting his body with mud or plant pigments, wearing the talons of beasts on the ends of his fingers, etc. The caster will be barred from polite society unless said society is in the direst need of his aide, specifically. The caster will also be barred from less privileged locales in civilization: inns, taverns mercantile establishments, etc. His appearance and manner drops him down three steps on the dice chain when rolling Personality checks required for interactions or negotiations with individuals from high society and one step on the dice chain for social interactions in all other civilized locales aside from outposts on the frontier of wild lands.

PATRON SPELLS: MAGOG

The Khan of conquest and humanoid subjugation grants three spells of his own devising, as follows:

Level 1: *Bloodlust*

Level 2: *Gutteral onslaught*

Level 3: *Ogremorph*

SPELLBURN: MAGOG

Magog transcended to a position of power in the Courts of Chaos through an ascetic, flagellant mysticism and he demands the same – and more – of his supplicants. When a caster utilizes spellburn, roll 1d4 and consult the table below. Use these examples as models for creating spellburn conditions that fit with how Magog's will manifests in your own campaign.

Roll   **Spellburn Result**

1   Magog reveals the path to power through purifying pain. The caster must pierce his flesh with fishhooks and then hang weights from the hooks (one cumulative pound of weights for each point of spellburn) and bear them stoically for one day for each point of spellburn. Every three pounds of weights (rounded down) reduces the caster's Agility and Fortitude by one point for the time that that caster bears them.

2   In his Writ of Silence it is inscribed: "Naught was ever wrought by hand save damnation." To power his use of spellburn, the caster must inflict wounds on his hands by a means of his choosing: holding them to a flame, shoving them into a hornet's nest, thrusting them the maw of a beast, etc. The wounds are minor, doing 1d3 points of damage, but this damage cannot be healed by magical means and the caster will be without the use of his hands for anything other than spellcasting for a period of time equal to one round per point of spellburn.

3   Magog preaches that to know power, an individual must know himself and that the only way to know oneself is to consume oneself. For each point of spellburn, the caster must consume a drachm (~1/4 pound) of his own flesh. Each drachm of flesh that a caster removes and consumes causes 1 hit point of damage that can only be healed by time, not by magical means.

4   Magog says: "To grow one must feed, to grow large one must feed at the source." To power the spellburn the caster must gorge on earthern materials: topsoil, silt, loam, sand, clay, etc. The caster must consume two drachms (~1/2 pound) of such materials for every point of spellburn. Once engorged, the caster will become bloated and stomach-sick, resulting in -5' of movement for every 2 drachms of earthern material consumed.

BLOODLUST

Level: 1 (Magog)	Range: Self	Duration: 1d7 rounds or more	Casting time: 1 action	Save: None

General
: Magog rewards followers who revel in martial combat with boosts to their prowess, ensuring them even bigger victories. The spell gives the caster bonuses to a future spell check roll for *invoke patron* proportional to damage they inflict on opponents in melee. Multiple bonuses earned in a melee combine into a single bonus to the next spell check rolled when casting *invoke patron* (e.g., a caster who earns three +1 bonuses from the use of this spell would add +3 to a spell check roll for *invoke patron*). While the spell is in effect the caster must make a Will save any round in which he wishes to cast a spell other than *invoke patron*. If the caster succeeds then he is able to control his bloodlust enough to gather the necessary focus for spellcasting.

Manifestation
: Roll 1d4: (1) blood drawn by the caster's weapon turns to red centipedes as it splashes to the ground; (2) the caster's weapon bleats in a pidgin version of Primeval Din as it strikes opponents; (3) the blood from opponents' wounds caused by the caster take the form of crude birds and fly about the battlefield; (4) the caster's skin takes on an increasingly bright red appearance as he wounds opponents.

1
: Lost, failure, and patron taint.

2-11
: Lost. Failure.

12-13
: When the caster engages in melee, every eight cumulative points of damage he does to opponents gives him a +1 on his next spell check roll to cast *invoke patron*. The caster must cast *invoke patron* by the end of the second round after he first earns a bonus or that bonus is lost. Any time the caster's point accrual has not yet reached eight and he goes three consecutive rounds without doing damage to an opponent, the accrual count resets to zero. The spell lasts d7 rounds and the caster cannot end the spell. The caster must succeed at a DC 14 Will save to cast a spell other than *invoke patron*.

14-17
: When the caster engages in melee this spell gives him a +1 bonus to his attack rolls. Every eight cumulative points of damage he does to opponents gives him a +1 on his next spell check roll to cast *invoke patron*. The caster must cast *invoke patron* within three rounds after first receiving a bonus or that bonus is lost. Any time the caster's point accrual has not yet reached eight and he goes three consecutive rounds without doing damage to an opponent, the accrual count resets to zero. The spell lasts d7+CL rounds and the caster cannot end the spell. The caster must succeed at a DC 13 Will save to cast a spell other than *invoke patron*.

18-19
: When the caster engages in melee, every six cumulative points of damage he does to opponents gives him a +1 on his next spell check roll to cast *invoke patron*. The caster must cast *invoke patron* within three rounds after first receiving a bonus or that bonus is lost. Any time the caster's point accrual has not yet reached six and he goes three consecutive rounds without doing damage to an opponent, the accrual count resets to zero. The spell lasts d7+CL rounds and the caster cannot end the spell. The caster must succeed at a DC 13 Will save to cast a spell other than *invoke patron*.

20-23
: When the caster engages in melee this spell gives him a +1 bonus to his attack rolls. Every six cumulative points of damage he does to opponents gives him a +1 on his next spell check roll to cast *invoke patron*. The caster must cast *invoke patron* within four rounds of first receiving a bonus or that bonus is lost. Any time the caster's point accrual has not yet reached six and he goes four consecutive rounds without doing damage to an opponent, the accrual count resets to zero. The spell lasts d7+CL rounds and the caster cannot end the spell. The caster must succeed at a DC 12 Will save to cast a spell other than *invoke patron*.

24-27	When the caster engages in melee, every six cumulative points of damage he does to opponents gives him a +1 on his next spell check roll to cast invoke patron. The caster must cast *invoke patron* within one hour after first receiving a bonus or that bonus is lost. Any time the caster's point accrual has not yet reached six and he goes four consecutive rounds without doing damage to an opponent, the accrual count resets to zero. The spell lasts 2d7 rounds but the caster can choose to end the spell. The caster must succeed at a DC 12 Will save to cast a spell other than *invoke patron*.
28-29	When the caster engages in melee this spell gives him a +1 bonus to his attack rolls. Every six cumulative points of damage he does to opponents gives him a +1 on his next spell check roll to cast *invoke patron*. The caster must cast *invoke patron* within one hour after first receiving a bonus or that bonus is lost. The spell lasts 2d7 rounds but the caster can choose to end the spell. The caster must succeed at a DC 11 Will save to cast a spell other than *invoke patron*.
30-31	When the caster engages in melee this spell gives him a +1 bonus to his attack rolls. Every six cumulative points of damage he does to opponents gives him a +1 on his next spell check roll to cast *invoke patron*. The caster must cast *invoke patron* within four hours after first receiving a bonus or that bonus is lost. The spell lasts 2d7 rounds but the caster can choose to end the spell. The caster must succeed at a DC 10 Will save to cast a spell other than *invoke patron*.
32+	When the caster engages in melee this spell gives him a +2 bonus to his attack rolls. Every six cumulative points of damage he does to opponents gives him a +1 on his next spell check roll to cast *invoke patron*. The caster must cast *invoke patron* within eight hours after first receiving a bonus or that bonus is lost. The spell lasts 3d7 rounds but the caster can choose to end the spell. The caster must succeed at a DC 8 Will save to cast a spell other than *invoke patron*.

Gutteral Onslaught

Level: 2 (Magog)   Range: Self   Duration: Varies   Casting time: 1 action   Save: Fort and/or Will vs. spell check

General	Magog's native tongue is the Primeval Din, one of the first languages of Chaos on the mortal plane. So utterly primal is The Din that to intone it is to unleash raw power into the world in the form of sound. Through this spell a wizard learns to form the equivalent of a babe's first words of Primeval Din - with devastating results. Though the raw power of Primeval Din penetrates normal or even substantial background noise, preternaturally loud noises such as the rush of a legendary waterfall or the roar of a dragon prevents the spell from having any effect. Similarly, any condition or effect that prevents the caster from speaking also prevents or cancels the spell.
Manifestation	Roll 1d4: (1) underneath the speech of the caster booms a nigh-subsonic basso comprised of distant thunder mixed with the footfalls of lumbering elephants; (2) as the caster speaks, animated, brightly-colored illusions of fierce primeval creatures leap from his mouth and cavort in the area of the spell's effect; (3) the caster spews forth a swarm of flying locusts as he speaks and his utterances are carried on the hum of their many wings; (4) as the caster speaks, lightning can be seen flashing in his mouth, nose and throat.
1	Lost, failure, and patron taint.
2-11	Lost. Failure.
12-13	Failure, but spell is not lost.
14-15	Upon hearing the Primeval Din, all creatures within 60' of the caster must make a Fortitude save or be lashed by the force of the sound. Creatures who fail their save suffer 1d4 points of damage, drop any items they are holding and are deafened.
16-19	All creatures within 60' of the caster must make a Fortitude save or suffer 1d7 points of damage, drop any items they are holding, fall prone and be deafened.
20-21	All creatures within 60' of the caster must make a Fortitude save or suffer 1d7+CL points of damage, drop any items they are holding, fall prone and be deafened. The audible onslaught is so terrible that all opponents within the area of effect must also make a Will save or be struck with fear, causing them to flee from the caster at top speed for one move action. The caster can sustain speaking the Primeval Din for a full round, preventing noises of shorter duration from cancelling the spell's effects.
22-23	All creatures within 60' of the caster must make a Fortitude save or suffer 2d7 points of damage, drop any

24-25	All creatures within 60′ of the caster must make a Fortitude save or suffer 2d7 points of damage, drop any items they are holding, fall prone and be deafened. Creatures that make their Fortitude save still suffer half damage (rounded up). The onslaught is so forceful that opponents within the area of effect who fail their save will be stunned and will be unable to take action during this round and the next. The caster can sustain speaking the Primeval Din two full rounds, preventing noises of shorter duration that would cancel the spell's effects from doing so.
26-29	All creatures within 60′ of the caster must make a Fortitude save or suffer 2d7+CL points of damage, drop any items they are holding, fall prone and be deafened. The onslaught is so forceful that opponents within the area of effect who fail their save will be stunned and unable to take action for 1d7 rounds. Creatures that make their save suffer half damage and are stunned for half as many rounds (rounded up). The caster can sustain speaking the Primeval Din for two full rounds, preventing noises of shorter duration that would cancel the spell's effects from doing so.
30-31	The caster has enough fluency in Primeval Din to shape its syntax in a way that spares his allies. All opponents within 60′ of the caster must make a Fortitude save or suffer 3d7 points of damage, drop any items they are holding, fall prone and be deafened. The onslaught is so forceful that opponents within the area of effect who fail their save will be stunned and unable to take action for 1d7 rounds. Creatures that make their save suffer half damage and are stunned for half as many rounds (rounding up). The caster can sustain speaking the Primeval Din for a full minute, preventing noises of shorter duration that would cancel the spell's effects from doing so.
32-33	The caster has enough fluency in Primeval Din to shape its syntax in a way that spares his allies. All opponents within 60′ of the caster must make a Fortitude save or suffer 3d7+CL points of damage, drop any items they are holding, fall prone and be deafened. The onslaught is so absolutely overwhelming that opponents within the area of effect who fail their save will be driven insane. Creatures that make their save suffer half damage and are stunned for 1d7 rounds instead of being driven insane. The caster can sustain speaking the Primeval Din for a full minute, preventing noises of shorter duration that would cancel the spell's effects from doing so.
34+	The caster has enough fluency in Primeval Din to shape its syntax to spare his allies. All opponents within 60′ of the caster must make a Fortitude save or suffer 4d7 points of damage, drop any items they are holding, fall prone and be deafened. The onslaught is so absolutely overwhelming that opponents within the area of effect who fail their save will be driven insane. Creatures that make their save suffer half damage and are stunned for 1d7 rounds instead of being driven insane. So potent are the utterances used by the caster to achieve this level of effect that his Din can penetrate any sound not issuing forth from a divine source.

Ogremorph

Level: 3 (Magog) Range: Touch Duration: Self Casting time: 1 action Save: None

General	The caster transforms himself into an ogre. If the caster possesses the Masticata and cannibalism patron taints, these do not affect him while he is in ogre form. Magog's spell *bloodlust* does not affect the caster when he is in ogre form. If the caster is slain in ogre form, he immediately reverts to his natural form and makes his Luck check for recovering the body two steps down on the dice chain. For ogre description and combat abilities, refer to the monster entry in the DCC RPG core rulebook, p. 422.
Manifestation	Roll 1d4: (1) darkness in the shape of a frock and cowl completely envelopes the caster, who then bursts forth in ogre form; (2) an ogre bursts out of the ground and swallows the caster; (3) an army of preternaturally large red ants swarm over the caster then retreat, leaving him changed into an ogre; (4) a single "word" in Primeval Din (one of Chaos' first languages) thunders out from the ether (sounding vaguely like "shuhzaym"), instantaneously transforming the caster.
1	Lost, failure, and patron taint.
2-11	Lost. Failure.

12-15	Failure, but spell is not lost.
16-17	The caster transforms into an ogre with 22 hit points. In ogre form, the caster's Intelligence drops four points. The transformation lasts 2d7+CL turns or until the caster chooses to end the effect.
18-21	The caster transforms into an ogre with 26 hit points. In ogre form, the caster's Intelligence drops four points but the caster becomes immune to fear-based spells. The transformation lasts 7d4+CL turns or until the caster chooses to end the effect. When the caster returns to his natural form, he heals 1d4 points of damage he received before the transformation.
22-23	The caster transforms into an ogre with 30 hit points. At this level of effect the caster's ogre form has a +6 bonus to attack and damage. In ogre form, the caster's Intelligence drops three points but the caster is immune to fear-based spells. The transformation lasts 1d7+CL hours or until the caster chooses to end the effect. When the caster returns to his natural form, he heals 1d4+2 points of damage he received before the transformation.
24-26	The caster transforms into an ogre with 36 hit points. At this level of effect the caster's ogre form has +7 attack and damage bonuses and its AC increases to 17. In ogre form, the caster's Intelligence drops three points but the caster is immune to fear-based spells. The transformation lasts 1d7+CL hours or until the caster chooses to end the effect. When the caster returns to his natural form, he heals 2d4 points of damage he received before the transformation.
27-31	The caster transforms into a fine specimen of the ogre. At this level of effect the caster's ogre form has 36 hit points, +7 attack and damage bonuses, acquires a second d20 action die, and its AC is 17. In ogre form, the caster's Intelligence drops three points but the caster is immune to fear-based spells. The transformation lasts 2d7+CL hours or until the caster chooses to end the effect. When the caster returns to his natural form, he heals 2d4+1 points of damage he received before the transformation.
32-33	The caster transforms into a prime specimen of the ogre. At this level of effect the caster's ogre form has 36 hit points, +8 attack and damage bonuses, a second d20 action die, and its AC increases to 18. In ogre form, the caster's Intelligence drops two points but the caster is immune to fear-based spells. The transformation lasts 3d7+CL hours or until the caster chooses to end the effect. When the caster returns to his natural form, he heals 3d4 points of damage he received before the transformation.
34-35	The caster transforms into an exceptional version of the ogre. At this level of effect the caster's ogre form has 38 hit points, +8 attack and damage bonuses, a second d20 action die, crits on a 20-21, and its AC is 18. In ogre form, the caster's Intelligence drops two points but the caster is immune to fear-based spells. The transformation lasts 24 hours or until the caster chooses to end the effect. When the caster returns to his natural form, he is at full hit points.
36+	The caster transforms into a **Dread Ogre:** Init +3; Atk slam +10 melee (2d4+8) or massive club +10 melee (2d6+8); AC 20; HD 7d10+7 (46 hp); MV 25'; Act 2d22; SP bear hug, hurling, regeneration, immunity to fear-based spells, crit on a 20–22; SV Fort +8, Ref +4, Will +2; AL as PC. The legendary ogre's bear hug does 2d4+10 damage. It can hurl stones (or other appropriate objects, e.g., wagon wheels, small pieces of furniture) as +4 missile fire (1d7+4, 60' range). The legendary ogre regenerates 1d4 hit points at the end of each round until its hit point total is at or below zero. In this form the caster has his normal Intelligence. The transformation lasts until the caster chooses to end the effect. When the caster returns to his natural form, he is at full hit points plus he gains 1d7 temporary hit points that are not restored once lost.

NHOOL

Nhool is the embodiment of warfare's destruction. Every battlefield is his banquet hall, every shattered fortress his throne room. He is the Prince of Ruins sitting atop the toppled thrones of a hundred score kingdoms. He is as old as bloodshed and as callous as a berserker's axe. Wherever peace and prosperity has fallen to conquest and violence, Nhool's has placed his three, gauntlet-covered hands.

Holding one-fifth of the power of the Court of Chaos under his command, Nhool is often sought as a patron by those servants of Chaos who revel in warfare and destruction. He has much to offer those who bend their knees to the Prince of Ruins.

Invoke Patron check results:

12-13   Nhool sends a wisp of chaotic power to enervate his lackey's weapon, causing the object (or servant's hands if unarmed) to shimmer with a dark, swirling, rainbow-hued light. The caster inflicts +4 damage on his next 1d4 successful attacks.

14-17   The caster is granted the power to destroy metal, stone, or wood with a touch. By smiting a single object no larger than the caster's size, the object shatters, falling into ruin. This power lasts for 1 turn or until used. Enchanted substances have a 75% chance of being unaffected by this ability.

18-19   Iridescent armor crawls across the caster's body, sheathing him in Chaos' mail. For the next hour, Nhool's servant gains +6 to his AC and enjoys a +2 bonus to all Fortitude and Reflex saving throws.

20-23   Nhool grants the caster the assistance of a ruinwrack (see below). It arrives on the following round and acts on the caster's initiative count. It follows all spoken commands by the caster and remains to assist him for 1d6+CL hours or until destroyed.

24-27   The caster gains the power to act as a living siege weapon capable of hurling rocks like a catapult. Boulders and other bombards of up to 400 lbs. in weight can be launched as a flat +10 missile attack (3d8+10; range 400'). This power lasts for one hour. Nhool does not provide ammunition for this power.

28-29   Nhool grants the caster the assistance of two ruinwracks (see below). They arrive on the following round and act on the caster's initiative count. The ruinwracks follow all spoken commands by the caster and remain to assist him for 1d6+CL hours or until destroyed.

30-31   The caster gains the powers of a ranking officer in the Army of Chaos. His body is encased in Chaos' mail, granting him a +6 bonus to AC and a +2 bonus to Fortitude and Reflex saving throws. His weapon (or bare hands if unarmed) become charged with Chaos' power, inflicting an additional 1d6+4 damage. He can also cast *Emirikol's entropic maelstrom* one time with a +10 bonus to the spell check. These powers last for 2d6+CL hours.

32+   As above, but the caster also gains the service of three ruinwracks (see below). They arrive on the following round and act on the caster's initiative count. The ruinwracks follow all spoken commands by the caster and remain to assist him for as long as he has the powers of an Army of Chaos officer or until they are destroyed.

Ruinwrack: Init +1; Atk slam +5 melee (1d10+2); AC 15; HD 3d12+3; MV 30′ or fly 20′; Act 1d20; SP demon traits; half-damage from non-magical weapons and fire; SV Fort +5, Ref +2, Will +1; AL C.

Ruinwracks are the demonic servitors of Nhool, appearing as three-armed animated suits of plate armor complete with massive, horrific helms. Swirls of blood-red ectoplasm writhe from inside the armor, occasionally wriggling out of the eye and mouth-holes of the helm to form ghastly streamers that appear to twist in an invisible wind. The ground beneath a ruinwrack becomes fractured and bloodstained if the creature stands still for more than a few moments.

PATRON TAINT: NHOOL

When patron taint is indicated for Nhool, roll 1d6 on the table below. When a caster has acquired all six taints at all levels of effect, there is no need to continue rolling any longer.

Roll	Result
1	The caster acquires the desire to see things, places, and people destroyed. Whenever the opportunity arises, he'll seek to break, burn, or otherwise ruin a person, place, or thing that holds no value or meaning to himself. If this result is rolled a second time, the caster *must* destroy someone or something every day or acquire a cumulative -1 penalty to all spell checks for each day he fails to cause destruction. Destroying a person or thing of at least minor importance or consequence (smashing a cup doesn't count, but breaking a farmer's hoe as he toils in the field does) removes the spell check penalty. If this result is rolled a third time, the caster loses the ability to cast any spell until he destroys a person, place, or thing of some magnitude every day. Causing destruction restores his power to cast spells.
2	The caster's skin acquires a crimson and black mottled pattern as if his body has been dirtied by blood and soot. If this result is rolled a second time, the stench of freshly spilled blood and burning wood wafts from his body no matter how well or often he bathes. If the result occurs a third time, his flesh sweats blood and smoke drifts from his pores constantly.

3	The caster grows a small vestigial arm from his torso. When this taint first manifests, it is the size of a baby's arm and inert, lacking strength or dexterity. If rolled a second time, the arm grows to the size of a young child's limb, possessing a Strength and Agility of 5. The caster can utilize the limb to take a second action each round, but any action performed by the limb suffers a -4 penalty to all rolls (plus ability penalties if the action is a melee or ranged attack) due to the caster's imperfect command of the alien limb. If this result is rolled a third time, the limb grows to normal adult size possessing the caster's normal Strength and Agility scores. The caster also gains better control over the limb and any action performed with the third arm now only suffers a -2 penalty. The caster will have to make modifications to clothing or armor to accommodate the adult-sized limb and most normal people will be horrified by the caster's unnatural appendage.
4	The caster's face acquires a metallic sheen as if his skin were dusted with iron flakes. If rolled a second time, actual metal plates emerge from the caster's face and skull, covering his head in a permanent crude helm. This bodily armament grants him a +4 AC bonus to any attack targeting his head, but limits his peripheral vision. His reduced visibility imparts a -4 penalty to any roll to detect hidden creatures or to avoid surprise. If this result is rolled a third time, the helm grows even larger, turning the caster's head into an iron covered, pumpkin-sized monstrosity. The caster gains a +8 AC bonus to any attack targeting his head, but his visibility is reduced to a mere sliver. The caster automatically fails any vision-related rolls to detect hidden creatures and is automatically surprised by any attack coming from the rear or to either side of him. In addition, the great weight of his head makes it impossible for him to sleep lying down. Should he ever fall unconscious in a recumbent pose, he must make a DC 10 Fortitude save or die from asphyxiation.
5	Small items are 25% likely to break when used by the caster. This include everything from normal tools (eating implements, hammers, drinking vessels, etc.) to weapons. Magical paraphernalia such as the caster's spellbook, wands, objects used in spell rituals, etc. are unaffected, as is any object not used by the caster himself (an opponent's weapon, for example). If this result is rolled a second time, the probability of breakage increases to 50%. If rolled a third time, items break 75% of the time.
6	The caster acquires a fondness for ruins, seeking to spend at least an hour wandering among the broken remains of the past whenever the opportunity arises. If this result is rolled a second time, the caster feels himself drawn to ruined places and must make a DC 10 Will save each week or become consumed by the desire to visit a ruined structure, city, or other shattered remnant of past glories. If this result is rolled a third time, the caster finds he can only rest inside the confines of a ruined structure or place. He cannot fall asleep when not within a ruin, gaining none of the benefits of a full night's rest and possibly other disadvantages (ability score loss, penalties to dice rolls, etc.) of the judge's choosing.

PATRON SPELLS: NHOOL

Lackeys of the Prince of Ruins eventually learn the three following spells:

Level 1: *Plunder the Ruin's Power*

Level 2: *Fist of Nhool*

Level 3: *War-gird*

SPELLBURN: NHOOL

Nhool responds to spilled blood, the clash of arms, and the screams of dying civilizations. Those who acquiesce to his desire for these things are rewarded with increased power in their incantations. When a caster utilizes spellburn, roll 1d4 on the table below or build off the ideas below to create an event specific to your home campaign.

Roll   Spellburn Result

1   Nhool shatters the spell caster's surroundings like the many city walls that have fallen beneath his mighty fists. Stone floors crack and become askew, walls shudder and break, ceilings shift and dust falls on those below. The blast shakes the caster's mortal frame (expressed as Strength, Agility, or Stamina loss).

2   The caster's flesh is assailed by the razor-sharp blades of Nhool's chaotic forces. The ghostly blades manifest around the caster, severing tendons, hacking away flesh, and gouging the caster's muscles (these wounds are expressed as Strength, Agility, or Stamina loss). The caster also suffers 1 point of damage for each ability point expended in the spellburn.

3   The caster is summoned before Nhool where he must recount the litany of his destructive acts and the names of

those who've fallen before him. The servant is whisked away to the Court of Chaos where the Prince of Ruins awaits to hear of the caster's deeds. The abrupt translocation across planar boundaries wracks the caster's body (expressed as Strength, Agility, or Stamina loss). The caster must either actually recount his deeds, role-playing the part of the servant addressing his master (played by the judge) or make a DC 15 Personality check if time is of the essence or the judge wishes to eschew role-playing. If the Personality check is successful or if the player does a good job of role-playing, Nhool is pleased with his servant's deeds and the caster gains twice the normal benefit of the spellburn (+2 modifier for each ability point spellburned). If the player does a poor job of accounting for himself or if the Personality check fails, he gains the normal benefit of the spellburn but the next time he attempts to spellburn, Nhool does not heed his request and he gains no benefit from the spellburn. The caster still takes ability damage, however. The PC is then whisked back to his location. No time has passed and his action continues as normal.

4 — Nhool demands blood before rewarding the caster, requiring his lackey to slice his own body with an edged weapon (expressed as Strength, Agility, or Stamina loss). But Nhool can be appeased even more by spilling the blood of another in his name. The cast spell is temporarily deferred for up to one additional round to allow the caster the chance to assuage the Prince of Ruin's lust for blood. If the caster causes injury to an unsuspecting creature in the current or following round, the cast spell immediately takes affect with the damage inflicted manifesting as spellburn. If the attack fails to injure another unwilling creature by the end of the next round after the spell is cast, it manifests with just the caster's own expended ability points as spellburn. This version of spellburning can only be used while the caster is not suffering from any additional spellburn ability loss. Thus, it can only manifest when the caster is at full ability scores and using spellburn for the first time during a given period. Once he's taken ability damage from spellburning (but not for other sources), this spellburn effect is not available to him. He must heal all spellburn ability loss before being able to use this effect again.

Plunder the Ruin's Power

Level: 1 (Nhool) | Range: Self | Duration: 1 round or longer | Casting time: 1 action | Save: N/A

General — The caster taps the lingering life force of those creatures that once dwelled in a ruined structure to power his own actions. This spell only works when cast in a ruin, a place purposely constructed by intelligent creatures to serve as living space, defensive emplacement, religious site, or other specific purpose. This spell has no effect if used within natural but ruin-like locations (caves, petrified forests, etc.) or intact buildings. The caster can leave the ruin after the spell is cast and retain the spell's benefit, but must return to a dilapidated structure to repeat this incantation.

Manifestation — Roll 1d4: (1) Ghostly images of the ruin's former occupants crowd around the caster, feeding black streaks of power into his body; (2) blue lightning seeps from the caster's feet and crawls across the ruin's floor and walls, drawing upon the structure's power; (3) whispers of the dead fill the air as the caster calls up the life energy of the past; (4) the surrounding ruin briefly appears restored and intact, revitalized by the tapping of past events.

1 — Lost, failure, and patron taint.

2-11 — Lost. Failure.

12-13 — The caster gains a +1 bonus on all attack and damage rolls, saving throws, ability checks, or spell checks for one round.

14-17 — The caster gains a +1 bonus on all attack and damage rolls, saving throws, ability checks, or spell checks for one turn.

18-19 — The caster gains a +2 bonus on all attack and damage rolls, saving throws, ability checks, or spell checks for one turn or can grant an ally within 30' a +1 bonus on all attack and damage rolls, saving throws, ability checks, or spell checks for one round.

20-23 — The caster gains a +2 bonus on all attack and damage rolls, saving throws, ability checks, or spell checks for three turns or can grant an ally within 30' a +1 bonus on all attack and damage rolls, saving throws, ability checks, or spell checks for one turn.

24-27 — The caster gains a bonus equal to his CL+1 on all attack and damage rolls, saving throws, ability checks, or spell checks for three turns or can grant an ally within 30' a +2 bonus on all attack and damage rolls, saving throws, ability checks, or spell checks for one turn.

28-29	The caster gains a bonus equal to his CL+1 on all attack and damage rolls, saving throws, ability checks, or spell checks for one hour or can grant an ally within 30' a +2 bonus on all attack and damage rolls, saving throws, ability checks, or spell checks for three turns.
30-31	The caster gains a bonus equal to his CL+1 on all attack and damage rolls, saving throws, ability checks, or spell checks for two hours or can grant an ally within 30' a +2 bonus on all attack and damage rolls, saving throws, ability checks, or spell checks for one hour.
32+	The caster drains the ruin of all its lingering life force to empower one single spectacular action. The caster gains a +15 bonus on one attack, damage, saving throw, ability check, or spell check roll. Once completed, the ruin is permanently drained of power and can never again serve as a site for the casting of this spell.

Fist of Nhool

Level: 2 (Nhool)　　Range: 60'　　Duration: 1 round or longer　　Casting time: 1 action　　Save: N/A

General	The caster conjures an oversized gauntlet. The large metal fist can be directed to strike opponents or bash its way through barricades and other obstacles.
Manifestation	Roll 1d4: (1) a brazen fist covered with verdigris and dripping blood; (2) a blackened-iron gauntlet adorned with spikes and studs; (3) an ogre-sized fleshy fist, blood-red in color and marred by weeping sores; (4) a scaly green hand covered with horny protrusions and bearing jagged nails.
1	Lost, failure, and patron taint.
2-11	Lost. Failure.
12-13	Failure, but spell is not lost.
14-15	The fist attacks a single target within range. This strike inflicts 1d8+CL damage. The fist vanishes after a single round.
16-19	The fist attacks a single target within range. This strike inflicts 1d8+CL damage. The fist has a duration of two rounds and can attack the same opponent or a different one on the following round.
20-21	**The caster can choose one of two effects:** A) The fist attacks a single target within range. This strike inflicts 1d10+CL damage. The fist has a duration of three rounds and can attack the same opponent or different ones on subsequent rounds. OR B) The fist strikes an inanimate barricade (door, wall, bars, shutters, etc.), ramming the barrier with a Strength of 20 (+4 bonus). The fist vanishes at the end of the round.
22-25	**The caster can choose one of two effects:** A) The fist attacks a single target within range. This strike inflicts 1d12+CL damage. The fist has a duration of four rounds and can attack the same opponent or different ones on subsequent rounds. OR B) The fist strikes an inanimate barricade (door, wall, bars, shutters, etc.), ramming the barrier with a Strength of 20 (+4 bonus). The fist remains for two rounds, allowing it to continue assailing the barrier, but not attack opponents.
26-29	**The caster can choose one of two effects:** A) The fist attacks a single target within range. This strike inflicts 2d8+CL damage. The fist has a duration of six rounds and can attack the same opponent or different ones on subsequent rounds. OR B) The fist strikes an inanimate barricade (door, wall, bars, shutters, etc.), ramming the barrier with a Strength of 20 (+4 bonus). The fist remains for three rounds, allowing it to continue assailing the barrier, but not attack opponents.

30-31	**The caster can choose one of two effects:** A) The fist attacks a single target within range. This strike inflicts 2d10+CL damage. The fist has a duration of eight rounds and can attack the same opponent or different ones on subsequent rounds. OR B) The fist strikes an inanimate barricade (door, wall, bars, shutters, etc.), ramming the barrier with a Strength of 20 (+4 bonus). The fist remains for four rounds, allowing it to continue assailing the barrier, but not attack opponents.
32-33	**The caster can choose one of two effects:** A) The fist attacks a single target within range. This strike inflicts 2d16+CL damage. The fist has a duration of ten rounds and can attack the same opponent or different ones on subsequent rounds. OR B) The fist strikes an inanimate barricade (door, wall, bars, shutters, etc.), ramming the barrier with a Strength of 24 (+5 bonus). The fist remains for five rounds, allowing it to continue assailing the barrier, but not attack opponents.
34+	A titanic, 5' cube-sized fist is conjured into existence. This hand streaks out from the caster in a straight 60' line striking anything in its path. Any creature in the way of the fist must make a DC 20 Reflex save or suffer 3d20+CL damage. Non-magical barricades such as doors, bars, and thin walls are 95% likely to be destroyed by the fist, allowing it to continue its movement. A barrier that survives the fist's strike stops it in its tracks, as does magical walls, doors, and stone barricades of 5' or more thickness.

War-Gird

Level: 3 (Nhool)	Range: Self	Duration: CL rounds or longer	Casting time: 1 action	Save: N/A

General	The caster calls upon the power of Chaos to invigorate him before entering battle, to strengthen his sword arm, and to protect him from harm while in the fray.
Manifestation	Roll 1d4: (1) roiling, gossamer armor of heavy plate wraps itself around the caster's body; (2) the caster's body ignites in sickly rainbow-hued flames; (3) the spectral appearance of Nhool manifests behind the caster for the duration of the spell; (4) scale-like plates of rusting, bloodstained iron emerge from the caster's skin.
1	Lost, failure, and patron taint.
2-11	Lost. Failure.
12-15	Failure, but spell is not lost.
16-17	The caster gains +4 hit points, a +2 bonus to AC, and a +2 bonus to all physical attack rolls for CL rounds.
18-21	The caster gains +6 hit points, a +3 bonus to AC, and a +3 bonus to all physical attack rolls for CL+1d3 rounds.
22-23	The caster gains +8 hit points, a +4 bonus to AC, and a +4 bonus to all physical attack rolls for CL+2d4 rounds.
24-26	The caster gains +12 hit points, a +6 bonus to AC, and a +6 bonus to all physical attack and damage rolls for CL+1d3 rounds.
27-31	The caster gains +12 hit points, a +6 bonus to AC, and a +6 bonus to all physical attack and damage rolls for CL+2d3 rounds.
32-33	The caster gains +16 hit points, a +8 bonus to AC, and a +8 bonus to all physical attack and damage rolls for one turn.
34-35	The caster gains +16 hit points, a +8 bonus to AC, and a +8 bonus to all physical attack and damage rolls for one hour.
36+	The caster gains +20 hit points, a +10 bonus to his AC and is immune to *magic missiles*, and a +10 bonus to all attack and damage rolls for CL hours.

OBITU-QUE

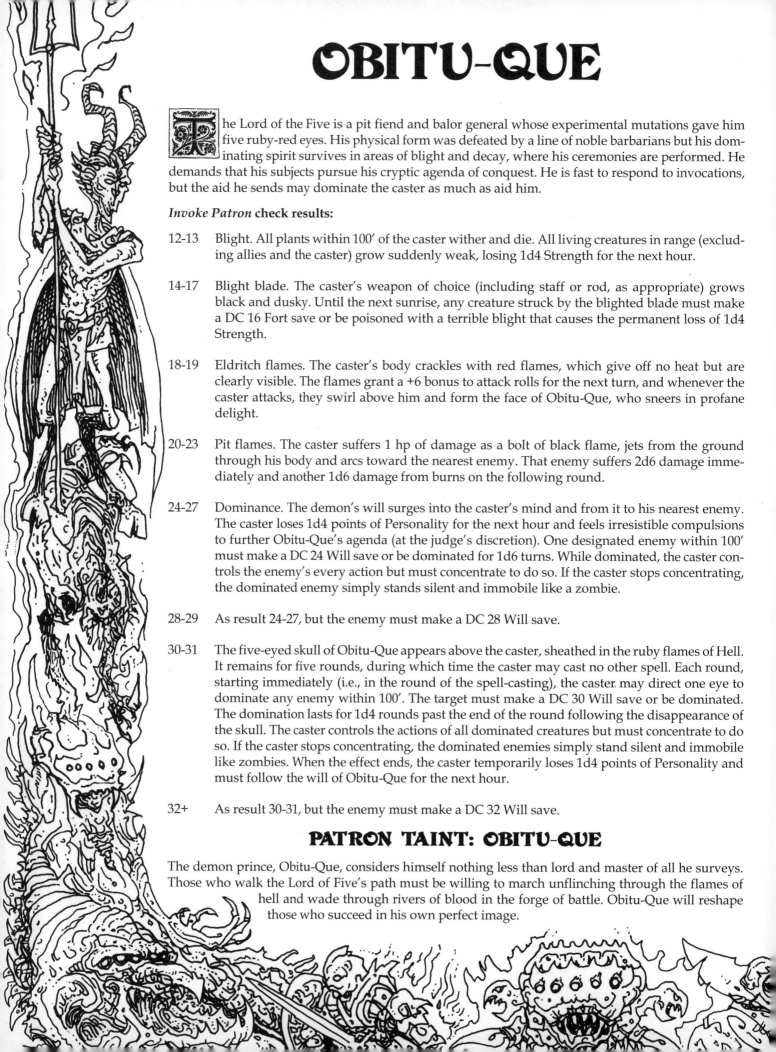

The Lord of the Five is a pit fiend and balor general whose experimental mutations gave him five ruby-red eyes. His physical form was defeated by a line of noble barbarians but his dominating spirit survives in areas of blight and decay, where his ceremonies are performed. He demands that his subjects pursue his cryptic agenda of conquest. He is fast to respond to invocations, but the aid he sends may dominate the caster as much as aid him.

Invoke Patron check results:

12-13   Blight. All plants within 100' of the caster wither and die. All living creatures in range (excluding allies and the caster) grow suddenly weak, losing 1d4 Strength for the next hour.

14-17   Blight blade. The caster's weapon of choice (including staff or rod, as appropriate) grows black and dusky. Until the next sunrise, any creature struck by the blighted blade must make a DC 16 Fort save or be poisoned with a terrible blight that causes the permanent loss of 1d4 Strength.

18-19   Eldritch flames. The caster's body crackles with red flames, which give off no heat but are clearly visible. The flames grant a +6 bonus to attack rolls for the next turn, and whenever the caster attacks, they swirl above him and form the face of Obitu-Que, who sneers in profane delight.

20-23   Pit flames. The caster suffers 1 hp of damage as a bolt of black flame, jets from the ground through his body and arcs toward the nearest enemy. That enemy suffers 2d6 damage immediately and another 1d6 damage from burns on the following round.

24-27   Dominance. The demon's will surges into the caster's mind and from it to his nearest enemy. The caster loses 1d4 points of Personality for the next hour and feels irresistible compulsions to further Obitu-Que's agenda (at the judge's discretion). One designated enemy within 100' must make a DC 24 Will save or be dominated for 1d6 turns. While dominated, the caster controls the enemy's every action but must concentrate to do so. If the caster stops concentrating, the dominated enemy simply stands silent and immobile like a zombie.

28-29   As result 24-27, but the enemy must make a DC 28 Will save.

30-31   The five-eyed skull of Obitu-Que appears above the caster, sheathed in the ruby flames of Hell. It remains for five rounds, during which time the caster may cast no other spell. Each round, starting immediately (i.e., in the round of the spell-casting), the caster may direct one eye to dominate any enemy within 100'. The target must make a DC 30 Will save or be dominated. The domination lasts for 1d4 rounds past the end of the round following the disappearance of the skull. The caster controls the actions of all dominated creatures but must concentrate to do so. If the caster stops concentrating, the dominated enemies simply stand silent and immobile like zombies. When the effect ends, the caster temporarily loses 1d4 points of Personality and must follow the will of Obitu-Que for the next hour.

32+   As result 30-31, but the enemy must make a DC 32 Will save.

PATRON TAINT: OBITU-QUE

The demon prince, Obitu-Que, considers himself nothing less than lord and master of all he surveys. Those who walk the Lord of Five's path must be willing to march unflinching through the flames of hell and wade through rivers of blood in the forge of battle. Obitu-Que will reshape those who succeed in his own perfect image.

When a patron taint is indicated, roll 1d6 on the table below. When a caster has acquired all six taints at all levels of effect, they will be reformed into a vessel worthy of Obitu-Que. Each time patron taint is indicated thereafter, the caster must make a successful Will save or be dominated by Obitu-Que forever. The Will save starts at DC 25, and increases by 1 each time patron taint is acquired.

Roll   Result

1   Beguiled by the whispered promises of Obitu-Que, the caster becomes convinced that he or she is the favored soul of the Lords of the Abyss. The caster takes on haughty and condescending airs. In any situation where the caster's group should employ stealth, retreat from battle, offer compassion, or keep their mouths shut, there is a 1 in 16 chance that the caster flies into a fit of rage, red-faced and choking with anger. The caster reacts immediately to reestablish their dominance, berating everyone within sight or rushing into battle. If this result is rolled a second time, the caster cannot ignore any perceived slight. The chance of the caster raging increases to 1 in 8. If this result is rolled a third time, the caster no longer tolerates any disrespect from puny mortals. The chance of the caster raging increases to 1 in 4.

2   Obitu-Que remolds the caster in his own im-

age. The caster's skull widens and the eyes move further apart. If this result is rolled a second time, pronounced ridges grow on the skull and a third blinking eye sprouts on the caster's forehead. The deformity can be concealed with a carefully positioned headband or hat. If this result is rolled a third time, a fourth and fifth eye appear on either side of the caster's eye and the third eye moves into alignment with the others. The ridges on the skull extend into devilish horns.

3   The Lords of the Abyss fling their filthy seed into the caster's soul. The caster's flesh takes on a reddish hue. If this result is rolled a second time, the air around the caster is unbearable hot. All spell manifestations are tainted by a demonic quality (e.g., lit from beneath by red light, surrounded by hellfire, buzzing with flies). If this result is rolled a third time, the air around the caster burns with the crimson flame of the Abyss when angered. All creatures within 5' burn for 1d3 damage, and must make a DC 15 Reflex save or burst aflame.

4   The caster's spirit is corrupted. The caster's alignment moves one step toward Chaos. If the caster is already of chaotic alignment, the deity of an order of lawful warrior priests feels a disturbance. The god commands his strongest followers to root out the source of evil. A war party consisting of 1d4+2 warriors and 1d3 clerics hunt the caster, arriving 1d6 days later to exterminate the evil-doer.

5   The caster's flesh is ripped apart and reformed into a shape more befitting of Obitu-Que's magnificence. The character undergoes an agonizing rapid transformation, taking 2d4 damage while growing 1' in height. If this result is rolled a second time, the caster takes 2d6 damage and becomes more muscular. Subtract 1 point of Intelligence and add it to Strength. If this result is rolled a third time, the caster takes 2d8 damage and grows another 1' as bulging ropes of musculature re-knit just below the skin. Subtract 2 points of Intelligence and add it to Strength.

6   The caster assumes a more demon-like form. A tail tipped by a spade extends from the caster's tailbone. If this result is rolled a second time, the caster's feet enlarge and become cloven hooves. The caster receives a -5' speed penalty until reaching the next level of experience while learning to walk with the new feet. If this result is rolled a third time, claw-tipped wings sprout from caster's back causing 2d6 damage. The caster may fly up to 20' for 1 plus Str modifier rounds per turn until the next level of experience, when they can fly with a movement speed of 30'.

PATRON SPELLS: OBITU-QUE

Obitu-Que grants three unique spells, as follows:

Level 1: *Blight*

Level 3: *Demonism*

Level 5: *Genocide*

SPELLBURN: OBITU-QUE

Obitu-Que is not moved by subtle pleas. To garner the attentions of the demon prince, the petitioner must make a display of dominance or unflinching cruelty—the grander, the better. When a caster utilizes spellburn, roll 1d4 and consult the table below or build off the suggestions to create an event specific to your home campaign. The table below should be used as a springboard for a player to invent ideas for the character to attract the favors of Obitu-Que.

Roll   **Spellburn Result**

1   The caster can sweeten his or her appeals to Obitu-Que by torturing or sacrificing a living creature in the most excruciating manner possible. Ripping the legs off a toad, biting the head off a bat, or slitting an enemy's throat and pulling its tongue through the fresh wound are but a few cruel examples.

2   Obitu-Que is impressed by casters that can inflict harm on themselves and show no pain. The ability point loss manifests through acts of self-mutilation such as jabbing needles into one's own eye, piercing nails through the flesh and leaving them there, or branding oneself with a red-hot poker.

3   Overactive adrenal glands dump an overdose of hormones into the caster's body triggering an episode of blind rage. In addition to the spell check bonus, the caster gains a +3 bonus to melee hit, melee damage, and Strength checks for 1d4 rounds. Afterwards, the caster's body is wracked by pain as the ability point loss take hold due to internal organs responding to the toxicity.

4   The caster drives a knife deep into his or her own body, seeking at arterial. The bloody display pleases Obitu-Que, but the caster must succeed in a DC 15 Fort save immediately after casting the spell, or fall unconscious for 1d3 rounds.

Blight

Level: 1 (Obitu-Que)	Range: Varies	Duration: Varies	Casting time: 1 round	Save: Fort vs. spell check

General
: The caster infects other creatures with blight, a supernatural disease that results in prolonged and agonizing death due to organ failure as the body decomposes from within.

Manifestation
: Roll 1d4: (1) yellow pus seeps from the caster's hands; (2) a black halo appears over the caster's head; (3) waves of heat emanate from the caster's hands; (4) a misty grinning skull appears above.

	When Cast on Enemy	**When Cast on Object**
1	Lost, failure, and patron taint.	Lost, failure, and patron taint.
2-11	Lost. Failure.	Lost. Failure.
12-13	A target within 10' becomes nauseous, and takes a -1 penalty to attack rolls for 1 round.	Failure, but spell is not lost.
14-17	A target within 10' is sickened, and takes a -1 penalty to all attack rolls, damage rolls, saving throws, skill checks, and spell checks for 1d3 rounds.	The caster's touch poisons the next potable item handled (flask size or smaller). Drinking the liquid causes 1d4 damage.
18-19	A target within 15' feels ill, and takes a -2 penalty to all attack rolls, damage rolls, saving throws, skill checks, and spell checks for 1 turn.	The caster's touch poisons the next potable item handled (flask size or smaller). Drinking the liquid causes 1d4 damage and a -1 penalty to all attack rolls, damage rolls, saving throws, skill checks, and spell checks for 1 day. Alternatively, the caster may choose any lesser effect.
20-23	A target (CL + 1 HD or less) within 15' falls to the ground vomiting and is unable to take any action for 1 round. All targets take a -2 penalty to all attack rolls, damage rolls, saving throws, skill checks, and spell checks for 1 turn.	The caster's touch poisons the next weapon handled. For 1 turn, the poisoned weapon causes +1 additional damage and a -1 penalty to all attack rolls, damage rolls, saving throws, skill checks, and spell checks for 1d3 rounds. Alternatively, the caster may choose any lesser effect.
24-27	1d3 targets (CL + 1 HD or less) within 20' begin vomiting and are unable to take any action for 1 round. All targets take a -2 penalty to all attack rolls, damage rolls, saving throws, skill checks, and spell checks for 1 round.	The caster's touch poisons the next weapon handled. For 1d6 turns, the poisoned weapon causes +2 additional damage and a -2 penalty to all attack rolls, damage rolls, saving throws, skill checks, and spell checks for 1d3 rounds. Alternatively, the caster may choose any lesser effect.
28-29	1d6 targets (CL + 2 HD or less) within 25' fall to the ground convulsing and are unable to take any action for 1 round. The targets take a -2 penalty to all attack rolls, damage rolls, saving throws, skill checks, and spell checks for 1d3 rounds.	The caster's touch poisons the next weapon handled. For 1 day, the poisoned weapon causes +1d4 additional damage and a -3 penalty to all attack rolls, damage rolls, saving throws, skill checks, and spell checks for 1d6 rounds. Alternatively, the caster may choose any lesser effect.
30-31	All targets (CL + 5 HD or less) within 50' begin bleeding from the eyes, are blinded for 1 turn, and are unable to take any action for 1d3 rounds. All targets take a -3 penalty to all attack rolls, damage rolls, saving throws, skill checks, and spell checks for 1 turn.	The caster's touch poisons a pond-sized or smaller water source. For the next 1d6 days, any creatures that drinks from the water takes a -3 penalty to all attack rolls, damage rolls, saving throws, skill checks, and spell checks for 1 day. Alternatively, the caster may choose any lesser effect.
32+	A number of enemies with a total HD of 3x CL within 100' are infected with blight. All targets must immediately make a DC 15 Fort save or die. Surviving targets fall unconscious for 1d3 rounds. When they awake, they take a -5 penalty to all attack rolls, damage rolls, saving throws, skill checks, and spell checks for 1 week. Any living creatures (of equal HD or less) they come into contact with must make a DC 10 Fort save or be infected with the same effect. After 1 week, infected creatures die unless subject to magic healing.	The caster's touch poisons a lake, river, or stream. For the next 2 weeks, any creatures that drinks from or bathes in the water must succeed in a DC 10 Fort save or contract blight. The creature takes a -5 penalty to all attack rolls, damage rolls, saving throws, skill checks, and spell checks for 1 week. Any living creatures (of equal HD or less) they come into contact with must make a DC 5 Fort save or be infected with the same effect. After 1 week, infected creatures die unless subject to magic healing. Alternatively, the caster may choose any lesser effect.

Demonism

Level: 3 (Obitu-Que) Range: Self Duration: 1 round per CL Casting time: 1 round Save: Varies

General	The caster takes on demonic traits for a limited time.
Manifestation	See below.
1	Lost, failure, and patron taint.
2-11	Lost. Failure.
12-15	Failure, but spell is not lost.
16-17	The caster summons a black trident burning with tyrannic malevolence. The caster can hurl the trident at one target within 50' with unerring accuracy for 2d6 damage.
18-21	The caster grows small horns and goat legs. The caster gains a 5' bonus to speed and a +1 bonus to melee attacks. The caster summons a shimmering ebon javelin that can be hurled at one target with 50' with unerring accuracy for 3d6 damage.
22-23	The caster takes on a demonic form 8' in height with long horns and wolf legs. The caster gains a 10' bonus to speed and a +2 bonus to melee attacks. The caster summons two smoldering hand-axes that can be thrown at targets within 50' with unerring accuracy for 2d6 damage each.
24-26	The caster takes on a demonic form 10' in height with spiral horns and stag legs. The caster gains a 15' bonus to speed and a +3 bonus to melee attacks. The caster grows fiery wings and can fly 20' per round. As a d20 action, the caster can breath a 30' cone of black and crimson flames that burns all targets for 2d6 damage (Ref save vs. spell check for half damage).
27-31	The caster takes on a demonic form 12' in height with single horn and warhorse legs. The caster moves at double speed and a +4 bonus to melee attacks. The caster grows fiery wings and can fly 30' per round. As a d20 action, the caster can breath a 40' cone of black and crimson flames that burns all targets for 3d6 damage (Ref save vs. spell check for half damage).
32-33	The caster takes on a demonic form 14' in height with ox horns and legs. The caster moves at double speed and a +5 bonus to melee attacks. The caster grows fiery wings and can fly 40' per round. As a d20 action, the caster can breath a 50' cone of black and crimson flames that burns all targets for 4d6 damage (Ref save vs. spell check for half damage).
34-35	The caster takes on a demonic form 16' in height with moose antlers horns and scaly legs. The caster moves at double speed and a +5 bonus to melee attacks. The caster grows fiery wings and can fly 40' per round. As a d20 action, the caster can breath a 50' cone of black and crimson flames that burns all targets for 4d6 damage (Ref save vs. spell check for half damage). A flaming whip appears in the caster's hand. The whip has a 10' melee reach, does 3d6 damage, and sets the target aflame.
36+	The caster transforms into a 20' tall balor. The caster moves at double speed and a +5 bonus to melee attacks. The caster's fiery wings fly 40' per round. As a free action, the caster can breath a 50' cone of black and crimson flames that burns all targets for 4d6 damage (Ref save vs. spell check for half damage). A flaming whip appears in each the caster's hand. Each whip has a 20' melee reach, does 3d6 damage, and sets targets aflame. At the end of the spell's duration, the caster suffers corruption; Roll 1d6: (1-3) caster falls unconscious 1d3 round; (4) minor; (5) major; (6) greater.

Genocide

| Level: 5 (Obitu-Que) | Range: Varies | Duration: Varies | Casting time: 1 round | Save: Varies |

General	The caster snuffs one creature, tribe, bloodline, or species out of existence forever.
Manifestation	Roll 1d4: (1) 5 crimson jewels float over the caster's head; (2) ghostly spirits rip from effected creatures as their bodies crumble to the ground; (3) black storm clouds forms into the shape of grinning skull crackling with thunder; (4) torrential black water wriggling with tadpoles rains from the heavens.
1	Lost, failure, and patron taint.
2-11	Lost. Failure.
12-17	Failure, but spell is not lost.
18-19	One target within 50' must make a DC 15 Fort save or die instantly.
20-23	One target within 50' must make a DC 20 Fort save or die instantly. In addition, 1d3 family members die, branded with the symbol of Obitu-Que. If the enemy group contains other creatures of the same race as the target, each creature has a 30% of being a family member of the slain target.
24-25	One target within 50' must make a DC 20 Fort save or die instantly. In addition, all creatures of the same race within 300' share the same fate. If the enemy group contains other creatures of the same race as the target, each creature has a 30% of being a family member of the slain target. Regardless of distance, the target's immediate family is killed. All slain targets are branded with the symbol of Obitu-Que.
26-28	One target within 100' must make a DC 25 Fort save or die instantly. In addition, all creatures of the same race within a half mile share the same fate. Regardless of distance, all living blood relatives of the target are killed, effectively ending their bloodline. All slain targets are branded with the symbol of Obitu-Que.
29-33	One target within 100' must make a DC 25 Fort save or die instantly. If any target fails the save, all creatures of the same race within the entire dungeon, city, or adventure locale share the same fate. The creatures are expunged from all wandering monster tables. Regardless of distance, all living blood relatives of the target are killed, effectively ending their bloodline. All slain targets are branded with the symbol of Obitu-Que and the caster's name.
34-35	One target of a single race within 100' must make a DC 30 Fort save or die instantly. If the target fails the save, all creatures of the same race within the entire continent share the same fate. Regardless of distance, all living blood relatives of the target are killed, effectively ending their bloodline. All slain targets are branded with the symbol of Obitu-Que and the caster's name. After 1 month, aggrieved survivors catch up with the caster wanting revenge.
36-37	1d3 targets of a single race within 200' must make a DC 35 Fort save or die instantly. If any target fails the save, all creatures of the same race within the Prime Plane share the same fate. Regardless of distance, all living blood relatives of the target are killed, effectively ending their bloodline. All slain targets are branded with the symbol of Obitu-Que and the caster's name. After 2 weeks, a war party of a random Law-aligned deity track down the caster to exact justice. After 1 month, aggrieved survivors catch up with the caster wanting revenge.
38+	1d6 targets of a single race within 300' must make a DC 35 Fort save or die instantly. A champion of the race immediately appears to prevent extermination of the entire species. In the case of non-intelligent creatures, a prime representation of the race appears. For intelligent races, one of their deities appears. Combat immediately ensues. If the caster is slain or retreats, the spell's further effects are negated. Otherwise, all creatures of the same race in existence in every plane or dimension are killed. The entire species is effectively exterminated from the campaign world. All slain targets are branded with the symbol of Obitu-Que and the caster's name. After 2 weeks, a war party of a random Law-aligned deity track down the caster to exact justice. Champions appear every 1d3 weeks thereafter to slay the caster for 1 year and 1 day.

SERBOK
The Slithering Shadow

While some scholars recognize the word "Serbok" as an archaic term for "serpent," there are few living today who know the word is also the legacy of a devious entity who stalked the worlds in epochs past. In the days when the serpent men laid claim to the world, the scaly sorcerers paid homage to the mightiest of their race, Serbok, also known as "He of the Scintillating Scales" or "the Slithering Shadow." It was Serbok who taught the serpent men guile, treachery, and brutality, ruling a hundred lesser kingdoms from the shadows by magic, blackmail, and fear.

Serbok is commonly depicted as either a serpent man of tremendous size or a human male with slitted pupils dressed in courtly finery. His true form is that of a reptilian humanoid with a cobra's hood and a serpent's body in lieu of legs. His scales glitter a thousand colors, ranging from the shining browns of a copperhead, the reds and blacks of a coral snake, and the vibrant emeralds of a forest boa.

Serbok is rarely sought after as a patron by non-serpent men, as few realize the Slithering Shadow still lives. Believed long dead, Serbok dwells in multiple disguises, pulling the strings behind the thrones of gods and devils alike. Those that do call upon Serbok for aid harbor similar ambitions, albeit on a mortal scale.

Invoke Patron **check results:**

12-13   Serbok lends assistance in the form of a ward against death by poison. The caster gains a +4 bonus on his next saving throw against poison.

14-17   Serbok reinforces the caster's will with his own, protecting his servant from magical control. The caster gains a +2+CL bonus on all Will saving throws against mental domination (including *charm person*, *hypnotism*, and *sleep*). The bonus lasts for 1d4+CL rounds.

18-19   The caster becomes supernaturally persuasive, able to convince others to serve him even if not normally inclined to. For the next CL rounds, the caster gains the spell, *charm person*, casting it with his base spell check modifier. If the caster already knows *charm person* or is a serpent-man with hypnotic gaze, he gains a +4 bonus to his spell check when casting that spell or using his hypnotic gaze for the next CL rounds. The duration of the *charm person* is determined by the spell check result and can exceed the number of rounds determined by the CL.

20-23   The caster can disguise his appearance as the serpent-man illusion ability (see DCC RPG p. 425) for a number of hours equal to 5+CL. If the caster is a serpent-man, the DC to pierce his illusion increases to 35 and he can alter his appearance twice in a single day instead of once.

24-27   The caster vanishes from sight, making him immune to direct physical and magical attacks. This disappearance is the result of mentally clouding his enemies' minds and not true invisibility. The caster remains undetectable for 2d6+CL rounds or until he breaks his concealment by attacking another. The caster can still be harmed by indirect attacks (such as being caught in a fireball's area of effect, for example) but this does not break his concealment. Certain divination spells such as a *detect evil* spell whose spell check exceeds the caster's *invoke patron* spell check will reveal the caster's presence.

28-29   A great venomous serpent appears to protect the caster. A giant viper (see DCC RPG p. 428) slithers up from the ground and obeys the caster's commands for 1d4+CL rounds before vanishing.

30-31   As result 28-29 above, but Serbok sends 1d3+1 giant vipers to assist his servant.

32+   The caster sheds his skin, removing all injuries and ailments along with it. This process takes two rounds to complete. Once the skin is shed, the process heals all damage, disease, and poison suffered by the caster. The shedding does not regrow lost limbs, remove corruption, cure paralysis, or end curses, but does cure blindness, deafness, broken limbs, and organ damage. Any injuries or baleful conditions received during the skin shedding process are applied to the rejuvenating caster as they occur, possibly slaying the caster before the transformation is complete.

PATRON TAINT: SERBOK

Servants of Serbok who suffer corruption begin manifesting his serpentine and treacherous attributes. When patron taint is indicated for Serbok, roll 1d6 on the table below. When a caster has acquired all six taints at all levels of effect, there is no need to continue rolling any more.

Roll	Result
1	The caster's skin undergoes a cosmetic alteration. If the caster is non-serpentine in race, his flesh becomes scaly and obviously reptilian. If the caster is of a reptilian race, his scales become colorfully mottled like that of his patron. Patches of red, yellow, copper, emerald, black, white, and tan scales cover his body.
2	The caster loses the ability to speak truthfully and becomes prone to telling falsehoods when directly questioned about important matters. Whenever asked a question where a truthful statement would be in the caster's best interests ("Do you need healing?" for example), the caster must make a DC 10 Will save to tell the truth. Otherwise, he must answer with a lie. Even telling the truth with gestures or incomplete statements is impossible if the save is failed, and the judge is free to require higher DC Will saves or assume temporary control of the character if this taint is not properly role-played.
3	The caster no longer derives nourishment from dead plants and animals, but subsists entirely on living creatures such as mice, rats, toads, and other small animals. The creature must be consumed while still living in order to satiate the caster's hunger. If the caster is already dependent on living creatures for nourishment, he must consume twice as many specimens at a meal as normal for his race in order to maintain his existence.
4	The caster's legs grow together and elongate, transforming into a 6' long serpent's tail. He suffers a -5' penalty to his speed as a result of moving about on the cumbersome appendage and obviously cannot pass as a normal biped without magical disguise.

5   The caster attracts serpents to his presence whenever in an area home to snakes. These serpents accumulate at the caster's location if he spends more than 12 hours in one place. Thereafter, snakes arrive at a rate of 1d3 each hour. There is a 50% chance each serpent is of the venomous variety. The caster has no control over the serpents, and while the snakes are not inclined to attack the caster outright, agitating them in any manner will likely result in a violent response.

6   The caster refuses to accept subjugation by others, be it physical, political or social. He deigns to take instruction or orders from anyone (excepting Serbok) and will attempt to usurp positions of power whenever possible. The caster need not openly assume command and is content with allowing another to "rule" in his stead while holding the reins of power from the shadows. If the caster cannot assume control of a group, power bloc, or social circle, he'll leave its ranks to pursue his own unfettered schemes.

PATRON SPELLS: SERBOK

Serbok grants three unique spells, as follows:

Level 1: *Child of the Serpent*

Level 2: *Skin of the Eel*

Level 3: *White Snake Immortality*

SPELLBURN: SERBOK

Serbock revels in delight when prideful man comes begging for assistance to augment their pitiful lives through the use of his power. In return, Serbock demands his followers assist his plan to prepare the world for a new 1000-year reign of serpent man rule. When a servant of Serbock employs spellburn, roll 1d5 on the table below, or create a similarly demanding request:

Roll   Spellburn Result

1   Serbock demands the caster shed his own skin. The caster must flay himself as if he were a molting snake. (Expressed as Stamina, Strength, or Agility loss.)

2   Serbock requires the caster's body act as a safe haven host for incubating a collection of snake eggs. For 3 days the caster's stomach will be painfully distended from the eggs lodged just beneath the skin. On the third day, the snakes will hatch and wriggle from the caster's navel.

3   The caster is shown Serbock's vision to install shape-shifting reptilian/human hybrids into positions of power and influence. The caster is tasked to travel to a nearby city and eliminate the political rival of a (magically camouflaged) serpent man bureaucrat. If the caster refuses, the spellburned points are lost and Serbock makes his displeasure known.

4   Serbock is offended by the caster's bipedal pride. For every point of spellburn expended, Serbock demands one hour where the caster must restrict all movement to crawling on his belly as a display of reverence to serpentine superiority. If the caster refuses, the spellburned points are lost and the displeased Serbock will deny spellcasting for 1 day per point of spellburn.

5   Predator birds are one of the few enemies of the snake. Serbock demands that within a fortnight the caster track down and destroy a giant eagle, roc, harpy, or other large avian predator.

Child of the Serpent

Level: 1 (Serbok) Range: Self Duration: Varies Casting time: 1 round Save: N/A

General	While Serbock tolerates the form of man and demi-humans when they pay homage to him, he is truly pleased when gazing upon the glorious likeness of the snake. By means of this spell, the caster may curry favor with Serbock by transforming themselves into one of his many likenesses, thereby benefitting from the power of his glorious serpentine form.
Manifestation	See below.
1	Lost, failure, and patron taint.
2-11	Lost. Failure.
12-13	Token transformation. Caster's tongue is temporarily forked, pupils become elliptical, and caster speaks with a hiss. In addition, the new sensitive forked tongue enables caster to "smell" gold and gems similar to a dwarf. Effects last for 1d6 rounds.
14-15	The caster's legs are replaced with a large, muscular tail, enabling the caster to move up to 40' and climb 25' per turn. Transformation lasts for 2d4 rounds.
16-19	The caster's head is replaced with that of a large rattlesnake, enabling the caster to use a fanged bite attack that does 1d8 damage plus Strength modifier. Upon a successful strike, the target must also make a DC 12 Fort save or suffer 2d6 poison damage. Transformation lasts for 2d7 rounds.
20-23	The caster's head and legs are both replaced, providing the caster all benefits listed for spell check results 12-19. Transformation lasts for 2d4 turns.
24-28	Snake man transformation. The caster's body is completely transformed into that of a snake man. The caster's AC is increased +2 from the thick snake skin, the bite attack gains +4 bonus, and the venomous bite now requires a DC 14 save or suffer 3d6 poison damage. Effects last for 2d8 turns.
29-31	Quetzalcoatl transformation. In addition to the effects listed for results 24-28, the caster takes on the appearance of the feathered serpent god Quetzalcoatl—one of Serbock's many aliases. As part of the snake man transformation, he springs bright green wings, and gains the ability to fly 25' per round. Effects last for 2d8 turns.
32+	Titanaboa transformation. The caster is transformed into the mighty Titanaboa — a giantic prehistoric snake 40 feet in length which has the ability to swallow man-sized creatures in a single bite. Effects last for 3d8 turns. **Titanaboa:** Init +5; Atk bite +10 melee (1d8 plus constriction); AC 20; hp +4d4 temporary hit points; SP constriction (1d8 damage each round), crit threat range 18-20. On critical hit, man-sized or smaller creatures must make a DC 12 Reflex save or be swallowed whole, suffering 2d10 damage plus 1d6 damage each additional round until freed. Constricted targets attempting escape must make an opposed Strength check (vs. Titanaboa's 4d6). Swallowed targets must make a DC 20 Agility check to escape back out the throat of the Titanaboa.

Skin of the Eel

Level: 2 (Serbok)	Range: Varies	Duration: Varies	Casting time: 1 round	Save: Varies

General	It pleases Serbock to imbue the caster with the traits of one of his favorite servants: the electric eel. The caster is thus enabled to defend himself or attack his foes with the electricity and thereby punish the enemies of the snake. As a side benefit, the caster is enabled with the ability to breathe underwater.
Manifestation	For 2d4 rounds after casting the spell, the caster's skin turns a dark, dull gray and gills form on the caster's neck. He also appears bald, with flat, black eyes, giving the caster the appearance of a grotesque eel/humanoid hybrid.
1	Lost, failure, and patron taint.
2-11	Lost. Failure.
12-13	Token transformation. The caster's skin is transformed into a shade of dark dull gray. Effects last for 1d6 rounds.
14-15	The caster's skin takes on a mild electrical charge. Any creature that makes a successful melee attack against the caster must make a DC 12 Fort save or take 1d8 points of electrical damage. In addition, the spellcaster is granted the ability to breathe underwater. Effects last for 1d6 rounds.
16-19	The caster's skin takes on a significant electrical charge. Any creature that makes a successful melee attack against the caster must make a DC 12 Fort save or take 2d4+CL points of electrical damage. Caster can breathe underwater. Effects last for 1d8 rounds.
20-21	The caster has the ability to shoot a bolt of electricity at a foe within 20'. One target takes 2d4+CL damage. Additionally, target must make a DC 15 Reflex save or catch fire, taking an additional 1d6 points of damage each round thereafter until flame is extinguished. Caster can also breathe underwater for 1d8 rounds. Effects last for one round per CL.
22-23	The caster can now launch two rays at a single target or multiple targets within 20'. Each ray does 3d5+CL damage. Additionally, target(s) must make a DC 15 Reflex save or catch fire, taking an additional 1d6 points of damage each round thereafter until flame is extinguished. Caster can also breathe underwater. Effects last for CL+1 rounds.
24-26	Electric barrier. The caster is able to create a circular barrier 15' in diameter around himself. Creatures touching the barrier take 4d6+CL damage (Fort save vs. spell check for half damage). Caster can also breathe underwater. Effects last for 1d3+CL rounds.
27-29	Human magnet. The caster can use his electric ability to turn himself into a powerful magnet. The caster can extend his hand and create a cone of magnetism extending from his hand 30 feet long and 10' to 30' wide. Any metal object not tethered will be drawn to the caster within 2 rounds. Creatures holding metal weapons must make a Reflex save vs. spell check or have their weapons wrested from their grasp. Creatures wearing metal must make a Strength check vs. spell check or be drawn to the caster at a rate of 10' per round. Effects last for 1d5+CL rounds.
30-33	Electrify ground. The caster can place his hand on the ground and, creating a charged vein in the earth 15' wide and up to 30+CL feet in length, inflict electrifying damage to all targets on the path. Targets take 4d6+CL damage (Fort save vs. spell check for half damage). Effects last for 1d5+CL rounds.
34+	Electric puppets. The caster can focus the electrical energy to galvanize the muscles within nearby corpses, turning them into "static zombies". The caster can manipulate up to 1d7+CL creatures, each having half of their original hit points and -2 from their original AC. As the creatures are not un-dead, per se, but merely corpses being manipulated, they cannot be turned. Effects last for 1d10+CL rounds.

White Snake Immortality

| Level: 3 (Serbok) | Range: Self | Duration: Varies | Casting time: 2 rounds | Save: N/A |

General	Serbock's power resides not only in massive strength and arcane knowledge, but also in his ability to harness and transfer the secrets of immortality. Powerful wizards willing to pledge years of service to Serbock will find their time rewarded in double via the patron's ability to extend a mortal's physical lifespan.
Manifestation	See below.
1	Lost, failure, and patron taint.
2-11	Lost. Failure.
12-15	Token benefit. A pale, ghostly aura briefly washes over the caster before quickly dissapating. The caster feels refreshed and alert. +2 bonus to Init rolls for 1d4 hours.
16-19	Light respite. Ghostly snakes emerge from the ground and crawl up the caster's body. Caster is provided 1d4 temporary hit points and +2 bonus to Init rolls for 1d4 hours.
20-23	Rejuvenating respite. A spectral boa constrictor envelops the caster's body for 2 rounds. Once it dissipates, the caster is granted 1d8 temporary hit points and is healed with 1 die of hit points, similar to cleric's *lay on hands*.
24-28	Light wounds are healed. Spectral snakes appear and lap at the caster's wound with darting, forked tongues. When they finish, caster is healed with 2 hit dice, similar to cleric's *lay on hands*.
29-31	Serious wounds are healed. A rattlesnake emerges from the caster's mouth carrying a bloody, dripping tumor symbolizing his wounds. The caster finds himself healed of 3 hit dice, similar to cleric's *lay on hands*.
32-33	Natural age extended 1 year. The great white snake spirit appears and briefly encircles the caster's body. When it unfurls, the caster is healed with 4 hit dice (similar to cleric's *lay on hands*), and 1 point of lost Stamina is permanently restored (not to exceed PC's originally rolled Stamina score). Requires at least 2 points of spellburn, including a minor quest to serve Serbock.
34-35	Natural age extended 2 years. The great white snake spirit appears and begins to constrict the caster. When the spell expires, the spirit releases the caster, who is revealed appearing younger and more vibrant. All lost hit points are restored. One lost point of Strength, Agility, or Stamina is permanently restored (chosen by PC, not to exceed original starting ability scores). If the PC has undergone minor corruption, it is removed. Minor effects of character aging (wrinkles, skin tone, etc.) are improved. Requires at least 5 points of spellburn, including a significant quest to serve Serbock.
36+	Natural age extended 5 years. The great white snake spirit appears and completely swallows the caster. When the spell expires, the spirit disperses and the caster is revealed appearing younger and more vibrant. All lost hit points are restored. Two points of lost Strength, Agility, or Stamina are permanently restored (chosen by PC, not to exceed original starting ability scores). If the PC has undergone minor or major corruption, those too are removed. Significant signs of character aging (baldness, liver spots, wrinkles, sagging skin, etc.) are removed. Requires at least 8 points of spellburn and must include at least a year of servitude to Serbock.

YILA-KERANUZ
The Lizard King

Yila-Keranuz is ancient and patient. He arose in the Primordial Days, crawling from the ooze to grasp the primeval world in his scaly claws. In that prehistoric epoch, Yila-Keranuz contested with Serbok and Schaphigroadaz for dominance, his fervent worshipers battling those of the Serpent and the Toad. When the end came in a flash of burning light and clouds of choking ash, Yila-Keranuz slipped into hibernation, awaiting a time when he and his children would once again dominate the world. Now, eons later, the Lizard King has awoken once again. His minions, although diminished in size and number, remain dedicated to their master and work anew to impose his will across myriad lands. Yila-Keranuz is mocked by his enemies as slow and lumbering, a clumsy thing left behind when the world moved on. He is content to allow his foes to believe these accusations for he knows that triumph is the ultimate reward for patience.

Yila-Keranuz is often the patron of wizards who prefer vengeance and survival over flashy magics and devastating first strikes. The Lizard King also counts a fair number of warriors amongst his loyal followers. These men and women honor his fortitude and his lethality. In the ancient days, Yila-Keranuz was served by the dinosaurs, but their numbers are scant and their intellect reduced in the current era. Nevertheless, some survivors from the Primordial Days still honor Yila-Keranuz with the Old Rites in verdant, steaming jungles and in secluded mountainous valleys. He and his followers remain dedicated foes of Serbok and Schaphigroadaz, seeking to thwart the schemes of Serpent and Toad at every turn. Those sorcerer servants binding themselves to the Lizard King will likely become soldiers in this scaly war.

Invoke Patron check results:

12-13   Yila-Keranuz rewards the patient servant. If the caster performs no action other than movement on the following round, the Lizard King grants him a +1d bonus to his next attack or spell check on the subsequent round.

14-17   A mass of small venomous lizards swarms one the caster's opponents inflicting 2d6 damage plus 1d3 Strength loss. A DC 13 Fort save reduces the damage to 1d6 and no ability loss.

18-19   Yila-Keranuz imparts the lizard's resilience upon his servant. The caster becomes immune to non-magical heat (including heatstroke, dehydration caused by arid climes, sunburn, and similar calamities) and gains a +4 bonus to saving throws against magical fire. His skin takes on a scaly appearance that grants a +4 AC bonus and the caster gains a temporary 10 hit points. These benefits vanish after 1d4+CL hours. The temporary hit points are lost first if the caster suffers damage.

20-23   The Lizard King dispatches a giant lizard (see DCC RPG core rulebook, p. 420) with maximum hit points to serve the caster for 1d6+CL turns. The lizard can be ridden as a mount, will guard the caster while he sleeps, and attacks its master's enemies upon command.

24-27   Yila-Keranuz transforms the caster into a huge lizard/man hybrid. Now standing 8' tall and bearing colorful scales and a lizard's head, the caster gains +6 to his attacks, damage, and AC, and receives an additional 20 temporary hit points. He also gains +5 to all saving throws against heat and poison. The transformation lasts for 2d4+CL turns.

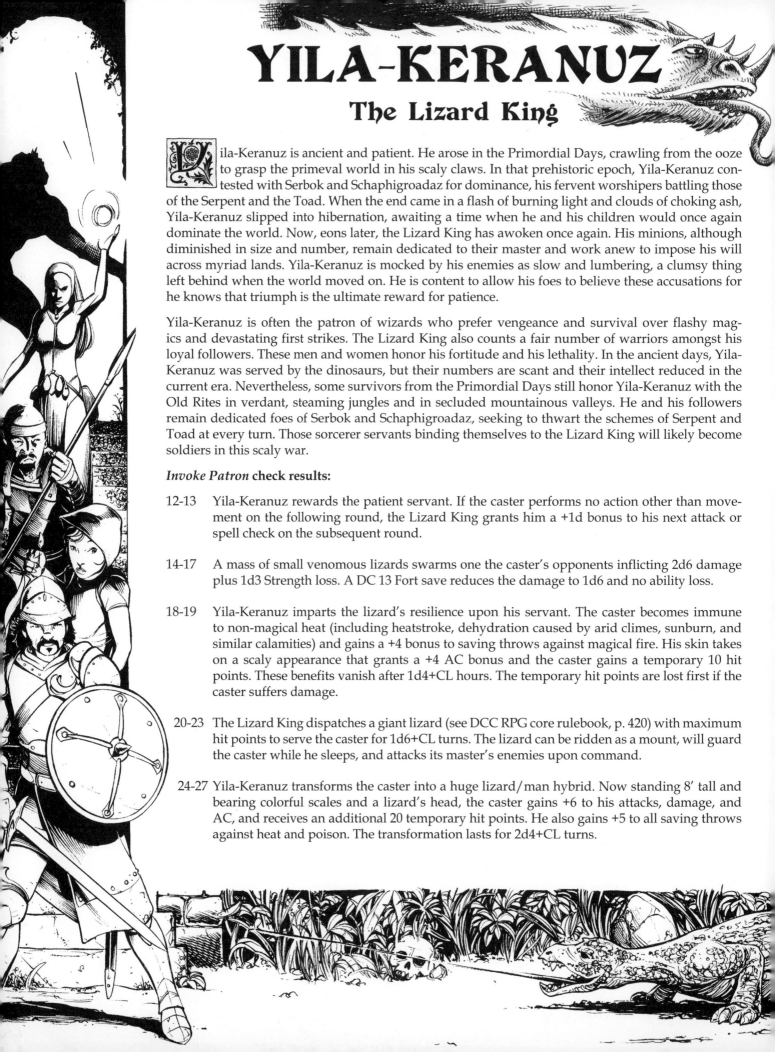

28-29	Yila-Keranuz calls upon one of its ancient servants from the distant past and summons a pterodactyl (DCC RPG, p. 424) for the caster's use. This creature serves the caster as the giant lizard in result 20-23 above for 1d3+CL days before vanishing. If slain before this time, the pterodactyl disappears in a burst of fetid, humid air. The Lizard King is not pleased his gift was sorely used and the next *invoke patron* check by the caster suffers a -2 penalty.
30-31	As above, but the caster is gifted with a small tyrannosaurus rex to aid him. The beast can be ridden as a mount, will guard the caster while he sleeps, and attacks its master's enemies upon command. It remains in the caster's presence for 1d5+CL days before vanishing. If slain before this time, the tyrannosaurus rex disappears in a burst of fetid, humid air. The Lizard King is not pleased his gift was sorely used and the next *invoke patron* check by the caster suffers a -4 penalty. **Tyrannosaurus Rex:** Init +0; Atk bite +8 melee (2d10+2); AC 15; HD 6d10+6; MV 50'; Act 2d20; SP none; SV Fort +10, Ref +2, Will +0; AL N.
32+	The Lizard King gifts the caster with the ability to go into a prolonged hibernation and avoid the ravages of age. The caster's body enters a state of suspended animation identical to death one hour after casting *invoke patron* with this spell check result. Beginning at that time, the caster no longer requires food or drink and does not age for the duration of his hibernation. The suspended animation lasts for up to 100 years per CL, but the caster can stipulate an earlier end to the hibernation before he goes into the suspended state if he desires. He awakens automatically when the hibernation ends or at the time he stipulated before entering hibernation. While hibernating, the caster's mind is in a meditative state and largely unaware of events occurring around his body. However, any attack or injury to his body has a chance of rousing his body and mind from suspended animation. Whenever the caster's body suffers damage he can attempt a DC 14 Intelligence check to end the hibernation and awaken early to deal with the danger to life and limb. If he fails, he may try again to awaken the next time he suffers damage, continuing the process until the hibernation ends or he is slain. However, he must *invoke patron* again and achieve this result to return to hibernation if the suspended state ends prematurely due to physical damage.

PATRON TAINT: YILA-KERANUZ

When patron taint is indicated for Yila-Keranuz, roll 1d6 on the table below. When a caster has acquired all six taints at all levels of effect, there is no need to continue rolling.

Roll   Result

1   The caster's blood begins to grow cold. When the first occurrence of this taint manifests, the caster becomes sluggish in cold weather, reducing his speed by 5' and suffering a -1 initiative penalty. If the result is rolled a second time, the initiative penalty is increased to -2 and he suffers 1d3 damage for each hour or part thereof he spends in temperatures of 60° F or less. If the result is rolled a third time, the caster goes torpid in cold conditions, effectively becoming paralyzed until he is removed to a place of warmth for 1 hour or more.

2   The caster's tongue increases in size. It regularly lolls from his mouth and licks his lips like a writhing worm. If this result is rolled a second time, the tongue increases in size and grotesqueness, resulting in the permanent loss of 1 point of Personality. If this taint occurs a third time, the Personality loss increases to -2 points and the tongue becomes large enough to act as an impediment to the caster's speech. He becomes difficult to understand (a DC 10 Intelligence check is required by any listener attempting to deduce what the caster is saying) and his spells suffer "loss, failure, or worse" results on a spell check result of a natural 1 or 2.

3   The caster develops a taste for warm climates. When this taint is first rolled, the caster must make a DC 5 Will save each month he is away from a sub-tropical, tropical, or hot desert environment. If the save fails, the caster succumbs to an uncontrollable urge to travel to the nearest such location and remain there for 1d7 days. Only physical restraint will stop him from traveling and he will walk the distance if he lacks the money to make more efficient travel arrangements. After the indicated time is spent living in the desirable climate, he no longer suffers from the urge and can travel at will. If this result is rolled a second time, the Will save increases to DC 10 and the caster must spend 2d7 days in the preferred environment. If this result occurs a third time, the caster must permanently move to such a locale and will only venture away from his beloved heat for 1d4 days each month.

4   The ancient battles Yila-Keranuz waged against the followers of the Serpent and the Toad echo through the caster's mind, instilling in him a hatred for such creatures and those who pay homage to them. The first time this result is rolled, the distaste is minor and the caster suffers a -2 penalty to all social rolls made with snake- or toad-like humanoids and those who worship powers associated with those animals. If the result is rolled a second time, the caster must make a DC 8 Will save to avoid attacking these creatures as well as normal snakes and toads when encountering them. If this result is rolled a third time, the DC increases to 14 and, even if the caster restrains his hatred, he still suffers a -4 penalty to all social interactions with such creatures.

5   The caster becomes a carrier for salmonella and is by no means immune to the disease. Unless strict sanitation practices are vigilantly followed, the caster and anyone coming into prolonged contact with him must make a DC 5 Fortitude save each week or lose 1d3 points of temporary Stamina. The ability loss heals as normal. If this result is rolled a second time, the DC increases to 8 and the Stamina loss rises to 1d4. If rolled a third time, the Fort save rises to DC 12 and the Stamina loss is 1d5. Spell effects that neutralize disease have no effect on this patron taint but some divine sources of healing might temporarily negate the taint for a short time at the judge's discretion.

6   The caster grows a reptile's tail, beginning with a short stub easily concealed by clothing. If this result is rolled a second time, the tail grows to 3' in length and 1' in diameter at its base. It may still be concealed by robes or flowing gowns. If this result occurs a third time, the tail grows to 6' in length. The appendage cannot be concealed by mere clothing and its unnatural nature imparts a -1 penalty to Personality. At the judge's discretion, the tail might improve the caster's initial reaction to reptilian races.

PATRON SPELLS: YILA-KERANUZ

Yila-Keranuz the Lizard King grants the three following spells to his servants:

Level 1: *Lizard's Tongue*

Level 2: *Gifts of the Lizard*

Level 3: *Shed the Lizard's Skin*

SPELLBURN: YILA-KERANUZ

Yila-Keranuz rewards his servants who abide by his core belief that the patient shall ultimately triumph over his enemies and decimate them entirely. Those who pledge themselves to the Lizard King must demonstrate the will to wait for the perfect moment to strike and to the utter destruction of their enemies by any means necessary when the time for the blow to fall finally comes. When the caster utilizes spellburn, roll 1d4 on the table below or build off the ideas presented to create an event specific to your campaign world.

Roll	Spellburn Result
1	A pair of spectral lizards with glittering eyes climb down the caster's arms as he casts his spell. At the height of the incantation, the lizards pounce, biting into the caster's skin and tearing at his flesh. The phantasmal wounds inflict stat point loss.
2	Yila-Keranuz assists the caster with his spell, but requires the caster give completely of himself to wreak havoc upon his foes. The caster must spellburn at least six points from his physical abilities to invoke a potentially phenomenal success. In return for giving his all, Yila-Keranuz matches the spellburn at a 2:3 ratio (for every two points of spellburn the caster performs, he gains +3 to his spell check). If the spell check results in the complete destruction of the caster's foes, he immediately heals a number of points of stat damage equal to his half his CL (rounded down) as Yila-Keranuz rewards him for his success.
3	The caster's skin slowly becomes scaly as he casts his spell, transforming into true scales at the moment the spell is completed. A moment after the spell's energy disperses, the scaly skin rips and tears, sloughing off completely by the end of the round. The trauma to the flesh and its sliding away manifests as physical stat point loss.
4	Yila-Keranuz refuses to aid his servant unless the caster demonstrates patience. The caster cannot spellburn this round, but if he purposely delays his spell until the next casting time increment required for the spell (his action, the following round, turn, hour, etc. as indicated in the spell's description), he enjoys a two-for-one bonus on spent ability points when spellburning. The spell is automatically delayed until the indicated time so long as the caster does not move or suffer damage. If either of those events occur, the spell automatically fails to go off, and the caster has a 50% chance of losing the spell for the day as if he failed the spell check.

Lizard's Tongue

| Level: 1 (Yila-Keranuz) | Range: Self | Duration: 1 round or longer | Casting time: 1 action | Save: N/A |

General	The caster's tongue transforms into a lizards's, forked and flickering. The sinuous tongue can be used to attack, cast spells, or as an additional appendage.
Manifestation	Roll 1d4: (1) caster's mouth widens as his tongue splits and lolls grotesquely from his mouth; (2) a glittering, semi-transparent lizard of particolored scales appears, crawling into the caster's mouth; (3) a halo of lizards, each a different color of the rainbow, momentarily manifests around the caster's head before vanishing; (4) caster grabs his tongue and yanks it from his mouth, molding it like clay.
1	Lost, failure, and patron taint.
2-11	Lost. Failure.
12-13	The caster's tongue forks and grows to a length of 2'. It remains in this state for one round, during which time the caster can use it as extra limb capable of lifting objects, wielding weapons, and engaging in simple actions requiring two fingers or less. The caster can also use it as a melee weapon which inflicts 1d4 damage on a successful hit.
14-17	As above, but the duration is extended to 1d3+CL rounds. If used as a weapon, the caster gains a +1 bonus to his attack roll and the tongue inflicts 1d6 damage on a successful hit.
18-19	As above, but the duration is extended to 1d5+CL rounds. If used as a weapon, the caster gains a +2 bonus to his attack roll and the tongue inflicts 1d8 damage on a successful hit.
20-23	The caster's tongue transforms as above for 1d6+CL, but also gains a poison-filled hypodermic fang at the end of each fork. A successful strike with the tongue at +2 to the attack roll inflicts 1d8+1 damage and requires the target to make a DC 8+CL Fortitude save or suffer an additional 1d4 damage.
24-27	The caster's tongue transforms as above for 1d7+CL, but also gains a poison-filled hypodermic fang at the end of each fork. A successful strike with the tongue at +3 to the attack roll inflicts 1d8+2 damage and requires the target to make a DC 10+CL Fort save or suffer an additional 2d4 damage.
28-29	The caster's tongue transforms as above for 1d8+CL rounds. The appendage splits multiple times to form a simple, scaly hand at its tip. This hand can wield weapons using the caster's normal attack bonus. The tongue also allows the caster to throw spells, granting him an additional 1d14 action die which can only be used to invoke magic.
30-31	The caster's tongue transforms as above for 1d10+CL rounds. The appendage splits multiple times to form a simple, scaly hand at its tip. This hand can wield weapons using the caster's normal attack bonus +2. The tongue also allows the caster to throw spells, granting him an additional 1d16 action die which can only be used to invoke magic.
32+	The caster's tongue transforms as above for 1d12+CL rounds. The appendage splits multiple times to form a simple, scaly hand at its tip. Each of the fingers of this rudimentary hand is tipped with a poison-filled hypodermic fang. The tongue and hand can be used as an extra limb to wield a weapon using the caster's normal attack bonus +4, or as a poisoned weapon that inflicts 1d10+3 damage and requires the target to make a DC 12+CL Fort save or suffer an additional 4d5 damage. The tongue also allows the caster to throw spells, granting him an additional 1d20 action die which can only be used to invoke magic.

Gifts of the Lizard

Level: 2 (Yila-Keranuz) Range: Self Duration: Varies Casting time: 1 action Save: N/A

General	The spell grants the caster an array of qualities associated with the different species of lizard that fill the known world. Each of these gifts is cumulative, allowing the caster to perform an astounding number of special actions with a high spell check result.
Manifestation	Roll 1d4: (1) a swarm of tiny skinks scamper across the caster's body, leaving the spell's effect behind when they abruptly vanish; (2) a reptilian shadow passes over the caster's body, leaving him with his gifts when it departs; (3) the sound of hissing lizards surround the caster; (4) the caster's skin ripples and his eyes become reptilian as the gifts transform his body.
1	Lost, failure, and patron taint.
2-11	Lost. Failure.
12-13	Failure, but spell is not lost.
14-15	The caster gains the ability to climb walls like a lizard. He gains a +20 bonus to climbing-related rolls while this power is in effect. He need not be barefoot or barehanded for this bonus to apply. This single power effect lasts for 2d6+CL rounds.
16-19	As result 14-15 above, plus the caster's skin transforms into hard scales that give him a +4 AC bonus. This power and the one above last for 1d3+CL turns.
20-21	As result 16-19 above, plus the caster can alter his coloration like that of a chameleon, allowing him to remain hidden from observers. The caster gains a +20 bonus to all stealth-related checks based on sight when using this power. This power affects both the caster's physical body and his possessions. He can change his coloration with a single action. All powers last for 2d6+CL turns.
22-25	As result 20-21 above, plus the caster gains the ability to run across bodies of water and other liquids without sinking. The caster suffers a -5' speed penalty, but otherwise treats the liquid as solid ground. He must remain moving for this ability to remain in effect. If he ceases to move for any reason, he sinks in the liquid immediately. All powers last for 1d4+CL hours.
26-29	As result 22-25 above, plus the caster grows a pair of poisonous fangs. The fangs grant him a bite +4 melee attack (1d6+Str modifier plus poison). Any creature bitten by the caster must make a DC 12 Fort save or suffer an additional 2d6 damage (half damage if save is successful). All powers last for 2d6+CL hours.
30-31	As result 26-29 above, but the caster's scales become harder and provide greater protection. His AC bonus increases to +8 and he gains a +4 Fort save bonus. All powers last for 3d6+CL hours.
32-33	As result 30-31 above, plus the caster is unaffected by great heat or arid conditions. Normal temperatures of 120° F or less have no debilitating effect on the caster and he can survive for long periods without the need of water. Additionally, he suffers half damage from magical heat-based attacks (one-fourth damage with a successful saving throw). All powers last for 24 hours.
34+	As result 32-33 above, plus the caster can completely transform himself into a giant lizard whenever he desires while the spell is in effect. The transformation takes an action to complete. When in this shape, the caster can still speak and cast spells. All his possessions are absorbed into the lizard's form and cannot be used while in lizard shape. As a giant lizard, the caster gains a total +10 AC bonus (includes benefits of above AC bonuses), MV 40' or swim 20', +15 hit points, and a bite +6 melee attack (3d4+Str modifier plus poison). The poison has the same effect as spell result 26-29 above. The caster can swap back and forth between his normal and giant lizard form as desired. This power and the ones above last for a number of days equal to his CL.

Shed the Lizard's Skin

Level: 3 (Yila-Keranuz)   Range: Self   Duration: Permanent   Casting time: 1 action   Save: N/A

General	The caster's skin sloughs away, taking injury, disease, poison, and similar afflictions with it at a cost to his physical body. The caster automatically loses the indicated number of ability points on a successful casting of this spell, but may choose which physical ability (Strength, Agility, and/or Stamina) may be affected.
Manifestation	Roll 1d4: (1) caster's skin becomes scaly and tattered, falling away in great ribbons that dissolve into green-tinted smoke; (2) minuscule lizards appear on the caster's body, nibbling away at his wounds and transforming it into unblemished skin; (3) a leathery egg encases the caster and then breaks apart, leaving him rejuvenated; (4) caster tears his flesh away with his bare hands to reveal unmarred flesh beneath it.
1	Lost, failure, and patron taint.
2-11	Lost. Failure.
12-15	Failure, but spell is not lost.
16-17	The caster's skin peels away like that of a shedding lizard, taking some of his wounds with him. The caster regains 1 hit point but loses 1 point from a physical ability of his choice in return.
18-21	The caster's skin peels away like that of a shedding lizard, taking some of his wounds with him. The caster regains 1 die of health but loses 1 point from a physical ability of his choice in return.
22-23	The caster's skin peels away like that of a shedding lizard, taking some of his wounds with him. The caster regains 2 dice of health but loses 2 points from one or more physical abilities of his choice in return.
24-26	The caster's skin peels away like that of a shedding lizard, taking some of his wounds with him. The caster regains 3 dice of health or cures himself of a single disease. The caster loses 3 points from one or more physical abilities of his choice in return.
27-31	The caster's skin peels away like that of a shedding lizard taking some of his wounds with him. The caster regains 4 dice of health, neutralizes the effects of a poison in his system, or cures himself of a single disease. The caster loses 4 points from one or more physical abilities of his choice in return.
32-33	The caster's skin peels away like that of a shedding lizard, taking some of his wounds with him. The caster regains 5 dice of health, neutralizes the effects of a poison in his system, or cures himself of a single disease. The caster loses 5 points from one or more physical abilities of his choice in return.
34-35	The caster's skin peels away like that of a shedding lizard, taking some of his wounds with him. The caster regains 5 dice of health, neutralizes the effects of a poison in his system, *and* cures himself of a single disease. The caster loses 6 points from one or more physical abilities of his choice in return.
36+	The caster's skin peels away like that of a shedding lizard, taking all of his wounds with him. The caster is restored to full hit points, cured of any diseases currently affecting him, and has any poison in his system neutralized. The caster loses 8 points from one or more physical abilities of his choice in return.

Chapter Eight
MAGIC ITEMS

for even the warrior can wield magic in a sword.

CRAFTING MAGIC RINGS

The crafting of magical items in *Dungeon Crawl Classics RPG* is not a labor undertaken lightly. The unpredictable nature of sorcery notwithstanding, the very process of creating and ensorcelling an object intended to rein in mystical powers is a complex undertaking capable of proving hazardous to life-and-limb. This article examines one possible method of crafting magical rings in a DCC RPG campaign.

The following information is provided as an option for judges to use in his game and should not be considered the 100% official, "this is the way it's done" method of magical ring enchantment. One of the most liberating traits of DCC RPG is that it's a game that readily lends itself to house ruling and judge creativity, allowing individual game masters to customize the game to their and their players' tastes. If this system works for your game, gladly embrace it, but if you prefer another method (or just want to keep your players on their toes), utilize that instead.

TO ENCHANT A RING

A wizard seeking to create a magical ring is essentially attempting to bind the wild forces of magic into a static state, limiting its highly chaotic nature by erecting metaphysical barriers to confine its fluctuations. Unlike when creating a scroll, potion, wand, staff, or other magical object that is expended with use, and thus allowing the imprisoned magic to return to its natural, wild state in the multiverse, a magic ring, like an enchanted sword, binds the ineffable paths of sorcery into an enduring and possibly permanent state. Doing so requires not only the knowledge of the proper spells to create an enchantment of a semi-predictable nature but also a uniquely created repository for that power.

Before a wizard or elf can embark on the creation of a magical ring, he must first acquire both the necessary mastery of the magical arts and discover the rare spell that binds sorcerous power into the ring to create the desired effects. In game terms this requires the spellcaster to achieve at least 7th level and to know the 4th-level wizard spell *enchant ring* (explained herein). This potentially allows the spellcaster to create a minor magical ring (see below). To manufacture a ring of more potent power, the spellcaster must rise to 8th or even 10th level! A spellcaster meeting both of these criteria can begin the task of creating a magic ring, but even with this knowledge, the chore is not an easy or safe one.

PROPOSING PROPERTIES

Before the wizard knows what steps are necessary to complete his task, the magnitude of the project must be evaluated. In order to gauge this, the spellcaster's player informs the judge of what properties he hopes to impart into the ring via the enchantment process. Although creating a magical ring is never simple, crafting one with minor powers is much easier than fabricating an object with nigh-legendary abilities.

Once the ring's desired powers are announced, the judge classifies the ring as either a *minor*, *major*, or *greater* ring. Each category has an effect on how difficult it is to successfully enchant the ring, what tasks must be undertaken to enspell it, and the ultimate cost of the enchantment.

A **minor ring** has a single power of small magnitude. Examples of a minor ring are ones that keep the wearer warm or cool in extreme climates (but provide no protection against magical heat or ice), grant the wearer infravision as if he were an elf or dwarf, or bestows a minor bonus to a single, mundane activity like swimming, climbing, carpentry, etc. (but not attack rolls, saving throws, AC, or spell checks). The ring's power is useful, but of limited impact.

A **major ring** possesses an enchantment superior to that of a minor ring. A major ring can duplicate a spell up to 3rd level in power, raise the wearer's abilities scores, or increase his AC, attack and damage rolls, or saving throw bonuses. Examples of major rings include the famous rings of invisibility, a ring that protects the wearer against magical fire, provides mystical armor, or fabulous strength. A major ring never bestows more than a single property or power on the wearer.

A **greater ring** is an object of immense power or one that can produce a number of different, lesser effects. Only the mightiest of wizards can create a greater ring. Greater rings can mimic spells of up to 5th level in power, bestow from two to five small bonuses or lower power spells on the wearer, grant the owner a single, spectacular benefit, or bind a powerful supernatural entity to it. Examples of greater rings include a ring of wishes, a ring that commands elementals, angels, or dragons, or a ring that transforms its wearer into a titan. Lifthrasir's Ring (see *DCC #85: The Making of the Ghost Ring*) is an example of a greater ring.

The judge is the final word on what class of ring the proposed item is based on the player's designs and may even rule that the player's goal is beyond the ability of mortal spellcasters to create if he deems the ring too powerful for the campaign. Tables 8-21, 8-23, and 8-25 below provide example powers of each ring class and will assist the judge in gauging the proposed power of a ring to determine its class. Once the classification is assigned, consult the following chart to determine if it's within the spellcaster's power to create, what the base penalty to the *enchant ring* spell check is, the minimum amount of time to create the ring, and the monetary cost of crafting it.

Table 8-14: Ring Class And Requirements

Ring Class	Minimum Spellcaster Level to Create	Enchant Ring spell check penalty	Creation Time	Crafting
Minor	7th	-4d	1 month	10,000 gp
Major	8th	-6d	5 to 8 (1d4+4) months	100,000 gp
Greater	10th	-8d	7 to 12 (1d6+6) months	500,000 gp

Before the caster can enchant a ring, he must first create the actual, physical ornament. Doing so requires painstaking labor combined with exotic substances, tools, and rare artisan techniques, making it a long and expensive process. The wizard first must spend half the ring's crafting cost as listed above to obtain rare, but mundane supplies prior to the fabrication of the ring. Once expended, crafting begins in earnest and the spellcaster can do nothing else during this stage but work on his ring (no adventuring) until the period given on the "Creation Time" column above has elapsed. Upon the conclusion of this time, the spellcaster can begin preparing the ring for its final enchantment by undertaking extraordinary measures.

STRANGE SUBSTANCES, FELL FORCES, AND WEIRD WORKINGS

Each class of ring imparts a base penalty to the spellcaster's action die when making a spell check for the *enchant ring* spell. Suffice to say that even a minor ring would require a substantial amount of spellburning to have a chance of success and a greater ring is impossible to fabricate with the applied penalty. Luckily for the spellcaster, this penalty can be reduced by undertaking various extraordinary steps during the creation process.

Theoretically, a wizard could spend the monies indicated on Table 8-14 above and create a jewelry masterpiece and potentially attempt to enchant it. Attempts to bind the wild forces of magic into such a base object, however, are likely to fail. In order for a ring to harness the power of sorcery, additional, highly unusual preparations must be undertaken. The caster might temper the ring in ghastly substances, employ supernatural assistants, bathe the band in eerie radiances, and otherwise go above and beyond the mundane to prepare the physical ring to receive enchantment. Each of these extraordinary steps increases the ring's suitability to house and constrain the magical forces placed within it. These extraordinary steps thereby reduce the difficulty of casting the final *enchant ring* spell.

In game terms, for each extraordinary step the wizard undertakes when crafting the ring, the base spell check penalty indicated on Table 8-14 is reduced by 1d. For example, a minor ring treated to four of the following unusual processes would have no penalty to the final *enchant ring* spell check. This fundamentally requires the wizard to go to extreme steps to create a magical ring, making the enchantment procedure far richer in atmosphere and more elevated in difficulty than simply expending time and money. This reflects the DCC RPG belief that magic is never mundane or predictable or without risk. As presented here, extraordinary efforts can only mitigate the *enchant ring* spell check penalty and never provide a bonus to the spell check even if the wizard undertakes more unusual methods than required to nullify the spell check modifier. However, there's nothing stopping a judge from granting a small bonus to the final spell check (+1 or +2 maximum) should he desire to reward a player who has demonstrated incredible determination and creativity during this stage of enchantment preparation.

The following charts provide a number of suggestions of unusual steps, substances, and other undertakings the spellcaster can employ. Some extraordinary steps affect rings of any class, while others may only affect one or two types of ring classes and be useless when crafting rings of grander power. Each suggestion bears notation in parentheses indicating the ring class(es) it affects.

Each table is also numerated, allowing the judge to randomly determine a specific requisite effect if desired. While the system provided in this article assumes the spellcaster will ultimately decide what extraordinary steps he undertakes to forge the ring, some judges may wish to assign the necessary steps themselves, creating a "recipe" for a specific ring that the spellcaster must follow explicitly to create a certain ring. In such cases, the judge need only roll on the tables below, rolling the appropriate die for the appropriate ring class: Minor, d10; Major, d8; Greater d4. Reroll if an effort is unsuitable or thematically inappropriate.

Table 8-15: Unique Band Materials

Roll*	The ring's band is made from…
1	A bone stolen from the Death Drake's animated skeleton (all).
2	Gold melted down from a gilded idol of the Goddess of Witches (all).
3	Iron plates ripped from a still-functioning golem (all).
4	Silver harvested from the Argent Mines of the Moon (all).
5	Wood carved from a treant's heart (minor or major).
6	The horn of a demon (minor or major).
7	Gold plundered from an archmage's tower (minor or major).
8	Platinum from a king's crown (minor or major).
9	The finger-bone of an apostate priest (minor).
10	Silver melted down from the coins on a dead man's eyes (minor).

Table 8-16: Jewels and Gemstones

Roll*	The ring is adorned with…
1	A fire opal stolen from the Temple of the Sacred Flame underneath the gaze of the Unforgiving Monks of Fiery Death (all).
2	A frozen tear of a fire giant (all).
3	A shard of amber containing a still-living abyssal fly (all).
4	An emerald stolen from the Serpent Demon-Queen's necklace (all).
5	A chip from one of the ruby eyes of the Horned Idol (minor or major).
6	A petrified bezoar cut from a medusa's stomach (minor or major).
7	One of the jewels of the Carnifax (minor or major).
8	A sapphire stolen from the brow of a lamia queen (minor or major).
9	A single diamond from the deepest jungles of the South (minor).
10	A pearl harvested from the giant, man-eating oysters of sunken Ru (minor).

Table 8-17: Unusual Assistants

Roll*	The ring is crafted with the aid of…
1	The spellcaster's twin from an alternate universe (all).
2	A hundred enslaved souls stolen from the Seventh Heaven (all).
3	A unicorn who inscribes the band with its horn (all).
4	A free-willed efreet (all).
5	A rival sorcerer's familiar (minor or major).
6	The ghost of an ancient dwarven master smith (minor or major).
7	The animated corpse of the wizard's true love (minor or major).
8	A blind jeweler from Far Kaathi of the Eastern Hell Wastes (minor or major).
9	An entire colony of helpful ants (minor).
10	A priest's shadow (minor).

Table 8-18: Strange Tempers

Roll*	The ring is tempered by/immersed in…
1	The frozen waters of the Sea of the Hollow World (all).
2	The blood-waters that surround the Court of Chaos (all).
3	The acidic tears of the Jester of Pandemonium (all).
4	The ghostly ichor of the First Sorcerer (all).
5	The dust of twenty mummy kings (minor or major).
6	The venom of a thirteen-headed hydra (minor or major).
7	The heart-blood of five score human sacrifices doomed on the Pyramid of the Green Sunset (minor or major).
8	The breath of a dragon (minor or major).
9	The blood of a virginal princess (minor).
10	The oily blood of a magical metal man (minor).

* For Tables 8-15 through 8-19: Roll the appropriate die depending on ring class: Minor, d10; Major, d8; Greater d4.

TABLE 8-19: EERIE RADIANCES

Roll*	The ring is exposed to the radiant power/vibrations of...
1	The ravaging solar winds of the Maelstrom Between the Stars (all).
2	A blast from the Horn of Hades sounded over the Unending Battlefield (all).
3	The sickening green glow spilling from the ruptured hull of an enchanted nuclear war engine (all).
4	The singing of a choir of angels (all).
5	The glowing eyes of the Troglodyte King (minor or major).
6	The howl of the Werewolf Lord (minor or major).
7	The light from the demon-haunted moon of Luhsaal (minor or major).
8	A newborn fairy's first laugh (minor or major).
9	The dying breath of an heirless emperor (minor).
10	A basilisk's gaze (minor).

There is no limit to how much time the caster has to apply extraordinary steps. Some rings require decades to properly treat as the wizard travels across the multiverse, undertaking daring measures to prepare the ring. Many a wizard dies before he completes this stage.

THE FINAL ENCHANTMENT

nce the spellcaster has completed all the extraordinary steps he intends to undertake, hopefully negating the spell check penalty in the process, the time has come for the final step: the enchantment of the ring. He pays the remaining 50% of the ring's crafting cost at this point and now holds a fully prepared ring in his hands.

The final enchantment of a ring is a process that cannot be stopped once begun, so the caster should be prepared both physically and magically (in good health, suffering no spellburn damage, ensconced in a sanctuary safe from surprise attacks, etc.). Should the enchantment process be interrupted, it results in a complete failure of the crafting of the ring and a loss of all expenses, ingredients, or benefits of extraordinary steps. Suffice to say, the wizard should ensure this does not happen!

If the spellcaster intends the ring to duplicate a spell effect such as *invisibility, fire resistance, magic shield*, etc. or if he desires the ring to be able to throw specific spells on command (*fireball, control ice, monster summoning*, etc.) he now casts those spell upon the ring. The spell check for each spell is made normally and the spellcaster may spellburn or expend Luck if desired. If the spell is successful, the judge notes the spell check result at this time. Should the spell fail, the caster must either spellburn to regain it and immediately recast it or forgo granting the ring that spell power or effect.

When the last spell is cast or if the ring is not intended to duplicate spell-like powers, the spellcaster casts *enchant ring*, spellburning, spending Luck, or otherwise influencing the spell check result. On a result of a natural 1, the crafting of the ring is a catastrophe and the spellcaster must start anew, losing all expended money, ingredients, etc. in the disaster.

If the spell check is successful, the judge consults the appropriate table noted in the *enchant ring* spell chart to determine the effectiveness of the ring. These tables also determine the potency of any spell or spell-like effect cast upon the ring during the final enchantment stage, including the maximum spell check result of a cast spell on the ring. Regardless of the result of the spell, its ultimate power cannot exceed the spell check presented on the tables. If the spellcaster's spell check is greater than the table allows, the imparted spell's effectiveness is reduced.

POTENCY TABLES

he following tables are used in conjunction with the *enchant ring* spell table to define the final power of a successfully enchanted ring. There is one table for each ring class (minor, major, and greater). Each ring class table also has an associated Ring Powers table. The Ring Powers tables are provided for two purposes: 1) to present a sample of potential powers a ring of each class might possess, allowing the judge to decide if a proposed ring is of that class type or not, and 2) to be utilized by the judge to randomly determine the magical properties and powers of a ring discovered by the party during their adventures. Simply roll on the subtable and apply the appropriate potency indicated on the main ring class table.

TABLE 8-20: MINOR RING POTENCY CHARACTERISTICS

Spell Check	D%	Power Range	Number of Uses	Maximum Benefit
18-19	01-50	A single skill.	Once per day	+1
20-23	51-75	A single skill.	Three times per day	+2
24-25	76-85	A single skill.	Three times per day	+4
26-28	86-90	A single skill or new physical ability or property.	Ongoing	+5
29-33	91-94	A single skill or new physical ability or property.	Ongoing	+7
34-35	95-96	A single skill or new physical ability or property.	Ongoing	+9
36-27	97-98	A single skill or new physical ability or property.	Ongoing	+10
38+	99-00	A single skill or new physical ability or property.	Ongoing	+12

Table 8-21: Minor Ring Powers

d10 Roll	Minor Ring Power
1	Grants bonus to a single physical skill (climbing, swimming, jumping, etc.).
2	Grants bonus to crafting skill of a single type (blacksmithing, brewing, carpentry, etc.).
3	Grants bonus to a single social activity (bargaining, performing, diplomacy, etc.).
4	Grants bonus to a single mental talent (poison identification, alchemy, history). Extraordinary skills such as spellcasting and *turn unholy* are beyond the power of a minor ring.
5	Grants bonus (or ability to use if not a thief) to a single thief skill (pick pocket, sneak silently, forge document, etc.).
6	Grants the wearer a physical racial ability of another species (infravision, smell gold, heightened senses, etc.). Extraordinary abilities such as a halfling's Luck is beyond the power of a minor ring.
7	Protects wearer non-magical from heat or cold (50/50 chance).
8	Allows wearer to alter a single minor physical characteristic (eye or hair color, skin complexion, facial hair, etc.).
9	Gives the wearer the ability to speak a single language (Roll on Appendix L table using "Wizard" column).
10	Allows the wearer to always know what direction is north.

Table 8-22: Major Ring Potency Characteristics

Spell Check	D%	Number of Uses (if bonus)	Number of Uses (if spell)	Maximum Bonus	Maximum Spell Check
24-25	01-75	Ongoing	Once per day	+1	17
26-28	76-85	Ongoing	Once per day	+2	21
29-33	86-94	Ongoing	Twice per day	+3	23
34-35	95-96	Ongoing	Twice per day	+4	26
36-27	97-98	Ongoing	Three times per day	+5	31
38+	99-00	Ongoing	Three times per day	+6	33

Table 8-23: Major Ring Powers

d10 Roll	Major Ring Power
1	Grants bonus to a single ability score.
2	Grants bonus to saving throws of a single type (Fort, Ref, or Will).
3	Grants bonus to AC.
4	Grants bonus to spell checks.
5	Grants bonus to attack or damage rolls. Roll 1d8: (1-3) attack rolls; (4-6) damage rolls; (7-8) both rolls.
6	Duplicates the effects of a 1st-level spell.
7	Duplicates the effects of a 2nd-level spell.
8	Duplicates the effects of a 3rd-level spell.
9	Gives the wearer the ability to speak a single language (Roll on Appendix L table using "Wizard" column).
10	Allows the wearer to always know what direction is north.

Table 8-24: Greater Ring Potency Characteristics

Spell Check	D%	Number of Uses (if bonus)	Number of Uses (if spell)	Maximum Bonus	Maximum Spell Check	Maximum Spell Check (if multiple spells)
34-35	1-90	Ongoing	Once per day	+5	29	21
36-27	91-98	Ongoing	Twice per day	+10	34	23
38+	99-00	Ongoing	Three times per day	+15	36	26

Table 8-25: Greater Ring Powers

d10 Roll	Greater Ring Power
1	Grants one wish per "# of uses (if spell)" per day.
2	Commands creature of a single type (dragons, giants, elves, etc.) as if under the effects of a *charm person* spell.
3	Wearer automatically succeeds on saving throws of a certain type (Fort, Ref, or Will).
4	Supernatural creature (elemental, efreet, demon, etc.) is bound to the ring and must serve his owner.
5	Grants wearer total immunity from a single form of attack (swords, clubs, teeth, claws, etc.).
6	Duplicates the effects of 1d4+1 1st-level spells.
7	Duplicates the effects of 1d3+1 2nd-level spells.
8	Duplicates the effects of 1d2+1 3rd-level spells.
9	Duplicates the effects of a 4th-level spell.
10	Duplicates the effects of a 5th-level spell.

Spell Check: The final *enchant ring* spell check result.

D%: This column can be used by the judge to determine the potency of a randomly discovered ring.

Power Range: Determines whether the ring grants a benefit to a skill or action or if it provides the wearer with a new physical ability or power.

Number of uses: Indicates the number of times per 24 hour period a ring's power can be called upon. Once per day allows the wearer to apply the benefit once to a single check. Three times per day allows three uses of the skill bonus. Ongoing means the wearer benefits from the bonus or can use the given ability whenever he desires so long as the ring is worn.

Maximum Benefit: The bonus the ring grants to skill checks (if applicable).

Maximum Bonus: The bonus the ring grants to a single activity, facet, ability, or other game property. This includes ability scores, AC, attack rolls, damage rolls, saving throws, spell checks, etc.

For Rory the Ringmaster, magical corruption had come in "handy".

EXAMPLE OF ENCHANTING A RING

Ekim the Numinous, still smarting from a spell duel with Sezrekan, decides to create a ring of fire to even the odds the next time the two meet. Ekim's player tells his judge that he wants the ring to both protect him from fire, allow him to throw fireballs, and summon a fire elemental. The judge reviews the request and easily determines the proposed ring would be a greater ring (multiple spell-like abilities). Reviewing the rulebook, the judge notes that all of the ring's proposed powers can be reproduced with 3rd-level or lesser spells, notably *fireball, fire resistance,* and *demon summoning* (with a little tweaking). The judge declares that Ekim can attempt to create the ring, but at a -8d penalty. This reduces Ekim's spell check die to a d5. He'll need to take some extraordinary steps to have a chance of success.

Ekim spends half of the ring's 500,000 gp cost acquiring the necessary materials to create the ring, a process which takes eight months (the judge rolls 1d6+6 and the result is 2 on the die). Once that period passes, during which time Ekim can only work on the ring, he can then undertake the extraordinary steps to ensure success. He begins by stealing a golden statue from the Plane of Fire to melt down and recast as the ring's band. While on that plane, Ekim also captures a wisp of fire from the Efreeti King's inner sanctum and acquires a flame ruby from the brow of the Inferno Queen. Returning to his home plane, Ekim next convinces an ancient dragon wizard to breathe fire upon the band, convinces a fire elemental to take it to the bottom of a volcano's throat, and sacrifices an elder flame salamander over the ring, spilling its smoking blood on the object. Finally, the wizard slays a brass golem and washes the ring in the construct's fiery fluids, and, as a last measure, blasts the ring with sunlight amplified by shining through the Conflagration Stone of Lost H'Lalag. These eight steps nullify the -8d penalty, bringing Ekim's spell check die back to d20. Note that Ekim could continue to take additional measures, but they would not further modifier his spell check die. Satisfied he's done his best to prepare the ring for enchantment, Ekim enters the final stages of the crafting process.

Looking to protect himself from magical fire, Ekim casts *fire resistance* on the ring, getting a spell check result of 26. The judge make a note of the spell check result. Next, Ekim attempts to bind a *fireball* spell into the ring, with a spell check result of 22. The judge notes this spell check result as well. Lastly, Ekim wants to give the ring the power to summon a fire elemental. Lacking a spell that specifically targets elementals but knowing a thing about demons, Ekim attempts to call a fire elemental using a modified version of *demon summoning*. The judge deems the attempt possible, but imparts a -1d penalty on the *demon summoning* spell check for the difficulties involved in conjuring an elemental without the appropriate spell. Ekim rolls a 2 on his *demon summoning* spell check which, even after applying his level and Intelligence modifiers, still fails. Ekim could spellburn at this point to regain *demon summoning* and attempt to cast it again, burn Luck to increase the failed spell check result or accept the failure. Deciding he'll need all the Luck and spellburning potential he can muster for the *enchant ring* spell check, Ekim sighs and accepts the failure, hoping he'll never need to conjure a fire elemental in the midst of battle.

With the two successful spells bound to the ring, Ekim finally casts *enchant ring*. Knowing he needs a minimum spell check result of 34 to create a greater ring, Ekim's player decides to spellburn 15 points and burn 3 points of Luck. Ekim's player crosses his fingers and throws the die, resulting a final spell check of 34! Ekim spends 2 more Luck for a final result of 36. The effort has left him a broken shell physically and unlucky, but he has successfully enchanted a magical ring.

The judge now consults **Table 8-24: Greater Ring Potency Characteristics** to determine the final results. Ekim's *fire resistance* spell check was 26, which exceeds the maximum spell check result for multiple spells as given on Table 9. The effective spell check (and therefore the protection of) the *fire resistance* spell is reduced to 23. The judge then compares the *fireball* spell check with Table 8-24. The *fireball* spell check of 22 does not exceed the maximum of 23 so is allowed to stand unmodified.

Ekim has successfully created a ring that allows him to ignore up to 10 hp of fire damage each round for 1 turn and protect nearby allies, as well as granting him a +4 bonus to fire-related saving throws. The ring can also throw a bouncing *fireball* that jumps to 1d4+1 different targets. Both of these power can be used three times per day. Although lacking the ability to call up a fire elemental, Ekim is nonetheless pleased. Once he recovers physically, he intends to visit Sezrekan for some payback!

PARTING WORDS

There is a scarcity of magical rings in the world and this article demonstrates precisely why that is. Crafting an enchanted ring requires not only a staggering level of magical knowledge, but a mountain of gold and the wherewithal to undertake life-threating steps to ensure success. And given that there is only a small minority of spellcasters capable of creating even a minor enchanted trinket, those who do succeed in reining in magical power and confining it into a ring are loathe to let the object out of their possession. A wizard who owns a magical ring either risked his life to craft it himself or—even more frightening—slayed one with the power to create it. Neither is likely to let another take it without a fight.

A PC spellcaster who forges a magical ring (or assists in the creation of one such as in *DCC #85: The Making of the Ghost Ring*) has achieved something few of his fellow sorcerers ever shall. His name will echo down the corridors of Time and the ring itself will serve as his legacy after his bones are dust. Are you wizard enough to scrawl your name on the pages of history and craft a ring to be remembered in future eons?

PATRON WEAPONS

As all wizards know, the contract between spellcaster and patron is built upon mutual respect. Through the exchange of gifts and acts of service, the bond between the two grows into a form of symbiosis. For those who remain respectful and strive to strengthen the relationship, serving a patron can be a rewarding experience.

Over time, though, some spellcasters become complacent or convinced of their own prepotency. Woe to those who forget the old adage: *The shark does not take direction from the remora.* It is never wise to undermine one's patron or fall into arrears in the delicate economy of favors. The numinous beings are notoriously mercurial, and the collection of overdue debt may arrive on wings both harsh and swift.

Enraged patrons have been known to afflict their most egregious debtors with boils, disease, and powerful hexes until the spellcaster makes good on overextended credit. In extreme cases, patrons have even imprisoned delinquents within weapons, armor, and other trinkets (though there is usually a quest that can be performed to regain freedom). These living weapons are called "patron weapons"—intelligent magic items created from living beings cursed by their former benefactors.

Such was the fate of Coefax the Clever. The quick-talking pyromancer possessed an even quicker temper, which he foolishly directed at his patron, Sezrekan the Elder. The Old Master imprisoned the impudent wretch's mind within three small rubies and set them into an iron ring. The item was dubbed the *band of fire* as it retained some of the arcanist's power. Coefax was cursed to remain imprisoned within the gemstones until his debt of service had been repaid, though the haughty pyromancer was never heard from again. The magic ring was lost many years ago, but the cautionary tale is whispered to this day. Never forget who is master and whom the servant.

LIVING WEAPONS

hough the actual manner of transformation can vary greatly, all those who have experienced transmogrification from living being to inanimate object describe it as agonizing and traumatic. Some patrons reshape warm flesh into cold steel while others prefer to rip the psyche from the body and implant it into an item of their choosing. Pick a manifestation for the patron's curse from the list below or create your own.

- The caster's body falls into a deep slumber and cannot be roused. The caster's mind awakes imprisoned within a patron weapon. The sleeping body must be cared for or it will waste away.

- The caster—including all carried possessions—polymorphs into a patron weapon. The transformation might be slow and painful (akin to lycanthropy), or sudden (e.g., a lightning bolt strikes the caster, who disappears and is replaced by a patron weapon that clatters to the floor).

- The caster is transported to an extradimensional prison plane, leaving behind a patron weapon. The caster dimly perceives and influences the material world through the patron weapon. While in limbo, the caster does not require food or water.

- The caster is transformed into a black gem that can communicate with anyone who touches it through empathy or telepathy. The gem has no other powers until it is placed in a ring, sword pommel, or other gemstone setting.

Being transformed into a patron weapon greatly reduces the afflicted character's agency. The character stops gaining experience points and levels for the duration of their imprisonment in the patron weapon. At this point, the player may choose to retire the character or the judge can come up with a way for this adventurer to remain in the campaign world. Several suggestions are listed below.

- The patron sends a new follower to collect the magic weapon. The follower has identical ability scores of the patron weapon character. This follower is essentially a clone of the original character, but restarts at level one.

- The character's mind is sucked into a carried item, though he or she can still control the body as long as the item remains in physical contact. Should the character be disarmed, the body falls to the floor in a coma state. Furthermore, the caster loses all normal spellcasting abilities outside of those granted through the patron weapon.

CREATING PATRON WEAPONS

atron weapons are created from living beings cursed by their former patrons. While it may seem a misnomer to call a shield a "weapon", all doubt is erased the first time a flurry of magic missiles bursts from

its surface. Regardless of the severity of the crime, there is always some task or condition that can be fulfilled to lift the patron's curse.

Follow the procedure below to create a patron weapon:

- First determine the item the character is imprisoned within by rolling on Table 8-26. Alternately, if the patron has a favored or iconic weapon, use that instead.
- If the item is a melee or ranged weapon, the item receives a bonus to attack and damage equal to half the caster's level (round down).
- If the item is a shield, the item receives a bonus to AC equal to half the caster's level (round down).
- Next, assign the item the same alignment and Intelligence score as the cursed character.
- Then, reference the imprisoned character's Intelligence score on Table 8-27. Powers come from the Sword Magic tables (DCC RPG, pp. 370-371). Normal spells are determined randomly from the cursed character's list of known spells. Patron spells are determined randomly from the entire list of the patron's unique spells, and the character need not have learned it. If the Intelligence score indicates a spell of higher level than the character knows, discard that portion of the result. The spell die indicates the action die used by non-casters using the patron weapon. Non-casters apply their class level as a bonus to the spell check, but not their Intelligence modifier. Wizards and elves make spell checks as normal.
- If the item has a power, roll d% on Sword Magic tables 8-7, 8-8, and/or 8-9 in the DCC RPG core rulebook for each power (pp. 370-371).
- Finally, roll on Table 8-27 to determine the conditions that must be met to release the character from the patron weapon. The trapped character must compel his or her bearer to complete the task.

Table 8-26: Item of Imprisonment

d10 Roll	Item
1-5	Melee weapon (same type as PC's primary melee weapon)
6-7	Ranged weapon (same type as PC's primary ranged weapon)
8-9	Shield
10	A ring, amulet, or other item of jewelry

Table 8-27: Patron Weapon Characteristics

Intelligence	Communication	Powers	Spells	Spell Die*
4-7	Empathy	25% chance of one type I power	1st-level patron spell (1/day)	1d10
8-12	Empathy	50% chance of one type I power	1st-level patron spell (1/day) and one 1st level spell (1/day)	1d12
13-15	Speech	One type I power, 25% chance of one type II power	One 1st–3rd-level patron spell (1/day) and two 1st-level spell (1d3/day)	1d16
16-17	Telepathy	Two type I powers, 50% chance of one type II power	One 1st–3rd-level patron spell (1/day), two 1st-level spells (1d3/day each), and one 2nd-level spell (1/day)	1d20
18	Speech and Telepathy	1d3 powers of type I or II (50% chance of either for each power), 25% chance of one type III power	Two 1st–5th-level patron spells (1/day each), three 1st-level spells (1d4/day each), two 2nd-level spells (1/day), and one 3rd-level spell (1/day)	1d24

* Spell die is for non-casters. Spell check is made as spell action die + class level.

Table 8-28: Curse Removal

Roll 1d30	Task
1	Seek out and slay an adult or older dragon, and then turn over the entire hoard to the patron's coffers.
2	Kill or capture the champion of a rival patron or deity.
3	Steal a powerful artifact from a stronghold of the world's largest thieves' guild and gift it to the patron.
4	Construct a monument in the image of the patron. Construction costs vary, but a suitable commemoration will cost upwards of 10,000 gp.
5	Extract three droplets of blood from the right breast of a queen and rub them on the patron weapon.
6	Infiltrate the ice tower of the demon-wizard Baalsha, sneak into his hibernation chamber, and cut off his beard without rousing him.
7	Travel to a distant land and bathe in the cool waters of the Fountain of Forgiveness.
8	Drive all the followers of a rival patron or deity from the city.
9	Induct 50 new followers into the service of the patron.
10	Protect the patron weapon's new bearer until he or she completes a difficult quest. If the bearer dies, the patron weapon must attract a new bearer and complete the task.
11	Behead the seventh son of a seventh son.
12	Slay a rival patron or lesser god, thereby extinguishing their magic from the cosmos for all eternity.
13	The weapon bearer must write the patron's name at the bottom of the deepest chasm beneath the sea.
14	The weapon bearer must write the patron's name on the top of the highest mountain peak.
15	Receive true love's kiss from a prince or princess.
16	Travel to a hostile plane and slaughter a black goat on the altar of an alien temple.
17	Receive a greater blessing from an archbishop or pope.
18	Topple a great wizard's tower. (The wizard must have a caster level of 9 or higher.)
19	Transfer the curse to another follower of the patron by cleaving or puncturing the follower's heart with the patron weapon.
20	Extinguish the life of three virgins.
21	Curry the favor of the Archwitch Wallace who will extract the curse in a physical form and boil it away in a bubbling cauldron.
22	Reflect the patron weapon's image at a medusa with a mirror.
23	Show kindness to a small woodland creature.
24	End the life of a true friend.
25	Show kindnesses three: give alms to a beggar; feed a hungry child; and wash the feet of an elderly cripple.
26	Strike a storm giant dead.
27	Show humility for a year and a day.
28	Dedicate the souls of one hundred hit dice of creatures to the patron.
29	Discover the true name of another patron.
30	Roll again twice.

WIELDING PATRON WEAPONS

Patron weapons are among the most coveted and rare of all armaments. The supernatural lords sometimes lead the followers that most please them to these mighty weapons. Followers of the patron receive an additional boon when wielding their patron's weapon. If the item is a melee or ranged weapon, the wielder gets an additional +1 bonus to attack and damage. In the case of shields, the follower does not incur the usual -1 check penalty for carrying a shield. Worn items—such as rings, necklaces, and circlets—grant a +1 bonus to all spell checks.

Extreme caution should be exercised when using the powers of a patron weapon around strangers. Openly brandishing one of these weapons in a city is sure to attract brigands and cutpurses looking to turn a fat profit. Wielders of patron weapons who are members of institutions such as an organized religion or thieves' guild may be strongly coerced to relinquish the weapon to a higher-ranking member.

Patron weapons are almost invariably created from mortals with intense personalities. It takes quite a bit of chutzpah to repeatedly defy a supernatural being. When attacking with or using one of the patron weapon's powers, there is always a chance that the weapon personality can overpower its bearer. Whenever a maximum number is rolled on an action die expended to use a patron weapon's attack or powers (e.g., a natural 20 on a d20, or a 24 on a d24), the bearer must make an ego check (a Will save opposed by the patron weapon's Intelligence). If the Will save fails, the bearer becomes dominated by the patron weapon's personality. The patron weapon yearns only to be free, and will act in its best interest to end the curse (though always in a manner consistent with its alignment). The bearer may attempt to regain control of their body with a reversed ego check (d20 + its weapon bonus opposed by the bearer's Intelligence). The reversed ego check can be attempted whenever a maximum number is rolled on a die, or in the following situations:

- If the bearer has a greater Intelligence score than the weapon, the reverse ego check can be made after a number of hours equal to the difference between the bearer and the patron weapon's Intelligence scores.

- If the patron weapon has a greater Intelligence score than the bearer, the reverse ego check can be made after a number of days equal to the difference between the bearer and the patron weapon's Intelligence scores.

As a nearly immortal being, there are no limits on the actions the patron weapon can make when it is in control of the bearer's body. If the weapon believes killing its bearer is in its best interest, it will do so without remorse. If the dominated bearer is slain, the weapon's Intelligence returns to its item of imprisonment. The domination effect can only be negated by destroying the patron weapon, a feat that can be achieved by throwing the item into an active volcano, an extremely successful *dispel magic* or *remove curse* spell, or other equally powerful means.

MYSTERIOUS MANUSCRIPTS, MONOGRAPHS AND MANUALS

A Narrative of Compelling Antediluvian Histories: This thick volume, bound in a cover of pale green fish scales, is a chronicle of the courtiers of ancient Poseidonis, telling of their loves, losses, duels and deaths. It is so compelling to the contemporary reader that having started, the reader must make a DC 14 Willpower save to stop reading the volume, which requires 5d3+3 hours. When completed, the reader must make a DC 14 save to resist the compulsion to seek out Volume II at any cost. The reader's absorption into the narrative is so complete that until such time as the Volume II is acquired the reader is able to breathe and move freely underwater, just as the subjects of the novel did.

The Manual of Obscene Predators: This useful book, bound between two plates of unearthly multi-hued metal, details the bizarre creatures that haunt the phlogiston, including descriptions of their weaknesses, methods and diets. The judge should endeavor to give the reader a clear advantage in-game for reading this tome, such as knowledge of how to tempt or trick the predator with its favorite prey, or where it lairs in order to catch it unawares. However, if no such knowledge is useful in a given scenario, the reader should have a +1d to attack and +1d to inflict damage upon the well-researched beast. For every creature so referenced, there is a cumulative 1% chance of accidentally summoning the phlogistonal entity to which a reader most recently referred.

The Testament of Q'rex the Damned: This bundle of brittle, yellowed pages is kept in a sack made from the skin of orphans. A DC 15 Intelligence check is needed to understand the eccentric script and ancient language of the author, a wizard of forgotten Metazothik. The opening pages promise to reveal great power if the work is read in its entirety. Unfortunately for the reader, the memoir is actually a ritualistic spell: Anyone perusing the tome's entirety must make a DC 16 Willpower save. Failing that, the reader will have the writer's intellect imprinted upon their own, immediately gaining the powers, personality and restrictions of the 6th-level wizard. A worshipper of Chaos, Q'rex will immediately set about finding his whalebone tower and pursuing his ancient grudge against Eesphew, the God of the Broken Claw.

The Almanac of Holcomb Hollow: This thin rose-colored cover hides a volume that is literally transporting. Ostensibly, the book appears to be a list of facts about a quiet, sleepy region untouched by war or want. Anyone perusing the first chapter disappears and is taken to a small pastoral acreage in a hidden dimension which accommodates a sunny, wind-rippled meadow and a pure, bubbling brook. The cozy one-room cottage has its own copy of the book and the reader must spend 2d3 hours reading the remainder to return to his reality. Each time the reader returns to the hollow, he must make a Luck check. A result of natural 20 indicates that the reality has been invaded by the Arch-Obscenity Lo-Kwan the Reality Eater, who will turn the pleasant bower into a hellish swamp of boiling blood habited by venomous living whips.

Rumptilion's Legacious Repository: This spellbook's front cover is a formed leathern replica of the caster's face, complete with a lifelike trailing white beard. Transcribed at the end of Rumptilion's long life, it includes 5 spells of each level. However the declining Rumptilion's transcriptions were imperfect and when learning a spell from the tome, the caster must roll 1d3 and take that penalty on the spell thereafter (unless relearned from a different source.) The last 18 pages are an off-putting account of the archmage's amorous exploits.

MALOPHOS

Malophos: Init +0; Atk by spell; AC 10; HD 2d4; hp 4; MV 30'; Act 1d16; SP spellcasting, aid casting (+2); SV Fort +1, Ref -2, Will +4; AL L.

Spells (+2 check): *cantrip, choking cloud, comprehend languages, magic shield, read magic, sleep,* and *ward portal.*

Malophos has acted as the living lectern of a cabal of wizards for decades. He began his career as a scullion, *charm*ed into this greater role as required, but soon his capacity for holding still for long periods, coupled with a surprising aptitude for harnessing occult forces, granted Malophos freedom from the kitchens. Indeed, although deformed by his new position, it has granted him high status among those who serve the cabal. Where once Malophos was ensorcelled to his task, he comes now proud and eager to the call.

When called upon to serve, various heavy arcane tomes are placed upon his back. So long has he performed this duty that he is permanently hunched over, his broad torso forming a stable platform for the occult volumes entrusted him. Malophos walks on all fours, using hands and feet with equal dexterity. Indeed, he can no longer stand in any other way.

His curious occupation has accustomed Malophos to magical energies, and he can intone incantations along with a wizard or elf reading from his back, granting a +2 bonus to the spell check. Over the years, he has learned several first level wizard spells, which he casts using 1d16+2 for his spell check. These are used to protect any grimoire he is entrusted with, as well as his own person and his sundry masters.

The judge should note that, although Malophos is lawful, and is devoted to the cabal he serves, his masters may be quite different in alignment. The servant's loyalty need not be reflected in those he serves.

THE LIVING BOOK BEARER OF FAN AGESTPO

Living book bearer of Fan Agestpo: Init -2; Atk none; AC 6; HD 2d8+4; MV 20'; Act 1d20; SP Personality drain, regeneration; SV Fort +5, Ref -2, Will -5; AL C.

It has been many aeons since the arch-warlock Fan Agestpo walked the surface of Áereth, yet many of his creations endure. Countless "living compositions" were shaped in the magician-artist's alchemical vats, but few evoke more pity or horror than the being Agestpo created to bear his grimoires.

This being has the headless body of a man and woman melded together front-to-back, so that their four legs provide crabwise locomotion. Their hands are free to hold open whatever book is placed upon them, or to turn pages as commanded. Upon the book bearer's abdomen is a face of an evil-visaged ape, which growls and gibbers incessantly. Although the being needs no food, it hungers, and it can only feed upon flesh, milk, or blood. The whole is garishly colored, as if painted by a madman with a brush.

The living book bearer seeks always to serve, but any who comes into contact with it (unless using special protections which Fan Agestpo kept secret) must make a DC 10 Will save or suffer a permanent loss of 1d3 Personality. If a being's Personality drops below 3 in this manner, they immediately seek another victim of the same process, to meld into a new book bearer. In this way, Fan Agestpo kept his lectory safe from the depredations of biblioklepts, and created additional servants to hold his books. The book bearer is not malicious, but does crave contact, and the judge may call for Luck checks to avoid contact when interacting with the creature. If a wizard or elf comes within 30' of the book bearer, it will automatically attempt to serve them, following them around as a repository for books the caster wishes to read.

In fact, it is only when the wizard is reading that the living book bearer remains absolutely still, and is of no danger to its new "master"!

This pitiful being cannot be slain by any mortal means. It regenerates 1d3 hp per turn, and even if completely disintegrated will reform over the course of 1d5 months. Additional book bearers created through contact with the original do not share this trait.

TABLE 8-29: BOOKS FOUND ON THE BACK OF A RANDOM BOOK BEARER

d20 Roll	Volume
1	*Linguistic Curiosities Within the Language of Heaven*, by Saint Ubration the Minor
2	*A Catalogue of Lost Volumes Purported to Be in the Lair of the Dragon Helluo Liborum*, by Fan Agestpo
3	*Folk Recipes from the Shudder Mountains*, by M. Curtis
4	*Occult Potentialities of Metal Lyrics*, by Bena S. Fugue
5	*Demons, Devils, & Diverse Beings in Illumination*, by Gudo Scovak
6	*Cantraips and Enchantments of Household Use*, by H. Shea
7	*Apoptosis for Occultists*, by Argute
8	*Alchemy of the Flesh Vats*, by Ostanes, the Persian
9	*Metallurgy and Medicine*, by Nágárjuna
10	*Canorous Songs of the Exsanguinated*, by Carmila Karnstein
11	*Kith, Elder Kith, and Elder Kindred: Evolutionary Connexions Between Planes and Worlds*, by the Honorable Torsh
12	*Alchemistry of Eviternity*, by Famulus
13	*Benthos of the Sunless Sea*, by A. J. Porter and A. Perry
14	*Vocal Projection and the Arte of the Pitchperson*, by Robert Edgefellow
15	*ACHROMA Service and Technical Manual*, v. 3.14 (no author given)
16	*Ye Theory & Practice of Transformation, or, Teaching Lead to become Gold Within the Human Form*, by Hermes Trismegistus
17	*Treasures of the Mudlarks*, by Merrythought
18	*Investigation of the Astroblemes of Madkeen*, by Al-Khazadar
19	*Occult Secrets of Beauty*, by Lord M. the Callipygian
20	*Under the Raven's Wing; Liturgy and Rituals of Malotoch*, by Phobis

NAMED SWORDS
LAKSHAMORDA

Marzalum Varza, the notorious pirate queen, made many enemies. Among the most terrible of them were the Seven Corsairs, elven raiders of great renown. While her fleet was mighty, and her band of reavers was stalwart, she was no match for the combined powers of the Seven Corsairs. The pirate queen would need an edge in her coming confrontation with them, so she sought a blade capable of thwarting the insolent elves and their baneful magics.

She summoned to her island fastness legendary smiths and wizards from every land, offering wealth and power to any who could fulfill her demands. Most refused her call, fearing the Seven Captains and their kin. Only one, Vorlonus the Blind, whose vendetta against the King of Elfland was legendary, would promise her the results she sought.

Vorlonus forged the blade from an alloy of mithril and steel, making it light and strong. The resulting amalgam of metals also enhanced the harmful effects of the iron to any elf cut with it. He engraved the blade with runes of protection against magic. The hilt and hardware were made in a brazen mockery of elven styles, Vorlonus going so far as to decorate it with the braided hair of the three elven maidens sacrificed to power the magic of its making. He named the blade *Lakshamorda* after the region of the Dreamlands where nightmares dwell.

Lakshamorda is a +2 scimitar (+4 to attacks and damage against elves and fey) with the following traits and powers:

- Intelligence 8.
- Causes obsession for taking by theft and piracy.
- When wielding the blade the user must make a DC 10+level Will save to retreat from battle with elves and fey.
- Detect elves at 500'.
- Critical hits against elves are made as a warrior of one level higher.
- Magic resistance (-2 to spells targeting wielder, and -4 to spells cast by elves).

HEKANHODA'S FINGERED FEMUR

efore ascending to the Court of Chaos, Hekanhoda, Lord of Grotesques, spell-forged a dagger. Tempering his blood and pus into a blade, and using one of his three deformed femurs as the hilt, Hekanhoda made a weapon to shape the multiverse into his own corrupted image. To ensure the blade sowed pain and sorrow, the Grotesque One used it to slay his own familiar, whose yellow-furred hide composes the scabbard.

To wield this formidable dirk, one must affix his own finger to the hilt; this completes the bond between wielder and weapon. The digit is consumed when the weapon spreads corruption, but the blade ensures that the wielder never runs out of fingers (see below). Prolonged contact causes minor corruption, unless the *Fingered Femur* is sheathed in its yellow-furred scabbard.

The history of the dagger's wielders is long, spanning races, classes, and even alignments. The most recent wielder of note is the grotesquemancer Nekros, though there are rumors that the quasit Elzemon has stolen it.

Use the following for running *Hekanhoda's Fingered Femur* in-game:

- +2 chaotic dagger, Int 12, communicates by empathy.
- Its goal is to spread arcane corruption.
- It refuses to be thrown, falling to the ground instead.
- The wielder is immune to disease; corruption does not suffer competition.
- On a critical hit, instead of rolling on his crit table, the attacker does 1d7 additional damage, and inflicts a randomly chosen corruption. He may make a DC 15 Will save to avoid this.
- Upon inflicting corruption, the PC grows 1d3 more fingers from some part of his body. The blade loses its abilities (including the +2 bonus) until the wielder attaches another of his fingers.
- Arcane casters wielding the blade automatically suffer corruption if a failed spell check indicates it as a possibility.

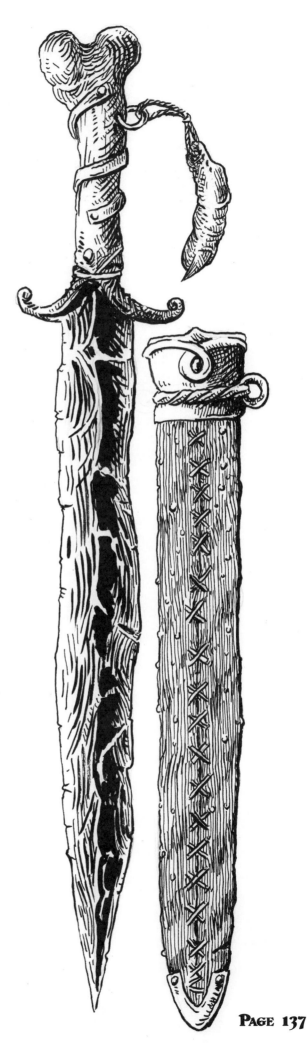

THE CRYMSTALLA

his short sword is made of living vermillion crystal from deep beneath Áereth. It glows with an unquenchable sanguine light equal to torchlight – even fully sheathed or wrapped, it gives off radiance equal to a candle.

This sword has a brooding, alien intelligence which sprang into existence before the first fish crawled from the sea. A shard from a greater crystal-based mind, it was first fashioned into a weapon by ancient reptilian pre-humans, and has been a weapon in one form or another ever since.

The *Crymstalla* is a +3 short sword, which increases the critical range of its wielder by 1 (i.e., a level 5 warrior armed with the *Crymstalla* rolls a critical hit on any successful attack of 17-20.) It is neutral, not caring about the eternal conflict between Law and Chaos.

When a creature is reduced to 0 hit points by the weapon, it becomes infected by minute shards left in the wounds (unless its body is completely destroyed by fire, acid, or magic). These shards grow at an astounding rate, converting the creature to crystalline un-dead over a period of 2d3 days. The creature then pursues its slayer with unceasing bloodlust. When the sword's owner is killed, all existing crystalline un-dead are reduced into fine crimson powder within the next 1d5 rounds.

Crystalline un-dead use the same statistics as their base creature, with the following changes:

- AC is increased by +3.
- Hit Dice become d12s, with hit points rerolled.
- All physical damage (bite, claw, etc.) is increased by +1d on the dice chain.
- Gain un-dead immunities, but can be turned by lawful and neutral clerics.
- Cannot be harmed by the *Crymstalla*.
- Retain special abilities of the base creature on a case-by-case basis, as determined by the judge. Physical abilities are retained, while supernatural ones may or may not be.

WITHERLEAF ELFSLAYER AKA S'KATH'S VENGEANCE

'kath S'karroth, the Lizard King, in his great cavernous realm eons ago, forged this cruel weapon to repel incursions of elvenkind from the valley above. A sorcerer and a flesh-weaver, S'karroth twisted the bodies and souls of captured elven lords and fused their warped essences onto a blade of cold iron, winding slices of their stretched skin onto the hilt of the very sword that he would use to slay their brethren.

Flaring with red-tinged golden spirals of energy coursing around the blade, this neutral two-handed +2 sword throbs like a frantic heartbeat if any living elf steps within 50'.

The crude runes on the iron translate roughly from lizard-speech to read, "Death to elvenkind," and "The forests must fall."

The sword's whispered communication is a rumble of guttural lizard-speech and corrupted elvish lamentations, with an Intelligence of 8, audible to anyone in contact with the hilt. The weapon has the following characteristics:

- Its goal is to destroy all elves.
- It seeks dark underground regions and loathes forested areas on the surface.
- Adds +1d to attack and damage vs. elves.
- Any mithril in contact with the blade is treated as if targeted by a shatter spell with an unmodified d30 die roll to determine the result (any result of 13 or lower simply counts as failure).
- The red-gold energy whirling around the blade creates a 10' radius of light.
- Green plant-life within 30' of the sword withers and dies while sentient plant life takes 1d6 damage per round.
- Any human or humanoid in possession of this sword for six consecutive days or more becomes bonded with it, losing 1d10 hit points from his maximum and taking 1d30 damage for each hour he is separated from the sword thereafter.
- The flesh-weaving sorceries that helped to craft this weapon remain captured in its whirling energy field, allowing a bonded wielder to cast polymorph on himself or anything touching the sword with an unmodified d30 die roll to determine the result – with "lost," "failure," "misfire," etc. still possible.

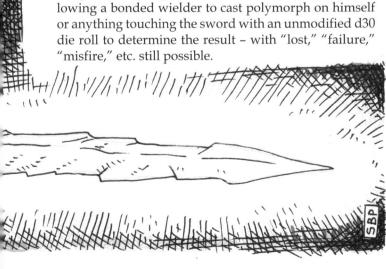

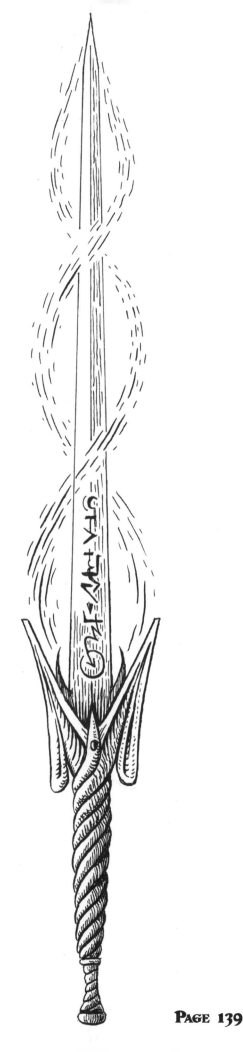

DRACO MAXILLAM HELIXA

Centuries ago, the notorious and feared despot Høck the Cruel commanded the champions of his domain to rid the lands of a menace whose appetite for death and power matched his very own: the ice dragon Helixa. Scores of human heroes and ancient elves perished in the ensuing melee, but eventually the great white wyrm Helixa lay dead.

And, lo, while it is well known that some breeds of dragons will re-grow teeth all their lives to replace those they've lost, Høck's dark mage's found a way to continue sprouting fangs on their jaws even in death! Armed with such knowledge, Høck the Cruel forced his black sages to sacrifice entire villages of children to fuel the demon sorcery needed to forge what was to become *Draco Maxillam Helixa*: the jaw of Helixa the ice dragon.

The bone-white shortsword is constructed from one of Helixa's jawbones, and is covered in the late dragon's razor sharp teeth. During combat, a tooth will sometime come loose, embedding itself into a victim, and a new tooth will eventually re-grow in its place.

Years later, the sword was eventually used to slay Høck the Cruel by his daughter, and its pommel was replaced with his shrunken skull, but that's another story…

Draco Maxillam Helixa has the following characteristics:

- +2 short sword.
- The sword communicates to its wielder via simple urges.
- The sword has 2 goals spawned from the latent desires of its dragon form: to locate and acquire gems, and to be reunited with its original skull.
- The sword enables its wielder to speak and understand the dragon language.
- On a critical hit, in addition to typical crit damage, the sword will lose 1d3 teeth which will embed themselves in the victim, each delivering an additional 1d4 points of damage. The teeth will regrow in 1d7 days.
- Once per week, the sword can release a cone of cold (Helixa's original breath weapon) for 3 points of damage per level of wielder.
- On a fumble, the angry soul of Høck the Cruel taints the PC, causing -1 to attacks and saves until the PC is subject to a *remove curse* spell.

OSZ-CROMACAR: "IRONSBANE," THE FLAWED BLADE

Aeons ago, dwarven smiths sought to forge arms for their elven allies that avoided the anathema of iron. But in their early efforts to work mithril, mistakes were made. *Osz-Cromacar* is reputed to be the first blade made of this wondrous metal, but imperfect crafting produced a blade improperly tempered, its brittleness countered only by its elven enchantments. These enchantments imbue *Osz-Cromacar* with a quintessentially elven combination of both near-permanence and mercuriality.

Each time it is borne the sword will eventually fail. The blade later rematerializes elsewhere and elsewhen, naked and without its furniture. Thus through the ages it has worn a variety of hilts, grips, and guards, but the blade itself is always the same: two-handed in proportion and neutral in alignment. Its relatively crude crafting makes it a mere +1 weapon, gives it low Intelligence (7) and limits it to communicating only simple urges. It is marked with notches, cracks and nicks that betray its inherent instability.

Osz-Cromacar exists to serve the elven races, so it will not voluntarily reveal its enchantment to non-elven wielders. Its battered appearance helps conceal this true nature.

An elven wielder can drain the power of the enchantments that hold the sword together – known as "revealing a flaw" – to activate special powers:

- *Osz-Cromacar* automatically increases its wielder's critical hit threat range by one. A wielder can increase this range by an additional +1 by revealing a flaw, and can do this after making an attack roll.

- Revealing a flaw turns the sword into an armor-breaker or a weapon-breaker (though not both simultaneously, and iron/steel weapons and armor only) as per DCC RPG, p. 371. This can be done during the same round that a wielder increases the sword's threat range.

- Revealing a flaw allows the wielder to cast the spell *shatter* on objects of iron or steel only, rolling a d24 spell check.

When found, the sword will have some level of enchantment strength remaining. Judges should secretly roll 6d6 to determine the number of flaws that can be revealed before the sword dematerializes once again.

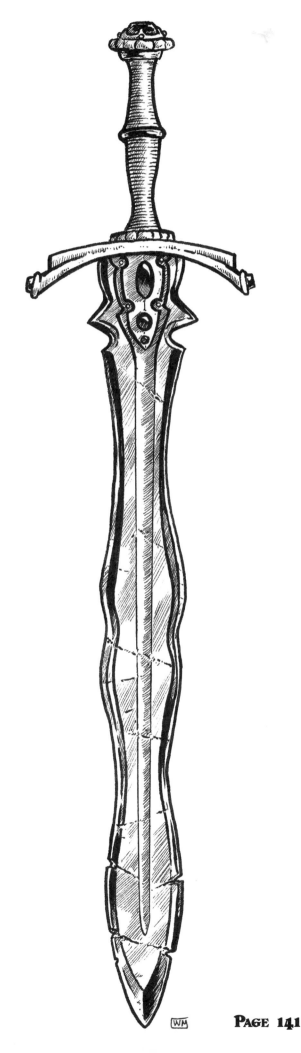

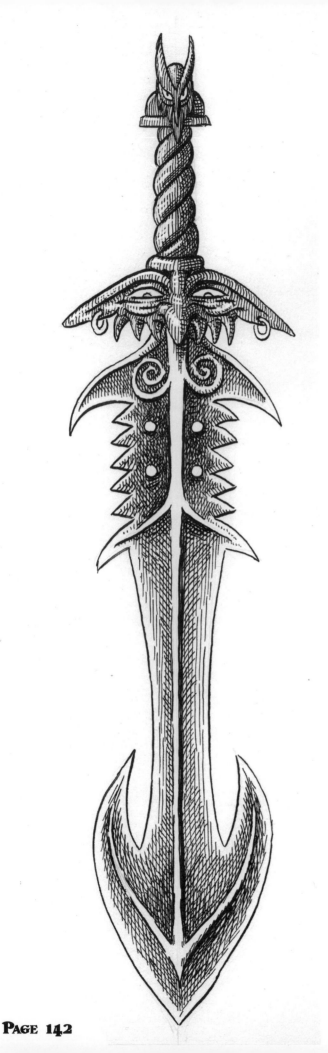

SEZREKAN'S SERVANT, AKA THE DEFEATED OF DARJR, AKA FANTAX'S FOOL, AKA AN OBJECT LESSON FROM ALAMANTER, ET.AL.

An arrogant wizard challenged the wrong opponent to a spell duel. In defeat, the wizard and his familiar were transmuted by the duel's victor into this exotic short sword. Some say it was Sezrekan who punished the upstart for his hubris, while others cite Darjr, Fantax, Alamanter, and a score of other archmages as the legendary victor. In truth, the identities of both victor and defeated are unconfirmed, and so the sword goes by many names. What is known is that the victor's spell included a clause for the defeated wizard's restoration — serve in sword form until its aide is lent in 1289 spell duels.

Whatever its origins, this +2, neutrally-aligned sword possesses the superior Intelligence of the transmuted wizard (16), but because it is a person-turned-inanimate-object its communication is limited to empathy.

The serrations of the sword's blade, the spurs of its langets, and the curves of its fullers form the shapes of mystical sigils that aide a wielder's magics. In combat, any time the wielder successfully hits with this weapon, he may cast *dispel magic* as an action in the next round, borrowing the necessary incantation from the sword's memory and then rolling a spell check as normal.

Pursuing its special purpose, in a spell duel the sword grants its wielder an extra action die that can only be used to make an attack with this sword. The attack is simultaneous with the caster's spell duel check. If the attack hits an opponent of the wielder involved in the spell duel, it adds its number of points of base damage (1d6) to the wielder's spell duel check roll.

The exact number of spell duels the sword has already assisted is unknown. One day, having has fulfilled the terms of transmutation, this weapon will polymorph back into a living wizard. On that day it will be learned whether his punishment taught the wizard humility or instilled in him instead a deep, dark resentment of any and all who exploited his imprisonment.

THE BEAK OF VA FEROUK

When Sword-Saint Madeline, one of the holiest servants of Justicia, felled the vulture demon Va Ferouk, the greater demons of the Abyss pledged that Va Ferouk would find redemption by becoming a servant to those sworn to defeat Justica. The demon council reconstituted the slain demon's corpse and with the assistance of sympathetic Chaos Lords forged The Beak of Va Ferouk, a semi-sentient chaotic weapon which still holds the remnants of the slain vulture demon's memories.

Wielders of the *Beak* frequently feel their minds clouded with chaotic ramblings of Va Ferouk urging the wielder into such acts as slaying the nearly dead, eating raw carrion, or attempting to take flight.

Goals:

- Re-establish the Scavengers of Va Ferouk and embolden the numbers of those that seek to serve the fallen vulture demon.
- Defeat Justicia and those who serve her.

Abilities:

- +2 to attack and damage.
- +4 to attack and damage against servants of Justicia.
- Fly: Once per day the *Beak* allows wielder to fly as per spell (1d6+1 turns).
- Beak's Precision: Warriors who attempt a Mighty Deed to disarm an opponent, or call a precision shot on an opponent's body, require only a 2 or greater on their deed die (as opposed to a 3).

Crits using the *Beak*:

- In additional to normal crit damage, Va Ferouk's spirit within the weapon adds the results of 1d8 on Crit Table DN: Devils and Demons (DCC RPG, p. 388).

Fumbles using the *Beak*:

- In addition to normal fumble results, there is a 1-in-4 chance the wielder also incurs some sort of minor chaotic taint from Va Ferouk (nose turns into beak, hands into talons, covered with feathers, etc.).

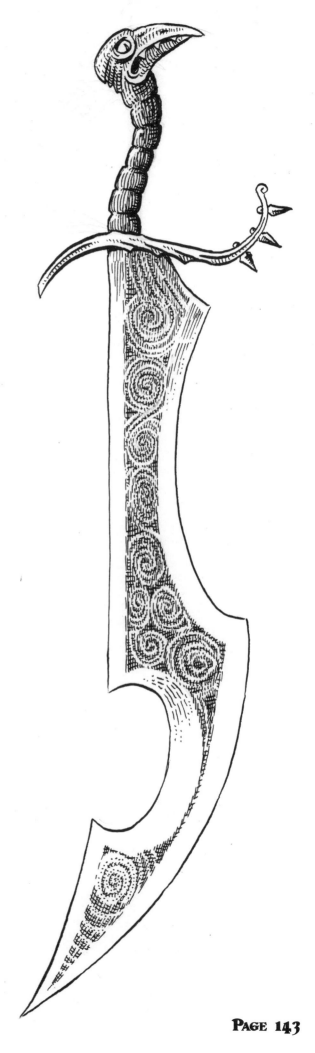

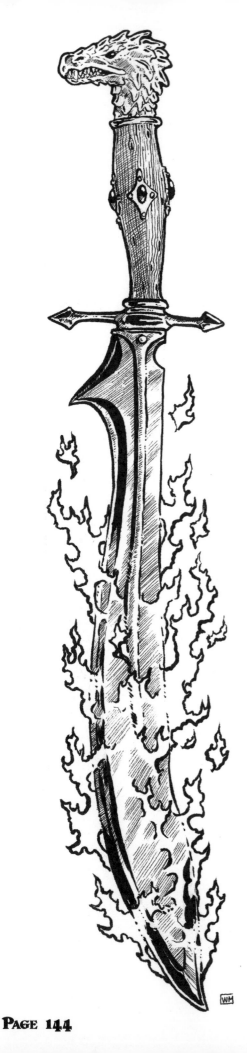

THE DRAGONTOOTH FLAMEBLADE OF AKIZA-MANNOTH

The great oracles of the ancient world prophesied that three portals would open at opposite edges of the world, allowing the combined armies of Fenwar the Fire God, Zhuhn the Infinite Void, and Klazath of the Crimson Banner to flow through and eradicate the puritanical paladins and angelic forces of Law.

Akiza-Mannoth, herald of the unyielding Chaos, rode his great bat-winged warhorse above the desolate desert lands, fire-capped peaks, and darkest jungles searching for the three portals that would bring forth such divine turmoil. Wrapped in gray bandages to protect his marble-white skin from the elements, Akiza-Mannoth quested for that which he would never find, but his scimitar grew increasingly powerful, tapping into an infinitesimal fraction of the strength of the chaotic gods who looked upon him with favor, even as their armies remained trapped on faraway planes.

Forces beyond his control held the three portals shut and when his aged, withered body finally collapsed, Akiza-Mannoth's sword sank to the bottom of the blue-green sea.

The scimitar acts as a +1 longsword in all respects, with these additional characteristics:

- Possessing Intelligence 5, this chaotic weapon communicates through simple urges, manifesting as subconscious desires in the wielder.
- It seeks to open the gates to the realms of Chaos and to free any locally-imprisoned or captured beings of chaotic alignment.
- The blade may become enflamed once per day per level of the wielder, granting it an additional +3 to attack and damage for 1d3 turns.
- Non-chaotic beings may wield this weapon, but they lose 1 Luck point for each successful hit or use of any sword abilities until they reach zero Luck — at which point they turn irrevocably chaotic and gain two major corruptions and 3d6 Luck points.
- The sword grants its wielder a limited planar step ability (as the wizard spell of the same name): roll 1d16 and add a +1 modifier for each living being slain by the weapon in the previous turn. (Increase the check roll to the action die of the wielder if used by a spellcasting class.)

THE BONESWORD OF THE SEA

When St. Brendan of Pelagia was set upon by the cannibal islanders of Huth, it is said that he defended himself and his shipmates with a jawbone wielded as a club. What creature this bone first came from, none can say, but it was later reformed into a primitive-looking bone sword, as strong as steel, with a mighty chopping blade. Black teeth embedded opposite the knapped bone edge give the weapon a fearsome appearance.

St. Brendan is now lost to the ever-changing vista of myth and legend. The *Bonesword* has gone on to change hands many times, being used by pirate captain and merchant mariner alike in the southern seas. It retains its power so long as it is within 50 miles of salt water, and has additional powers if that water is tropical.

The *Bonesword* is considered to be a +2 short sword, but inflicts a base 1d7 (rather than 1d6) damage. The teeth opposite its blade can be used to gain a +1d bonus to Mighty Deeds intended to disarm opponents. The sword has an Intelligence of 13, and can communicate telepathically with any who holds its grip. Entirely devoted to Pelagia, the *Bonesword* demands the same fealty of its wielder, or it withholds the use of its special powers.

Within 50 miles of salt water:

- Storms are calmed and waters placid within 500' of the sword.
- Clerics of Pelagia gain a +2 bonus on spell checks within 15' of the unsheathed blade.
- Wielder gains a +2 bonus to all saves against spells while in direct contact with the *Bonesword*.

If that water is tropical:

- Wielder makes any swimming checks using 1d30.
- Wielder gains an additional +1 bonus to attack rolls and damage with the sword.
- Wielder can speak with dolphins and whales.

"I got all the stretch goals!"

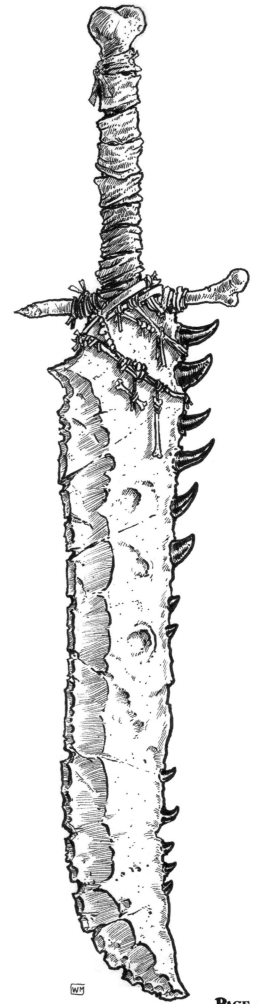

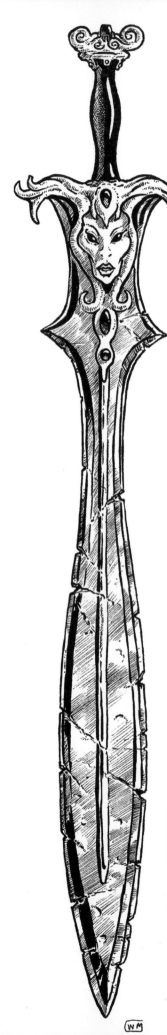

OPLEMA'S SONGSWORD

Most mariners feel a cold chill upon hearing the name "Oplema," but only if they're male. The siren sorceress has lured many men to their deaths, from enchanting them to walk into the ocean, to beckoning them to sail into ship-sinking rocks.

A betrayed lover unfairly exiled from the Sunken Kingdom of Ru, Oplema began a vengeful crusade to eliminate men of all races. To aid her cause, she sculpted a blade from one of her favorite victims, the kopoacinth Slurrg, a sea gargoyle of tremendous power. Adorning the short sword with her own image, accented by black pearls, Oplema infused it with her hatred for men, her love for the sea, and her sorcerous voice, all while keeping some of the blade's inherent kopoacinth nature.

Oplema's Songsword seeks a woman to continue its maker's crusade of male gendercide. Although famous wielders have been female, such as Pirate Queen Nimhail Negrain, the songsword will endure a man wielding it, but restricts its powers, and ultimately leads him to death through seductive betrayal. Its unique composition of organic marine stone requires it to soak in saltwater at least 12 hours per week. Failure results in a weakened blade (details below). One smells salty air and hears crashing waves when gripping the hilt.

- +3 neutral short sword, Int 14, speech and telepathy (-2d on attacks and damage if weakened).

- 2d6 damage (instead of 1d6) vs. males of any race.

- Bearer breathes underwater, and suffers no penalties to underwater combat.

- Siren's Beckon (2x/day, female wielders only): The sword croons for a man to follow its wielder. Target makes a DC 15 Will save or follows the bearer anywhere for 2d4 rounds.

- Stonestance (1x/day, female wielders only, only if not weakened): The wielder becomes an unbreathing statue, taking half damage from mundane attacks, though magic damages her normally. She can maintain the form up to a number of turns equal to her Stamina.

ZLABADO'S WAND

labado's Wand, named for its maker, the mad wizard-tinker Zlabado, was made specifically to kill creatures of Law and Chaos, and the blade is notorious in both Courts. The Lords of Law and Chaos each desire the blade, and will spare no effort to find and destroy it.

Each part of *Zlabado's Wand* has its own powers.

Zlabado forged the blade from the forked tongue of SKRSOWXWGJFEZAZX, a demon from the Hell of Thirteen Metals, and it contains a portion of that chaotic entity's intellect and ego.

- Blade attack (as longsword) +1 to attack and damage (+2 vs. lawful).
- Can communicate simple urges (Int 5).
- Light 20' radius.
- Magic resistance (-2 to spells cast against wielder).

The hilt was formed from the living body of an ultamalox, a flying, turtle-like being, capable of free travel across all the planes of existence. The ultamalox is a favored messenger of the Court of Law, capable of understanding any spoken language. This particular ultamalox was captured by Zlabado, locked in planar stasis, and shrunk to a thirteenth of its normal proportions. Its body shields the sword's wielder from the blood-thirst of the infernal blade. Should a non-chaotic user grasp the hilt, the ultamalox will beg for release from its suffering, for the uncanny magics used to bind the lawful creature to the chaotic blade cause it relentless pain, as its lawful essence battles that of the chaotic demonic relic.

- Hilt attack (as club) +2 to attack and damage (+3 vs. chaotic, demons, and wizards).
- Capable of speech (Intelligence 11).
- Detects traps within 30'.
- Comprehends languages (when hilt is grasped the ultamalox translates unknown languages).
- May burn up to 3 points of hilt's Int (heals in full each night). Doing so makes it lose language-based powers until healed.

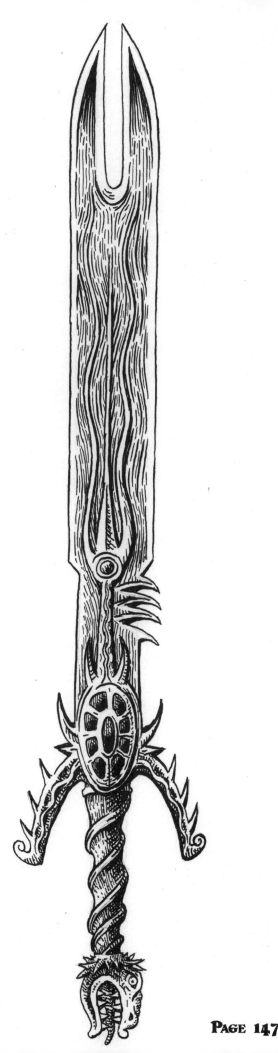

Chapter Nine
MONSTERS

The greatest monster is a black heart.

MAKING BUGS MORE INTERESTING

Giant ants, beetles, centipedes, flies, mantids, mosquitoes, scorpions, spiders, cave crickets, and killer bees all plague the intrepid and unlucky. Here are some stats for giant bugs and some randomized tables to add a twist of the unusual to such creatures.

GAME STATS FOR GIANT BUGS

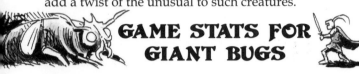

Black widow, giant: Init +1; Atk bite +1 melee (1d4 plus poison); AC 10; HD 1d4; MV 30′; Act 1d20; SP poison (DC 22 Fort save or lose 1d4+4 Strength permanently; success results in temporary loss of 1 Strength), *web* (10′ diameter, see General description of spider web spell, DCC RPG, p. 196); SV Fort -1, Ref +2, Will -1; AL C.

Despite only being the size of a small dog, the giant black widow is justly feared for its aggressive behavior and potent venom. Distinguished by their glossy black exoskeleton and red hourglass abdominal marking, these giant spiders also spin tangled, irregular webs in which the unwary may become snared.

Fly, giant: Init +5; Atk bite +1 melee (acid vomit and disease); AC 13; HD 1d4; MV fly 40′; Act 1d20; SP acid vomit (1d4 damage for two rounds), diseased (DC 12 Fort save or lose 1d3 from each ability score for 1d6 days); SV Fort +1, Ref +5, Will –2; AL C.

Giant flies are foul, pestilential creatures attracted to carrion, refuse, and sewage where they vomit on organic materials before sucking them up to digest. These small creatures seldom attack unless threatened, but lay many eggs on decaying matter which hatch into pallid, pulsating maggots the size of a fist. Due to their unsavory, disease-ridden nature, they are actively exterminated where they are found.

Mantid, giant: Init +6; Atk claw +8 melee (1d6+2, special); AC 14; HD 4d8+4; MV 30′; Act 2d20; SP grasp and bite (if both limbs strike the same target, the target is grasped and may be automatically bitten for 1d10 damage each round until it escapes; breaking free requires a DC 14 Strength check), camouflaged (+10 to attempts to hide in native habitat); SV Fort +4, Ref +2, Will +1; AL N.

Among the most terrifying of giant insects, mantids are solitary, still, and patient hunters that strike with alarming speed, grasping victims in their barbed forelimbs before devouring them alive. Well-camouflaged, they can be mistaken for the branches, limbs, and leaves of vegetation, striking as soon as prey comes within reach.

Mosquito, giant: Init +0; Atk bite +1 melee (1 plus blood drain and disease); AC 11; HD 1d4; MV fly 30′; Act 1d20; SP blood drain (automatically drains 1d4 hit points per round until slain), diseased (DC 12 Fort save or lose 1d3 from each ability score for 1d6 days), stealthy (+10 to attempts to move silently); SV Fort -1, Ref +1, Will –1; AL C.

A plague in areas of marsh, jungle, and swamp, giant mosquitoes fly and approach warm-blooded victims silently before alighting to drain their fill (4 hit points of blood). Tragically, even in cases when these creatures are detected before they sate themselves, they still carry a very real threat of disease.

Tarantula, giant: Init +2; Atk bite +6 melee (1d8 plus poison) or bristle cloud (special); AC 14; HD 3d8; MV 30′; Act 1d20; SP poison (DC 20 Fort save or lose an extra 3d4+4 hit points and 4 Strength temporarily; success results in loss of additional 1d4 hit points only), bristle cloud (10′ range, DC 14 Ref save or –2 penalty on all actions until treated), stealthy (+10 to attempts to move silently); SV Fort +2, Ref +1, Will -1; AL C.

Huge hairy spiders the size of a horse, giant tarantulas will attack nearly any living thing that ventures near their tunnel lairs. If under threat, once every 1d4 rounds a giant tarantula can use its action to flick irritant hairs from its abdomen in a small cloud in front of it. Although too large to easily hide, giant tarantulas are quiet and very, very patient.

Wolf spider, giant: Init +3; Atk bite +4 melee (1d6 plus poison); AC 14; HD 1d8; MV 40′ or jump 30′; Act 1d20; SP poison (DC 15 Fort save or lose an extra 2d4 hit points and 1 Strength temporarily; success results in loss of additional 1d4 hit points only), camouflaged (+10 to attempts to hide in native habitat); SV Fort +1, Ref +3, Will +0; AL C.

Swift, agile and active hunters, giant wolf spiders are the size of bear cubs, and while some are solitary like their mundane relatives, others hunt in packs with a frightening level of cooperation and cunning. They have keen vision and can see up to 90′ in the dark, preferring to hunt under cover of darkness where their natural camouflage is only enhanced.

RANDOM TABLES FOR BUG GENERATION

D24	Bug Color
1-3	Black
4-9	Brown
10-12	Green
13-14	Red
15-16	Yellow
17-18	White
19	Blue
20	Turquoise
21	Iridescent (color shifts between two differing colors as it catches the light)*
22	Abdomen is one color striped with bands of a second color*
23	Abdomen and thorax one color, legs another*
24	Abdomen, thorax, and legs each a different color*

*Roll color(s) using 1d20.

"Looks like someone's been using the random monster generator again."

D24 Bug Physical Traits

1. Abdomen is long and slender
2. Abdomen is huge and bulbous
3. Abdomen is broad, tapering quickly to a point
4. Abdomen bears a striking marking (skull, hourglass, etc.) in a contrasting color
5. Large, feathery antennae
6. Short, horn-like antennae
7. Long, thin antennae that curve backwards over the head
8. Long thin antennae that curl into spirals
9. Glossy, smooth exoskeleton
10. Exoskeleton is covered in hairs
11. Exoskeleton is rough and slightly spiky
12. Eyes are huge and compound
13. Eyes consist of two large front-facing orbs surrounded by smaller ones
14. A ring of eyes surrounds the head
15. Head is vaguely human
16. Legs are short and thick
17. Legs are bizarrely long and thin
18. Legs are slender and moderately long
19. Has a strangely floral odor
20. Has an odor that is acrid and unpleasant
21. Wings are short, stubby, and transparent, like those of a fly*
22. Has two pairs of long, slender, transparent wings, like a dragonfly*
23. Has resplendent, multi-colored wings like a butterfly*
24. Has powdery, dull, moth-like wings*

Wings may be for appearances only and useless for flight.

D100 Bug Special Abilities

1-2. **Alchemical honey.** The bug produces honey with miraculous properties. A number of doses of this honey can be found in its lair equal to the bug's HD. Roll 1d7 to determine the honey's property: (1) fire resistance; (2) giant strength; (3) growth; (4) healing; (5) shrinking; (6) speed; (7) water-breathing. See the Master Potion List (DCC RPG, pp. 224-225) for details.

3-4. **Amphibious.** The bug can breathe underwater and swim effortlessly.

5-7. **Beweaponed.** The bug bears a natural weapon of great power such as scything mandibles, wicked claws, chitinous horns, or even a combination of these. This increases the damage dice of its melee attacks, so a 1d6 damage bite would become 1d8 instead, for example.

8-9. **Bioluminescent.** The bug glows in the dark, whether to attract curious prey or mates.

10-11. **Blinding flash** (1/hour). The bug can emit a blinding flash from its abdomen. Anyone within 15' in front of the bug must make a DC 15 Ref save or be blinded for 1d4 rounds.

12-14. **Blood sucker.** Following a successful bite attack, the bug automatically drains 1d4 hit points from its victim each round until slain.

15-16. **Brood mother.** When slain, an insect swarm bursts forth from the bug's body, attacking those nearby (see DCC RPG, p. 419).

17-18. **Burrow.** The bug can "swim" through sand and dirt at its normal speed.

19-21. **Camouflaged.** The bug's exoskeleton changes color and pattern constantly to blend with its surroundings. It gains +10 to all attempts at hiding.

22-23. **Caustic blood.** The bug's blood is a potent acid. Anyone damaging the bug in melee must immediately make a DC 15 Ref save to avoid being splashed with the foul substance or suffer 1d4 acid damage.

24-25. **Diseased bite.** The bug's bite carries a terrible wracking disease. Anyone bitten must make a DC 12 Fort save or lose 1d3 from each ability score for a duration of 1d6 days.

26-27. **Extra head(s).** Roll 1d6: (1-5) bug has one extra head; (6) bug has two extra heads. Each extra head grants the bug an extra action die, and an extra Will save to resist magics or emotional or intellectual influence.

28-30. **Extra limb(s).** Roll 1d6: (1-3) bug has one extra pair of limbs; (4-6) bug has two extra pairs of limbs. An extra pair of limbs provides the bug with an extra action die, and increases the bug's MV by 10'.

31-33. **Fast reflexes.** The bug's Ref save is increased by +4.

34-35. **Grasping limbs.** The bug's front pair of limbs are spiked grasping limbs like those of a mantis. This provides two 1d8 melee attacks. If both limbs strike the same target, the target is grasped and may be automatically bitten each round until it escapes. Breaking free requires a Strength check (DC 10 + bug's HD).

36-41. **Huge eyes.** The bug's eyes are large and bulbous compound eyes, or multitudinous. Unless a foe approaches using invisibility or a similar means of avoiding any visual detection, the bug cannot be surprised or snuck up on.

42-43 **Human shape** (1/day). The bug can transform into a human of appropriate gender, assuming all physical traits of that creature.

44-45 **Immunity.** The bug is immune to (roll 1d4): (1) acid; (2) fire; (3) cold; (4) poison.

46-47 **Infravision 100'.**

48-49 **Irritant bristles** (1/1d4 rounds). The bug can spend an action to flick a cloud of irritant bristles from its abdomen, these irritating the eyes or lungs of those breathing them. Anyone within 15' of the front of the bug must make a DC 14 Ref save or suffer a –2 penalty on all actions until treated.

50-52 **Leaping.** The bug can leap up to 50' in any direction with grasshopper-like legs.

53-55 **Lightning strike.** The bug attacks with blinding speed, increasing its initiative by +4.

56-57 **Pincers.** The bug's forelimbs are equipped with crushing, scorpion-like pincers that inflict 1d8 melee damage.

58-60 **Poisonous bite.** The bug gains a poisonous 1d6 bite attack if it does not already possess one, or simply the benefits of a poison if it already has a bite attack that powerful or moreso. Poison type (roll 1d5): (1) black widow; (2) giant centipede; (3) scorpion; (4) tarantula; (5) giant wasp. Details can be found in Appendix P: Poisons (DCC RPG, p. 446).

61-62 **Regeneration.** The bug regenerates 1 point of damage at the end of every round but still dies when reduced to 0 hit points. Damage caused by fire or acid cannot be regenerated.

63-64 **Scalding spray** (1/hour). The bug can fire a cone of scalding fluid from its abdomen 20' long and 20' at its widest point. Damage is equal to half the bug's hit points, but a successful Ref save (DC 10 + bug's HD) halves damage.

65-66 **Scorpion tail.** The bug possesses a scorpion's muscular, telson-tipped tail. It can make a melee attack with it for 1d6 damage plus poison (DC 15 Fort save or death in 1d4 rounds).

67-72 **Spider climb** (at will). The bug can climb any surface as if it were a spider.

73-74 **Spines.** Short, thorn-like spines cover the bug's carapace. Any creature making an unarmed attack on it automatically suffers 1d4 damage.

75-76 **Spit acid** (1/1d4 rounds). The bug may spit a globule of acid at its foes, attacking at +10 to a range of 50', and inflicting 2d6 acid damage. The spit automatically causes 1d6 acid damage per round thereafter until neutralized.

77-78 **Spit glue** (1/1d4 rounds). The bug can spit a ball of glue up to 50' with a +4 attack bonus. Anyone struck must make a DC 15 Str check or Ref save to work free or be unable to act. The glue dissolves after 1d6 hours.

79-81 **Stealthy.** The bug moves with deathly quiet in its native habitat, gaining a +10 bonus to attempts to move silently.

82-83 **Stench** (1/day). Once per day the bug can unleash a stench so vile that that anyone coming within 10' must make a DC 12 Fort save each round or succumb to a fit of retching (-2 to all rolls while retching).

84-85 **Sticky.** Sticky hairs cover the bug's exoskeleton. Any creature or object touching or striking the bug requires a DC 15 Str check to pull away. Stuck creatures have a –2 penalty to all attack rolls.

86-87 **Stupifying scent** (1/hour). The bug can unleash an invisible chemical cloud that stupifies others. Anyone within 10' when the cloud is sprayed must make a Will save (DC 10 + bug's HD) or be stupified and unable to act for 1d6 rounds.

88-90 **Tough exoskeleton.** The bug has a particularly hard exoskeleton, increasing its AC by +4.

91-92 **Trapper.** Intelligent or not, the bug crafts a variety of crude traps (pits, deadfalls, and snares) around its lair using local materials.

93-94 **Water walker** (at will). The bug can walk across or stand upon the surface of relatively calm bodies of water as if they were ground.

95-97 **Web spinner** (1/day). The bug can spin a web 30' in diameter that lasts for 1d6 days before dissolving. For details see the General description of the *spider web* spell (DCC RPG, p. 196).

98-00 **Winged.** Bug gains MV fly 30'.

CHAOS LORDS, MUTANTS, DEGENERATES, SYCOPHANTS, SERVITORS, AND JUGGERNAUTS:

A COMPILATION OF CREATURES FOR DCC RPG

One of the main design goals of DCC RPG is that the players (and thereby their PCs) should never know what to expect when it comes to meeting new monstrous foes in dank dungeons, the tangled wilderness, or on the field of battle. Each enemy is a mystery, with the party unsure of what weird power or horrible ability their foe might possess. To this end, DCC RPG encourages judges to tweak the monsters provided in the rulebook and to create their own horrible threats. But even the most creative judge can find his or her imagination being taxed when forced to constantly make new threats for the party to face. Luckily, this article is here to help! In the following pages you'll find sniveling servitors, disgusting degenerates, malignant mutants, and even stranger things to prowl the dark corners of your campaign. Use them as provided or to serve as inspiration for even more fiendish foes of your own concoction.

BYEMGEIRD

Byemgeird: Init +2; Atk mental thrust +1 ranged (DC 10 Will save or 1d5+1; range 40'); AC 11; HD 1d6+2; MV fly 30'; Act 1d20; SP magic and corruption absorption, mystic emanations; SV Fort +1, Ref +3, Will +2; AL Any.

Byemgeirds are magical servitors given life by forgotten sorcery millennia ago. Few remain in this age, and those that survive are either serving a wizard master or lie awaiting discovery in crumbling ruins. A byemgeird appears to be a floating human or humanoid skull embedded in a transparent blob of ectoplasm. Tendrils dangle from beneath the viscous globule, giving the byemgeird the appearance of a flying man-o-war jellyfish with a grinning skull set in its bubble-like body.

Byemgeirds were created to serve wizards as both a sorcerous bodyguard and a means to divert the malignant touch of corruption. Once bound to a wizard or elf, the byemgeird can be fueled with magical energy, allowing it to produce a number of mystic emanations or be left "empty" to allow it to absorb the taint of corruption in place of its spell-casting master.

A wizard or elf that binds a byemgeird to his service can charge the creature by casting spells directly upon it. Any successfully cast spell does not manifest as normal, but is instead absorbed like an electrical charge, allowing the byemgeird to produce a small number of magical effects on command. A byemgeird can hold up to ten "charges" to create these effects. Each spell cast upon the creature grants it a number of charges equal to its spell level. Any spell that would cause the creature's internal magical battery to exceed ten charges has a 50/50 chance of either failing or man-

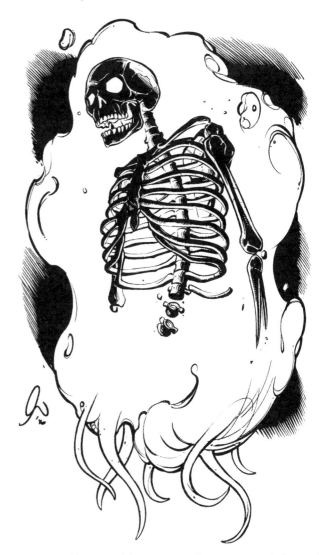

ifesting normally, possibly injuring the creature if the spell is offensive in nature.

Every round the byemgeird can expend charges from its battery to produce one of the following effects. Each effect drains the indicated amount of power from the creature until its battery is exhausted.

- **Magic missile (3 charges):** Three magic missiles streak from the creature to strike up to three different targets within 100'. Each missile does 1d6+1 damage.

- **Heal master (1 to 3 charges):** The creature transfers stored power to its master, healing the spellcaster of 1 to 3 dice of damage. Each die of healing drains 1 charge from the creature's battery. The byemgeird must be within 20' of the spellcaster to use this power.

PAGE 153

- **Illumination (1 charge):** The byemgeird glows with the brilliance of a lantern, throwing light in a 30' diameter. This magical illumination produces no heat and lasts for 1 hour. The radiance can be dismissed by the spellcaster with a word, but another charge must be spent to reinstate the light.
- **Erode magic (5 charges):** The byemgeird throws up a field of magical interference that withers the potency of a magical effect as it materializes. This power allows its master to make two saving throws against a spell on the round it takes effect and keep the better result. When this power is used, the byemgeird acts on the same initiative count as the spell but can perform no other action that round. If the byemgeird has already acted during the round, it loses its action the following round.

If a byemgeird is slain, any stored magical power disperses back into the multiverse, producing a colorful but harmless pyrotechnic display.

A byemgeird has a second, extremely useful power. If the creature's battery is left empty, a spellcaster about to suffer corruption from a miscast spell or other source can shunt the corrupting energy into the byemgeird instead. This action automatically destroys the byemgeird, but the wizard suffers no ill-effects from the corruption.

A byemgeird lacking charges in its magical battery has a single offensive capability. It can produce a 40' long thrust of mental power that lances through a target's brain, inflicting 1d5+1 damage if a DC 10 Will save is failed.

A wizard or elf who discovers a byemgeird unbound to a living master can attempt to take the creature as its servitor. To do so, the caster must first make a DC 15 Personality check, adding his caster level to the roll. If this check is successful, he must also immediately feed the creature one or more charges by casting a spell upon it. Failing to do so angers the byemgeird and it either leaves the spellcaster's presence immediately (75% chance) or attacks the caster (25% chance).

DHWYGHT

Dhwyght: Init +2; Atk club +0 melee (1d4) or knife +2 missile fire (1d4; range 10/20/30'); AC 11; HD 1d6; MV 30'; Act 1d20; SP master's element (varies by type), benefits from master's saving throws; SV Fort +0, Ref +2, Will -1 (but see below); AL N or C.

Some men and women are born to serve. Lacking the drive, intelligence, personality, or wherewithal to advance themselves, they devote their lives to serving a more powerful figurehead. And when this figurehead is not a mere earthly leader but a malignant un-dead creature, mad scientist, or foul fiend, the servant becomes a dhwyght—a human (or other race) touched by his master's evil.

A dhwyght appears as a normal specimen of its race, although these creatures, by the sheer circumstances that led them to servitude, tend to be ugly of countenance, twisted of limb, possess dim intelligence, or be outright mad. They neglect their appearance, dressing in whatever shabby robes, discarded clothing, or stained raiment their masters gift them, and arm themselves with simple weapons. Dhwyghts are poor opponents in physical combat, but possess two abilities that make them potentially formidable.

Every dhwyght is influenced by his master, subconsciously and magically leeching off a small portion of his superior's power and skill. The dhwyght can manifest this power to his and his master's benefit. The specific ability each dhwyght is capable of producing is based on his master's type (un-dead, infernal, scientific, etc.). The four types of masters given below are just some of the possible figureheads that may be served by dhwyghts and the judge should expand the possibilities as needed. There are reports of dhwyghts found serving lycanthrope masters, invisible criminal geniuses, and reptilian monsters from the blackest of lagoons.

- **Un-dead master:** Roll on Table 9-6: Traits or Properties of Un-dead (DCC RPG core rulebook, p. 381; base save DC is 10 if applicable).
- **Infernal master:** Throw hellfire and brimstone. This is a +4 ranged attack that does 3d6 damage (DC 10 Reflex save for half damage) to a single target up to 60' away.
- **Scientific master:** Electrical grasp. Electrical power courses through the dhwyght's body and he can make a touch attack (+3 melee) that inflicts 2d8+2 damage to the victim. The dhwyght also heals if exposed to electricity, regaining 1 hit point for each damage die the lightning or other electrical field would normally inflict.
- **Faerie master:** *Color spray.* The dhwyght uses a d20 with no modifiers when making his spell check. The dhwyght never misfires, suffers corruption, or loses the spell so long as his master is alive.

Dhwyghts enjoy a second benefit from their devoted servitude. So long as their master lives and is within sight of the dhwyght, the servant uses his boss's saving throw bonuses instead of his own if the master possesses better modifiers.

If the dhwyght's master is slain and the servant survives, he loses his special ability within 24 hours. A master-less dhwyght is likely to end his own life unless another master can be found. A master gives the creature purpose; without someone to serve, his life lacks meaning.

GRILLUS

Grillus: Init +2; Atk bite +4 melee (1d8+2) or nauseating touch +3 melee (DC 14 Fort save or retch); AC 13; HD 3d10; MV 30'; Act 1d20; SP inflict nausea; SV Fort +4, Ref +2, Will +3; AL C.

Grillus are broad-shouldered, obese humanoids with a singular spectacular feature: their heads reside in their torsos instead of atop their bare shoulders, peering out from their abdomens. The face of a grillus possesses a huge, tooth-lined mouth, flat noses with broad nostrils, and beady, piggish eyes. The first grillus were gluttonous degenerates who lived only to feast. For their hedonistic ways, legends say,

a spirit of the gods cursed them and their heads replaced their stomachs, a fitting fate as they only thought of food and feasting. In their cursed state, grillus literally live only to eat and no amount of food can end their relentless hunger. Grillus will devour anything edible, but prefer fresh meat consumed raw off the bone. Travelers and explorers are their favorite meals.

Grillus attack by initially touching their prey, sending a quiver of revulsion flowing through their bodies. Any creature suffering the touch of a grillus must make a DC 14 Fortitude save or retch, vomiting up their most recent meal (which the grillus will eat later). The vomiting is so powerful that the target cannot act for 1 round and suffers a -1d penalty on all rolls for the next 1d4 rounds. A creature can only be affected by a grillus' touch once in a six hour period. After a victim is impeded by nausea, the grillus attacks with its mouth, attempting to eat the creature alive.

Some sages speculate that a massive amount of food delivered instantaneously to a grillus would immobilize the creature for up to a full day or possibly even remove the curse that plagues it. A cleric casting *food of the gods* on a grillus, for example, and achieving a spell check of 24+, might produce one of these theoretical results at the judge's discretion.

MAGEMELT

Magemelt: Init +1; Atk claws +2 melee (1d4+1) or makeshift sword +1 melee (1d6+1) or makeshift javelin +1 missile fire (1d6; range 30/60/90'); AC 12; HD 2d6+2; MV 30'; Act 1d20; SP caustic gas; SV Fort +2, Ref +2, Will +1; AL C.

Magemelts are the unintended side-effects of alchemical experimentation in large cities. The hazardous substances utilized by alchemists and wizards are sometimes carelessly discarded and find their way into the city's sewers. Homeless vagrants, criminals, the insane, and other unlucky souls come into contact with these caustic and/or trasmutative materials that melt and warp their flesh, changing them into magemelts. Magemelts vary in appearance, but all are ghastly with skin that seems to have melted like wax and large, discolored pustules defacing their exposed flesh.

These degenerate creatures attack anyone entering their subterranean territory, raking enemies with horn-like claws or attacking with weapons they've constructed from discarded junk or broken tools. Although individually magemelts are not overly formidable, they tend to congregate in colonies and overwhelm enemies with their numbers.

Complicating fights with magemelts are the pustules covering their skin. A successful physical attack on a magemelt ruptures one or more of these sacs, causing a noxious alchemical pus to spray out. The pus turns gaseous when exposed to air, creating a 10' diameter cloud around the creature. All opponents within the gas must make a DC 12 Fortitude save or suffer a -2 penalty to all rolls and take 1 point of damage each round for 1d4 rounds. The damage continues even after the affected creature exits the cloud unless the alchemical pus is washed off, requiring a round to do so. The gas dissipates after a single round, but further physical attacks on the magemelt creates new clouds and those caught within them must make additional saving throws. The effects of multiple exposures to the gas are cumulative. Magemelts are unaffected by their own alchemical gas.

MOAI-MAN

Moai-Man: Init +2; Atk slam +25 melee (6d10+15) or hurled stone +15 missile fire (3d10+15; range 400'); AC 25; HD 30d10; MV 60'; Act 2d20; SP crit on 15-20, roar, immune to poison/gas/suffocation/blindness, immune to mind-affecting spells; SV Fort +20, Ref +6, Will Immune; AL N.

Travelers to distant lands report of natives who venerate a giant stone head embedded in the ground. Sacrifices and prayers are offered up to this unmoving idol, and the tribesmen who worship the monolith are considered primitive and simpleminded by the supposedly more world-wise visitors. Little do these travelers know that the religious rites are performed to keep a powerful monstrosity in check.

The stone head that rises from the ground is but a small part of a juggernaut buried in the earth. This colossus was constructed by unknown beings many eons ago, perhaps given life by the ancient but more technologically advanced ancestors of the people who now pay it homage. So long as the religious rites are performed, this monster, the Moai-Man, continues to sleep in the ground. Should the veneration be interrupted, however, the colossus awakens and unleashes a swath of destruction upon the world.

When unearthed, the Moai-Man stands 100' tall and is of humanoid appearance. Its body is fashioned from rough, volcanic rock. It pummels people, buildings, livestock, and

PAGE 155

anything else that gets in its path with fearsome fists, and hurls shattered stone like a giant casts boulders. The Moai-Man's rocky head contains a primitive brain that is immune to any mind-affecting spell and it automatically succeeds on all Will saving throws.

The Moai-Man can unleash a tremendous roar capable of making even the most stalwart warrior flee in terror. All creatures within 100' of the creature must make a DC 15 Will save or flee for 2d7 rounds. Once a successful save is made, the hearer is no longer affected by the roar.

The Moai-Man, once roused from its torpid state, can only be stopped by either destroying it or appeasing its anger with acts of profound piety. What constitutes such an act is left to the judge to decide, but possibilities include a massive sacrifice, the destruction of vast wealth or powerful magical objects in the name of the Moai-Man, or the gift of a humongous quantity of wine to the stony juggernaut.

VIMSWAIN

Vimswain: Init +0; Atk bite +3 melee (1d10+1); AC 15; HD 3d12+3; MV fly 40'; Act 2d20; SP argument; SV Fort +7, Ref +2, Will +10; AL C.

A vimswain is an uncanny creature resembling three grotesque humanoid heads set one atop the other, with each growing out of the cranium of the one beneath it. Each head is slightly smaller than the one below, giving the vimswain a vaguely triangular shape. Bushy black mustaches adorn the lips of each head and the bottommost mouth has sharp teeth to gnaw enemies with. Lacking bodies of any sort, a vimswain moves via flying, levitating through the air at modest speed.

The vimswain is usually discovered arguing with itself over a trivial matter. They therefore seldom surprise opponents who easily hear the creature approaching. When confronted by enemies (or perhaps just to spread discord), a vimswain can instill in others an argumentative, confrontational urge, leading to disagreements among even boon adventuring companions. The vimswain chooses a victim within sight and that creature must make a DC 14 Will save or become infected by a magical contradictory state. This state lasts for 1d6 turns or until a *remove curse* spell is successfully applied.

While in the argumentative state, the victim refuses to agree to any proposed action or decision presented by others, arguing instead why another option is better. This includes targets of attack, spells to cast, and other important commands and suggestions offered in the midst of combat. The argumentative state does not render the victim stupid, so reverse psychology may or may not be effective depending on how well he knows those he's arguing with. For example, if his fellow adventurers, known to be greedy, suggest the victim take all the treasure discovered in a chest, he'll know they want him to do otherwise and take 90% of the loot to both spite them and disagree with their instructions. In the case of strangers with unknown goals, the victim isn't likely to know their true desires (unless blatantly obvious) and may thereby succumb to reverse psychology.

The victim can also command others to not perform an action, contradicting their desires with supernatural effectiveness due to the argument infection. Each round the victim must choose someone within view and demand they not do what they intend to. The victim and the target both make Will saves and compare the results. If the victim rolls higher, the target loses his action for the round while he argues why he should be able to act as he intends. This is a magical effect that overrides the target's logical mind. If the target's result is better than or equal to the arguer's, he may act as normal that round. The arguer's target is best determined randomly each round, with either the judge or the player rolling to determine who receives the brunt of the disagreement. All intelligent creatures the arguer can see are potential targets, so enemies, allies, and bystanders are all likely to be targeted. The vimswain itself is immune to the argument and does not count as a potential target. The ability to spread the argumentative infection ends when the original victim is no longer under the effects of the vimswain's power.

The origin of the vimswain is unknown, although some sages point to an old cautionary tale of three wizards whose argument over magical mastery led to a spell duel that resulted in their bodies becoming fused into one. Somehow, the original trio may have magically reproduced themselves, giving birth to the vimswains encountered today.

WASTE REAVER

Waste Reaver: Init +3; Atk scimitar +4 melee (1d8+2) or saw-edged crossbow disk +3 missile fire (1d6 plus 1 per round for 1d4 rounds; range 80/160/240'); AC 14; HD 3d8+2; MV 25'; Act 1d20; SP blood squirt; SV Fort +5, Ref +3, Will +2; AL C.

From out of the Flash Wastes, a region of arid desolation said to be the product of unholy technological wars waged eons ago by dead nations, come the waste reavers. These badland brigands are a hybrid of man and horned lizard and stand 7' tall. They cover their spiny, dun-colored flesh with linen wrappings and weatherworn leather scavenged from their victims. Spikes, both those naturally adorning their skin as well as manufactured ones that pierce the flesh, are considered signs of beauty and power among the waste reavers and nearly all of them sport sharp body ornamentation.

Waste reavers survive as bandits, killing their victims with savage scimitars and curious crossbows that hurl spinning, saw-toothed disks through the air. Anyone struck by one of these missiles loses 1 additional hit point each round as the jagged wound continues to bleed. Staunching the bleeding requires an action but ends the hit point loss.

Due to their horned lizard heritage, waste reavers can squirt a stream of blood from their eyes at a single target up to 15' away. The target of the bloody blast must make a DC 13 Reflex save or be blinded for 1d6 rounds. A waste reaver can only produce one blood squirt per day.

Waste reavers travel across the Flash Wastes and other arid regions on sail-propelled, triangular-shaped, three-wheeled vehicles. These unusual transports can move up to 30 miles per hour in a strong breeze and are capable of crossing 100 miles of desert in a day (terrain and weather allowing).

ZHIL, THE SATRAP OF KNIVES

Zhil, the Satrap of Knives: Init +10; Atk razor +22 melee (3d12+6) or storm of knives +22 missile fire (5d8+6 to all targets in 20' diameter, DC 25 Ref save for half damage; range 100'); AC 28; HD 30d12+60; MV 50'; Act 2d20; SP infravision, immune to weapons of less than +4 enchantment and natural attacks of 9HD or less creatures, teleportation, astral and ethereal projection, crit on 16-20, wounding glare, blood fascination; SV Fort +25, Ref +30, Will +30; AL C.

Zhil, the Satrap of Knives is a titanic humanoid standing 40' tall. His flesh is a mass of serrated blades, which both overlap like scales and jut out chaotically in disordered clusters. Despite his razor-sharp skin, Zhil is uncannily handsome by human standards, with sharp cheekbones, narrow chin, slashing eyebrows, and limpid eyes the color of bright blood. He dresses in anachronistic fashions, wearing everything from Grecian togas to Victorian gentleman's evening wear to tailored Italian three-piece suits.

In ages long past, Zhil was a Chaos Lord with a seat at the Court of Chaos. The constant internal struggles and political gambits of the Court ultimately unseated Zhil, stripping him of his rank in the Host and casting him back down Chaos' ever-changing hierarchy. He craves nothing more than to recover his former status and to avenge himself against Hekanhoda, the Lord responsible for his ousting. Although Zhil lost much of his power when his seat was usurped, he remains a devastating foe. Only the greatest of warriors and wizards stand a chance of surviving a confrontation with the Satrap of Knives.

Zhil wields a massive straight razor in melee combat, but seldom allows himself to be drawn into close quarters with enemies. He prefers to conjure up a storm of slashing knives that fill a 20' diameter area like slashing hornets when direct confrontation is necessary.

Zhil has the ability to open old wounds in a target with a mere glare. The target, which must be visible to the Satrap, must make a DC 25 Fortitude save or suffer damage equal to his hit die type +5. Thus, a wizard failing the save would take 1d4+5 points of damage while a warrior would endure 1d12+5 damage as old, long-healed wounds reopen and bleed anew. Zhil can use this ability as an action, but can't target the same victim twice in the same round. Subsequent glares on following rounds are possible.

The Satrap can also cause freshly-spilled blood to acquire a macabre allure, forcing targets seeing the gore to become fascinated by it. This fascination can manifest in three different forms.

- If Zhil uses this ability on his own blood, even that of the smallest wound, all creatures capable of seeing the ichor must make a DC 26 Will save or obey the Satrap's commands as if under the effects of a powerful *charm person* spell (victim acts as if Zhil is a friend, but will not perform suicidal actions; Will save vs DC 26 at intervals to shake the effect). A viewer who successfully makes his saving throw is immune to this effect for the remainder of the encounter but possibly affected if he sees the enchanted blood at a later date.

- If the spilled blood is due to another creature's wound, Zhil can cause that wound to fascinate the injured creature. A wounded creature failing a DC 26 Will save can do nothing but watch his blood flow, reveling in its red majesty. The affected creature ignores everything else and can perform no action during a round. Healing the wound or a successful *remove curse* spell ends the fascination.

- Lastly, Zhil can impart a blood thirst into any creature bearing a bloodied weapon, be it blade, tooth, claw, etc. Zhil chooses a target with a blood-stained weapon and that creature must make a DC 26 Will save or fall into a bloodthirsty rage for one hour or until the blood is cleansed from his weapon. During the rage, the affected creature attacks randomly, striking at anyone he is able to. If no opponents are viable, he departs to search for someone or something to slay. Zhil himself cannot be targeted by the affected and the judge should determine the raging creature's opponent randomly.

Zhil is a terrifying opponent and the judge should not use him as an enemy lightly. However, given his reduced status in the ranks of the Host and his desire to retake his seat and avenge himself against Hekanhoda, the Satrap of Knives could prove to be a useful—although not completely trustworthy—ally if the PCs have made enemies in the Court of Chaos (after playing through DCC RPG #80: *Intrigue at the Court of Chaos*, for example). Zhil will assist the party so long as their actions align with his own. He may even reward them should he regain his seat, if the urge moves him.

DCC CONSTRUCTS

Some monsters are born, but others are made: androids, golems, iron shadows, and living statues. These tables customize such creatures, and provide several new golem types to supplement those on page 203 of Dungeon Crawl Classics RPG. As in the rulebook, the new golem types assume roughly human size and shape, so judges will need to adjust these numbers to reflect larger or smaller creations.

Straw Golem: Init +0; Atk slam +3 melee (1d4+1); AC 10; HD 3d8+3; MV 30'; Act 1d20; SP double damage from fire; SV Fort +0, Ref +4, Will +4; Int 8, Str 14, Agi 10. Construction costs: 10,000 gp + 500 gp.

Rope Golem: Init +0; Atk slam +3 melee (1d4+2); AC 10; HD 4d8+4; MV 30'; Act 1d20; SP double damage from fire; SV Fort +1, Ref +4, Will +4; Int 8, Str 16, Agi 10. Construction costs: 10,000 gp + 750 gp.

Glass Golem: Init +0; Atk slam +3 melee (1d8+2); AC 10; HD 4d8+4; MV 30'; Act 1d20; SP double damage from lightning, subject to *shatter* spells; SV Fort +1, Ref +4, Will +4; Int 8, Str 16, Agi 10. Construction costs: 10,000 gp + 1,000 gp.

CONSTRUCT'S LAST PURPOSE AND FOCUS

General Purpose (1d5): (1) Destroy; (2) Detain; (3) Guard; (4) Obey; (5) Protect.

Focus: Once the construct's general purpose is decided, select an appropriate focus from the below:

People: Group Members (individuals identified by specific garment, symbol, password, or other identifying feature), Specific Individual (creator, creator's beloved, creator's enemy, creator's employer, etc.), Specific Race (human, dwarf, elf, halfling, orc, etc.)

Place: Entire Building/Complex/Dungeon, Specific Room (oubliette, treasure room, armory, laboratory, etc.), Location (this forest, this village, etc.)

Thing: Creature Type (demons, dragons, giants, hybrids, wicked humanoids, etc.), Specific Object (the *Accursed Quill of Niloc*, this sealed scroll, etc.), Object Type (coins, gemstones, weapons, etc.)

For example: If a flesh golem's general purpose is Destroy, you might select its focus as Specific Race (humans) meaning that the golem is tasked with continually hunting and slaying any humans it encounters, ignoring any other tasks or targets unless attacked or otherwise interfered with.

D14	Construct Appearance
1-4	Crudely made but effective.
5-12	Smooth and well-constructed, but otherwise unremarkable.
13-14	Intricately wrought whether woven, decorated, etched, or otherwise crafted to a high degree of finish.

D20	Construct Body Shape
1	Ape-like proportions with barrel-chest, long arms, and short legs.
2-3	Beast-headed: human-like body with head crafted to resemble that of a beast. Roll 1d6: (1) bull; (2) cat; (3) cobra; (4) crocodile; (5) falcon; (6) jackal.
4-5	Dwarf proportions: short, stocky, and broad.
6-7	Elf proportions, tall and slender.
8-16	Human proportions.
17-18	Skeletal. Looks like a skeleton made of the material used.
19-20	Unnatural, e.g., conical body with cylindrical head and multi-jointed arms.

D100	Construct Abilities
1-3	**Armored surface.** The construct's AC is increased by +4.
4-5	**Berserk.** When damaged, the construct goes berserk, gaining +2 to all attacks, damage, and saving throws until combat ends.
6-8	**Beweaponed.** The construct's striking surfaces are powerful weapons such as spiked bludgeons, spinning saws, or serrated metal horns. This increases the damage dice of its melee attacks by +1d, so a 1d8+2 damage slam would become 1d10+2 instead.
9-10	**Bleeding wounds.** The wounds inflicted by the golem continue to bleed until bound or healed. Each wound causes the loss of an additional 1 hit point per round until dealt with.
11-12	**Blessed.** The construct has been blessed by a cleric; it benefits from a +2 bonus to attack and damage creatures considered unholy by the blessing cleric.
13-14	**Blinding flash** (1/hour). The construct can emit a blinding flash from part of its form. Anyone within 15' in front of the construct must make a DC 15 Ref save or be blinded for 1d4 rounds.
15-16	**Blood drain.** Due to a sharp, tube-like protuberance it extends, hollow fingertips, or a syringe-like inbuilt device, the construct can drain blood from a victim, possibly storing it for collection by its creator. Following a successful slam attack, the construct automatically drains 1d4 hit points from its victim each round until slain.
17-18	**Breath weapon** (1/day). The construct can eject a hazardous substance once per breath weapon type (roll 1d3): (1) fire; (2) cold; (3) poison gas. Save, damage, and shape are as per Table III: Dragon Breath Weapon (DCC RPG, p. 407).

19-22 **Camouflaged.** The construct has the uncanny ability to hide in plain sight, appearing as a column, wall-carving, totem pole, statue, series of flagstones, item of furniture, pile of boulders, or other inoffensive element of the environment based on the material of its construction. This enables it to surprise others 50% of the time.

23-24 **Cause tremor** (1/day). The construct can create a tremor centered on itself. Earth shakes for several seconds. Creatures within 30' of the construct must make a Reflex save or be knocked prone. Concentration of enemies is disrupted.

25-27 **Caustic core.** The core of the construct contains a perilous substance. Type of substance (1d3): (1) acid (anyone damaging the construct in melee must immediately make a DC 15 Ref save to avoid being splashed with the foul substance or suffer 2d4 acid damage); (2) magma (anyone damaging the construct in melee must immediately make a DC 15 Ref save to avoid being splashed with the lava or suffer 2d4 fire damage); (3) toxic ooze (DC 15 Ref save to avoid being splashed; if failed, must make DC 10 Fort save or be permanently paralyzed [only paralyzed for 1d4 days if successful]).

28-30 **Damage reduction.** The construct's tough exterior reduces the damage of all blows against it by 1d6 points (roll at time of creation).

31-32 **Darkness** (at will). The construct can cloak an area of 30' radius into absolute darkness. Target any spot within 100'.

33-35 **Detection** (at will). The construct can detect object of one type within 100' at will with precision. Object of detection (roll 1d6): (1) same substance as golem; (2) any living creatures; (3) men; (4) dwarves; (5) elves; (6) un-dead.

36-37 **Earth to mud** (1/hour). The construct can transform an area of earth into sticky mud. The area transformed can be up to 50'×50' in size. The mud, up to 3' deep, slows movement to half speed for all within.

38-39 **Earth to stone** (1/day). The construct can transform an area of earth into solid stone. The area transformed, up to 100'×20'×5', is permanently changed into stone.

40-41 **Electrified.** Electricity constantly courses through the construct's body, adding +1d4 damage to its melee attacks and causing 1d4 damage to anyone who touches it unarmed or with a metal melee weapon.

42-44 **Energy blast.** As an action, the construct can unleash an unerring bolt or ray of energy at a target up to 100' away, doing 3d6 damage. A Reflex save (DC 10 + golem's HD) halves damage. Energy type (roll 1d5): (1) cold: (2) electricity; (3) fire/heat; (4) light; (5) magical force.

45-48 **Extra slam.** The construct has an extra arm, pair of arms, or tail-like appendage that allows it to make an additional slam attack each round.

49-50 **Fly.** Whether through arcane levitation, a strange pack-like array, or some other means, the construct gains MV fly 50'.

51-53 **Frightful presence.** The construct's visage and sheer implacability are absolutely terrifying. All who look upon it must make a Will save (DC 10 + golem's HD) or flee in terror (duration 1d4 turns or until a safe distance is reached).

54-55 **Heat metal** (1/turn). The construct can heat one metal object within 50' to painful levels. This ability inflicts 1d8 damage per round to characters holding heated objects or 1d10 damage per round to characters wearing heated armor.

56-57 **Healing energy.** When struck by a specific type of energy, the construct is not damaged, but instead repaired, regaining 1 hit point for each 5 points of damage normally inflicted. Type of energy (roll 1d6): (1) fire; (2) cold; (3) electricity; (4) acid; (5) force attacks (i.e., *magic missile*); (6) sonic attacks.

58-61 **Immunity.** The construct is immune to (roll 1d6): (1) fire, (2) cold, (3) electricity, (4) acid (5) force attacks (i.e., *magic missile*), (6) sonic attacks.

62-63 **Infravision 100'.**

64-65 **Light** (at will). The construct can bring the full light of daylight into an area of 30' radius. Target any spot within 100'.

66-67 **Magic resistance.** All spells cast against the construct are subject to a 50% chance of failure before saves are rolled.

68-69 **Magnetic touch.** A strong magnetic charge runs through the construct's surface. Any metal implement touching it becomes stuck. It requires one action and a successful DC 15 Strength check to pull a stuck object or weapon free.

70-72 **Pass substance.** The construct can walk or swim through anything made of the same material at its normal speed (so a stone golem could walk through stone walls, a wood golem could pass through a wooden door, and so on).

73-74 **Petrifying touch.** The construct can petrify targets with its touch. A creature struck by the construct must make a Will save (DC 10 + golem's HD) or be permanently changed to stone.

75-76 **Ray attack** (1/turn). As an action, the construct can unleash a ray of strange energy up to 100', attacking with a +4 bonus. Ray type (roll 1d2): (1) paralysis ray (target is paralyzed for 2d4 turns, DC 15 Fort save negates); (2) strength drain ray (target loses 1d4 Str for 1 hour, DC 15 Ref save negates).

77-78 **Resonate.** The construct vibrates when physically hit, producing a painful sonic wave for 1d3 rounds. This inflicts a –1 penalty on all actions for those within 30', and makes spellcasting impossible within that area.

79-80 **Rusting touch.** The construct's merest touch causes rust in all normal metal objects. As a result, its successful attacks cause metal armor to crumble to useless rust immediately, and weapons used to attack the construct crumble to rust upon touch (although magic armor and weapons are immune).

81-84 **Self repairing.** The construct self-repairs, regenerating 1d6 hit points at the end of every round, though it cannot restore lost limbs and is still completely destroyed at 0 hit points.

85-87 **Spikes.** Tough spikes cover the construct's exterior, whether carved from its own substance or made from metal or stone spikes driven into it. Any creature making an unarmed attack on it automatically suffers 1d6 damage.

88-89 **Sticky globules** (1/1d4 rounds). The construct can hurl a ball of a sticky substance such as alchemical glue, fast-hardening liquid crystal, or clay up to 50' with a +4 attack bonus. Anyone struck must make a DC 15 Str check or Ref save to work free or be unable to act. The glue dissolves after 1d6 hours.

90-91 **Tendrils.**  1d5+1 tendrils extend from the construct's body, be these woven vines, ropes, iron chains, or lengths of bloody sinew. The construct can use an action to attack with a tendril as if slamming at distance (though the damage dice are stepped down by -1d) or, more commonly, to whip around and grab a target. On a successful melee attack intended to grab, no damage is inflicted, but the victim is bound and unable to act save trying to free themselves. Bound creatures can attempt to escape with a Strength check (DC 10 + construct's HD). The construct does not have to expend actions to maintain its hold on a bound victim.

92-93 **Terrible wounds.** The construct's melee attacks leave sharp fragments in the wounds it inflicts, doubling the hit point cost of healing them.

94-96 **Weapon-resistant exterior.** The construct's armor is so thick that it takes half damage from mundane weapons. Magical weapons do normal damage.

97-00 **Wheeled or multi-legged.** Instead of a normal pair of legs, the construct has wheels, rollers, machine-like treads, or a multi-legged lower torso, giving it a land-based MV 50'.

GIANTS

The giants of myth, legend, and Appendix N exhibit great variety in appearance and power, the only constant being that of huge stature and generally humanoid form. While many may be brutish, foul of mien, and lacking in intellect, others can be fair of face, canny, or possessed of mystical powers. Use the following tables to craft your own unique giants. The giant's personality should be decided by the judge as suits his needs.

GENERIC GIANT ENTRIES

Judges may use the tables presented to modify existing cyclopes and giants as presented in the DCC RPG rulebook, or may use the following generic giant entries as starting points.

Giant, small (12' tall, 1,200 lbs.): Init -2; Atk weapon +15 melee (2d8+6) or hurled object +7 missile fire (1d8+4, range 100'); AC 16; HD 8d10; MV 30'; Act 1d24; SP crit on 20-24, roll 1 Giant Ability; SV Fort +10, Ref +5, Will +6; roll Giant's Alignment.

Giant, average (14' tall, 2,000 lbs.): Init –1; Atk weapon +19 melee (3d8+8) or hurled object +9 missile fire (2d8+6, range 200'); AC 18; HD 13d10; MV 40'; Act 2d24; SP crit on 20-24, roll 1 Giant Ability; SV Fort +11, Ref +6, Will +7; roll Giant's Alignment.

Giant, large (16' tall, 3,000 lbs.): Init +0; Atk weapon +23 melee (4d8+10) or hurled object +7 missile fire (2d8+8, range 300'); AC 20; HD 17d10; MV 50'; Act 3d24; SP crit on 20-24, roll 2 Giant Abilities; SV Fort +12, Ref +6, Will +8; roll Giant's Alignment.

Giant, huge (20' tall, 10,000 lbs.): Init +1; Atk weapon +26 melee (5d8+12) or hurled object +13 missile fire (3d8+10, range 400'); AC 21; HD 20d10; MV 50'; Act 4d24; SP crit on 20-24, roll 2 Giant Abilities; SV Fort +16, Ref +8, Will +12; roll Giant's Alignment.

Giant, colossal (30' tall, 30,000 lbs.): Init +2; Atk weapon +29 melee (6d8+14) or hurled object +14 missile fire (3d8+12, range 500'); AC 22; HD 23d10; MV 60'; Act 5d24; SP crit on 20-24, roll 3 Giant Abilities; SV Fort +18, Ref +8, Will +13; roll Giant's Alignment.

Giant, titanic (40' tall, 50,000 lbs.): Init +3; Atk weapon +32 melee (8d8+16) or hurled object +16 missile fire (4d8+14, range 600'); AC 23; HD 26d10; MV 70'; Act 6d24; SP crit on 20-24, roll 3 Giant Abilities; SV Fort +20, Ref +8, Will +14; roll Giant's Alignment.

GIANT SIZE

All giants are gigantic compared to the likes of humans and demi-humans, but some giants are giants to their kin. Hurled objects can include anything large and heavy enough such as boulders, trees, and horse carts.

D20	Giant Size
1-6	Small
7-12	Average
13-16	Large
17-18	Huge
19	Colossal
20	Titanic

GIANT TRAITS

Although giants are often dim, those dealing with them should be aware that not all are mentally challenged, and some can match wits with even the keenest of human minds.

D20	Giant's Intellect
1-6	Painfully stupid and easily confused
7-12	Notably dim
13-16	Possessed of low cunning
17-18	Surprisingly canny if not intellectual
19	Astute and thoughtful
20	Of genius intellect

D12	Giant's Alignment
1	Lawful
2-3	Neutral
4-12	Chaotic

D24	Giant Personal Traits
1	Unusual hair: mohawk, braids, ponytail, topknot, corn rows, balding (possibly with a clumsy comb-over), etc.
2	Broken or missing front teeth
3	Bad acne (on a gigantic scale)
4	Broken nose
5	Buck teeth
6	Only one eye; other eye is covered by homemade patch

PAGE 161

7	Noticeably long, dirty fingernails and toenails
8	Missing several fingers on each hand
9	Missing an arm, severed at the elbow
10	Unusual facial hair: handlebar moustache, mutton chops, goatee, etc.
11	Highly visible tattoos (face, arms, hands, or legs)
12	Unusually fragrant odor (may smell of musk, spice, flowers, or something else equally odd but not unpleasant)
13	Cyclopean, the single large eye natural, animalistic or gem-like in appearance
14	Extremely hirsute, possibly even fur-covered
15	Utterly hairless, lacking even eyebrows and eyelashes
16	Heavily scarred (may be wounds caused by attacks, marks left by disease, or decorative scarification)
17	Many piercings (may be bone or metal, precious or otherwise)
18	Gangling and skeletal but surprisingly tough
19	Constantly drools and sucks the spittle back while talking
20	Encrusted in filth (and likely extremely pungent)
21	Grossly obese (likely slower and heavier than normal)
22	Deformed (may be hunchbacked, club-footed, twisted of limb or face, or even wholly gnarled in form)
23	Triclopean (has an extra eye in the middle of the forehead)
24	Strikingly well-proportioned and attractive

D30	Giant Abilities
1	**Amphibious.** The giant can breathe underwater and swim effortlessly.
2	**Armored hide.** The giant's AC is increased by +4.
3	**Bestial head.** The giant's head is that of an animal, providing access to that creature's natural senses. Bestial head type (roll 1d3): (1) goat; (2) lion; (3) rooster.
4	**Bestial legs.** The giant's legs are those of a beast. Increase MV by 10'. Bestial legs type (roll 1d3): (1) goat; (2) lion; (3) snake's tail.
5	**Beguiling song.** The giant's voice is eerily melodious. If the giant forgoes one action to sing, all creatures within 300' must make a DC 13 Will save or stand enraptured, unable to do aught but listen entranced. A save may be made each round the song continues.
6	**Beweaponed.** The giant bears natural weapons of great power such as great horns, wicked talons, terrible tusks, or even a combination of these. This changes the damage dice its melee attacks to d10s instead of d8s, so melee damage of 3d8+10 would become 3d10+10 instead, for example.
7	**Blood sniffer.** The giant's sense of smell is infallible and can automatically detect the scent of flesh and blood up to 100' away. This does not necessarily permit the giant to pinpoint the scent's exact location, however.
8	**Breath weapon.** The giant can breathe a hazardous substance a number of times per day equal to its HD divided by 6 (round down). Breath weapon type (roll 1d4): (1) fire; (2) cold; (3) electricity; (4) poison gas. Save, damage, and shape are as per Table III: Dragon Breath Weapon (DCC RPG, p. 407).
9	**Change shape** (1/day). The giant can transform into another creature, assuming all physical traits of that creature. Creature type (roll 1d5): (1) human of appropriate gender; (2) raven; (3) boar; (4) fish; (5) viper.
10	**Command weather** (1/day). Once per day, the giant can control the local weather as per the *weather control* spell (DCC RPG, p. 302) with no chance of corruption and a casting ability of 1d20+10.
11	**Damage reduction.** The giant's tough hide reduces the damage of all blows against it by 1d4 points (roll at time of creation).
12	**Deathless.** Unless fully dismembered and cremated or dissolved in acid, the giant cannot be truly slain. The giant regenerates 1d8 points of damage at the end of every round, even after death, limbs crawling back to reattach and so on. The body will even stoop to retrieve and replace its severed head. Only damage by fire or acid cannot be regenerated.
13	**Earth shaker** (1/round). The giant can use an action to slam or stomp the ground beneath them, causing the ground to ripple and shake. All creatures within an area equal to the giant's HD in feet take 1d3 buffeting damage and must make a Reflex save or be knocked prone. Concentration of enemies is disrupted, buildings are shaken, etc.
14	**Evil eye** (1/day). One of the giant's eyes possesses terrible power. Usually kept closed, the giant can spend an action to open it and gaze into the eyes of a target. A creature that meets the giant's gaze must make a Will save (DC 10 + giant's HD) or suffer the effects. Evil eye effect (roll 1d3): (1) permanently turned to stone; (2) –1 penalty to all rolls for 24 hours; (3) struck blind. The type of effect is determined at the time of creation.

15. **Extra arm(s).** Roll 1d6: (1-4) giant has one extra arm in the middle of his chest; (5) giant has a pair of extra arms; (6) giant has 1d4+2 extra arms. Apart from giving the giant the potential to make more grab attacks, each full extra pair of arms provides the giant with an extra action die.

16. **Extra head(s).** Roll 1d6: (1-5) giant has one extra head; (6) giant has two extra heads. Each extra head grants the giant an extra action die as well as an extra Will save to resist magics or emotional or intellectual influence, though oft-times the heads may disagree and bicker.

17. **Frightful presence.** The giant's visage and sheer mass are absolutely terrifying. All who look upon it must make a Will save (DC 10 + giant's HD) or flee in terror (duration 1d4 turns or until a safe distance is reached).

18. **Immunity.** The giant is immune to (roll 1d4): (1) poison; (2) fire; (3) cold; (4) electricity.

19. **Infravision 100'.**

20. **Panoptes.** Truly freakish to behold, the giant's flesh is covered in eyes. Unless a foe approaches using invisibility or a similar means of avoiding any visual detection, the giant cannot be surprised or snuck up on, even when asleep, for some eyes are always vigilant.

21. **Peerless smith.** The giant possesses the ability to craft arms and armor of exceptional quality, and given time may even create magical artifacts. The services of such giants are avidly sought, though the payments they demand can be the cause of legendary quests. At the judge's discretion, the arms the giant itself bears may be enchanted or at least of exceptional quality.

22. **Prophecy.** The giant is gifted with futuresight, and may peer through the mists of time to catch glimpses of what is to come. The results should always be slightly vague, and are left to the judge's discretion. Such giants may be eagerly sought and consulted, though most giants will make great demands to use their ability for others in this way.

23. **Putrid.** The giant's stench is so vile that that anyone coming within 50' must make a DC 12 Fort save each round or succumb to a fit of retching (-2 to all rolls while retching).

24. **Sandman** (1/day). Once per day, the giant may breathe a glittering cloud of sleepdust at those nearby (cloud in front of the giant, radius 1d4×10'). Those within the cloud must make a Fort save (DC 10 + giant's HD) or fall asleep for 1d6 hours. Furthermore, the giant possesses the ability to send dreams to those in slumber, be they nightmares or more pleasant imaginings.

25. **Snatch attack.** The giant can forgo doing damage with a melee attack to try to snatch a target. If the attack is successful, the target is grabbed. The giant cannot make the corresponding melee attack while a creature is snatched. A snatched creature takes 1d6 crushing damage each round if the giant desires. Snatched creatures can attempt to escape with a Strength check (DC 10 + giant's HD).

26. **Sorcerous.** Whether by dint of study and intellect or the prowess of an idiot savant, the giant can cast spells as a wizard of level 1d4+2.

27. **Speak with animals** (1/hour). The giant can designate one animal and communicate effectively in that animal's native tongue for the remainder of the hour. The animal still cannot communicate beyond the limits of its intelligence and physical abilities. Many giants with this ability are accompanied by several bestial pets such as bears.

28. **Stealthy.** Despite his great size and mass, the giant moves with preternatural quiet, barely betraying even the whisper of a sound. The giant gains a +8 bonus to attempts to move silently.

29. **Sun's curse.** If ever subjected to direct sunlight, the giant will be instantly and permanently turned to stone until such a time as spell, artifact, or divine power acts to restore him.

30. **Turn invisible** (1/hour). The giant can turn invisible for up to 1 turn.

GIANT'S WEAPON

The type of weapon used rarely makes any difference to the melee (or missile) damage inflicted, but may indicate a certain style or appearance.

D12	Giant's Weapon
1-2	Axe (could be a rough stone-and-wood affair, or a huge, intricately-engraved battleaxe)
3-9	Club (may be little more than a ripped-up tree trunk, but could also be a beautifully-carved and polished bludgeon)
10-11	Spear (whether a stone head crudely lashed to a rough shaft, or a well-crafted weapon of war) – may also be thrown as a hurled object
12	Sword (indicates some craftsmanship, but could be rusty, roughly-forged iron or an exquisite well-balanced steel arm)

MAKE YOUR FREAK UNIQUE! (MUTATIONS)

Exposure to chaotic energies, devotion to Chaos itself, the results of foul magic gone awry, the unforeseen and random results of terrible experiments—all of these things and more may twist and warp the flesh, bringing mutation. Sadly, mutants are often insane, driven mad by the profound and painful changes their bodies endure.

This article provides a means for rolling random mutations for beasts and characters. A roll can determine how many mutations an individual has, and what those mutations are.

Any contradictory rolls can either be re-rolled, or may represent a second twisting of the mutant with one mutation being replaced by another. This is up to the judge. Similarly, with a little creativity, any given result may be interpreted in different ways. For instance, a "Head, Relocated" result, with the right hand as the random body part location, might mean the entire right hand has been replaced with the individual's head, or might mean the palm of the right hand features the individual's face, but in miniature.

Suffice to say, mutations may change a mutant's senses; a wolf-headed mutant, for example, could be naturally assumed to have great senses of smell and hearing at the judge's discretion.

Mutations providing natural weaponry rarely provide extra attack actions, but provide the mutant with more options for attacking others. The damage inflicted by mutations assumes a mutant of roughly human or demi-human size; the judge may scale up or down the damage caused by certain mutations for creatures of notably larger or smaller size.

CREATING A MUTANT

1) Take a base creature (often a Subhuman, as per DCC RPG core rulebook, p. 429).

2) Determine the number of mutations by rolling on this table:

NUMBER OF MUTATIONS

D6	Mutations
1-4	1
5	2
6	1d3+2

3) Roll for each mutation and apply any results creatively.

Several mutations indicate that **random body parts** must be rolled. For these, use the table below.

RANDOM BODY PARTS

D24	Location
1-2	Head
3-7	Torso, front
8-12	Torso, back
13-14	Right Arm
15-16	Left Arm
17	Right Hand
18	Left Hand
19-20	Right Leg
21-22	Left Leg
23	Right Foot
24	Left Foot

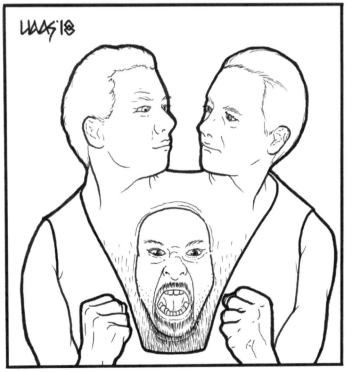
"Why do I always have to be the ideas guy?"

RANDOM MUTATIONS

D100   Mutation and Description

1-2   **Bestial Armor.** Gains substantial natural armor[2] be it (1) thick rhino-like hide, (2) a leathery turtle shell, (3) a glistening black insectile carapace, or (4) tough crocodilian skin.

3-5   **Bestial Arms.** One or more arms have been replaced (roll 1d3): (1) left arm; (2) right arm; (3) both arms. Replacements include (roll 1d6): (1) mantis-like spiked grasping forelimbs[6], (2) reptilian hands with gecko-like pads (provide +1/+2 to climb), (3) crab or scorpion-like pincers[6], (4) large octopoidal tentacles or masses of smaller ones, (5) frog-like webbed hands (provide +1/+2 to swim), or (6) spindly, clawed insectile forelimbs[4].

PAGE 165

6-7	**Bestial Eyes.** Eyes are (1) bulbous, like a frog, (2) compound, like a fly, (3) independent and scaly like a chameleon, (4) slit like a cat, (5) yellow like a wolf, or (6) on stalks like a crab.		

6-7 **Bestial Eyes.** Eyes are (1) bulbous, like a frog, (2) compound, like a fly, (3) independent and scaly like a chameleon, (4) slit like a cat, (5) yellow like a wolf, or (6) on stalks like a crab.

8-10 **Bestial Head I*.** Head of a (1) bear[6], (2) ram[3], (3) rat[4], (4) ape[4], (5) tiger[6], or (6) wolf[4], as well as thick bristly fur all over.

11-13 **Bestial Head II*.** Head of a (1) vulture[3], (2) raven[3], (3) owl[3], or (4) eagle[4], as well as dense coat of feathers all over.

14 **Bestial Head III*.** Head of a (1) frog, (2) octopus[3], (3) squid[3], or (4) salamander, as well as mottled, clammy flesh all over. Fully amphibious.

15-17 **Bestial Head IV*.** Head of a (1) snake (1d2 damage plus DC 10 Fort save or lose 1d4 Sta permanently), or (2) lizard[3], as well as iridescent scales all over.

18-20 **Bestial Head V*.** Head of a (1) elephant[5] with prehensile trunk, (2) bull[5], (3) horse, or (4) rhino[6], as well as thick, leathery skin[1] all over.

21-23 **Bestial Head VI*.** Head of a (1) fly (can consume decaying matter with no ill effect), (2) spider (1d2 damage plus DC 10 Fort save or lose 1d4 Str permanently), (3) cockroach[3], (4) mosquito (1d2 damage plus 1 hp/round blood drain), (5) centipede (1d4 damage plus DC 10 Fort save or paralyzed for 1d7 hours), or (6) ant[4], as well as dark, shiny skin all over.

24 **Bestial Head VII*.** Head of a (1) barracuda/pike[4], (2) shark[6], (3) manta ray, or (4) moray/conger eel[4], as well as thin, silvery scales all over. Also has Gills mutation.

25 **Bestial Head VIII*.** Head of a (1) crab, (2) lobster, or (3) prawn, as well as a tough, smooth exoskeleton[2] all over. Also has Gills mutation.

26-28 **Bestial Legs.** One or both legs have been replaced (roll 1d3): (1) left leg; (2) right leg; (3) both legs. Replacements include (1) furred goat-like legs with cloven hooves, (2) both legs merged into a long snake-like or worm-like tail, (3) frog-like legs with webbed feet, (4) clawed, bird-like legs and feet, (5) furred, feline or canine legs, or (6) long, spindly, clawed insectile legs.

29-30 **Bestial Mouth.** Mouth and nose have merged and changed into a (1) bird-like or octopoidal beak[3], (2) spider's chelicerae (1d2 damage plus DC 10 Fort save or lose 1d4 Str permanently), (3) elephant's mouth, tusks[5] and prehensile trunk, (4) smilodon's muzzle and sabre-teeth[6], (5) snake's mouth and nostrils (1d2 damage plus DC 10 Fort save or lose 1d4 Sta permanently), (6) mosquito's proboscis (1d2 damage plus 1 hp/round blood drain), (7) frog's mouth and sticky tongue, or (8) lamprey-like rasping mouth[3].

31 **Biped/Quadruped.** If a biped, limbs have twisted, stretched, and reset so as to allow to crawl at normal speed, but no longer walk. If quadruped or similar, forelimbs have become arms and hands and creature now walks upright on rear limbs.

32 **Blood Change.** Blood is completely replaced with (1) acid (attacker causing damage in melee must make DC 12 Ref save or be splashed suffering 1d4 damage, then 1d4 damage again the following round), (2) living insects (swarm attacks when host is slain), (3) slime (primeval slime of same HD as host attacks when host is slain), or (4) poison (anything biting must make DC 10 Fort save or be paralyzed for 1d7 hours).

33 **Boneless Mass.** Bones are dissolved. Becomes a pulsing, moving skin-sack that can hold vaguely normal form when needed, but may ooze through small gaps.

34 **Brain, Enlarged.** Brain enlarges to double its normal size. +2d2 Intelligence.

35 **Brain, Shrunken.** Brain shrinks to half normal size. -2d2 Intelligence. Roll 1d6 each round: (1-3) stands confused and drooling; (4-6) acts normally.

36 **Cyclopean.** Eyes merge into single large orb. Poor depth perception increases range penalties by one increment (e.g. Short range becomes Medium).

37 **Deadly Spit.** 1d3 times/day, may spit a glob of (1) acid (1d4 damage, then 1d4 damage the next round), (2) fire (1d4 damage, may ignite flammables), or (3) poison (DC 10 Fort save or lose 1d4 Sta permanently). Range is 20'.

38-39 **Features, Enlarged.** One or more natural features are grossly enlarged to triple their normal size (roll 1d6): (1) one ear; (2) both ears; (3) one eye; (4) both eyes; (5) mouth; (6) nose. If mouth is enlarged, increase bite damage by one die (+1d). Others provide +1 bonus to use appropriate sense.

40-41 **Features, Extra.** Gains 1d4 extra features located on a **random body part**. These are extra (1) ears, (2) eyes, (3) mouths, or (4) noses.

42-43 **Features, Inhuman.** Face is (1) devoid of mandible form, leaving a flapping wet mess in place of the mouth and nose, (2) stripped of flesh leaving a grinning skull, (3) covered in eyes with no other features visible, (4) is a mass of wriggling worm-like tendrils, (5) a twisting, pulsing knot of bloody flesh and bone, or (6) distorted and rent by twisted alien metal barbs and hooks. Creatures of 1 HD or less must make a DC 10 Will save or flee for 1 round.

44-45 **Features, Jumbled.** All of the features are jumbled. The mouth might be where an eye normally is, the nose where the mouth normally is, an ear where the nose normally is, and so on.

46-47 **Features, Missing.** One or more features are missing altogether (roll 1d8): (1) one ear; (2) both ears; (3) one eye; (4) both eyes; (5) mouth; (6) nose; (7) roll twice; (8) all of them. May incur -2 penalty to use sense or may not be able to use at all.

Somewhere on the streets of Punjar between the Temple of the Moon and the Charnel Pits! (See DCC #74: Blades Against Death)

48-49	**Features, Relocated.** One or more features are relocated to **random body parts** (roll 1d8): (1) one ear; (2) both ears; (3) one eye; (4) both eyes; (5) mouth; (6) nose; (7) roll twice; (8) all of them.			

48-49 **Features, Relocated.** One or more features are relocated to **random body parts** (roll 1d8): (1) one ear; (2) both ears; (3) one eye; (4) both eyes; (5) mouth; (6) nose; (7) roll twice; (8) all of them.

50-51 **Features, Shrunken.** One or more features are shrunk to a third of their natural size (roll 1d8): (1) one ear; (2) both ears; (3) one eye; (4) both eyes; (5) mouth; (6) nose; (7) roll twice; (8) all of them. If mouth is reduced, bite damage is reduced by one die (-1d). Others incur -1 penalty to use appropriate sense.

52 **Fetid.** Constantly emits horrendous, vomit-inducing fetor. Creatures within 5′ must make a DC 12 Fort save or be sickened for 1d4 hours (-1 to all actions while ill).

53 **Fragrant.** Constantly emits intoxicating aroma. Creatures within 5′ make a DC 12 Will save per round or stand rapt.

54 **Frame, Corpulent.** Gains bodyweight in rolls of fat. Halve speed, -2 Agility, -1 Ref save, +50% hp.

55 **Frame, Skeletal.** Sheds all but the thinnest veneer of flesh and skin, like a living skeleton. Halve weight, -2 Str, -2 Sta.

56 **Gills.** Gains the ability to (1) breathe water and air, or (2) breathe water only.

57-58 **Head, Enlarged.** Head enlarges to triple its natural size, wobbling about atop the neck.

59-60 **Head, Extra.** Gains 1d2 extra heads. These are (1) located in the same general area, or (2) located at **random body parts**. Extra head is (1) agreeable with original, or (2) argumentative. Extra heads may provide extra actions at the judge's discretion.

61-62 **Head, Relocated.** Head is shifted to a **random body part**.

63-64 **Head, Shrunken.** Head shrunken to a half natural size. -2d2 Intelligence. Reduce bite damage by one die (-1d). Roll 1d6 each round: (1-3) stands confused and drooling; (4-6) acts normally.

65 **Hive Flesh.** Surrounded and physically inhabited at all times by a swarm of (1) ants, (2) flies, (3) wasps, or (4) mosquitoes. Swarm may attack opponents in melee range.

66-67 **Limbs, Enlarged.** One or more limbs have doubled in size (roll 1d6): (1) left arm; (2) right arm; (3) left leg; (4) right leg; (5) both arms; (6) both legs. +2 Strength using the limb. MV +10′ if both legs enlarged.

68-69 **Limbs, Extra.** Has gained 1d4 extra limbs (roll 1d2): (1) arm; (2) leg. These are (1) located in the same general area, or (2) located at **random body parts**. No extra speed or actions gained.

70-71 **Limbs, Jumbled.** One or more legs and arms have swapped places (roll 1d2):. (1) one leg and arm; (2) both legs and arms.

72-73 **Limbs, Missing.** One or more limbs have disappeared altogether (roll 1d7): (1) left arm; (2) right arm; (3) left leg; (4) right leg; (5) both arms; (6) both legs; (7) one arm and one leg.

74-75 **Limbs, Relocated.** One or more limbs are relocated to **random body parts** (roll 1d7): (1) left arm; (2) right arm; (3) left leg; (4) right leg; (5) both arms; (6) both legs; (7) one arm and one leg.

76-77 **Limbs, Shrunken.** One or more limbs have shriveled to half their normal size (roll 1d7): (1) left arm: (2) right arm; (3) left leg; (4) right leg; (5) both arms; (6) both legs; (7) one arm and one leg. -2 Strength using the limb. MV -10′ if both legs shrunk.

78-79 **Natural Weapons I.** Bite enhanced with (1) small fangs[3], (2) boar-like tusks[4], (3) saber-like canines[6], or (4) elephantine tusks[5].

80-81 **Natural Weapons II.** One or both hands enhanced or replaced with animalistic weaponry (roll 1d3): (1) right hand; (2) left hand; (3) both hands. These may be (1) replaced by scorpion-like pincer(s)[6], (2) fingers tipped with small, retractile claws[3], or (3) fingers tipped with long, bear-like claws[6].

82-83 **Natural Weapons III.** Horns sprout from head. These are (1) small harmless pedicles, (2) curling ram's horns[3], (3) sweeping antelope horns[4], (4) broad bull's horns[5], (5) a rhino's horn[6], or (6) a spiraling unicorn's horn[4].

84 **Regeneration.** Heals 1d6 hit points per round except for damage from fire or acid. Regeneration cannot resurrect.

85 **Size Change, Huge.** Doubles in size. +2 HD, natural damage increased by two dice (+2d), MV increased 50%.

86 **Size Change, Small.** Halved in size. -2 HD, natural damage decreased by two dice (-2d), MV halved.

87-88 **Spined Hide.** Flesh is covered in (1) sharp eruptions of bone, (2) porcupine-like spines, or (3) plant-like thorns. This provides +1 AC, and any melee attackers must make a DC 10 Ref save or take 1d3 damage.

89-90 **Strange Hair/Fur.** Hair/fur is replaced with (1) feathers, (2) writhing tendrils, (3) scales, (4) a crest, (5) a mane, or (6) bony growths or is (7-8) bizarrely colored (as per Strange Skin mutation).

91-93 **Strange Skin.** Skin is a strange color or pattern (roll 1d8): (1-4) a single color; (5) striped (two colors); (6) mottled (two colors); (7) spotted (two colors); or (8) chameleon-like (+2 bonus to hide). Determine colors as (1) red, (2) orange, (3) yellow, (4) green, (5) blue, (6) purple, (7) white, (8) black, (9) brown, (10) silver, (11) gold, or (12) transparent.

94-96 **Tail.** Gains a tail that is (1) prehensile and may hold objects and grip things, (2) tipped with a spiked bony club[6], (3) a scorpion-like tail and telson (1d4 damage plus DC 10 Fort save or lose 1d4 Str permanently), or (4) finned like a fish or eel, doubling swimming speed.

97-98 **Wings.** May fly with (1) bat-like wings, (2) dragonfly-like wings, (3) feathered wings, (4) butterfly-like wings, or (5) patagia (may glide only). Flying/gliding speed is double normal movement rate.

99-00 **Judge Creation.** Get creative!

1. Natural +1 AC
2. Natural +2d2 AC
3. Natural attack 1d3 damage
4. Natural attack 1d4 damage
5. Natural attack 1d5 damage
6. Natural attack 1d6 damage

* Mutants with the Bestial Head mutation are frequently called Beastmen.

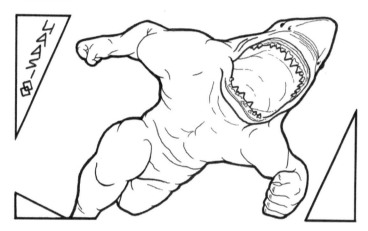

EXAMPLE OF MUTANT CREATION

This example shows how the table can be used to create a group of four subhuman mutants:

SUBHUMAN MUTANT 1

 # Mutations: 1

Mutations: (59) Extra Head

Rolled two extra heads. The first is located next to the original head, and another roll reveals it's agreeable with the original. The second is located at a random body location, and a roll reveals "Torso, front". We can interpret that to mean the mutant has an ugly face peering from the middle of its chest. A final roll reveals it's disagreeable with the original head! Because the mutant has two main heads, the judge also decides that each head controls an arm independently, and so grants the mutant an extra action die.

"Three-Face": Init -1; Atk club +3 melee (1d4+2); AC 13; HD 1d8+2; hp 7; MV 30'; Act 2d20; SP two heads; SV Fort +2, Ref +1, Will -2; AL C.

You hear several voices in the gloom ahead, but see only one figure, a figure with two heads perched atop its shoulders and a rough-hewn club in each hand. The heads seem to be arguing with a third voice, and as the mutant turns, you see a hideous, snarling face peering out from its chest, mouthing obscenities at the two heads above it.

SUBHUMAN MUTANT 2

 # Mutations: 1

Mutations: (24) Bestial Head VII

Rolling gets a shark's head (can bite for 1d6 damage), silvery scales all over, and the Gills mutation for free. It's a Beastman!

"Render": Init -1; Atk bite +3 melee (1d6+2); AC 13; HD 1d8+2; hp 9; MV 30'; Act 1d20; SP breathe underwater; SV Fort +2, Ref +1, Will -2; AL C.

A dull silvery-gray sheen reflects off the skin of the filth-encrusted mutant ahead of you…a sheen that does not reflect at all in the merciless black eyes of its shark-like head! It charges forward, hungry maw agape with rows of gore-encrusted teeth, gills fluttering in its bullish neck!

SUBHUMAN MUTANT 3

 # Mutations: 2

Mutations: (36) Cyclopean and (81) Natural Weapons II

This mutant's eyes have been replaced by a single large ugly eye (poor depth perception; this mutant is terrible at ranged attacks), and a couple more rolls reveal that the left hand has been replaced by a twisted, scorpion-like pincer (1d6 damage).

"Gromm": Init -1; Atk pincer +3 melee (1d6+2); AC 13; HD 1d8+2; hp 8; MV 30'; Act 1d20; SP ranged attack penalties; SV Fort +2, Ref +1, Will -2; AL C.

Mouth twisted in rage, its single eye burning with hate, the cyclopean mutant bellows a warcry and lunges forward, intent on snapping your neck or crushing your skull between the massive pincers that form its left hand!

SUBHUMAN MUTANT 4

 # Mutations: 3

Mutations: (30) Bestial Mouth, (02) Bestial Armor, and (73) Missing Limbs

This mutant's mouth has been replaced by an elephant's prehensile trunk, mouth, and tusks (1d5 damage) while the rest of the head remains that of a normal subhuman. Bestial Armor rolls grant the mutant a +3 AC bonus and indicates that it has tough, rhino-like hide. A final roll indicates that both the mutant's arms are utterly missing! Good thing it has that trunk!

"Slammoth": Init -1; Atk tusks +3 melee (1d5+2) or club +3 melee (1d4+2); AC 16; HD 1d8+2; hp 10; MV 30'; Act 1d20; SP no arms; SV Fort +2, Ref +1, Will -2; AL C.

Storming forward, the leader of the mutants swings a vicious club from its elephantine trunk, cracked tusks stained, human eyes staring wildly! Gnarled, sagging hide covers its filthy naked form — a form whose only trace of arms are withered, crooked fingers sprouting from its shoulders!

REPTILES

Basilisks, giant lizards and snakes, lizard-men, snake-men, and troglodytes: reptilians are staples of fantasy fiction, and the following tables can be used to help customize such creatures.

D20	Reptilian Personal Traits
1	Endlessly patient and economic of action
2	Bony neck frill projects from back of skull
3	Frenetic and ceaselessly in motion
4	Smooth glossy hide
5	Pebbled hide
6	Flicks out tongue to taste the air constantly
7	Cocks head oddly to side when regarding things
8	Legless and serpentine
9	Runs on all fours but stands on hind limbs to observe surroundings
10	Dull rough hide
11	Impressive crest tops head
12	Tail tipped with rattle of dried scales
13	Hide is naturally carved with fine grooves and whorls
14	Possesses a large neck frill that it displays when agitated
15	Large decorative scales thrust up along the whole length of the spine
16	Covered in feathers
17	Inflates frill at throat to display for mates
18	Aggressive and seemingly fearless
19	Hisses loudly when angry or threatened
20	Odd erratic gait

REPTILIAN COLOR

The reptilian's color may be dictated by its habitat, but sometimes it stands out against it surroundings.

D16	Reptilian Color
1	Pure white or albino
2	Pale green
3	Emerald green
4	Dark green
5	Light turquoise
6	Electric blue
7	Dark brown
8	Tan
9	Rust
10	Pale yellow
11	Bright yellow
12	Black
13	One primary color with stripes of a second color running the length of the back. Roll 1d12 to determine each.
14	One primary color (Roll 1d12 to determine) with intricate patterns of black and white scales
15	Head is one color, body another. Roll 1d12 to determine each.
16	One primary color with throat and underside a second color. Roll 1d12 to determine each.

"What did you roll?"

D100	Reptilian Abilities
1-2	**Acidic skin.** The reptile constantly oozes a caustic acid from its skin. This adds +1d4 acid damage to any of its natural attacks, and any unarmed strikes against it suffer 1d4 acid damage automatically. Mundane weapons striking the reptile suffer a –1 damage modifier as it corrodes them.
3-5	**Amphibious.** The reptilian can breathe underwater and swim effortlessly.
6-7	**Beguiling dance.** The reptile can spend an action die to dance, its sinuous, smooth movements entrancing others. Any sapient and/or living creature gazing upon the reptile must succeed on a Will save (DC 10 + reptilian's HD) or be transfixed. Entranced creatures can take no action save to defend themselves while the dance continues. The victim can attempt to throw off the beguilement by attempting a new Will save each round.

Page 170

8-10 **Beweaponed.** The reptile bears a natural weapon of great power such as a great horn, wicked talons, terrible fangs, or even a combination of these. This increases the damage dice of its melee attacks by +1d, so a 1d6 damage bite would become 1d8 instead.

11-13 **Blinding spray** (1/1d4 rounds). The reptile can spray a narrow stream of mild venom unnerringly at a target's eyes. The victim must make a DC 15 Reflex save or be blinded until appropriately treated.

14-15 **Breathe cold** (1/1d4 rounds). The reptilian can spray a cone of blasting cold 30' long and 20' wide at its terminus. All within the area must make a DC 15 Ref save or take 3d6 cold damage and be stunned for 1 round.

16-17 **Breathe fire** (1/1d4 rounds). The reptile may issue forth a flaming jet at its foes, attacking at +10 to a range of 50' and inflicting 3d6 fire damage. Targets must make a DC 15 Ref save or catch fire for another 1d6 damage per round until they pass a subsequent Reflex save or otherwise have the fire extinguished.

18-20 **Burrow.** The reptile can "swim" through sand and dirt at its normal speed.

21-23 **Chameleon skin.** The reptile's skin changes color and pattern constantly to blend with its surroundings. It gains +10 to all attempts at hiding.

24-26 **Constrictor.** The reptilian possesses a long, muscular tail or tentacular appendages that permit it to bind and crush its victims. With a successful melee attack that does not cause damage, it grasps its victim. Each round thereafter it constricts its target for an automatic 1d6 points of damage. Breaking free requires a Strength check (DC 10 + reptilian's HD).

27-28 **Extra head(s).** Roll 1d6: (1-4) reptilian has one extra head; (5) reptilian has two extra heads; (6) reptilian has 1d4+1 extra heads. Each extra head grants the reptilian an additional action die as well as an extra Will save to resist magics or emotional or intellectual influence, though oft-times the heads may disagree and bicker in the case of sapient reptiles.

29-30 **Extra limb(s).** Roll 1d6: (1-3) reptile has one extra pair of arms; (4-6) reptile has one extra pair of legs. An extra pair of arms provides the reptilian with an additional action die, while an extra pair of legs increases the reptile's MV by 10'.

31-33 **Fast reflexes.** The reptilian's Ref save is increased by +4.

34-36 **Gecko climb** (at will). The reptile can climb any surface as if it were a gecko.

37-39 **Gliding membranes.** Gliding membranes extend from the reptile's sides, allowing it to descend from any height undamaged though it cannot actually fly.

40-41 **Human shape** (1/day). The reptile can transform into a human of appropriate gender, assuming all physical traits of that creature.

42-44 **Hypnotic stare.** The reptilian can hypnotize targets with its gaze. The reptilian can gaze into the eyes of one target per round using one action die. A creature that meets the reptile's gaze must make a Will save (DC 10 + reptilian's HD) or stand stupefied, unable even to defend itself, as long as the reptile holds its gaze.

45-47 **Immunity.** The reptilian is immune to (roll 1d4): (1) acid; (2) fire; (3) cold; (4) poison.

48-49 **Independent eyes.** The reptilian's eyes are large and bulbous, moving independently and constantly like those of a chameleon. Unless a foe approaches using invisibility or a similar means of avoiding any visual detection, the reptilian cannot be surprised or snuck up on.

50-52 **Infravision 100'.**

53-55 **Lashing tongue.** The reptilian's tongue is long and muscular. As a melee action it can lash this tongue out to 20', a successful hit grabbing a target and pulling it instantly towards the reptile. Getting free requires a Strength check (DC 10 + reptilian's HD).

56-58 **Lethal tail.** The reptile's tail terminates in a crushing bludgeon or a bristling array of boney spikes, giving it an extra attack in the form of a tail strike that deals 2d6 damage.

59-61 **Lightning strike.** The reptile attacks with blinding speed, increasing its initiative by +4.

62-63 **Petrifying gaze** (1/hour). The reptile can petrify targets with its gaze. The reptilian can gaze into the eyes of one target per round using one action die. A creature that meets the reptile's gaze must make a Will save (DC 10 + reptilian's HD) or be permanently changed to stone.

64-66 **Poisonous bite.** The reptile gains a poisonous 1d6 bite attack if it does not already possess one, or simply the benefits of a poison if it already has a bite attack that powerful or moreso. Poison type (roll 1d4): (1) adder; (2) asp; (3) cobra; (4) viper. Details can be found in Appendix P: Poisons (DCC RPG, p. 446).

67-69 **Regeneration.** The reptilian regenerates 1d3 points of damage at the end of every round and can even regrow lost limbs given a week or so of time, but still dies when reduced to 0 hit points. Damage caused by fire or acid cannot be regenerated.

70-72 **Shell.** The reptilian has a turtle-like shell, increasing its AC by +4.

73-75 **Speak with reptiles** (at will). The reptilian can communicate effectively with any reptiles they encounter. The animal still cannot communicate beyond the limits of its intelligence and physical abilities. Many reptilians with this ability are accompanied by several bestial pets such as giant lizards or snakes.

76-78 **Spines.** Short, thorn-like spines cover the reptile's skin. Any creature making an unarmed attack on it automatically suffers 1d4 damage.

79-80 **Spit acid** (1/1d4 rounds). The reptile may spit a globule of acid at its foes, attacking at +10 to a range of 50' and inflicting 2d6 acid damage. The acid automatically causes 1d6 acid damage per round thereafter until neutralized.

81-83 **Spray venom** (1/hour). The reptilian can spray a cone of poison 30' long and 20' wide at its terminus. All within the area are affected by the reptilian's poison (determine as per Poisonous bite).

84-86 **Stealthy.** The reptile moves with deathly quiet in its native habitat, gaining a +10 bonus to attempts to move silently.

87-89 **Stench** (1/day). Once per day the reptilian can unleash a stench so vile that that anyone coming within 10' must make a DC 12 Fort save each round or succumb to a fit of retching (-2 to all rolls while retching).

90-92 **Thick scales.** The reptilian's AC is increased by +2.

93-95 **Venomous skin.** The reptilian's skin oozes a contact poison. Any creature touching or making an unarmed attack on it must make a DC 15 Fort save or be paralyzed for 1d6 turns.

96-97 **Water runner** (at will). When moving at full speed, the reptile can run across the surface of relatively calm bodies of water as if they were ground.

98-00 **Winged.** Reptile gains MV fly 50'.

DCC THERIANTHROPES

The ravening werewolf, the seductive snake-woman, the mischievous foxwere: all are therianthropes, a mixture of the natures and physicalities of man and beast. How the therianthropy itself started varies greatly, as does the individual's social status; a thrope may be unique, the first of a line, or of an old shapeshifting lineage or tribe. In human form these shapeshifters are just as vulnerable as other men and women, though they may possess physical tells that clue in the wise as to their dual nature. In beast form they come in a multitude of human-beast blendings, though all are superior animal specimens, and all are highly resistant, if not immune, to mundane forms of damage.

Regardless of their origins and form, all assume their natural form when slain, and most damage suffered in one form is cured upon changing to the other—though marks of such damage will remain, such as cuts or burns. Extreme damage, such as the loss of a limb, is carried over.

To create a base form for the thrope, use details of one of the following animals, and apply the Beast Form Modifiers below (as well as any other changes wrought by the shape of the thrope's beast form):

Typical Thrope Animals: Cobra/Viper, Crocodile, Fox/Jackal, Hyena, Jaguar/Leopard, Lion/Tiger, Wolf (DCC RPG, p. 431).

Cobra/viper: Init +6; Atk bite +2 melee (1 plus poison); AC 13; HD 1d6; MV 20' or climb 20'; Act 1d20; SP 25% spitting, poison (DC 18 Fort save or permanently blinded; see DCC RPG p. 446); SV Fort +0, Ref +4, Will +0; AL N.

This represents a particularly large specimen of a snake such as a king cobra. Once per hour, 25% of these animals may spit their venom at a single target up to 10' away.

Crocodile: Init +1; Atk bite +5 melee (3d4); AC 15; HD 3d8; MV 20' or swim 40'; Act 1d20; SP camouflage, roll; SV Fort +3, Ref +0, Will −2; AL N.

These reptiles hide beneath the surface of water with great skill (+10 bonus to such attempts). They may also grasp victims in their jaws and roll them. Any creature successfully bitten must succeed at an opposed Strength check. For purposes of this check, the crocodile has a +10 modifier. If the crocodile wins, it rolls the target underwater. While trapped in this manner, the victim begins drowning. Each round the target takes 1d6 temporary Stamina damage. When Stamina is reduced to 0, the target dies. A crocodile occupied in this manner cannot attack other targets, and the ensnared victim can attack only at a −4 penalty.

Fox/jackal: Init +4; Atk bite +1 melee (1); AC 13; HD 1d3; MV 40'; Act 1d20; SP stealthy; SV Fort +0, Ref +4, Will +0; AL N.

These creatures are sneaky and enjoy a +10 bonus to all attempts to move silently.

Hyena: Init +2; Atk bite +2 melee (1d6+2); AC 12; HD 1d6; MV 30'; Act 1d20; SV Fort +3, Ref +1, Will +1; AL L.

Jaguar/leopard/puma: Init +5; Atk claw +3 melee (1d4) or bite +3 melee (1d4); AC 14; HD 2d4; MV 40'; Act 2d20; SP camouflage, stealthy; SV Fort +2, Ref +4, Will +1; AL N.

Due to their ability to hide and move silently, they enjoy a +10 bonus to both these activities.

Lion/tiger: Init +5; Atk claw +5 melee (1d6) or bite +5 melee (1d6); AC 14; HD 3d6; MV 40'; Act 2d20; SP camouflage, stealthy; SV Fort +4, Ref +4, Will +1; AL N.

Due to their ability to hide and move silently, they enjoy a +10 bonus to both these activities.

THERIANTHROPE BEAST FORM MODIFIERS:

- Maximum hit points for Hit Dice, +1 per die. For example, a 1d3 HD thrope would have 4 hit points in beast form, and a 3d6 HD thrope would have 21 hit points.
- Add 1d3 to each of the following: initiative, AC, attack bonuses, saves.
- The beast form's mystical nature reduces the damage of all blows against it by 2d4 points (roll to determine at creation), save those of magic and the thrope's bane.
- Increase any damage dice by 1 die (minimum 1d4).
- Increase action die by +1d.
- Add infravision 100'.

D7	Therianthropic Beast Form Shape
1	**Beast-man (i.e., the classic wolf-man):** Reduce bite damage to that of normal for the animal type, MV becomes 40', gains claws that inflict 1d6 damage (or the same damage as the creature's claws already do, if higher). Also gains one extra action die to make an additional claw attack.
2	**Humanoid animal (furred biped with beast head):** MV becomes 40', gains claws that do 1d6 damage (or the same damage as the creature's claws already do, if higher). Also gains one extra action die to make an additional claw attack.
3	**Normal animal:** No change.
4	**Normal animal but with disturbingly human face:** Reduce bite damage to that of normal for animal type, but may talk normally if desired.
5	**Normal animal but with hand-like forelimbs/paws:** Reduce claw damage to normal for that animal type (if any), but therianthrope may manipulate objects such as door handles.
6	**Normal animal but with human eyes:** No change.
7	**Normal animal but with no tail:** No change.

D16	Therianthropic Origins
1	Beast that became human/human-like by devouring people
2	Beast that learned to become human/human-like
3	Bitten by a thrope
4	Blessed by a patron/deity
5-6	Cannibal who became a beast
7-8	Cursed by beast whose skin they stole
9-10	Cursed by deity for transgression
11-12	Cursed by ghost of someone they slew
13-14	Cursed by witch
15	Inhabited by evil spirit
16	Natural shapeshifter

D20	Control Over Bestial Form
1-2	Constantly transformed – only assumes human or natural animal form when slain
3-9	Transforms every full moon
10-14	Transforms every night
15-19	Transforms whenever angered/hurt/enflamed with lust
20	Voluntary – can shift form at will 1d4 times per day

D12	Tells in Human Form
1	Constantly hungry
2	Curved fingernails
3	Eyebrows meet in the middle
4	Eyes gleam in light
5	Eyes those of beast
6	Fur/scales under the tongue
7	Hairy palms
8	Has bestial tail
9	Howls/hisses when startled
10	Low-set ears
11	Unusually long canines
12	When cut, fur/scales are seen beneath the skin

D12	Therianthropic Diet
1-3	Corpse-eater
4-10	Man-eater
11-12	Normal for animal

D8	Therianthropic Bane
1-2	Damaged by holy water and other implements as if un-dead, and may be turned by clerics of any alignment
3	Damaged by organic implements (bone, wood, fists, fangs, and claws of animals, etc.)
4-8	Damaged by silver

D16	Unusual Therianthropic Abilities
1	**Balefire breath** (1/1d4 rounds). The beast's eyes glow an eerie hue, and it may issue forth a flaming jet of the same color at its foes, attacking at +10 to a range of 50' and inflicting 3d6 fire damage. Targets must make a DC 15 Ref save or catch fire for another 1d6 damage per round until they pass a subsequent Reflex save or otherwise have the fire extinguished.
2	**Blood sniffer.** The beast's sense of smell is infallible and can automatically detect the scent of flesh and blood up to 100' away with pinpoint precision.
3	**Cursed bite.** Anyone bitten by the thrope and survives, must make a DC 12 Fort save or become a therianthrope of the same type themselves, albeit subject to the utter control of their "parent". The transformation takes 1d4 days.
4	**Damage immunity.** The thrope is completely immune to mundane sources of damage, and is only harmed by magical attacks and those of their bane.
5	**Diseased bite.** The beast's bite carries a terrible rotting disease. Anyone bitten must make a DC 12 Fort save or lose 1 Stamina per day until dead or cured.
6	**Fast reflexes.** The beast's Ref save is increased by +4.
7	**Great speed.** Double the thrope's MV.
8	**Hypnotic gaze.** The thrope can gaze into the eyes of one target per round using one action die. A creature that meets the beast's gaze must make a Will save (DC 10 + thrope's HD) or stand stupefied, unable even to defend itself, as long as the beast holds its gaze.
9	**Lock-bane.** Mundane doors, locks, and catches automatically undo themselves when the beast comes within 10'.
10	**Poisonous teeth/claws.** The thrope's bestial attacks are venomous. Any that do damage force the victim to make a DC 12 Fort save or be paralyzed for 1d6 hours.
11	**Regeneration.** The beast regenerates 1d3 points of damage at the end of every round and can even regrow lost limbs given a week or so of time. Damage caused by the therianthrope's bane cannot be regenerated.
12	**Seductive** (at will). In human form the thrope exudes powerful animal attraction. Anyone of the

appropriate sexuality within 5' of the human-form thrope must make a DC 12 Will save or fall under the thrope's control, utterly smitten by them. This acts as the *charm person* spell check result of 14-17 (DCC RPG, p. 131) but the victims are not marked by the influence and the influence itself is not magical.

13 **Speak with beasts** (at will). Even in human form, the thrope can communicate effectively with any normal animals of their type. The animal still cannot communicate beyond the limits of its intelligence and physical abilities. Additionally, all animals of the thrope's type within 50' must make a DC 12 Will save or automatically become friendly towards them. Many thropes with this ability are accompanied by several bestial allies.

14 **Stealthy.** The thrope moves with deathly quiet, gaining a +10 bonus to attempts to move silently.

15 **Terrible teeth.** Increase the damage of the thrope's beast form bite by +1d (a 1d8 bite would become 1d10, for example).

16 **Vampiric.** Following a successful bite attack, the beast automatically drains 1d6 hit points per round until slain.

MONSTROUS PATRONAGE

"Lousy, stinking adventurers," Gruggle the goblin muttered as he gingerly placed a side of rat steak on the black eye he was nursing, courtesy of a cleric's mace. "Just when you t'ink you got 'em dead, one of those bozos in a robe shouts out and da tide gets turned!"

"Tell me about it," Shungo the orc sighed, commiserating with his friend while trying to staunch the blood pouring from where his left ear once was. "I remember one time me and da boys had a group of dese jokers cornered and was set to give 'em a good ol' Mordor blanket party when, all o' a sudden, de wizard's patron sends a friggin' treeman to beat us up!"

"Treeman? Dat's nothin'! Me and some other gobbos had this scrawny elf trapped on the edge of Bottomless Canyon once, all ready to shove 'im of de cliff. Know what 'e did? 'E went back in time and warned 'imself we wuz gonna do that! I mean, how can a hardworkin' monster expect to compete with dat sorta thing?!"

Shungo slowly lowered the bloodstained rag from his head and looked thoughtfully at the goblin. "Maybe der's a way," he said slowly and softly. "Maybe der is a way…"

or far too long, the adventuring wizard and elf have enjoyed great advantage over their monstrous foes. The ability to bond with a powerful supernatural entity and draw upon that being's power is a potent one, leaving even the toughest monsters at a disadvantage at times. Many judges know the heartbreak of planning a climactic battle to end an adventure or campaign, only to watch it dissolve in a single *invoke patron* spell check.

This article introduces new and devilishly delightful ways of granting the monstrous residents of a DCC RPG campaign the power to invoke their own patrons. From the Mother of Monsters to Magog the Beast, the inhuman dungeon denizens now have formidable allies and awesome powers of their own to drawn upon and the PCs will soon learn what it's like to be on the other end of a patron's invoked might.

MONSTER PATRONAGE

As every good DCC RPG judge should know, monsters don't play by the rules and this article doesn't either. Rather than introduce a new *patron bond/invoke patron* system for monstrous spellcasters, it provides a mechanic that any monster—from the lowliest goblin to the most powerful of dragons—might use to draw power from a patron. This new mechanism is called the **monster patron die**.

The monster patron die is a die of varying size that is rolled along with the creature's typical attack, spell check, or saving throw action die. The result on the monster patron die is compared to the roll of the action die, and if lower than the action die result, the monstrous patron steps in to aid his servant.

A typical servant of a monstrous patron typically uses a d20 as its monster patron die, but more esteemed or powerful servants might roll a d16 or d14 instead, thus increasing the probability of patron aid when facing powerful foes.

If the monster patron die result is less than the unmodified action die roll, the judge compares the **monster patron die** roll to the corresponding entry on the table for the appropriate monstrous patron (see Tables 9-16 and 9-18) and applies the results.

If the monster patron die roll is equal to or greater than the creature's unmodified action roll, one of two things occur: either nothing happens as the patron ignores its servant, allowing the creature to attempt to invoke his patron again at a penalty; or the monstrous entity becomes enraged at the temerity of its servant and punishes it accordingly.

A higher result on the monster patron die than the action die roll produces no unfortunate effects if the roll is 19 or less. The monster can attempt to call upon his patron on a subsequent round, but the monster patron die increases by +1d on the die chain. Thus, the typical servant of a monstrous patron would roll a d24 on its next attempt to invoke its patron, while a more favored assistant's monster patron die might increase from a d16 to a d20.

A monster whose initial attempt to invoke the power of his patron failed can continue to try to call on the entity's assistance until either his monster patron die would exceed a d30 (usually after three failed attempts) or if displeasure is provoked: when the monster patron die results in a roll of 20 or greater, the patron is displeased with its servant and visits a punishment known as monstrous patron displeasure. The judge consults the Patron Displeasure Table for the appropriate entity using the **action die roll**, then applies the corresponding effects upon the unfortunate creature. Unless the displeasure effect stipulates otherwise, the displeasure transpires immediately.

Once a monster successfully invokes the aid of his monstrous patron, he usually cannot do so again during that same encounter or combat; but at the judge's discretion, exceedingly powerful monsters such as dragons, un-dead, and similar creatures might be able to call upon their patron for assistance multiple times but only by using an increased monster patron die to do so. This monster patron die suffers the same +1d penalty for each subsequent attempt as if the creature had failed its attempt.

WHO CAN INVOKE A MONSTROUS PATRON?

Although it is possible for any intelligent monster to procure the patronage of a supernatural entity, in reality it is only the exceptionally evil, cunning, and twisted who succeed in attracting the attention of these potent beings. The measures required to gain the notice of one of these powerful entities are grueling, even potentially lethal, and only the hardiest and most determined monsters survive them. It would be extraordinarily rare for the average goblin warrior or kobold cutthroat to live through the dangerous rites to earn the patronage of a powerful entity—but that doesn't mean

PAGE 177

sual observer untrained in monstrous lore or supernatural knowledge is likely to expect the monster is attempting something unusual.

The judge can create his own list of special rites and acts required to invoke a monstrous patron, or choose or roll randomly on the following table to determine what the invoking monster does to call down the might of its horrible master.

TABLE 9-15: MONSTROUS PATRON INVOCATION ACTIONS

Roll 1d20	Result
1	The monster cuts fresh wounds in its skin, allowing the blood to fall freely onto the ground.
2	The monster bites off the head of a small animal (bat, rat, cat, dog, etc.).
3	The monster speaks the Seven Profane Words in its native tongue. Thunder sounds and lights grow dim.
4	The monster breaks a sacred bone across its knee and scatters the pieces in an esoteric pattern.
5	The monster stabs an allied creature, automatically doing 1d4 points of damage.
6	The monster bites off one of its fingers or toes.
7	The monster burns its flesh with fire or an acidic substance.
8	The monster consumes fresh offal or bodily waste.
9	The monster slices strange symbols into its flesh.
10	The monster notches its ears, nose, or arms with sacred marks.
11	The monster shakes a bone rattle dedicated to its patron and cries out to the heavens (or down to the hells).
12	The monster shouts the Ancient Phrase of Power.
13	The monster sings a rhythmic, rhyming chant in its native language.
14	The monster drives rusted nails, broken glass, razor-sharp metal, or similar painful objects into its body.
15	The monster claws at its face, carving bleeding runnels into its own skin.
16	The monster punches itself in the mouth repeatedly until a tooth or fang is knocked free.
17	The monster consumes a vile concoction of liquids, clumps of exotic herbs, dried animal brains, or similar gross matter.
18	The monster flays its own body with a specially consecrated whip with lashes bearing embedded shards of sharp bone.
19	The monster makes bizarre and somewhat obscene gestures in the air or over its weapon.
20	Roll again twice.

it's utterly impossible, and the judge is free to use the PCs' expectation against them to keep them on their toes.

It is far more likely, however, for creatures such as sentient un-dead, dragons, giants, subhuman cultists, corrupted nature spirits and Unseelie faeries, deep ones, monstrous humanoids of 2 HD or better (minotaurs, ogres, shrooman, etc.), and the elite ranks such as shamans and chieftains amongst lesser humanoid monster types (goblins, orcs, gnolls, bugbears, hobgoblins, et al.) to serve a monstrous patron.

The rites a monster might need to perform or the actions necessary to attract the attention of a monstrous patron make for excellent adventure seeds and a reason for the PCs to come into conflict with the new monstrous servant. For example, if the monster must horrifically murder the occupants of several human farms on the night of the new moon to engage in a compact with its patron, the party is certain to hear of the massacre and possibly intervene. They might expect a particularly nasty band of goblins or orcs are behind it, but are surprised to discover only a single monster—now with supercharged powers—is the culprit.

INVOKING THE PATRON

The game mechanic for invoking a monstrous patron is simple, but the in-game methods a monstrous servant must employ to call upon its master's power are anything but. The monster must make special gestures, speak certain words, wield potent talismans, or perform specific ritualistic measures if it hopes to attract its patron's attention. Even a ca-

ASSUAGING THE ANGER OF A MONSTROUS PATRON

After the first failed attempt to invoke the assistance of a monstrous patron, the chance of attracting its displeasure increases in the form of an increased monster patron die size. In some cases, the servant's attempts to call upon his patron's aid become hopeless due to repetition (the monster patron die increased beyond a d30). The long term effects of such penalties are usually not needed by the judge (the monster is slain by the PCs before it can attempt to make amends to its patron, for example), but in rare cases it might be required for the judge to see how long it takes for a servant to assuage the anger of its patron and reduce the chance of incurring displeasure.

The simplest way is to say the monster patron die resets after 24 hours have passed, so long as the monster didn't incur a displeasure result. If the servant was struck by patron displeasure, the penalty drops by 1d every 24 hours. Thus, if the monster patron die was increased to d30, it would take two full days for the die to return to a d20 or three full days to return to a d16. At the judge's discretion, the monster can perform a sacrifice, usually a living creature, in his patron's name to reduce the penalty by 1d should he need to quickly reestablish himself into his master's good (or evil) graces.

NEW MONSTROUS PATRON: THE MOTHER OF MONSTERS

Every monster culture has myths of a primordial deity that spawned their numbers. Amongst the serpent men, this deity is known as "She-Without-Pity." The hobgoblins call their goddess "The Womb of the Culling Tooth." Dragons know her as "Kalimat of the Colorless Scales." Each of these monikers, however, refers to a single ghastly goddess, the origin of the multiverse's nightmares: the Mother of Monsters. No matter what species a monstrous creature might be born to, the Mother of Monsters can be called upon to aid those who recognize her as the origin of all terrible life.

Table 9-16: The Mother of Monsters Invocation Table

Monster Patron Die Result	Monster is Attacking	Monster is Spellcasting	Monster is Making a Saving Throw
1-2	The monster's weapon (natural or constructed) causes bleeding wounds that inflict an additional 1d6 damage each round for five rounds.	A horrible laughter echoes around the monster as the Mother of Monsters bolsters its sorcery. The monster gains a +10 bonus to its spell check.	Ghostly, monstrous arms manifest around the servant, protecting it from harm. The monster automatically succeeds in its saving throw regardless of DC.
3-4	The fire of primordial creation erupts around the monster. It gains a +2 bonus to AC, a +4 bonus to attacks and damage, and an additional d16 action die for 2d10 rounds.	Purple larvae burst from the monster's flesh as the Mother of Monsters amplifies its casting. Monster gains a +9 bonus to its spell check.	The monster is covered with a bloody, slimy caul that grants a +8 bonus to its next 1d3 saving throws.
5-6	A 10' square primordial slime with random special properties appears (DCC RPG pp. 423-424) and acts on the behest of the monster. It remains until slain or 2d8 rounds elapse.	A crack of thunder and a ghostly, monstrous female face appears over the caster. The monster gains a +8 bonus to its spell check.	A pair of scaly hands appear before the monster, batting away the effect being saved against and granting a +7 saving throw bonus.
7-8	The Mother of Monsters speeds up her servant, granting the monster a second attack with a +4 bonus for 1d5 rounds.	The monster is struck with agonizing birth pains and suffers 1 point of damage. It gains a +6 bonus to its spell check in return.	A ragged, ethereal bat wing drapes itself over the monster, providing a +6 saving throw bonus.
9-10	Caustic juices cover the monster's weapon(s). Successful attacks inflict an additional 1d6 damage. The burning liquid endures for 2d6 rounds.	Tiny, ghastly fetuses dance around the spellcaster and amplify its castings. The monster receives a +5 bonus to its spell check.	A wall of tentacles bursts from the ground in front of the monster, deflecting the effect being saved against and granting a +5 saving throw bonus.
11-12	In addition to dealing damage, the monster's attack covers its target with a constricting caul of scaly flesh. The target must make a DC 12 Ref save or become entangled. The victim cannot attack or move until it breaks free with a DC 12 Strength check.	A terrible scream of primordial creation resounds around the monster. It enjoys a +4 bonus to its spell check.	The monster's flesh produces a slick film of curdled milk that provides a +4 bonus to its saving throw.
13-14	A swarm of gnawing monster babies emerges from the servant's mouth, crawling over its target. These carnivorous children attack for 1d3+1 rounds with a bite (+3 melee, 1d5 damage). They are immune to all attacks and spells and vanish after the duration elapses.	The ground shudders as if in the midst of birth pangs as the Mother of Monsters makes her presence known. The monster gains a +3 bonus on its spell check.	A gruesome mouth filled with jagged teeth manifests before the monster and consumes some of the effect being saved against. The monster gains a +3 saving throw bonus.
15-16	Viscous fluids of unholy origin flow over the monster, imparting the Mother's power to it. Its attack and damage rolls gain a +2 bonus for the next 1d4+1 attacks.	The monster's flesh darkens as the Mother of Monsters touches the spellcaster, granting it a +2 bonus to its spell check.	A wisp of breath stinking of rancid mother's milk blows past the monster and grants a +2 bonus to its saving throw.
17-18	A pustule-covered tongue protrudes from a rift in time and space to lick the monster's weapon(s). It next two damage rolls gain a +2 bonus.	The wailing cry of a horrific infant rings through the air. The monster gains a +1 bonus to its spell checks on its next two spells.	The Mother of Monsters erects a fragile shell around the monster. It shatters under the effect the monster is saving against, but provides a +1 bonus to its saving throw.
19+	The monster gains a +1 bonus to its next attack roll as the Mother of Monsters imparts a scrap of her power into the creature's weapon.	The Mother of Monsters intercedes and twists the skein of magic. The monster can make another spell check (without rolling a monster patron die) and take the better spell check result.	A horrible, translucent infant monster appears to take a portion of the effect being saved against. The monster can roll two saving throws and take the better result.

TABLE 9-17: THE MOTHER OF MONSTERS PATRON DISPLEASURE TABLE

Action Die Result	Displeasure Effect
1	The Mother of Monsters's anger is terrible indeed! She slays the irritating servant outright, blasting its body into a red slime that evaporates into a stinking black cloud.
2-3	A swarm of gruesome, flying monstrous infants appears and gnaws the servant with piranha-like mouths before vanishing. The monster suffers 1d5 points of damage.
4-5	Agonizing pains afflict the monster. It can take no action for the next 1d3 rounds. At the end of that time, the creature gives birth to a twisted homunculus of itself that capers off, tittering madly.
6-7	The monster's flesh sprouts tiny, egg-like pustules filled with tiny monsters. The pustules burst the following round, unleashing a horde of tiny terrors. The birth of these creatures inflicts 1d3 points of damage and causes a -1d penalty on all action dice rolls for the following round. The monsters run off to grow into new terrors.
8-9	The monster's body becomes swollen as if in the last stages of pregnancy. The creature suffers a -2 penalty to attack rolls, skill checks requiring grace or agility, and Ref saves. This effect is permanent unless the servant somehow convinces the Mother to reverse the effects.
10-11	The monster suffers birth pangs and must make a DC 8 Fort save each round for 1d4 rounds. On a failed save, it suffers a -2 penalty to all its actions for that round.
12-13	The monster is reduced to a mewling infant, incapable of doing anything but bawling and crying for 1d5 rounds. After this time, it returns to normal size.
14-15	The monster is chastised by the Mother. Tentacle-like whips appear from a rift in time and space to lash the creature. These blows inflict 1d6 points of damage and impart a -1d penalty on all the creature's rolls for 2d4 days.
16-17	A horrific maw opens in the ground beneath the monster. It must make a DC 10 Ref save or fall into the mouth, suffering 1d6 damage and being unable to move for 1d5 rounds.
18-19	The monster is immediately transformed back into an infant and must once again grow up, reliving childhood to reach adulthood. Depending on the monster type, this could take decades. The monster is defenseless as an infant, but some kind-hearted adventurers might take pity on the poor thing.
20+	The Mother of Monsters snatches away her servant, transporting it to her Womb of Pain, where the creature undergoes 1d7 days of instructional torture. The monster reappears from where it was taken after this time with a single hit point remaining.

NEW MONSTROUS PATRON: MAGOG THE BEAST

One of the feared Hosts of Chaos, Magog the Beast is often called upon by the monstrous and bestial to aid them in their hatred of the goodly races and the sowing of chaos and destruction. A callous power, Magog cares only for the pleasurable sensation of spilling blood, tearing out the throats of one's enemies, and consuming their still-warm flesh in an orgy of violence and gore. Magog is a common patron of ogres, minotaurs, and other bestial giants.

Table 9-18: Magog Invocation Table

Monster Patron Die Result	Monster is Attacking	Monster is Spellcasting	Monster is Making a Saving Throw
1-2	A pair of elephantine trunks ending in six-fingered hands sprout from the monster's body. These appendages grant two additional attacks (+5 melee, 2d4+1 damage each) using a d20 action die every round for 2d6 rounds.	Animalistic power rushes through the monster. It gains a +8 spell check bonus. In addition, if the spell is one that causes damage, the evocation automatically inflicts maximum damage.	Empowered by Magog's bestial power, the monster not only automatically succeeds but reflects the effect being saved against back at its source, which must save against its own effect (if applicable).
3-4	Magog drains the blood of the monster's victims, infusing its servant with a portion of their vitality. The monster gains a number of hit points equal to the damage of a successful attack. These stolen hp can exceed the monster's usual maximum and last for 24 hours or until removed by injuries.	Magog's rage fuels the spellcaster, granting a +7 bonus to its spell check. In addition, any saving throw against the spell suffers a -2 penalty due to the ferocity of the magic.	The monster's flesh becomes thick and wrinkled, like that of a hellish pachyderm. The monster gains a +8 bonus to all saving throws for 2d8 rounds.
5-6	A clawed animal-like arm sprouts from the monster's chest. This arm provides a second attack each round (+4 melee, 1d5 damage) using a d20 action die. The arm remains for 2d3 rounds.	Savage sorcery born from Magog's hunger flows through the monster. It gains either a +6 bonus to its spell check or receives a +3 bonus and can cast a second spell immediately afterward using 1d16+3.	Enraged at the audacity of targeting his servant, Magog intervenes on the monster's behalf. It gains a +6 bonus to its saving throw and, if the save succeeds, enjoys a +1d bonus on its next action or saving throw.
7-8	Magog innervates the monster's body, increasing his strength and vitality. The creature gains a +4 bonus to attacks and damage and 10 temporary hit points. The hit points are lost first if the creature is injured; otherwise these vanish after 1 hour.	A monstrous roar sounds as the caster completes his casting. Magog amplifies the spell with a +5 spell check bonus. However, the creature must make a physical attack the following round: Magog desires bloodshed.	Magog allows the monster to draw upon its own life to shrug off the effect. The monster can reduce its hit points to gain a bonus on a 1:1 basis. It can spend up to 10 hit points to gain a +10 saving throw bonus.
9-10	The monster turns ferocious, its attacks fueled by hatred. It receives a +3 bonus to attacks, but any that strike inflict maximum damage. This effect lasts for 1d6 rounds.	Magog intercedes in the casting. The spellcasting creature can spellburn after the spell check has been made, spending up to CL+3 points of spellburn to bolster his spell.	Scales and bone plates appear on the creature's body, protecting it from some harm. These provide a +5 saving throw bonus for 1d4 rounds, then vanish.
11-12	Magog's animalistic power imparts cat-like reflexes on the creature. He gains a +2 bonus to attack and a +2 AC bonus for 1d4 rounds. Additionally, during that time, he can attempt to parry one melee attack directed at him each round. If the creature rolls a d20+2 and it beats the attacker's roll to hit, the attack misses.	The fury of Magog grants the caster a +4 spell check bonus. If the spell inflicts damage, the damage roll also gains a +4 bonus; otherwise there is no additional effect.	A pair of gigantic six-fingered hands appears and tear the effect causing the saving throw to shreds. The monster gains a +4 saving throw bonus.

Table 9-18: Magog Invocation Table (continued)

Monster Patron Die Result	Monster is Attacking	Monster is Spellcasting	Monster is Making a Saving Throw
13-14	Magog transforms the monster's blows into deadly wounds. The next 1d3 successful attacks made by the monster are automatic crits.	Magog has no time for his servants who will not bleed for him. He grants a +3 spell check bonus, but if the spell is a damaging one, the creature can spend his own hp on a 1:1 basis to increase damage up to an additional +5.	A ghostly robe resembling the stinking rags Magog wears cloaks the creature. It gains a +3 saving throw bonus for two rounds.
15-16	The monster's body hums with Magog's power, granting him a +2 bonus to all attack rolls and an additional d16 action die that can be used to make melee attacks.	Magog imparts a fragment of power upon the creature, increasing his spell check by +3 if it is a damage-causing spell or +2 if it is a spell of another type.	The power of the Host of Chaos emerges around the creature. Roll 1d5 to determine the bonus the creature receives to its saving throw: a 1 adds +1, a 2 adds +2, etc.
17-18	The monster goes into a bestial rage. It is immune to fear effects, never checks morale, and gains a +2 bonus to attacks and damage. This rage lasts for 1d6+1 rounds.	The ferocity of Magog grants the spellcaster a +2 bonus to his spell check and, if the spell causes damage, allows the caster to roll damage twice and take the better result.	A thick coat of matted hair and scales emerges from the monster's flesh. This provides a +2 saving throw bonus against physical effects, but only +1 against mental ones.
19+	The monster receives a portion of Magog's strength, gaining a +1 bonus to the attack. If it is a bite attack, it also gains a +2 bonus to damage.	The animal power of the Beast allows the monster to make two spell checks and take the better result.	Magog has little pity for the monster. The Beast begrudgingly grants a +1 saving throw bonus.

Table 9-19: Magog Patron Displeasure Table

Action Die Result	Displeasure Effect
1	Magog craves the blood and flesh of his servant. A rending mouth appears and consumes the monster, slaying it in a tide of blood and shredded flesh.
2-3	Tearing claws appear around the monster, ripping its body and inflicting great pain. The creature suffers 1d6 damage and must make a DC 14 Fort save or pass out from the agony for 2d10 rounds.
4-5	Magog consumes some of the creature's life force. The monster is immediately reduced to 2 hit points and is paralyzed for 1d3 rounds as Magog drains its essence.
6-7	Magog inflicts a bestial mutation on the creature. Roll 1d7 to determine the type: 1) elephant ears; 2) goat horns; 3) itching scales; 4) non-prehensile tail; 5) weak sucker pads; 6) cow udders; 7) skunk's tail.
8-9	Magog desires to teach his servant a lesson. The creature becomes bestial and rage-filled for 1d5 rounds. During that time, it cannot cast spells, speak, or compose rational thoughts. It can only make physical attacks.
10-11	Magog marks his irritating servant with his sign: the six-fingered hand. The creature's hands become oversized and six-fingered, causing clumsiness that imparts a -2 penalty to physical attacks and skill checks requiring dexterity. This effect is permanent unless the creature somehow convinces Magog to reverse the transformation.
12-13	Magog drains a portion of his servant's blood to satiate his bestial hunger. The monster suffers either 2d4 points of damage or 1d4 points of temporary Stamina drain (judge's choice).
14-15	Magog transforms the creature's nose into a limp, elephantine trunk ending in a six-fingered hand. The trunk is not prehensile and hangs lifeless, a symbol of Magog's displeasure. It is permanent unless somehow Magog is persuaded to reverse the transformation.
16-17	A tremendous six-fingered hand bursts from the earth and slaps the offending monster. The blow knocks him prone and inflicts 1d4 damage. The monster suffers a -4 penalty to all rolls for the next 2d3 rounds.
18-19	A terrible roar of displeasure directed at the monster splits the air. Dazed by the roar, it suffers a -2 penalty to all rolls for the next two round and must make a DC 15 Fort save or be knocked prone.
20+	The creature is overwhelmed by a feeling of terror and becomes paralyzed with fright. He can perform no action but cower before Magog's might for 1d4 rounds.

Appendix M
Moustaches

A moustache is a serious thing.

THE 'STACHE STASH: MAGIC MOUSTACHES FOR DCC RPG

In the world of Dungeon Crawl Classics RPG, the threads of magic that infuse the world with power and definition are often drawn to places of awesome natural beauty – majestic waterfalls, towering mountains, breathtaking live oak trees. Occasionally, the magical power of the universe finds its way into that most spectacular of natural wonders: the rock solid 70's style ultra groovy moustache.

When an adventurer of some note, 2nd-level or higher, grows a truly righteous 'stache they might just catch the attention of the Sub Naribus, a mysterious power of exacting aesthetics who may choose to infuse that cookie duster with a fraction of his amazing power.

Not everyone can grow a moustache by normal means – i.e., just not shaving. If your character decides it's time to rock a truly righteous 'stache they must make a Personality check – this roll is made exactly once and the result is permanent. Success means they can actually grow a decent 'stache and not just some embarrassing peach fuzz that just makes him look shifty and weird. Scoring a 20 or better on that roll means characters can grow a seriously epic 'stache that makes the world stand up and take notice.

Once your 'stache is grown, the judge determines if it is so righteous that Sub Naribus himself notices, and decides to test the character to see if he is worthy. This can take whatever form the judge chooses. The Mighty Cosmic 'Stachanator always tests his chosen ones secretly. He might send them on a quest, using cat's-paws and indirectly changing the circumstances to put an adventure in the character's path, to see if they handle it with real gusto. Mighty Sub Naribus might test them in other ways, like appearing as a student barber offering gold for a chance to skin his lip so he can practice his hot shave.

Whatever the case, if the 'Stache-rocker is deemed worthy, Sub Naribus imbues the moustache in question with a fraction of his cosmic power, and that character is now the proud possessor of a Magical Moustache. Aw yeah.

You could roll randomly, but we suggest that you have the judge, as Sub Naribus the All-Grooming, choose a good Magic Moustache for the newly 'Stache Anointed. Different types of magical moustaches are described below. Each moustache power is activated via a certain action (see below) and comes with a unique manifestation (also described below).

Every Magic Moustache draws power from the character's Whisker Points.

Whisker Points = Character's Personality bonus + Luck bonus, minimum 1.

Each use of the Magic Moustache costs one Whisker Point. Whisker Points regenerate at a rate of one per night spent in rest and careful grooming.

MOUSTACHE MANIFESTATION

Every Magic Moustache manifests its power differently. Roll to see how the Moustache activates, and what unique effect it creates.

d10	Moustachial Effect
1	A demon in a tuxedo appears, hands you an item then disappears. Item is (1d5): (1) a cocktail; (2) a menu with pictures of everyone you are about to fight in it; (3) a lit cigar; (4) a 9 iron; (5) a shot of something you are likely going to regret in the morning.
2	A pair of sunglasses appears on your face for 1d6 rounds when you activate the power. Style (1d5): (1) aviators; (2) giant sparkly disco stars; (3) highway patrol; (4) wayfarers; (5) futuristic punk rock monoblock.
3	All of your allies grow their choice of badass facial hair when you activate any 'Stache ability. These new facial features are permanent until they shave.
4	Every creature you point at grows an amazing moustache – no exceptions. This also works on inanimate objects that have a face. You can give a moustache to a statue, an elf maiden, a fire elemental, your horse, etc. Once shaved these moustaches do not regrow, unless the 'Stache Warrior decides to give them another one at some point.
5	For 1d6 rounds after you activate a 'Stache power you develop a soundtrack that can be clearly heard 100' away. Style (1d8): (1) 70's funk with a handclap; (2) maw chikka mau-mau; (3) one long, sustained, metal power chord; (4) Western saloon piano; (5) dangerous guitar and castanets; (6) chorus of angels singing down the godlights; (7) old school breakbeats; (8) soundtrack to a movie with elves in it.
6	You break out in awesome, rock star permanent tattoos, the general theme being (1d6): (1) sexy dragons; (2) everything you ever killed; (3) Ronnie James Dio vs. King Diamond; (4) serious hotties; (5) tribal; (6) photorealistic family and friends.
7	You break out in weak, regrettable permanent tattoos, the general theme being (1d5): (1) bands I used to really, really like; (2) discount hotties; (3) I was totally in the Navy and totally saw hula girls!; (4) jail was sooooooo booring; (5) Speling is for Cyssies!

8   You have a second magically awesome hair symptom (1d7): (1) amazing head of shagadelic curls; (2) chest like a bear skin rug; (3) Prussian mutton chops; (4) stage IV hairy hands; (5) Farah Fawcett wings; (6) Paulie Walnut wings; (7) Hobbit feet you could comb.

9   Your hair morphs into a new permanent hair style. You can get it cut, or even shave your head, but it just grows back the exact same way overnight. Style (1d8): (1) a serious hockey mullet; (2) sick dreads; (3) insane mohawk; (4) weak-ass fauxhawk; (5) Wall Street tycoon; (6) supreme afro; (7) 70's glam shag; (8) full Kojack, baby!

10   Your outfit changes along with your 'stache. You keep the benefit of your armor, shield, and any other armaments or magic devices; only your appearance changes. Change is permanent until you can get you some new threads. Effect (1d10): (1) biker leathers; (2) cig advert cowboy; (3) disco whites; (4) everything the same except now it all has the Motörhead logo; (5) full S&M; (6) Hawaiian shirt, acid washed jeans, Foster Grants; (7) Kung Fu pajamas; (8) steampunk Zeppelin pilot; (9) tangerine Speedo/bikini; (10) tuxedo/little black dress.

MOUSTACHE ACTIVATION

Roll to see how you activate your 'Stache abilities.

Mustacheafestation: Roll 1d7: (1) lip twitching; (2) sneering; (3) straightening; (4) touch up waxing; (5) tongue brushing; (6) twanging out a rogue hair; (7) twirling.

TYPES OF MAGICAL MOUSTACHES

The Chevron, AKA the Hugh

This is the classic manly moustache. Not for the faint of heart, this is a serious heartbreaker of a lip rug.

The Hugh confers the following abilities upon its wearer:

- You are one tough son of a bugbear. By spending one Whisker Point, you can heal back 1d6 worth of hit points.
- You can spend a Whisker Point to add 1d4 to any saving throw.
- People have a hard time looking you in the eye and lying. By spending 1 Whisker Point, the Chevron wearer makes lying to him impossible for 10 minutes. Would-be liars can't get the words out, instead stuttering and shaking.

The Italian Stallion, AKA the Super Mario

This is a dapper little moustache, at once disarmingly charming and devastatingly sexy.

The Italian Stallion confers the following abilities to its wearer per Whisker Point spent. Only one ability can be in effect at a given time:

- You double your maximum jump for 1 turn.
- Once per day you can cast *enlarge* on yourself, rolling 1d20 + character level for the spell check. The manifestation is your growing large in stages while a snappy musical refrain plays. A "Lost and worse" result de-activates the power of your Italian Stallion for 24 hours – no corruption is possible.

- For 1 hour, whenever you smash an easily crushable man-made object, such as a bottle or tiny barrel, there is a 10% chance that you will find a silver piece in the debris. When you hit 5th level, this increases to a 20% chance of finding a gold piece.

The Matador, AKA the Sidewinder

The ultimate in suave. Two well defined lines descend your lip as if they were painted there by El Greco. You suddenly possess the self-confidence of a much taller person.

The Matador confers the following abilities:

- You are adept at sidestepping enemy attacks. Burning one Whisker Point gives you an AC bonus equal to your character level for 1 turn.

- You will not be spoken to like that! You can spend Whisker Points to re-roll a missed saving throw against the following spells: *charm person, scare, sleep, forget, slow*, or *word of command*. The judge may allow this reroll against other charm or fear-based effects.

- In a non-combat situation where there is decent music playing, you can spend a Whisker Point to charm a dancer into performing one dance with you, save DC = 1d24 + CL + Personality bonus. No matter what the victim's or your own background, for that one dance you are an unforgettable duo dancing in splendid synchronicity.

The Girl 'Stache, AKA the Kahlo

The Girl 'Stache has two modes. The first is stealthy – utterly undetectable until its bearer comes close enough to kiss, whisper a secret, or headbutt the daylights out of someone. At that point the previously unaware party becomes very aware of two facts – one, that this woman is rocking a bitchin' lip-tickler, and two, that it is working for her – big time. In the second mode, the owner of a Girl 'Stache can make it visible and utterly blatant, and people just have to rethink their stance on lady whiskers because she is straight up OWNING it. Switching from stealth mode to in-your-face is instant, requiring just a quick look in something reflective.

The Girl 'Stache confers the following abilities to its wearer:

- Girl 'Stache rockers can slay with sarcasm. It takes 1 Whisker Point to activate the ability, and once activated it lasts for 1d4 rounds. She chooses a target within 60' who needs a talking to. The 'Stache Warrior gives the target a little bit of her best wit, the kind of amazingly subtle yet unmistakable insult you can see shimmer though the air at the target like a major league fastball. The victim must make a Will save (DC = 1d20 + character level + Personality modifier) or take 1d6 damage. Victims who roll a 1 on their save actually get tears in their eyes and start sniveling like little bitches. This ability does an additional 1d6 damage against creatures who just said something amazingly sexist in hearing range of the 'Stache weilder. The Sarcasm Blast can be done once per round in addition to any other attacks or movement. At 5th level the base damage increases to 2d6.

- The Girl 'Stache wielder can spend a Whisker point to reroll any missed Personality check.

- The Girl 'Stache owner can spend a Whisker point when she walks over a threshold – when she passes through to the other side, she will instantly be wearing the perfect outfit for whatever may be on that other side. If the room beyond holds a potential combat encounter, the new outfit gives an AC bonus of +1d4. The new outfit lasts for 1d6 hours before reverting to whatever it was before the point was spent.

The Villain 'Stache, AKA the Dick Dastardly

This is two darty-looking lightning bolts coming out neatly, right out from under your nostrils. You may as well go ahead and get a top hat and opera cloak to go with it because your look is definitely wanting to go that way.

The Villain 'Stache confers the following abilities:

In combat, the possessor of the Villain 'Stache can actually steal one of the following rules from other fine RPG systems (1d5, rolled whenever the power is activated, each use costs 1 Whisker Point):

1   For 1d3 rounds he has Advantage, and rolls twice for every action die roll, taking the best result.

2   For 1d4 rounds he is Specialized, and gets a bonus

attack every other round at their highest possible action dice with whatever weapon they had in hand when they activated the power. At 5th level this becomes Double Specialization, and they get a bonus attack with their Specialized weapon every round.

3. For 1d5 rounds anyone he hits must make a Sanity Check (Will save DC = 5 + damage done) or go Partially Insane. Partially Insane characters always look a bit squirrely, tend to wax on and on about the horror of existence, and run in terror from anything they see with tentacles. Villain 'Stache characters at 5th level drive victims who fail their save Whoo Boy Insane; those sad souls spend a lot of time screaming, catatonic, or running amuck until a same-alignment cleric uses the *lay on hands* ability to cure the insanity (requires a result of 3 dice). Whoo Boy Insane player characters go under the control of the judge, who is granted Complete and Utter License to use them to create all possible chaos and mayhem.

4. For 1d6 turns the Universe changes within 1 mile of you, and during that time all creatures speak an alignment language, which will allows all intelligent creatures and domesticated animals the ability to communicate with all other intelligent creatures of their same alignment. Turns out your horse thinks you are a slave-driving bastard who actually *doesn't* need a second helping of rations, please and thank you.

5. For 1d7 hours your team has a Mojo Pool equal to your Personality score. These points can be given by any player to any other player and can be added to any Action Dice check. People can't give points to themselves, and if they ask for points from the pool they may not receive any points from this particular Mojo Pool. Mojo Points must be offered before the die roll. The Mojo Pool does not refresh, and completely disappears at the end of the duration or when it is spent down to zero.

MOUSTACHE DUELS

When two creatures with Magic Moustaches come within 1 mile of one another they are instantly aware of each other's presence. Either can choose to find the other. While the path might meander, perhaps past a tavern where some hip bards are playing something especially funky, they always eventually lead the two 'Stache Rockers together.

There is no rule that says folks with Magic Moustaches who meet up have to have a duel. Sometimes the characters just do something really moustachey, like standing in front of a sunset leaning against a hitching post, smoking and arguing over the best breed of horse to get you through the desert. Or they might carry a rowboat down to a river, sit in it, and start reeling in big mouth bass. But sometimes things get ugly, and then folks with a 'stache must have a clash.

If both mustachioed parties decide to duel, they each put a d14 in front of their character sheet; this is the Moustachum Tracker, and they both begin with it set at 7.

The duelers start showing off their 'staches to maximum effect. This can take the form of posing, glaring, combing, giving meaningful looks, judgmental eye tracking, and similar. The participants each roll 1d20 and add their Luck and Personality modifiers. High roll wins, and the winner moves his tracker up by one. Each check takes one round.

If the two checks are identical there is a cosmic rift as the conflicting power of the two amazing 'Stashes unleash a Phlostachian Disturbance. Roll on the table below to see the effect.

Keep rolling until somebody hits 14 on the tracker and wins the Moustache Duel. The winner gains +1d5 Whisker Points. The loser's moustache droops listlessly for 24 hours, during which he can access none of his moustache abilities.

Phlostachian Disturbance, roll a d5:

1. The duelers wink out of existence. They find themselves suddenly on horseback, riding across a picturesque desert landscape in a pocket dimension created by the Phlostachian Disturbance. The ride lasts for 1d5 turns. Each turn the riders must make a DC 13 Stamina check – failure means they fall from the horse, exhausted. Once someone falls they return to their original location, as if no time had passed, and the dueler who managed to stay mounted gains 1d3 points on the Moustachum Tracker.

2. A group of onlookers appears from nowhere and starts to hoot and holler, rooting for a good contest. Each one has an amazing and unique 'stache – these are the Ancient Masters of Facial Hair, and their approval is all. They remain there until the end of the contest, at which point they each come and shake hands with the winner, who gains 1d3 points of Luck.

3. The entire battle becomes a full blown song and dance extravaganza. Suddenly the competitors are amazing dancers in a synchronized battle dance. Musical accompaniment comes from everywhere and is entirely appropriate to the scene. Onlookers are helpless to resist the dance, although if they are in combat they can continue to fight, dancey-style. The battle continues this way until there is a winner.

4. Both combatants feel a tingling sensation, and their moustaches begin to grow. They grow 1d6" each round until the contest is over.

5. A mustashioed demon shows up and declares that the loser of the contest forfeits his soul and must return with him to the dark eternity of the underworld. The catch: the demon can't actually back that up, and the loser can absolutely refuse and just not go. If they go without resistance they subject themselves to a lifetime of infernal servitude.

D200 Random Stuff Chart

1. Bramble Staff
2. Friendly Cat
3. Backpack
4. Rusty Dagger
5. Old Helm
6. Poodle
7. Chicken
8. Spade
9. 3 Gallon Iron Pot
10. Wineskin
11. Bag of Klartesh
12. Small cage with three blind mice
13. Book, Ink, Pen
14. Holy Symbol
15. Skeleton Key
16. Crowbar
17. Longsword
18. Mustard Jar
19. Bag of Marbles
20. 10ft Rope
21. 20ft Rope
22. Spiked belt
23. Strong Wire ball
24. Cleets
25. Pony
26. White flag
27. Potion of what?
28. Spear
29. Bugle
30. step ladder
31. cookies wrapped in paper
32. Rusty Manacles but NO key
33. Wheel Barrow
34. Bag of broken glass
35. Telescope
36. Basket of Eggs
37. Pipe and Tobacco
38. Ceramic Spoon
39. Compass
40. Boar Spear
41. Book of Monster identification
42. Silk Spider Sniper Scarf
43. Giraffe skull
44. Ornate Club
45. Ornate chair leg
46. Shield
47. Rattle
48. 10 foot chain
49. wooden short sword
50. 6 torches in hemp bag
51. Bear trap
52. Bag of Cotton
53. 3d4 cp
54. 1d30 sp
55. Goat
56. Needle and thread
57. Hourglass
58. 3 legged dog
59. fighting rock
60. collection of sharpened sticks
61. scrawny cur
62. small trinket
63. meat cleaver
64. pitch fork
65. fishing net
66. cudgel
67. rope (3d6 x10 ft)
68. canvas sack filled with alien rocks
69. steak knife & great fork
70. wooden shield
71. holy symbol
72. skull cap
73. leather apron
74. hatchet
75. sling
76. extra large banded leather
77. lantern
78. Blacksmith hammer
79. stout staff
80. sack of yams
81. leather brassiere
82. girdle of matrimony
83. mule
84. stretcher or thimble
85. roll twice or roll three times for someone else
86. snare supplies
87. heavy insulated mats
88. face scarf
89. push broom
90. dagger
91. torch
92. spiked glove
93. wheat thresher
94. scythe
95. bamboo spear
96. grandma's ring
97. flask of bad wine
98. backpack
99. Eyes of the Overworld*
100. small flawed garnet
101. Thieves picks
102. 1000 year old egg
103. suit of fine clothes
104. musical saw
105. stripped hose
106. empty scroll case
107. jar of paint with no brush
108. ½ pound of salmon
109. wind chimes
110. Jew's harp
111. empty black bag
112. green chalk
113. cloak with hidden pocket
114. bloody rags
115. six crucifixtion nails
116. bishop's mitre
117. wire brush
118. time travel soup can
119. three hand rolled cigars
120. glass eye
121. blank leather book
122. cheese made of steel
123. hacksaw
124. anti-gravity raisin
125. bronze bowl
126. shot glass
127. lock of hair
128. wooden toe ring
129. canary in cage
130. spool of tin wire
131. jar of whale fat
132. Locked iron box (no key)
133. red vial labeled "aether"
134. ornamented human skull
135. purple tunic
136. tall hard boots
137. rolling pin
138. iron dagger
139. small silver bell on chain
140. 1 EP
141. mithril needle
142. bag of quickling powder
143. jug of moonshine
144. wool shirt
145. six bronze tipped arrows
146. goat horn
147. sword breaker
148. coyote pelt
149. rabid raccoon bile
150. paper airplane
151. leather belt
152. single pink glove
153. Martian shingle
154. plastic bubble helm
155. fireplace poker
156. shitty spear
157. snakeskin hat
158. wooden cube
159. four walnuts
160. ornate rod
161. sun dress
162. face powder
163. cart wheel
164. fecal prod
165. Hijab
166. crochet knee pads
167. tree tap
168. voodoo cat head
169. smuggler's hand drum
170. antiquated sword
171. Small Energy Cell
172. William's Lucky Coin
173. Human Skin Purse
174. Kate's Sandals
175. sack of feed corn
176. waxed canvas hip waders
177. horse skull
178. religious pamphlet
179. brass candle snuffer
180. chisel
181. ball of string
182. loin cloth
183. jar of pickled pig ears
184. drum sticks
185. wooden mug
186. preserved aardvark heart
187. map
188. grey hooded cloak
189. leg warmers
190. mittens
191. box of nails
192. pliers
193. rat skin
194. chewing tar
195. ½ page from spell book
196. profane femur
197. tiny knife
198. pin
199. wasps nest
200. tofu bag

*If you've read the Jack Vance book of the same name and feel confident in doing some seat-of-your-pants judging, you should go for it. Maybe make the character realize they were under a spell all along to return the eyes to Iucounu the Laughing Magician. If not, make it a shovel or a can of beans or something else, then read *The Eyes of the Overworld*. If you're already running DCC RPG, you won't regret it.

INDEX

Absolve 21
Accountancy of the occulted eye 81
Akiza-Mannoth 144
Almanac of Holcomb Hollow, The 133
Baneful gaze 70
Beak of Va Ferouk 143
Black Temple Prayer 19
Black widow, giant 150
Blessing of the Flesh 25
Blight 101
Bloodlust 88
Bonesword of the Sea 145
Book bearers 135
Bugs 150
Byemgeird 153
Cadixtat 6
Call of the wild hunt 77
Canticles 9, 14, 18, 22, 27, 31, 36
Capsule campaign 43
Carnifex 50
Chaunt of the Unmoving Mountain 14
Child of the Serpent 107
Cleanse 21
Cleric titles 7, 12, 17, 21, 25, 30, 34
Cloak of the Carnifex 53
Cobra/viper 174
Constructs 158
Court of Chaos 78, 92, 94, 122, 157
Crocodile 174
Crymstalla 138
Crystals, Murn 45
Daenthar 11
DCC #80 .... 78, 157
DCC #85 120
Death Touch 18
Defeated of Darjr 142
Demonism 102
Detect deception 60
Dhwyght 154
Disapproval 7, 12, 17, 21, 25, 30, 35
Divine favors 7, 21, 25, 30, 34
Downtime 40
Draco Maxillam Helixa 140
Dragontooth Flameblade of Akiza-
 Mannoth 144
Dwarven acolyte 14
Dwarven priest 14
Dzzhali 56
Excoriate energy 63
Executioner's blade 54
Fantax's Fool 142
Fiend fatale 57
Fist of Nhool 96
Fly, giant 150
Fox/jackal 174
Genocide 103
Giants 161
Gifts of the lizard 115
Golems 158
Grillus 154
Gutteral onslaught 89
Hand of Chaos 10
Heart of chaos 7
Hekanhoda 64, 137
Hekanhoda's Fingered Femur 137
Hekanhoda's homunculus 68
Hidden Lord, The 16, 33
Hidden Path 16
Høck the Cruel 140
Hold liquid 30
Horned King 72
Hound 71
Hound, eldritch 77
Hyena 174
In-between escapades 40
Inflict anguish 61
Interesting occurrences 40
Invoke patron ... 50, 56, 64, 72, 78, 84, 92, 98,
 104, 110
Ironsbane 141
Jaguar/leopard/puma 174
Justicia 20, 143
Klavgorok 78
Klavgorok's astounding artificer 83
Klavgorok's merciless gaze 82
Lakshamorda 136
Lay on hands 7, 12, 16, 21, 25, 30, 34
Ley lines 45
Lion/tiger 174
Living book bearer of Fan Agestpo 134
Lizard's tongue 114
Lost Continent of Mu 43
Lunar Glow 36
Magemelt 155
Magog 84, 182
Malophos 134
Malotoch 24
Mantid, giant 150
Manual of Obscene Predators, The 133
Martyr's Reward 22
Metamorphosis 9
Moai-Man 155
Monster patron die 177
Monsters 150
Monstrous patronage 177
Moonsense 34
Mosquito, giant 150
Mother of Monsters 179
Motivational Shanty 31
Moustache duels 189
Moustaches, magic 186
Mu .... see Lost Continent of Mu
Murder Hymn 27
Mutations 165
Mysterious manuscripts 133
Name of the quarry 76
Named swords 136
Narrative of Compelling Antediluvian
 Histories, A 133
Nhool 92
Nigodow's Septichromatic Orbs 37
Obitu-Que 98
Object Lesson from Alamanter 142
Ogre, dread 91
Ogremorph 90
Oplema's Songsword 146
Order of the Sundered Scale 20
Osz-Cromacar 141
Patron taint 51, 58, 66, 73, 79, 86, 93, 98,
 105, 112
Patron weapons 128
Patron weapons, wielding 132
Pelagia 29, 145
Plunder the ruin's power 95
Psalm of Secrets 18
Psalm of the Flesh-Eater 27
Psalm of the Hallowed Forge 15
Raven Moon 25
Reckoning braid 34
Reptiles 170
Requiem of the Surrendered Flesh 28
Righteous Freedom 22
Rings, magic 120
Ruinwrack 93
Rumptillion's Legacious Repository 133
Serbok 104
Sezrekan's Servant 142
Shed the lizard's skin 116
Shroud of death 55
Shul 33
Shul's Shining One 36
Siren's Call 31
S'kath's Vengeance 139
Skin of the eel 108
Slaying strike 75
Song of Stone 14
Speak with Messenger 25
Spellburn 52, 59, 67, 74, 80, 87, 94, 100,
 106, 113
Summon minor sea life 30
Tarantula, giant 150
Tattered Veil of Chance 9
Templar's Might 22
Temple of the Sacred Wave 29
Testament of Q'rex the Damned, The ... 133
Therianthropes 33, 174
Turn unholy 12
Tyrannosaurus Rex 111
Vimswain 156
War-gird 97
Waste reaver 156
Water breathing 30
Water's True Name 31
Weavers of the Divine Flesh 6
White snake immortality 109
Will of the axe 7
Witherleaf Elfslayer 139
Wolf spider, giant 150
Wracking Plague 69
Yila-Keranuz 110
Zhil, Satrap of Knives 157
Zhuhn 6, 144
Zlabado's Wand 147

TABLES

Table	Ref	Page
Books Found on the Back of a Random Book Bearer	8-29	135
Bug Color		150
Bug Physical Traits		151
Bug Special Abilities		151
Construct Abilities		158
Construct Appearance		158
Construct Body Shape		158
Control Over Bestial Form		175
Curse Removal	8-28	131
Eerie Radiances	8-19	123
Giant Abilities		163
Giant Personal Traits		161
Giant Size		161
Giant's Intellect		161
Giant's Alignment		161
Giant's Weapon		164
Greater Ring Potency Characteristics	8-24	124
Greater Ring Powers	8-25	125
Interesting Occurrences In-between Adventures		40
Item of Imprisonment	8-26	130
Jewels and Gemstones	8-16	122
Number of Mutations		165
Major Ring Potency Characteristics	8-22	124
Major Ring Powers	8-23	124
Magog Invocation	9-18	182
Magog Patron Displeasure	9-19	183
Minor Ring Potency Characteristics	8-20	123
Minor Ring Powers	8-21	124
Monstrous Patron Invocation Actions	9-15	178
The Mother of Monsters Invocation	9-16	180
The Mother of Monsters Patron Displeasure	9-17	181
Moustachial Effect		186
Patron Weapon Characteristics	8-27	130
Phlostachian Disturbance		189
Random Body Parts		165
Random Mutations		165
Reptilian Abilities		170
Reptilian Color		170
Reptilian Personal Traits		170
Ring Class and Requirements	8-14	121
Strange Tempers	8-18	122
Therianthropic Beast Form Shape		174
Therianthropic Diet		175
Therianthropic Origin		175
Tells in Human Form		175
Unique Band Materials	8-15	122
Unusual Assistants	8-17	122
Unusual Therianthropic Abilities		175

This printing of DCC RPG Annual Vol. 1 is done under version 1.0 of the Open Gaming License, and the System Reference Document by permission from Wizards of the Coast, Inc. Designation of Product Identity: The following items are hereby designated as Product Identity in accordance with Section 1(e) of the Open Game License, version 1.0: Dungeon Crawl Classics, DCC RPG, Mighty Deed of Arms, spell check, Luck check, spellburn, mercurial magic, corruption, disapproval, all spell names, all proper nouns, capitalized terms, italicized terms, artwork, maps, symbols, depictions, and illustrations, except such elements that already appear in the System Reference Document.

Designation of Open Content: Subject to the Product Identity designation above, such sections of Chapter One: Characters and Chapter Four: Combat as derive from the SRD are designated as Open Gaming Content.

Some of the portions of this book which are delineated OGC originate from the System Reference Document and are copyright © 1999, 2000 Wizards of the Coast, Inc. The remainder of these OGC portions of these book are hereby added to Open Game Content and, if so used, should bear the COPYRIGHT NOTICE "DCC RPG ANNUAL VOL. 1, copyright © 2019 Goodman Games, all rights reserved, visit www.goodman-games.com or contact info@goodman-games.com"

Dungeon Crawl Classics Role Playing Game is copyright © 2012 Goodman Games. Open game content may only be used under in the terms of the Open Game License.

OPEN GAME LICENSE Version 1.0a

The following text is the property of Wizards of the Coast, Inc. and is Copyright 2000 Wizards of the Coast, Inc ("Wizards"). All Rights Reserved.

1. Definitions: (a) "Contributors" means the copyright and/or trademark owners who have contributed Open Game Content; (b) "Derivative Material" means copyrighted material including derivative works and translations (including into other computer languages), potation, modification, correction, addition, extension, upgrade, improvement, compilation, abridgment or other form in which an existing work may be recast, transformed or adapted; (c) "Distribute" means to reproduce, license, rent, lease, sell, broadcast, publicly display, transmit or otherwise distribute; (d) "Open Game Content" means the game mechanic and includes the methods, procedures, processes and routines to the extent such content does not embody the Product Identity and is an enhancement over the prior art and any additional content clearly identified as Open Game Content by the Contributor, and means any work covered by this License, including translations and derivative works under copyright law, but specifically excludes Product Identity. (e) "Product Identity" means product and product line names, logos and identifying marks including trade dress; artifacts; creatures characters; stories, storylines, plots, thematic elements, dialogue, incidents, language, artwork, symbols, designs, depictions, likenesses, formats, poses, concepts, themes and graphic, photographic and other visual or audio representations; names and descriptions of characters, spells, enchantments, personalities, teams, personas, likenesses and special abilities; places, locations, environments, creatures, equipment, magical or supernatural abilities or effects, logos, symbols, or graphic designs; and any other trademark or registered trademark clearly identified as Product identity by the owner of the Product Identity, and which specifically excludes the Open Game Content; (f) "Trademark" means the logos, names, mark, sign, motto, designs that are used by a Contributor to identify itself or its products or the associated products contributed to the Open Game License by the Contributor (g) "Use", "Used" or "Using" means to use, Distribute, copy, edit, format, modify, translate and otherwise create Derivative Material of Open Game Content. (h) "You" or "Your" means the licensee in terms of this agreement.

2. The License: This License applies to any Open Game Content that contains a notice indicating that the Open Game Content may only be Used under and in terms of this License. You must affix such a notice to any Open Game Content that you Use. No terms may be added to or subtracted from this License except as described by the License itself. No other terms or conditions may be applied to any Open Game Content distributed using this License.

3. Offer and Acceptance: By Using the Open Game Content You indicate Your acceptance of the terms of this License.

4. Grant and Consideration: In consideration for agreeing to use this License, the Contributors grant You a perpetual, worldwide, royalty-free, non-exclusive license with the exact terms of this License to Use, the Open Game Content.

5. Representation of Authority to Contribute: If You are contributing original material as Open Game Content, You represent that Your Contributions are Your original creation and/or You have sufficient rights to grant the rights conveyed by this License.

6. Notice of License Copyright: You must update the COPYRIGHT NOTICE portion of this License to include the exact text of the COPYRIGHT NOTICE of any Open Game Content You are copying, modifying or distributing, and You must add the title, the copyright date, and the copyright holder's name to the COPYRIGHT NOTICE of any original Open Game Content you Distribute.

7. Use of Product Identity: You agree not to Use any Product Identity, including as an indication as to compatibility, except as expressly licensed in another, independent Agreement with the owner of each element of that Product Identity. You agree not to indicate compatibility or co-adaptability with any Trademark or Registered Trademark in conjunction with a work containing Open Game Content except as expressly licensed in another, independent Agreement with the owner of such Trademark or Registered Trademark. The use of any Product Identity in Open Game Content does not constitute a challenge to the ownership of that Product Identity. The owner of any Product Identity used in Open Game Content shall retain all rights, title and interest in and to that Product Identity.

8. Identification: If you distribute Open Game Content You must clearly indicate which portions of the work that you are distributing are Open Game Content.

9. Updating the License: Wizards or its designated Agents may publish updated versions of this License. You may use any authorized version of this License to copy, modify and distribute any Open Game Content originally distributed under any version of this License.

10 Copy of this License: You MUST include a copy of this License with every copy of the Open Game Content You Distribute.

11. Use of Contributor Credits: You may not market or advertise the Open Game Content using the name of any Contributor unless You have written permission from the Contributor to do so.

12 Inability to Comply: If it is impossible for You to comply with any of the terms of this License with respect to some or all of the Open Game Content due to statute, judicial order, or governmental regulation then You may not Use any Open Game Material so affected.

13 Termination: This License will terminate automatically if You fail to comply with all terms herein and fail to cure such breach within 30 days of becoming aware of the breach. All sublicenses shall survive the termination of this License.

14 Reformation: If any provision of this License is held to be unenforceable, such provision shall be reformed only to the extent necessary to make it enforceable.

15 COPYRIGHT NOTICE

Open Game License v 1.0 Copyright 2000, Wizards of the Coast, Inc.

System Rules Document Copyright 2000 Wizards of the Coast, Inc.; Authors Jonathan Tweet, Monte Cook, Skip Williams, based on original material by E. Gary Gygax and Dave Arneson.

DCC RPG Annual Vol. 1, copyright © 2019 Goodman Games, all rights reserved, visit www.goodman-games.com or contact info@goodman-games.com FIRST PRINTING

REAVERS FACE THE UNKNOWN

… For when you positively, absolutely, NEED to know how much damage your flock of two headed, fire-breathing chickens can dish out! **Critters, Creatures, & Denizens** provides:

• A wide selection of DCCRPG compatible critters from the mundane to bizarre aberrations from beyond the spheres.
• Detailed Mutation Tables
• New spells, & much more…

Liber Arcanum, a wizard's grimoire of new DCC RPG compatible lore providing:
• 6 new patrons, 46 new spells,
• New powers & banes for magic weapons & a lot more...

Available at: drivethrurpg.com

Campaign Elements

Compatible With DCC RPG

Having Your First Funnel, Adventure Lies Before You
Now You Need to "Quest For It!"

Commit a legendary burglary
Locate an unique wizard patron
Meet the Osmons in an alien swamp
Master new combat techniques
Eliminate a psionic threat in a radioactive ruin
Resist the machinations of the Crimson Void

Every Campaign Needs a Unique Element or Two

It is Time for A DCC Campaign
(Available at Rpgnow from Purple Duck Games)

Hope Dies Eternal...

Black Sun Deathcrawl

Available at www.kickassistan.net

Compatible With DCC RPG

Crawl!

The original fanzine compatible with Dungeon Crawl Classics RPG!

Scrawl!
Spells, scrolls and other magic.

Sprawl!
City, wilderness and, of course, dungeon adventures.

Maul!
Weapons and 10-foot poles.

Fan created options, classes, monsters, treasure, patrons, spells and more!
All to help make your gaming awesome!
Folded into an old-school zine format!

Compatible With DCC RPG

Available now at:
www.crawlfanzine.com

STRAYCOUCHES PRESS
www.straycouches.com

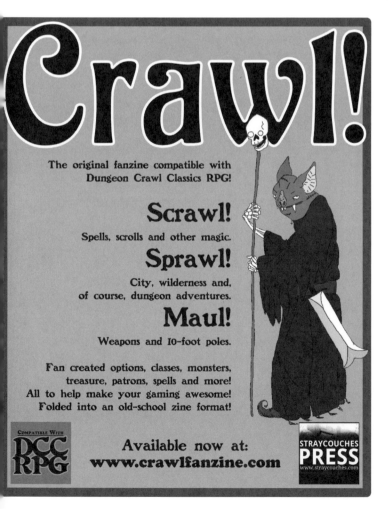

---

crawljammer.blogspot.com

CRAWLJAMMER

LASER SWORDS AND RAY GUNS IN THE PHLOGISTON FLUX!

MOON DICE GAMES (12)

Compatible With DCC RPG

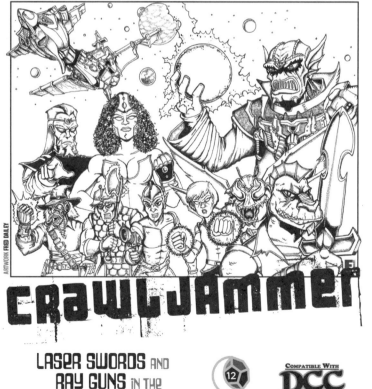

PAGE 197

Crawling Under a Broken Moon

Compatible With DCC RPG

A fanzine dedicated to bringing gonzo post apocalyptic content for the Dungeon Crawl Classics RPG from Goodman Games

crawlingunderabrokenmoon.blogspot.com

LET THE INVOCATIONS BEGIN!

Available now at RPGNow.com
Follow us: shinobi27games.blogspot.com.au

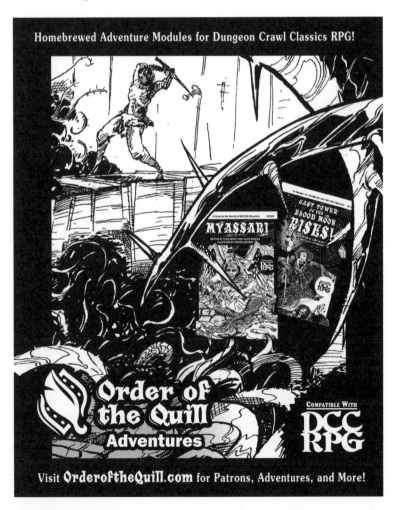

Visit OrderoftheQuill.com for Patrons, Adventures, and More!

Divinities & Cults
Classic Deities for DCC RPG!

Written by Dan Osarchuk
Illustrated by Luigi Castellani, Bradley K. McDevitt, Fred Dailey, and Traci Meek

Each with unique:
- Tenets
- Allowed Weapons & Armor
- Holy Symbols
- Divinity Magic
- Healing Side-Effects
- Disapproval Tables
- Spell Lists

Plus:
- Random Encounter Tables, organized by deity
- Lots of optional rules
- And Monsters!

http://divinitiesandcults.blogspot.com/

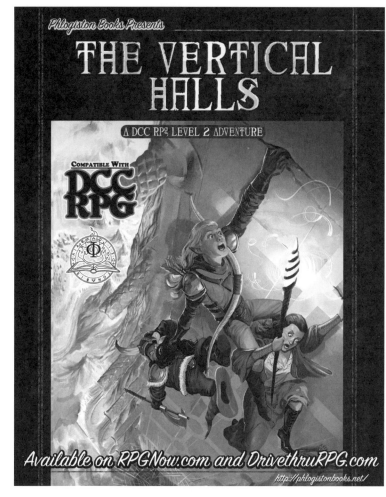

Mystic Bull Games

Your Companion Into the Weird

www.mysticbull.com

100 years have passed since Mankind revolted and slew the Sorcerer Kings.

Now, the survivors of five ancient empires begin to rebuild, placing new lives and hopes on the ashes of old. However, even as life continues an ancient and forgotten evil stirs awaiting its moment to strike against mankind.

Explore a war-torn land where the struggle for survival continues as new kingdoms arise to impose their will upon the masses. Vicious warlords fight to control territories carved out of the Fallen Empires. Imposing magicians emerge claiming the legacy of the Sorcerer Kings. High Priests of long forgotten gods and goddesses amass wealth in the name of divine right while warrior-monks, devoted to a banished god, patrol the lands bringing justice to people abandoned by their rulers.

Tales of the Fallen Empire is a classic Swords and Sorcery setting compatible with the *Dungeon Crawl Classics* Role Playing Game. Within these pages is a detailed post-apocalyptic fantasy setting taking you through an ancient realm that is fighting for its survival and its humanity. Seek your fortune or meet your fate in the burning deserts of the once lush and vibrant land of Vuul, or travel to the humid jungles of Najambi to face the tribes of the Man-Apes and their brutal sacrificial rituals.

Within this campaign setting you will find:

- 6 new classes: Barbarian, Witch, Draki, Sentinel, Man-Ape, & Marauder
- Revised Wizard Class (The Sorcerer)
- New Spells
- New Creatures
- Seafaring and Ritual Magic Rules
- A detailed setting inspired by the works of Fritz Lieber, Robert E. Howard, Lynn Carter, H. P. Lovecraft, Michael Moorcock, and Roger Corman

Tighten the straps on your sandals, grab your weapon, and head forth into a land of trouble and turmoil. Adventure awaits those foolhardy to enter the wastelands or for those who fear not the unknown.

  Available at DriveThruRPG – The Largest RPG Download Store!  WWW.CHAPTER13PRESS.COM

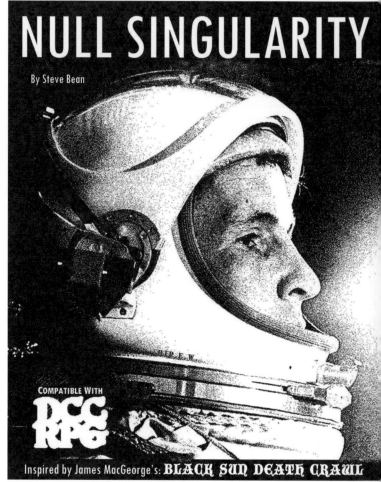

NULL SINGULARITY
By Steve Bean

Compatible with DCC RPG

Inspired by James MacGeorge's: **BLACK SUN DEATH CRAWL**

SANCTUM SECORUM
A LITERARY PODCAST FOR DCC RPG

ENTER... AND BE INSPIRED.

AVAILABLE AT HTTP://SANCTUM.MEDIA

14 dice sets in 9 colors

Compatible With DCC RPG

All the dice you need for your next adventure for Dungeon Crawl Classics
Available at impactminiatures.net

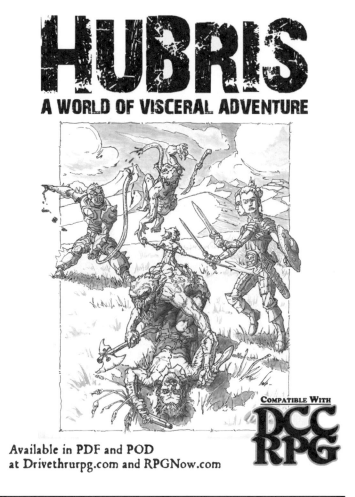

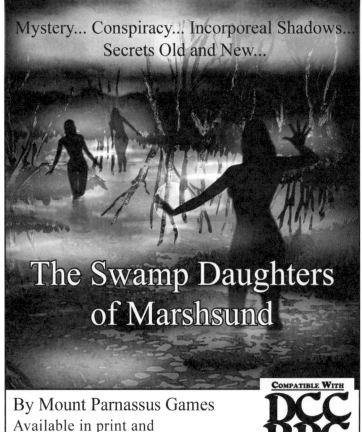

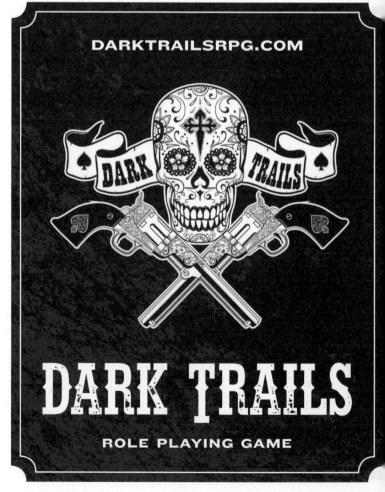

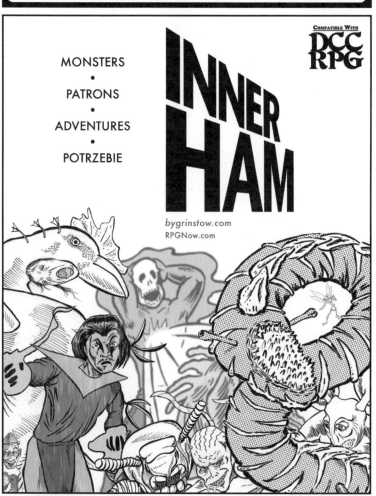

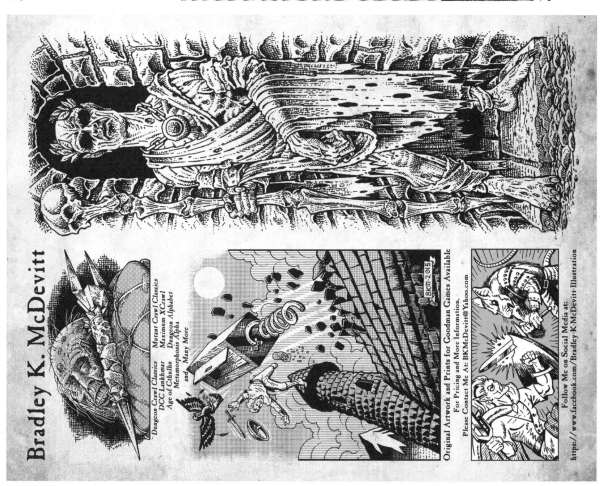

THE HOBONOMICON

Many are the tales of woe told of the book of the void, the legendary shadow tome of doom architects and fallen chaos martyrs. Penned in an obscene combination of the tears of false prophets, the sweat from sated succubi, and the blue-black blood of the Cats of Zar,

HOBONOMICON.COM

The Hobonomicon's volumes include *Death of a Reaver*, the unfolding story of the DCC Band in graphic form , as well as varied and sundry materials used to run after hours convention games. Each book contains more art and klartesh inspired waking dreams from the mind of Doug Kovacs and his collaborators.

We're with the band.

The band of adventurers, that is. Join us in the pages of Dungeon Crawl Classics adventure modules. Stand-alone, world-neutral, all new, and inspired by Appendix N. Learn more at www.goodman-games.com.

DCC RPG